FREEFALL

Gravity slammed Howe against the seat as he fought to regain control of the plane. Bile filled his mouth and nose; it stung his eyes, ate through the sinews of his arms. He pulled back on the stick, but the plane didn't respond.

He wanted to cough, but couldn't. The helmet pounded his skull, twisting at the temples. The F/A-22V threatened to whip into a spin. He pushed the stick to catch it, jammed the pedals.

Nothing worked. The Velociraptor's control system had gone off-line. That ought to have been impossible.

Engines gone.

Backup electricity to run the controls should automatically route from the forced-air rams below the fuselage.

Nothing. Too late.

Out, time to get out!

"Starts fast and keeps getting faster, with fascinating characters and a great finish . . . I loved it all."

—**Larry Bond,** *New York Times*
bestselling author of *Red Phoenix*

CYCLOPS
ONE

JIM DeFELICE

POCKET STAR BOOKS
New York • London • Toronto • Sydney • Singapore

This book is a work of fiction. Names, characters, places and incidents are products of the author's imagination or are used fictitiously. Any resemblance to actual events or locales or persons, living or dead, is entirely coincidental.

An *Original* Publication of POCKET BOOKS

A Pocket Star Book published by
POCKET BOOKS, a division of Simon & Schuster, Inc.
1230 Avenue of the Americas, New York, NY 10020

ISBN: 0-7434-6422-2

First Pocket Books printing October 2003

10   9   8   7   6   5   4   3   2   1

POCKET STAR BOOKS and colophon are registered trademarks of Simon & Schuster, Inc.

For information regarding special discounts for bulk purchases, please contact Simon & Schuster Special Sales at 1-800-456-6798 or business@simonandschuster.com

Cover design and illustration by James Wang

Printed in the U.S.A.

For the guys putting their lives on the line . . .

ACKNOWLEDGMENTS

To properly thank everyone who's helped me get this book in shape I'd need another four hundred pages. But I'd be remiss if I didn't mention a few people who have helped me, some in ways I can't begin to adequately acknowledge.

First and foremost, I have to thank Dale Brown, who's been an idol of mine even before I started pounding computer keys. Just talking with Dale is like taking a graduate seminar, and I was extremely lucky to catch a few pointers from him as I worked on this book.

I'd also like to acknowledge another long-time hero of mine, Stephen Coonts, whose kindness and generosity buoyed me along the way. Larry Bond also added some critical moral support at a crucial moment.

My editor, Kevin Smith, had many useful ideas and kept me moving in the right direction. He also provided important baseball commentary, though it didn't make it into the book.

Publisher Louise Burke has been a real source of support and an enthusiastic ally; no writer could ask for more. Art director Paolo Pepe and designer James Wang blew me away with the cover and the "package." Copyeditor David Chesanow prevented me from making many embarrassing mistakes. And a big thanks to the rest of the Pocket Books team for their help and hard work on my behalf.

My agent Jake Elwell not only made the whole thing happen but helped me sort out the initial story-line. Plus he smokes a mean cigar.

Thanks also to Tom, Bob, the Motion Poets, "Blaze," Mark, Beefy, Fred, and to various and sundry E-mail correspondents who have provided counsel, cheer, and technical data, as well as kindly pointing out errors. Also, a big wave to the folks in Green Bay, especially Marty and Larry.

Finally, thanks and love to Deb and Bobby, as always.

AUTHOR'S NOTE

Though real technology is discussed and detailed in this book, it is a work of fiction. The commercial entities, machinery, and procedures described do not exist in real life; nor do the people. As always, I've taken some liberties in concocting the yarn.

Some of the details regarding the firebombing of Tokyo were inspired by my reading of *Inferno* by Edwin P. Hoyt. While I respectfully disagree with some of his opinions, his work is provocative and well written.

PART ONE
MIA

CHAPTER

1

At least fifty yards separated Colonel Thomas Howe from the dozen people clustered around the nose of the test plane, but even at that distance she seduced him. A thick flight suit and a layer of survival gear obscured the soft curves of Megan's body, but he could still sense the sway of her hips. His lips tasted the perfumed air around her; his thumb caught the small drop of sweat forming behind her ear. Megan York had her back to him, but she pulled him forward like a mermaid singing to a castaway.

If he'd stopped there, fifty yards away—if Howe had turned and gone across the cement apron to where his own plane waited at the edge of the secret northern Montana airstrip—a dozen things, a million things, might have been different. Or so he would tell himself later.

But Howe didn't stop. He continued toward her, drawn by the warmth he had felt the night before as he had undressed her. Blood rushed to his head; the air grew so thick he could barely breathe.

When he was about ten yards from her, Megan turned. Seeing him, she frowned.

Her frown was a bare flicker, lasting only a fraction of a fraction of a second, but in that instant a hole opened in his chest. Despair, then anger, erupted from it.

Had he been alone in a house or a building, Howe would have punched the wall or whatever fell in range. But he was not alone, and this fact and his training as a combat pilot made him cock a smile on his face.

"Hey," he said.

"Hey yourself."

"What's up?"

"What's up with you?"

The others standing nearby seemed to fade back as they stared at each other. Finally, Howe blinked and slung a thumb into the side of his survival vest. His anger returned for a half moment, and then he felt a great loss, as if they hadn't made love for the first time only a few weeks before but for the ten thousandth time, as if they'd grown old in each other's arms and now she wanted to leave.

Until that moment he hadn't realized he was in love. It hadn't been real, like a bruise on his arm or a broken rib. Until that moment desire had been just sex, not something that could cling to his chest like a tight sweater you could never take off.

"Looks like it's going to rain," she said.

"Hope so," he said.

Rain—heavy rain—was the purpose of the exercise today. The Cyclops laser in Megan's modified 767-300ER had not been fully tested in foul weather. Developed as a successor to the airborne laser (ABL) missile-defense system, the weapon's COIL-plus chemical oxygen iodine laser projected a multifaceted beam of energy through a nose-mounted ocular director system that was in many ways reminiscent of the nose turrets on World War II aircraft. The laser could strike moving and nonmoving objects approximately three hundred miles away. Using targeting data from a variety of sources, it could destroy or disable up to fifty targets on a mission, at the same time directing advanced escorts in their own more conventional attacks, thanks to a shared avionics system.

The escorts were themselves impressive weapons systems: F/A-22Vs, specially built delta-wing versions of the F/A-22 Raptor prepared by the National Aeronautics Development and Testing Corporation (NADT), which was also overseeing Cyclops's final tests before production. The F/A-22Vs—generally called Velociraptors—traded a small portion of their older brothers' stealth abilities for considerably greater range and slightly heavier weapons carriage, but their real advance lay in the avionics system they shared with Cyclops. With a single verbal request, the Velociraptor pilot could have an annotated, three-dimensional view of a battlefield three hundred miles away, know which targets Cyclops intended to hit, and have suggestions from a targeting computer on how to best destroy his own. The system was scalable; in other words, it would work as well with two Velociraptors as with twenty.

In theory, anyway. Only four F/A-22Vs currently existed in all the world, and there were only two Cyclops aircraft, though presumably today's test would lead to funding for a dozen more.

"We ready?" Megan asked Howe.

"You pissed at something?" Howe said instead of answering. Besides flying chase, he was in charge of overseeing the system's integration for the Air Force, the de facto service boss of what was in theory a private program until it proved itself and was formally taken over by the military. He was the top "blue suit," or Air Force officer, on the project, though the hybrid nature of the program diluted his authority.

Dominic Gregorio pushed his big jaw between them, saying something about how they'd better hit the flyway before the weather got too tremendously awful. The forecast had the storm continuing for two or three days.

"Pissed?" asked Megan. "Why?"

A phony answer, he thought.

"We ready to hit the *flyway?*" repeated Dominic.

He giggled. For some reason the engineer thought *flyway* was the funniest play on words ever concocted in the English language.

"Kick butt," Megan told Howe. She slugged his shoulder and swept toward her plane.

By the time the altimeter ladder on Colonel Howe's heads-up display notched ten thousand feet an hour later, he had nearly convinced himself he hadn't seen her frown. Howe pushed the nose of his F/A-22V right, swinging toward the south end of the test range. Megan's 767 was just settling into its designated firing course about three hundred yards ahead, wings wobbling ever so slightly because of the severe turbulence they were flying through. The synthesized radar image in Howe's tactical display showed the plane as well as its course; its annotations critiqued Megan's piloting skills, noting that she was deviating from the flight plan by .001 degree.

Howe's Velociraptor, with its delta wings and nose canards, had been designed to work with Cyclops as a combination long-distance interceptor and attack plane, able to switch seamlessly from escort to bombing roles. The long weapons bay beneath its belly would include a mix of air-to-air AMRAAM-pluses and air-to-ground small-diameter GPS-guided bombs; the bays at the side would have either a heat-seeking Sidewinder or an AMRAAM-plus, an improved version of the battle-tested AIM-120. Roughly a dozen feet longer than a "stock" Raptor, the Velociraptor's massive V-shaped wings allowed it to carry nearly twice the fuel its brother held. Its rear stabilizers were more sharply canted and included control surfaces operated with the help of a hydrogen system to radically change airflow in milliseconds, greatly increasing the plane's maneuverability.

"Birds, this is Cyclops. We're in the loop," said Megan, alerting Howe and his wingman that the test sequence was about to begin.

"Bird One," acknowledged Howe. He looked down at the configurable tactical display screen in the center of his dash, which was synthesizing a view of the battle area ahead. The computer built the image from a variety of sources over the shared input network of the three planes; Howe had what looked like a three-dimensional plot of the mountain below. The large screen showed not just the target—an I-HAWK MIM-23 antiaircraft missile site—but the scope of its radar, a yellowish balloon projecting from the mountain plain. A red box appeared on the missile launcher, indicating that the laser targeting gear aboard Cyclops was scanning for the most vulnerable point of its target; the box began to blink and then went solid red, indicating it was ready to lock. Had this been a real mission, they could have fried it before it presented any danger at all.

Howe pushed his head back against the ejection seat, trying to will his neck and back muscles into something approaching relaxation.

Far below in the rugged Montana hills, the Army I-HAWK battery prepared to fire. The missile launcher was twenty nautical miles due north, a thick dagger in Cyclops's course. When the 767 drew to within five miles, the battery would fire its weapon. A millisecond after it did, the phased-array radar built into Cyclops One would detect it. The turret at the nose would rotate slightly downward, like the giant eye of the Greek monster the weapon had been named for. Within seconds the laser would lock on the missile and destroy it between three and five hundred feet off the ground.

The only thing difficult about the test was the thick band of storm clouds and torrential rain between the plane and the ground. The rain was so bad the normal monitoring plane, a converted RC-135, which would have had to fly at low altitude through the teeth of the storm, was grounded. Cyclops had handled simultaneous firings from two I-HAWK batteries handily in clear-sky trials three weeks before; it had nailed SAMs, cruise missiles, tanks, and a bunker during its extensive trials. Only the bunker had given it problems; the beam was not strong enough to defeat thick, buried concrete, and the system relied on complicated image analysis to attempt to find a weak point, generally in the ventilation system. The analysis could take as long as sixty seconds—something to work on for the Mark II version.

"Hey, Colonel, what's your number?" said Williams over the squadron frequency.

"Three-five-zero."

"Got five even."

Howe snickered but didn't acknowledge. The crews had a pool on the altitude where the laser would fry the missile. Three-five-zero was 350 feet, and happened to be the average of the last four trials; five meant five hundred, the theoretical top of the target envelope. Given the results of the past tests, a hit there would be almost as bad as a complete miss. Williams was just a hard-luck guy.

"I can't see a thing here," added Williams. "What do you think about me dropping down to five thousand feet?"

"We briefed you at eight," said Howe. "Hang with it."

"I'm supposed to see what's going on, right? My video's going to get a nice picture of clouds."

"Okay, get where you have to get. Just don't get in the way."

"Oh yeah, roger that. Don't feel like becoming popcorn today."

Howe flicked his HUD from standard to synthetic hologram view, in effect closing his eyes to the real world so he could watch a movie of what was happening around him.

The grayish image of the sky blurred into the background, replaced by a blue bowl of heaven. Bird Two ducked down through faint puffs of clouds, its speed indicated as functions of Mach numbers in small print below the wing.

The holographic view could not only show the pilot what was happening in bad weather or night; using the radar and other sensor inputs, the Velociraptor's silicone brain could synthesize an image of what was happening up to roughly 150 miles away. The image viewpoint could be changed; it was possible to essentially "see" what Williams saw through his front screen by pointing at the plane's icon in the display and saying "first-person" to the computer. (The command was a reference to point-of-view directions in movies and books.) And this was only a start: The real potential of the computing power would be felt when unmanned aerial vehicles or UAVs were integrated into the system, which was scheduled to begin after the Air Force formally took over the program; for now, UAV data could only be collected aboard the 767 at a separate station.

Howe found the synthetic view distracting and flipped back to the standard heads-up ghost in front of the real Persipex that surrounded him before scanning his instrument readings. Speed, fuel burn, engine temperature—every reading could have come straight from a spec sheet. The F/A-22Vs had more than a hundred techies assigned as full-time nannies; the regular Air Force maintenance crewmen, or "maintainers," were augmented by engineers and company reps as well as NADT personnel who were constantly tweaking the various experimental and pre-production systems they were testing.

"Alpha in sixty seconds," said Megan.

Something in her voice sparked Howe's anger again. He squeezed the side stick so tightly his forearm muscles popped. For a moment he visualized himself pushing the stick down and at the same time gunning the throttle to the firewall. An easy wink on the trigger would lace the Boeing's fuselage with shells from the cannon. The plane's wings, laden with fuel, would burst into flames.

Why was he thinking that?

Why was he so mad? Because she hadn't smiled when he wanted her to? Because he was in love and she wasn't?

Screw that. She loved him.

And if not, he'd make her love him. Win her, woo her—whatever it took.

Howe nearly laughed at himself. He was thinking like a teenager, and he was a long way from his teens. At thirty-three, he was very young for his command but very old in nearly every other way. *Emotionally mature beyond his physical years,* Clayton Bonham had written when picking him from three candidates to head the Air Force portion of the project. *Steady as a rock.*

Except when it came to love, maybe. He just didn't have that much experience with it, not even in his first marriage.

Megan did love him. He knew it.

"Thirty seconds. What's Bird Two doing?" snapped Megan.

"Dropping for a better view," he answered, his tone nearly as sharp as hers.

"That's not what we briefed."

Howe didn't bother answering. They were flying into the worst of the storm. Lightning streaked around him. A wind burst pushed on the wings but the flight computer held the plane perfectly steady, making microadjustments in the control surfaces. Forward airspeed pegged 425 knots—very slow for the Velociraptor, which had been designed to operate best in supercruise mode just under Mach 1.5.

"Fifteen seconds," said Megan.

More lightning. The only thing he could see in the darkness beyond the glass canopy were the zigs of yellow, heaven cracking open.

"Ten," said Megan.

An indicator on the RWR panel noted that the I-HAWK radar had locked on the stealthy chase planes as well as Cyclops.

"Five seconds," she said.

Howe blew a full wad of air into his mask. He felt her legs again, her smallish breasts against his chest.

Blow her away with something special: a week in Venice. They were going to have some downtime once these tests were done.

"Alpha," said Megan.

His HUD screen flashed white. In the next moment, Howe's Velociraptor plunged nose-first toward the ground.

He couldn't see. He couldn't breathe. Everything Thomas Howe had ever been furled into a bullet at the center of his skull. His head fused to his helmet and for a brief moment his consciousness fled. His heart stopped pumping blood and his body froze.

In the next moment something warm touched the ice.

Megan. Smiling, last night on the bed.

It was only a shard of memory, but it made his heart catch again.

Gravity slammed Howe against the seat as he fought to regain control of the plane. Bile filled his mouth and nose; it stung his eyes, ate through the sinews of his arms. He pulled back on the stick, but the plane didn't respond.

He wanted to cough but couldn't. The helmet pounded his skull, twisting at the temples. The F/A-22V threatened to whip into a spin. He pushed the stick to catch it and jammed the pedals.

Nothing worked.

The Velociraptor's control system had gone off-line. That ought to have been impossible.

Engines gone.

Backup electricity to run the controls should automatically route from the forced-air rams below the fuselage.

Nothing. Too late.

Out, time to get out!

But the engines were still working. He could feel the throb in his spine.

Out—get out! You'll fly into the ground.

The computer controlled the canopy. If it was gone, if that was the problem, he'd have to go to the backup procedure.

Set it. Pull the handle.

Out!

The controls should work. Or the backups. Or the backups to the backups.

Howe hit the fail-safe switch and clicked the circuit open manually.

Nothing.

Out!

Howe forced his head downward and forced himself to hunt for the yellow handle of the ejection seat. The blackness that had pushed against his face receded slightly, enough to let him think a full thought. Without control of the plummeting plane, he was no more than a snake caught in the talons of an eagle; the yellow handle was his only escape.

The fingers on his right hand cramped hard around the stick at the right side of the seat. He looked at them, trying to will them open.

They were locked around the molded handle. He looked at them again, uncomprehendingly: Why were they not letting go?

He pulled back on the stick, then pushed hard to each side several times. If the controls worked, the plane would shake back and forth violently, trying to follow the conflicting commands. But it did nothing.

A black cone closed in around his head. *Let go,* he told his hand.

Finally his fingers loosened. He reached for the ejection handle, wondering if the F/A-22V had started to spin. He could no longer tell.

Augering into oblivion.

Something stopped him as his gloved finger touched the handle. He looked up and saw the large hulk of the Boeing bearing down straight at him.

Instinct made him grab the stick again. It was a useless, stupid reaction in an uncontrollable airplane; if he pulled the eject handle, he might at least save himself. The dead controls had no way of stopping the collision.

Except that they did. The F/A-22V responded to his desperate tug, pushing her chin upward and steadying on her left wing. The 767's tail loomed at the top of the canopy for a long second, the stabilizer an ax head above his eyes. Then it disappeared somewhere behind him.

Two very quick breaths later Howe had full control of the plane. He wrestled it into level flight. He called a range emergency—it was the first thing he could think to say—then tried to hail Cyclops.

Empty fuzz answered.

"Bird One to Cyclops," he repeated over the frequency they had all shared. Ideas and words blurred together, his mind several steps behind his instincts; he couldn't sort out what he needed to say, let alone do. "Two? Williams, where are you? Cyclops? Bird Two? No joy! Shit—lost wingman! Break off! Shit."

Howe sent a long string of curses out over the radio before finally clicking off to listen for a response. He put his nose up, trying to get over the weather. Worried that he would hit either his wingman or the Boeing, he kept his gaze fixed on the sky over the heads-up display until he broke through the clouds. Only then did he look back down at his instruments.

Everything was back, everything. All systems were in the green. The only problem seemed to be the radar: completely blank.

The techies would pull their hair out over this one. He reached for the radar control panel on the dash, manually selecting search and scan mode. The auxiliary screen flashed an error message listing several circuit problems.

Then it cleared. The screen tinged green before flashing a light blue, the color of empty sky. NO CONTACT appeared in the right-hand corner. His position indicator showed he was now over Canada, just north of the intended test area.

Howe keyed the self-test procedure for his radar. As it began, he tried reaching Cyclops again.

"Bird One to Cyclops. Hey, Megan, you hear me or what?"

Howe waited for her to snap back with something funny. He felt ashamed of his anger now.

"Bird One, this is Ground Unit Hawk. What the hell is going on up there?"

"I had a major equipment flakeout," he told the ground controller at the I-HAWK station. "Controls just disappeared. Looks like I still have a problem with my radar. Until your transmission I thought my radio was gone as well. I can't reach Cyclops or my wingman."

"Neither can we."

"Give me a vector," he said, twisting his head around to look for the planes.

"Negative. We don't have them on our radar."

"What?"

"We have you and that's it. Cyclops and Bird Two are gone. Completely gone."

CHAPTER

2

Timing was everything. Light up too soon, and either the attendant would notice or the smoke alarm would go off. Too late, and he'd miss at least two drags on the Camel.

Andy Fisher fingered his lighter as the Gulfstream dropped into its final approach to the runway. On a commercial flight, the most the stewardesses would do if he lit up now was tsk-tsk on the way out. But this was an Air Force plane, and the attendant wasn't exactly a piece of eye candy: The sergeant looked like he could bench-press the plane. He also reeked of health freak, and had frowned when the FBI Special Agent asked for a refill after his fourth cup of coffee.

Still, a smoke was a smoke, and it didn't make sense to miss a nice hit of nicotine because a Neanderthal was breathing down your neck. Fisher was already late for the meeting he was supposed to be at, and it was doubtful that the others on the task force would allow smoking there. Not that he would let that sort of thing bother him under normal circumstances, but this being a military matter, there was bound to be a full complement of uniformed types with guns available to enforce even the most egregious government usurpation of personal smoking rights.

The jet's tires squealed loudly as they hit the runway. The plane settled onto the concrete with a slight rocking sensation, but Fisher had no trouble firing up the end of the cigarette.

"You ought not smoke," growled the sergeant, sitting two rows back. "Pilot'll have a fit."

"He owns the plane?"

The sergeant threw off his seat belt and came forward, looming over Fisher.

"Thinks he does, the prick."

Without a word Fisher handed the sergeant the pack. Both men were midway through their second cigarettes when the Gulfstream finally rolled to a stop. A lieutenant barely old enough to shave was waiting for Fisher with a driver and a Humvee.

"Welcome to North Lake, sir," said the lieutenant as Fisher shambled down the steps, overnight bag slung over his shoulder. The man stood at attention, hand seemingly stapled to his forehead.

"You looking for change or a salute?" said Fisher, taking a final drag from the cigarette as he reached the tarmac.

"Uh, no, sir." The lieutenant made a stiff grab for his bag, but Fisher held it tightly. It had most of his smokes; no way he was letting go of it.

"Where's the water?" asked Fisher.

"Sir?"

"If this is North Lake, where's the water? All I saw were mountains coming in."

"Uh, I'm not following. The water supply is a well."

"Deep subject."

"Oh yes, sir." Still playing puppy, the lieutenant jerked around and ran to open the back door of the Hummer for him. Fisher got into the front instead.

"I think we're running behind," Fisher told the airman at the wheel. "Let's kick some butt."

The driver complied, nearly sending the lieutenant through the back window as he whipped around on the blacktop. Fisher slumped against the door, starting another cigarette.

The base had been laid along the saddle of two mountains; what wasn't concrete was rock. Two small hangars sat at the far end of the runway. A large concrete mouth yawned beyond them, the low-slung opening narrowing the profile to a secure hangar. Three small, pillboxlike structures sat about a hundred yards beyond it. They didn't seem big enough to house latrines.

"Have a good flight?" asked the lieutenant from the backseat as they pulled toward the pillboxes.

"I didn't puke," said Fisher. "That was a plus."

They stopped about ten feet from the smallest structure, a dark brown box of cement maybe seven feet wide and a little taller. A steel door sat in the middle. It reminded Fisher of the entrance to the rooftop stairwell in Brooklyn where he'd lost his virginity at age fourteen.

"The Ritz, sir," said the driver.

As Fisher slid out of the vehicle the lieutenant went over and flipped the cover on a panel at the center of the door, revealing a small numeric keypad. He punched a set of numbers, then pressed his palm against a reddish-black square directly below. The door slid open.

"You'll have to press your palm against the sensor on the doorjamb," said the lieutenant as Fisher started to follow him.

"Which?"

"See the gray blotch there?" The lieutenant pointed toward the side. He added apologetically, "Once I'm in, I can't step out or the door will slam and everything will freeze."

Fisher sighed, then laid his palm against the sensor so it could be read.

"Um, and the cigarette, sir: I'm afraid there's no smoking."

"Alarms?" asked Fisher.

"And sprinklers."

Fisher eyed him suspiciously. The kid's peach fuzz was too obvious for him to be lying. Reluctantly the FBI agent finished the Camel and tossed it as he stepped through the doorway.

An elevator waited beyond the threshold. "More security downstairs," said the lieutenant as they started downward. "They're going to want to search your bag. And you'll be escorted everywhere."

"They know I'm one of the good guys, right? See, my white hat's back home and it seems like a real pain in the ass to run back and get it."

The lieutenant's laugh sounded tinny against the pneumatic rush of the plunging elevator. "Yes, sir. But the nature of the project, and then with yesterday's, er, incident . . ."

"I've been through this sort of thing before, kid," said Fisher. "Otherwise I wouldn't be here, right?"

"Yes, sir."

They did have more security downstairs—a lot more. The narrow hallway was lined with Air Force security personnel holding M16 rifles with thick laser scopes at the top. There were at least six video cameras in the ceiling, and two sets of crash gates. Farther along, four men in civilian clothes guarded the entrance to a corridor that led to the main sections of the underground complex. The men looked like linebackers preparing to blitz a rookie quarterback.

"Jesus, what the hell are you guys expecting?" Fisher said as his bag was inspected for a second time.

"What are *you* expecting?" said a voice from down the hall. "The scan in the elevator showed you brought a dozen cartons of cigarettes and no change of underwear."

"I ain't planning on crapping my pants, Kowalski," said Fisher. "I'm not part of the DIA."

"You wouldn't last in the DIA," said Kowalski, appearing from down the hall. The Defense Intelligence Agency officer had worked with Fisher several times before.

"Oh, I'd make it—just get a double lobotomy and I'd fit in fine," said Fisher.

"Yuck, yuck. Same old Fisher."

"Same old Kowalski. Same old frumpy brown suit," said Fisher, taking his bag back. "Add any ketchup stains since England?"

"Come on, they're starting. Stay close to our friend here," added the DIA officer, thumbing toward a large Air Force security type in battle dress with a flak vest and a very large gun holster at his side. "You can't go anyplace without a minder no matter who you are. It's worse than Dreamland. By the way, Jemma Gorman's running the show."

"Shit."

"Yeah, that was about her reaction when she heard you were coming."

Jemma Gorman—officially, Air Force Colonel Jemma Gorman, special aide to the Air Force chief of staff temporarily assigned to the Office of Special Investigations—was holding forth in front of a wall of white erase boards as Fisher entered the small amphitheater briefing area behind Kowalski. Her reaction to Fisher's arrival was friendlier than he expected: She ignored him, continuing her lecture without stopping.

"The planes disappeared precisely eighteen hours and fifteen minutes ago," she told the audience of military and civilian investigators. "In that time we have conducted a thorough search of the continental United States. Neither Cyclops nor the missing F/A-22V landed at an airport in North America. We have two working theories. Theory One: There was some sort of catastrophic event. The planes collided, or something similar. They crashed—"

"Gee, you think?" said Fisher, just softly enough for her to pretend she didn't hear. Gorman continued speaking, her eyes focused on some hapless speck of dust in the back of the room.

"—and because of the difficult weather conditions, locating them has been delayed." Gorman pulled down a large map at the front—she'd always been good at visual aids—and indicated that the search area was mountainous and currently obscured by severe weather, which wasn't supposed to break for several more hours. "You'll note that a good portion of our grids are in Canada," she said, segueing into a summary of the arrangements with the Canadians. Their major concern seemed to be the possible effects of the search on the local moose, rumored to be in rutting season.

"In addition to assets from the project team directed by General Bonham and NADT, USAF has conducted and will continue to conduct the search," she added. "Major Christian is our lead on that aspect. He will keep us updated on the progress." Gorman glanced sternly toward the second row, where an Air Force officer nodded grimly. Her own expression grew even graver, her brows furrowing on her forehead. "The other theory, Theory Two, is that the planes have been stolen. Unlikely. But we will exhaust that possibility in parallel to the search. Mr. Kowalski will head that team."

"Pet," said Fisher in a loud whisper. Kowalski, who had sat in the row in front of him, bobbed his head backward but said nothing.

"Kevin Sullivan from Aerodynamics Linx will head the technical team. We'll have a subsection on sabotage to rule it in or out; Major Yei from CID will take the lead, along with the technical team headed by Al Biushi. You may remember Mr. Biushi from the NASA project last year. The malfunctions on the F/A-22V that landed have yet to be explained," said Gorman. Her hands jabbed the air as if she were a conductor signaling the cannon for the *1812 Overture*. "That will be a priority for the Velociraptor technical team, which will be headed by Jack Meiser from Locker Aircraft."

Fisher pulled his cigarette pack from his pocket and slumped back in his seat, unwrapping the cellophane as

Gorman went through administrative information about meeting places and quarters. Anyone else would leave this sort of minutiae to an aide or even a handout, but Gorman's hands worked into a frenzy and she actually smiled while reciting, from memory, the telephone extensions of the various subgroups assigned in the base's encrypted phone system.

The cellophane wrapper stuck at the corner of the pack. Fisher pulled it off with a loud flourish; one or two of the people in front of him shot nasty looks over their shoulders, as if he'd set off a stink bomb.

"Howard McIntyre from the NSC will be joining us from Hawaii via closed circuit this afternoon," said Gorman sharply, a buried Brooklyn accent filtering into her words. "Most of you know Mr. McIntyre, but for those of you who don't, he is the assistant to the national security advisor in charge of technology. He's flying to Hawaii for the augmented-ABM tests, which are due to start tomorrow, but he's also been tasked to keep the President updated. As you can well imagine, the White House is extremely interested in what's going on here. I don't have to tell you all how sensitive this is, not only in terms of national security, but politically. Especially politically. I expect all of you to be discreet."

She looked directly at him as she said that.

"Discreet—my middle name," said Fisher in a whisper. "Hey, Kowalski, who's Bonham?"

"Retired two-star Air Force general who heads the National Aerospace Development and Testing Corporation, which is NADT," whispered Kowalski. "The big boss of the project. NADT's a contract agency with serious clout. They've developed a half-dozen weapons including the modified F/A-22s, and they're responsible for testing and refining a bunch more, including Cyclops. Part of the drive to privatize non-warfighting military functions and save some cash. Bonham's the main man."

"Yeah, but get to the good stuff. What kind of underwear?"

"That's more your department, but I'd guess boxers."

"What about the little boss?"

"You mean Howe?"

"Sure."

"Almost bought it in the chase plane."

"Prime suspect."

"Yeah, right."

"Who else is important?"

"Guy named Williams in the other chase plane. Gone. Air Force. Never heard of him." Kowalski stopped to look at his notes. "Lady named, uh, Megan York."

"Air Force?"

"Contract test pilot. Works directly for NADT, like just about everybody else here. She's about thirty. Supposed to be a dish. Haven't seen the photos yet."

"Put me in for the eight by ten. What kind of underwear does she wear?"

Gorman frowned severely in their direction, then looked back to her groupies in the front row. "I'm in the process of requesting more people for the monkey work. Again, I remind you: Everywhere you go on this base, you go with security. You know the drill. Questions?"

"I have one," said Fisher quickly. "Where's the smoking lounge?"

"For those few of you privileged not to know Special Agent Andrew Fisher, that is him in the rumpled gray suit. He is our lone representative from the FBI, assigned to be as annoying as possible. Obviously the Bureau does not believe this is a very important case. Agent Fisher likes to play class clown, though fortunately today he has left his red nose and floppy shoes at home. He will act as FBI liaison and attempt to grab as much glory as he can, while at the same time doing nothing more than drinking coffee and smoking cigarettes, though not in that order."

"I thought grabbing glory was your job," said Fisher innocently.

Gorman gave him some dagger eyes, then turned to answer other questions from the assorted teacher's pets. The only one that interested Fisher was the one she shrugged in answer to: Why hadn't the emergency locator beacons on the downed planes been picked up yet?

The answer was, there were no locator beacons. Because of the nature of the project, the planes flew without ident gear that would identify them if properly queried. They didn't have black boxes or any of the otherwise useful gear that would, presumably, have made them easier to find. In fairness, all the monitoring gear they were carrying for the trial exercises would ordinarily be more than enough to supply pinpoint positions in the case of an emergency. But whatever had blanked the systems in all the planes had made them impossible to track as well.

As the questions faded, Fisher got up to leave. A few people nodded at him, but with the exception of Kowalski and Gorman he didn't know anyone here very well. Probably just as well: It would make it easier to bum cigarettes the first few days.

"Hold on, Andy," said Gorman as he started toward the door.

"Hey, Gorgeous."

"Knock off the crap. This is my show."

"I saw your name in lights outside."

"Just do your job."

"And save your ass like in Italy?"

"There are two opinions on that."

"Yours and everyone else's?"

"Oh, you're a master comedian."

"Yeah, I'm doing Vegas next week," said Fisher. "Look, I'd love to trade bon mots with you, but I'm dying for a smoke. Where do I find the pilot of the F/A-22. Howe, right?"

"Who says you're talking to Colonel Howe?" Gorman's cheeks not only colored red but seemed to rise on her face. "I just went through the various assignments. This—"

"If you're going to be a pain, we can call General Whatzhisname and ask him to read that long paragraph from DOD Memorandum 17-85B. The verbiage is a bit obscure, but I think it says something to the effect that you have to cooperate with me or get a good spanking. Of course, if that's what you're interested in . . ."

"Just stay out of my way," said Gorman, walking away so quickly her escort had to double-time down the hall.

"Let's go, Kato," Fisher said to the sergeant looming at his elbow. "Smoke, food, meaning of life. More or less in that order."

"Sir?"

"You can knock off the 'sir' routine," he told the noncom, who looked to be about thirty. The patch on the pocket of his combat camos declared his name was JHNSN. "I know you don't mean it. Just call me Fisher. Or Andy, if you're pissed off. Come on, I need a smoke."

"We have to go outside."

"Yeah, or the men's room," Fisher told him. "But today we'll go outside, because it's always nice to make a good first impression."

CHAPTER
3

Howard McIntyre settled into his first-class seat, indulging in a fantasy about the stewardess who was pouring the champagne. He was just removing her bra when one of the two cell phones he carried in his suit jacket—he had a third in his briefcase, along with an encrypted phone—rang.

The attendant was just good-looking enough to tempt him not to answer, and he might not have if the call hadn't been on his "A" phone, a special encoded satellite phone with global coverage reserved for his boss, National Security Advisor Michael Blitz.

"McIntyre," he said.

"Where are you?"

"Sitting on the airplane, about to take off for Hawaii," McIntyre told Blitz.

"Get off and call me."

"It may be too late. We're about to taxi."

"Then find a parachute."

"Doc—"

"Don't give me the Doc line and don't call me Professor," said Blitz. "Get off the plane and call me back."

McIntyre stifled a curse and got out of his seat, reminding himself for the one millionth time in the past year that being a public servant meant putting off personal pleasure in hopes of much greater rewards in the future.

Though at times it was hard to imagine what those rewards could possibly be.

Twenty minutes later McIntyre found himself standing in the middle of the rental car lot, briefcase and carry-on in one hand, secure KY-118 phone–handheld computer in the other.

"Mac, what's the latest?" asked Blitz. The NSC head was already in Hawaii, which was obvious from the background noises of the reception.

McIntyre could have played dumb, but that would only lessen the already infinitesimal chance that he could talk Blitz into changing his mind about what he wanted him to do. Both men knew each other well enough—McIntyre had been Blitz's graduate assistant a million years before—to guess exactly what the other was thinking.

"Uh, nothing new on Cyclops One as of two hours ago, Doc. I had a secure videoconference with them to do the rah-rah thing, but—"

"I want you up there ASAP."

"Aw, Professor."

"To the best of my knowledge, my current employer is the U.S. government, not Harvard."

"I'm due in Hawaii for the augmented-ABM tests," pleaded McIntyre. "I mean, my main area is technology, and if that's not technology . . ."

"There are plenty of people here. More than we need."

"But, uh . . ." It was difficult to argue that he was needed in Hawaii—in fact, almost no one was, outside the actual work crews who monitored the test missile firings. Three different company coalitions were taking part in the tests, which called for long-distance, low-altitude strikes of small warheads, such as those that could be carried by cruise missiles.

The augmented system would greatly enhance "standard" ABM capabilities, closing a serious gap in the defense system and making the U.S. impervious to attack. While the tests involved surface-launched missiles, the production model would include satellite batteries that would eventually provide global coverage. It would be the last and most powerful part of a complicated blanket that would include tactical coverage from Cyclops laser planes—great at short-range interception but very limited beyond three or four hundred miles—and high-altitude ballistic interceptions from the "normal" ABM system, which couldn't target short-range warheads, let alone cruise missiles. When built, the augmented ABM system would revolutionize warfare. It might even make it obsolete.

Assuming, of course, the system could be made to work. Surprisingly, none of the companies responsible for the standard ABM system had done very well in the tests so far. The surprise winner in the simulations had been a team headed by Jolice Missile Systems.

McIntyre didn't particularly like the Jolice people—arrogant rich bastards well connected in Washington. He expected them to fall on their asses in the Hawaii tests, though not before their hospitality party—which, if past was prologue, would feature the best available babes in Hawaii.

"You're stuttering, Mac," said Blitz.

"I don't know that I can do anything Gorman and Bonham can't. They assured me twenty minutes ago that they'd be recovering the planes anytime now," said McIntyre.

That didn't draw an immediate response, so McIntyre added, "There's a couple of hundred—must be a thousand—people involved in the search. The weather was a bitch, and that's the only reason it hasn't been wrapped up yet."

"The President just asked me why you weren't there."

"Yes, sir," said McIntyre. "So, how do I get to North Lake?"

"I have a jet en route from Edwards right now."

Dr. Michael Blitz paced the length of the room, his right hand rubbing the nubby outline of his goatee, his left hitched back into his belt. It was a pose the students in his international relations seminar at Harvard would have recognized as presaging a major pronouncement, more than likely some wild metaphor comparing a campaign in the Napoleonic Wars to a Cold War tête-à-tête between Nixon and Mao Zedong, with a snide reference to Henry Kissinger thrown in for laughs.

But this wasn't Harvard. And while the suite of rooms in the Hawaiian hotel where he was pacing was considerably more luxurious than his usual academic haunts, at the moment he would have gladly exchanged the surroundings.

Not the job, just the surroundings.

The two floors below him swarmed with contractors whose companies had staked billions on the right to build the next phase of America's global augmented ABM system. The name itself was anachronistic, considering that the intent of the next phase was actually to defend against non-ballistic warheads, but it was difficult enough to get the administration and Congress to agree on a goal; changing the name to something more appropriate—long-range, high-speed automated interceptor, for example—would have required political skills beyond even Blitz's impressive repertoire. Integrated with the standard ABM system and short-range weapons such as the airborne laser and theater defenses, the augmented ABM system would provide a true, extendible shield for the world, finally fulfilling the Reagan vision of the 1980's of making nuclear weapons obsolete.

For Blitz, the system represented an opportunity for an entirely new view of the world. America wouldn't simply be the most powerful country on the globe; it would be the ensurer of peace. The augmented ABM system represented a chance at completely altering global politics, and even though he was cautious and conservative by nature, he couldn't help but be awed by the possibilities.

On the other hand, the missile system would also make many rich people even richer. Thus, the representatives of the three coalitions in Hawaii for the tests were like rival motorcycle gangs who'd happened to pick the same town to rampage through. They were nice to Blitz, of course—overly nice, and very eager to run down their competition. Rumors of malfeasance, chicanery, and corruption were more common than the olives in the hospitality suites. And there were a lot of olives.

The tests were hardly Blitz's only or even main worry at the moment. Losing Cyclops One and its F/A-22V escort during testing, probably over Canada, was a major headache, though he might be able to use it to persuade the President to dispense with NADT and the other quasi-governmental agencies and independent firms that had moved into place during the last administration to facilitate weapons development and procurement. To Blitz's mind, farming out national security to private interests undermined the military and therefore national security itself, but it was a difficult notion to sell in these days of shrinking government.

Even the Cyclops accident paled next to the situation in India and Pakistan. Blitz and the rest of the National Security Council were receiving hourly updates on tensions there. Militants on both sides of the border were pushing for a serious confrontation, not just in Kashmir, but across the Rann of Kutch to the southeast. U.S. intelligence estimates had both countries mobilizing large parts of their armies and placing their nuclear forces at or near their top levels of alert.

"Dr. Blitz, it's time for the conference call with the Japanese defense minister," said Blitz's assistant, Mozelle Clark, calling through the door. "And, uh, room service left a coffee cart outside. And, uh, goodies."

Blitz had ordered the coffee but not the dessert. He opened the door. *Goodies* was an understatement: A two-tiered cake stood in the middle of several hundred assorted Italian cookies, along with a phalanx of profiteroles and rum cakes. An envelope stood amid the pile in the corner of the table, undoubtedly announcing which contractor had bestowed the sweets.

"Make sure there's no cash in the envelope," said Blitz. "Then dump the cookies."

"Want me to give them to the security people?"

"No way," insisted Blitz. "Take them downstairs to the lobby, find some four- or five-year-old, and tell them it's an early Christmas."

"They look good," said Mozelle, who was eyeing one of the rum cakes.

"The Devil always does. Please, before I'm tempted to find out who sent them and hold it against them."

"Secretary of State's office called: They want another conference on India and Pakistan in half an hour. Word is, the secretary wants to send a delegation," added Mozelle.

"Just great. You volunteering?"

Mozelle laughed, then grew serious. "You are joking, right?"

"Yes." Blitz folded his arms. "All right, I give in."

Mozelle gave him a quizzical look.

"Give me one of those cookies. Then get rid of the tray."

CHAPTER

4

Howe sat in the steel chair, staring at the blank white board at the front of the room, arms crossed, feet flat on the floor. The latest of the marathon debriefings had ended only a few minutes before, more or less as the others had ended: with his voice trailing off mid-sentence and the investigators standing around nervously waiting for him to continue.

Most likely they thought he was haunted by the accident, affected because he'd lost his wingman and lover. That wasn't it: He just didn't know what else to say. He'd gone over and over and over it until the words had no connection to what had happened.

Probably they didn't know Megan was his lover. They'd always been pretty careful about that, and no one had brought it up yet.

He could feel her next to him, laughing.

"You've never seen Ben-Hur? *The greatest movie ever made?"*

She'd said that three weeks ago, in the Starr Bar, the little place they'd found "off campus" a good fifty miles away. Megan had started to explain the movie to him, shifting her body to take the different parts in the chariot race, moving fluidly in the dim light of the small room, mesmerizing him. She'd continued after they paid up and walked to the car, pausing for a kiss, continuing as they rode down the deserted highway back to North Lake.

That was the moment he'd realized there could be many conversations like that—long, meandering talks in the middle of the night. When they lived together, or got married, conversations would go on for hours and days, even; he'd hear her talk and watch her hands moving through the air, mimicking the beautiful curves of her body.

When they got married. . . ? Had he thought that then?

No. That was something he was thinking now. He—they—hadn't gotten that far. It wasn't even hinted.

Howe had been married once, and it was a bust. But Megan was different, ideas flowing from her, thoughts—

And the sex, of course.

She had promised to buy *Ben-Hur* from Amazon.com so they could see it. The DVD had to take a roundabout route because of the covers involved in protecting the secrecy of the base; it hadn't arrived yet.

It wasn't so much her death as her complete disappearance that drove a hole in his chest.

"You're Colonel Howe, right?"

Howe jerked his head around. A tallish man with a pallid face stood in the doorway, shadowed by a tall Air Force security sergeant. The civilian wore a somewhat disheveled gray suit; he might be athletic under it—he didn't look fat or particularly thin—but his body slouched in a way that made it hard to tell.

"Who are you?" asked Howe.

"Fisher, FBI."

"You think the planes got kidnapped?" said Howe, getting up. He decided he'd been interviewed enough today.

"Actually, I think they were used in a bank robbery. Got a minute?"

"No," said Howe. "I have to go check on the search."

"Ah, Jemma can screw that up on her own," said Fisher. "And if not, she has about a million people helping her. I want to know about Captain Williams."

"What about him?"

"What kind of guy was he?"

"What do you mean?"

"As a person."

Howe shrugged.

"Did he like money?" asked Fisher, as if he knew the answer was yes.

"Money?" The other investigators had gone over the flight procedures and the myriad details of what had happened ad infinitum, but this came completely out of left field. "What the hell are you getting at?"

"How about York?"

"Megan York's family's richer than hell. One of her cousins is a congressman. What is it you want, Mr. Fisher?"

"Rest of the people on her crew? There were four all together, right, counting her?"

"You think we crashed the planes for money?"

" 'We'? "

Howe's anger had risen so quickly it surprised even him. He felt as if he were looking at himself from across the room, watching his body pitch forward, his arms stiff at his sides, hands balled into fists. He stuck his face about six inches from the FBI agent's; they were nearly the same height, with Fisher maybe an inch taller.

The agent didn't flinch. His expression, in fact, remained the same: quizzical puzzlement mixed with a certain reserve wariness. Howe pulled his face back, sensing he'd been purposely provoked.

"I was just thinking those planes are worth a hell of a lot of cigarettes," said Fisher.

"I don't have time for this," said Howe. He pushed past and out the door.

"Quick temper," Fisher told the sergeant trailing him as he worked his way out of the rat-maze of administrative offices beneath the control-command level of the underground facility. "If this were *Perry Mason*," said the FBI agent, "we'd figure he had something to hide."

"I wouldn't know about that," said the sergeant.

"Johnson, if I accused you of taking a bribe, you'd get pissed off."

"Yes, sir."

"And if I accused your friend of taking a bribe, you'd probably also get pissed off."

"Yes, sir, I would."

"Yeah, me too. I can't see why it changes anything for Perry. But he's the man. Come on, let's go see if the search parties have their coffee situation straightened out."

CHAPTER
5

Captain Timothy "Blaze" Robinson—known as Timmy to his friends—pulled the F-16 through its turn gently, moving his whole body as he pressured the control stick. The Falcon did a graceful bank three thousand feet above the closest peak, tiptoeing around the Canadian Rockies as if afraid to wake them. Timmy nudged the aircraft straight and level, his movements the minimum needed to keep the plane on its course. He leaned his head toward the canopy, staring out at the terrain he'd been given to comb.

The search force included a half-dozen helicopters, several small propeller-driven craft that could fly low and slow in the mountains, a J-STARS aircraft with a bushel of sensors, and a U-2R providing near-real-time IR imaging. Still, Timmy flew as if finding his downed comrades were entirely on his shoulders. No high-tech sensor, no satellite image, could do a better job than his own eyes as they hunted through the shadowy slopes below. Two other pilots had taken this same workhorse F-16 over this same terrain on earlier shifts, but Timmy tracked over it as if it were virgin territory, sure that he would see something through the haze and persistent, lingering clouds.

By rights, Timmy should be the guy they were looking for. He was one of the F/A-22V pilots and ordinarily flew as Williams's wingman; Colonel Howe had bumped him for the test, taking lead and slotting Williams behind him.

Timmy scanned his instruments, double-checking to make sure all systems were in the green. The F-16 had a smooth, easygoing personality, a can-do attitude that matched its versatility. She wasn't particularly well suited to the SAR role, however; the propeller-driven and helicopter assets involved in the search could fly lower and slower much more comfortably, and had more eyes available for the search. That fact was reflected in Timmy's assigned area, well out of the primary search grid. But neither the pilot nor the F-16 herself would have admitted this. Muscling her ailerons against the sharp wind vortices tossed off by the crags, the Falcon stiffened her tail and held off the breeze, sailing across the valley with the calm aplomb of a schooner on a glass lake.

The shared radio frequency being used to coordinate the search buzzed with voices. Grandpa—the J-STARS control that was coordinating the search—shifted assets around as the clouds slowly made their way off the mountains.

In a combat zone, a specific protocol governed when an airman would "come up" or broadcast on Guard frequency, the radio channel reserved for such emergencies and monitored by all of the searchers. These special instructions or spins conserved the limited battery power of the radios and made it more difficult for an enemy to detect or home in on the transmissions. But in this situation—and sometimes even in combat—a broadcast might be made at any time, especially if the downed airman heard a search plane overhead.

Timmy tried willing a broadcast into his ear; he heard only static, and even that was faint.

This long after a crash, what were the odds that someone had survived?

Not particularly good. Nor was it likely that one of the crew would be this far north. But it was possible. Moving at a couple of hundred miles an hour, you could travel relatively far in ten minutes, fifteen. There was no radar cover close to the mountains, and it was possible the planes had stayed in the air even longer. Punch out over the clouds, get pushed around a bit by the wind, hit your head somewhere—it *was* possible, if unlikely.

The searchers suddenly began chattering. They'd spotted something in a ravine. Metal.

Though the discovery was over a hundred miles to the west, Timmy felt his pulse jump. He slipped into another turn, dipping his wing and throttling back so he was just barely above stall speed, tiptoeing over the rough terrain. Something was there. He slipped around for another look.

The F-16's General Electric F110-GE-129IPE power plant developed roughly 30,000 pounds of thrust and could move the Fighting Falcon out to Mach 2 in a heartbeat. The power plant had been engineered specifically to increase acceleration and performance at low altitude, allowing a pilot on a bombing run to accelerate quickly after his bombs were dropped. But here he wanted to do the opposite, and the engine grumbled slightly as the pilot dialed its thrust ever lower.

Timmy flew over the spot four times, making sure it was just a rock he'd seen, not a body. On his last pass he flew barely fifty feet from the ground, moving dangerously slow, just over 140 knots. Still, it was difficult to get a good glimpse of the ground, and the interplay of terrain and shadows played tricks on his eyes. Once more he broadcast his location on Guard, asking if Williams or anyone could hear him.

Going from the F/A-22V to the F-16 was a little like trading a BMW M5 for a Honda Civic. Both aircraft were well made, but the ideas behind their designs were very different. The base F/A-22 was a cutting-edge design aimed at creating the world's best interceptor. All of the political wrangling and bureaucratic BS involved in its procurement—such as what Timmy viewed as the absurd designation change from F-22 to F/A-22—couldn't gum up what was, at its core, a great fighting machine.

The F/A-22V took that design considerably further— without, he might have added, the political BS, since the work was all handled "off-line" by NADT. Specially designed to work with Cyclops as part of a new-era battle element, the aircraft was arguably the most versatile and capable ever constructed.

The F-16 was a lower-cost (though not cheap) jack-of-all-trades. Depending on its configuration, it could operate as an attack plane, a Wild Weasel or anti-SAM aircraft, a close-air-support mud fighter, or an interceptor. This Block 50/52 aircraft represented a substantial improvement over the original Block 15, the Air Force's first production model, which nudged off the assembly line in the 1970's. Even so, its base technology was older than Timmy and even Colonel Howe, and after flying the F/A-22V, the pilot would have felt severely handicapped in the F-16 in a combat situation.

Not overmatched, though. The F-16—which was known as the Viper as well as the Fighting Falcon, its more "official" nickname—had excellent maneuverability and acceleration at near-Mach and Mach-plus speeds, attributes that played well in a knife fight. The original lack of BVR or beyond-visible-range killing ability had been corrected with the fitting of AIM-120 AMRAAMs some years before, and the Block 50/52 aircraft's APG-68 radar, with a range between thirty and forty-five miles and the ability to track up to ten targets simultaneously, was at least arguably as capable as anything the F-16 was likely to encounter.

Assuming, of course, that it didn't encounter an American plane.

Timmy came to the end of the area he'd been assigned to patrol and began to track back south. As he did, the controller in the J-STARS coordinating the search effort hailed him.

"Florida Three," he acknowledged.

"Florida, we have an area for you to check out, possible debris picked up by our Eyes asset."

Eyes was a U-2 helping with the search.

"Florida Three acknowledges, Grandpa," answered Timmy. "Feed me a vector."

He selected military power, climbing quickly and tracking toward the area, which was so far north and east of the test area that he guessed it had to be a false lead. The mission specialist in the J-STARS gave him a detailed description of the terrain as he flew, saying there seemed to be a large piece of metal in or on a rockslide at the base of a sheer cliff in the foothills of the Canadian Rockies about two hundred miles due west of Edmonton. He described it as a broken silver pencil stuck in the side of a thousand-meter rockslide.

As Timmy neared the spot he took the plane down, asking the J-STARS specialist to describe the area again. J-STARS were E-8A or E-8C Boeing 707-type aircraft that had been developed as a joint project by the Air Force and Army. The aircraft had considerable surveillance equipment of their own, including a Norden AN/APY-3 multimode Side-Looking Airborne Radar. The complement of operators—there were a minimum of ten consoles, with room for up to seventeen, depending on the plane and mission—could process and coordinate information from a seemingly infinite variety of sources. They could direct and download targeting information to properly equipped Air Force attack planes as well as provide comprehensive battlefield intelligence to ground commanders. In this case, the operator was using a newly developed variant of the Joint Tactical Information Distribution System (or JTIDS) data link to pass an infrared feed directly from the U-2R to his console. Some F-16s were already equipped with gear that would have allowed the specialist to punch a few buttons and relay the image directly to Timmy's cockpit. Had he been flying one of the F/A-22Vs, the data would have been added to the synthesized three-dimensional rendering of the area on the tactics screen. The plane's computer would have calculated his best approach and likely time to target, along with a fuel matrix and a suggested wine.

Timmy oriented himself, tucking down toward the cliff side. He took the first pass too fast and too high, streaking by the mountain so quickly, he couldn't spot anything. His heart had started to pound; he realized as he pulled the nose of his plane back away from the ground that his hand was shaking.

He cut his orbit, pushing his wing down and falling back toward the target area. He backed his speed off and even considered putting down his landing gear to help slow down.

He didn't see the grayish object until the third pass. From the air, it looked like the bottom half of an old ballpoint pen buried under some loose gravel. It seemed too small to be an airplane and had no wings. Timmy banked to his right, circling around to get another view. He leaned forward from the canted seat of the F-16, pushing around, slowing the aircraft down to a walk. This pass was a tiptoe so close that his left wingtip nearly clipped the side of the hill.

There was definitely something in the crevice of the ravine. The bodies of both missing planes were covered with a dull gray next-generation radar-resistant skin—not the black coating of B-2s but something considered more durable and nearly as slippery. It was extremely difficult to see against the gray rocks and shadows.

But it was there. Or something was there.

Timmy spun back over it, this time going so slow that the aircraft bleated out a stall warning.

He could see a wing farther along, an almost perfect isosceles triangle sheered from an aircraft.

The Velociraptor.

He clicked his microphone to call the airborne search coordinator.

CHAPTER

6

Clayton T. Bonham waited impatiently as the MH-60G Pave Hawk helicopter he'd commandeered pitched through the mountains toward the area where the piece of metal had been found. He was just twenty minutes behind the initial-response team, which itself had arrived barely a half hour after the call from the flight that had made the find, but to Bonham it was too damn late already. When he gave an order, he expected it filled immediately, if not sooner. The Pave Hawk was moving close to its top speed, but that was hardly fast enough for him.

Bonham had been retired from the Air Force for nearly five years. Nonetheless, he still thought and acted like a two-star general; he even insisted on his subordinates calling him General.

Not insisted, exactly. Encouraged.

After all, as head of NADT, he was owed a certain amount of respect. He was responsible for developing the most important weapons the United States had developed since the hydrogen bomb.

An exaggeration, surely, and yet, one with some justification. When fully implemented, a Cyclops battle element could destroy anything from a hardened ballistic-missile complex to a terrorist one-man basement bomb factory, with minimal collateral damage. The possibilities were endless and, without exaggeration, revolutionary.

One of the crewmen standing in the rear of the helicopter with Bonham tugged at him slightly as a reminder that he was leaning across open space. Bonham glared at the young man, though the crewman had only been concerned about his safety. The helicopter settled into a hover; Bonham was out on the ground before the wheels hit dirt. He trotted across the road to where an Air Force major from the first team in waited to make his report. The major was flanked by a Special Tactics sergeant with an M16, as well as a civilian whom Bonham didn't recognize.

"General," said the major, bobbing his head in an unofficial salute.

"What do we have?"

"Piece of fairing from a large aircraft, very possibly a 767 type, though we're still not sure."

"Definitely a 767," said the civilian.

Bonham glanced at the man, who had a cigarette in the corner of his mouth. The general liked definite opinions, and so gave the civilian only half the scowl he normally would have for interrupting. Obviously the man was one of the experts brought in by the Air Force to help with the operation.

"We're going to airlift it out, get the technical people to take a look at it," said the major.

"Waste of time," said the civilian.

"This way, General," said the major. He walked up the road about twenty yards, then began hiking up a short embankment. Bonham and the others followed. The metal had definitely come from an aircraft; it appeared to be one of the underside flap track housings that ran front to back on both winds beyond the engines on the 767. While it was certainly possible for an aircraft to lose one and remain airborne, as a practical matter, finding something that had been part of a wing meant the rest of the aircraft was somewhere nearby.

In a lot of pieces.

The civilian walked to one end of the metal and kicked it. "Dropped just about flat," he said after a long drag on his cigarette.

"I can't recall your name," said Bonham, turning to him.

"Probably 'cause you don't know it." He blew a wad of smoke in Bonham's direction.

"Well, let's share it." Bonham put his hands on his hips.

"Andy Fisher." He waved the hand with his cigarette. "You're going to find this piece of aircraft was dropped here. It didn't come from a crash. It's proof there wasn't a crash."

"Andy Fisher is with who?" said Bonham. "What company do you work for?"

"I'm with the FBI," said Fisher. "And it's *with whom*. Nuns were sticklers for grammar."

"What are you doing here, Mr. Fisher?"

"At the moment I'm looking for a cup of coffee."

"I don't have time for bullshit, Mr. Fisher."

"Yeah, neither do I," said Fisher. "I'm kind of interested in that plane part, though. Figure out how it got here and we figure out who stole your plane."

Bonham suddenly felt a cold chill on the back of his neck. *Stole?*

He jerked his thumb to the side and the FBI agent followed him a few feet away.

"Why do you think the plane was stolen?" Bonham asked.

"Well, where is it?"

"Obviously it crashed further north than the, uh, experts thought it did. In these mountains, with the weather we've had and are having, it can take quite a while to locate. We have a vector now; the search can take shape."

"Yeah." Fisher took a long pull on his cigarette. "You think your guys ran into each other?" asked Fisher.

"Of course not."

"So what else could've happened?"

"Crashes happen for a lot of reasons."

Fisher shrugged. Bonham couldn't tell whether he was blowing smoke—literally—about the accident *not* being an accident or not.

"How do you know the metal piece isn't from the plane?" asked Bonham.

"Oh, it is. It definitely is," said Fisher. "I just think somebody put it out here for you to find."

"Why would they do that?"

"Look at it: It's not banged up enough to have fallen from, what, thirty thousand feet? Forty?"

"Try three or four hundred over the mountain," said Bonham, now fairly sure the FBI agent was an idiot. "And you can't go by how banged up something is in a crash."

"True. I've seen weird things." Fisher shrugged. "I think it's bullshit."

"How many crashes have you investigated?"

"A couple." The agent took a very long drag on his cigarette, bringing it down to his fingertips. "Maybe a few more than that. I don't really like crashes, though. Pretty much the technical people run the show."

"Well, we have plenty of technical people," said Bonham. "Why aren't you back at the base?"

"This is more interesting than staring at Jemma Gorman's tight ass all day." Fisher took a long draw and then threw away the cigarette.

"Thank you for your opinion," said Bonham sarcastically. Gorman actually wasn't that bad-looking, but she was definitely a tight-ass.

"Hey, it's free," he said, walking back down the hill.

"Sir?" asked the sergeant who had been following Fisher.

"Stick with him," said Bonham. "Make sure he gets the hell back where he belongs."

"Yes, sir." The sergeant scrambled down to follow.

"Double the search assets in this sector. Use this point as a starting point and assume the plane broke up as it went north," Bonham told the major when he returned to where he was standing.

"Sir, uh, with respect, Colonel Gorman is in charge."

Bonham glared at him.

"Yes, sir," said the major.

One of the crew members from the Pave Hawk came hustling down the hill toward them. "General! Search teams are reporting a find about a hundred and fifty miles from here, due east."

"A hundred and fifty miles?"

"Yes, sir. They think it's the F/A-22V."

"Let's go," said Bonham, starting back toward the landing area.

One of the other helicopters had just brought in a small ATV with a plow on it, and a pair of airmen were using it to cut a narrow zigzag trail down to the mountain crevice where the airplane had been found. The trail looked to be about wide enough for a shopping cart, but the two men certainly seemed to be having a hell of a time running the vehicle, and Fisher saw no reason to tell them their effort was probably a waste of time, since a heavy-duty lift helicopter was already en route from the base. Crushing personal initiative was a military job, and besides, one of the airmen had lent him a lighter.

Fisher also saw no need to go down and look at the wreck; it would be fairly jumbled, and his naked eye wasn't going to tell him anything the technical people couldn't. Besides, the one person worth talking to about it wasn't going to answer any more questions in this lifetime.

What was interesting, however, was watching Bonham direct the response teams down toward the wreckage. Though well into his fifties, the ex-general hustled around as if he were in his mid-twenties. He wasn't a stay-on-the-top administrator: The arms of the denim shirt were covered with grime, and his work shoes were well scuffed. Fisher had had a boss like that once, a real pain in the ass who basically wanted to solve every case himself. Had it ended there, it wouldn't have been bad, but he was such a control freak that he had informants in every diner in the city, making it difficult to cop a cup and a smoke on Bureau time. And as far as he was concerned, every minute you breathed was Bureau time.

A doctor had gone down to check on the pilot's body before it was removed. He trudged up the hill now, his green T-shirt soaked with sweat. As soon as he got to the apex of the trail, he collapsed on the pile of rocks there. Fisher slid down from his vantage point and went over to him.

"Hey, Doc. Hot down there?"

The doctor grunted something. It was summer, but it was probably only about sixty degrees.

"So, it was Williams, right?" asked Fisher, taking out his cigarettes. "Still strapped in, right?"

"You're Fisher."

"That's what the cred says," said Fisher. "Picture kind of looks like me, if you squint."

The doctor grimaced. "Those things'll kill you."

Fisher held out the pack. "Want one?"

The doctor hesitated, then reached for the pack.

"Pretty gruesome, huh?"

"Let's just say *severe trauma*," said the doctor. He took a long breath on the cigarette, held it nearly thirty seconds, then exhaled. "Autopsy'll have the details."

"You think he was dead before the crash?" asked Fisher.

The doctor's hand shook as he brought the cigarette to his mouth and took a drag.

"Was his body bruised?" Fisher prompted. "I'm kind of wondering, because if he was dead, well, then obviously that's one line of expectations, and if he was alive, well, that's another. It'd be pretty obvious on the face—"

The physician turned abruptly and began to vomit. Fisher had never met a weak-stomached doctor before, and looked on with scientific interest.

"You all right?" Fisher asked when the doctor finally stopped retching. He appeared to have had some sort of meat dish for lunch.

"Ugh," muttered the man. Fisher took out a handkerchief and gave it to him.

"Not much left of the face," managed the doctor.

"Warm?"

"I think he was alive at impact, yes," said the doctor. "My g-guess would be unconscious. I've never seen such, such— The impact tore—"

He turned away and began to retch again.

"Fisher, what the hell are you doing? Why are you bothering my people?" demanded Bonham. "Why are you even here?"

"You commandeered my helicopter, remember?"

"*Your* helicopter?"

"I'm a taxpayer. When I remember to file."

"There's a time and place for everything. Show some respect."

Fisher put his cigarette into his mouth, considering Bonham's words. They seemed almost biblical.

Psalm-like, actually.

"So how do you figure the plane got so far north?" he asked Bonham.

The general gave him as exasperated look.

"Blacks out like Colonel Howe's did, but then keeps flying?" asked Fisher. "Two hundred miles?"

"It's probably less than one-fifty," said Bonham. "I'm sure the crash experts will be able to compute it."

"Yeah, they're whizzes at this stuff. God bless 'em." Fisher heard a helicopter arriving at the LZ and decided to see if he could hitch a ride back. "Keep the handkerchief," he told the doctor. He looked up the hill for his bodyguard. "Come on, Johnson. Time for us to head home. I'm down to my last pack of cigarettes."

Flying back on the helicopter, Fisher got involved in a philosophical discussion with the crew chief about whether the inventor of lite beer ought to be hanged or simply jailed for life. Because of that, he wasn't prepared for the attack that met him on the tarmac.

"Fisher, who the hell do you think you are, screwing up a rescue operation?"

"Hey, Jemma. You're looking particularly pallid today. Wanna cigarette?" said Fisher, walking toward the pillbox that housed the elevator into the bunker complex.

"You can't smoke on this base," said Jemma. "There's all sorts of jet fuel and flammable materials."

"Write me up." Fisher poked out a Camel and lit up. He had a hankering for a Marlboro, but his Indian suppliers didn't go for the image, so they were hard to get. "How come you're outside during the day? Aren't you afraid of melting?"

"Fisher, what the hell were you doing?" She placed herself in front of him in a pose that convinced Fisher she had been a linebacker in a previous life.

"Looking at a piece of metal from our plane," he said. "Then Bonham decided to have me tag along to the F/A-22V crash. Damn far north, don't you think?"

"They have the course already computed."

"Sure, *now* they do: Why the hell didn't they figure that out before? Would've saved a lot of trouble. You're going to have to get all your little men on the situation board to shift north, right? What are the Canadians saying about this?"

"Computing crash sites isn't as easy as you think."

"Which is why Cyclops is still missing, right?"

Gorman pulled the bottom of her uniform jacket down, smoothing it.

"Better off pressing it," said Fisher. "That's what you get for sleeping in it."

"I don't sleep in my uniform."

"Pink jammies with fuzzy feet?"

"What did you see up there? Was the pilot alive when the plane hit, or what?"

Fisher studied his cigarette a moment. It seemed to him that the burn tilted slightly to the west, no matter how he held it. Maybe it was a magnetic thing.

Figure it out and he could use it as a compass.

"Well?" asked Gorman.

"Doc thought so. I don't think he has much experience, though. Make sure they check the blood for carbon dioxide levels, but I'd almost for sure rule that out. Say, tell me about Bonham. How old is he?"

"How the hell do I know?"

"If he's not in the Army—"

"*Air Force.*"

"Yeah. So he's retired, right? But everyone calls him general and acts like he's hot shit."

"It's an honorific. And he's head of the NADT. He *is* hot shit, as you put it."

"He's a pain in your ass, isn't he?"

Gorman's cheeks shaded dark red. "I'm sure I don't know what you're talking about."

"He thinks he's running the investigation."

"This is an Air Force investigation. I am in charge here."

"I didn't say you weren't. Getting any pressure from Congress?"

"Congress? Why?"

"York's cousin's a congressman."

Gorman shrugged. She obviously hadn't known that, though she was about as likely to admit that as the pope was to confess he'd smoked pot in seminary. "Tell me about that piece of metal," she said, changing the subject. "Was it from Cyclops One or not?"

"Oh yeah. We can discard the accident theory. Plane was definitely stolen."

"What?"

"I'm going to start going through the personnel files. I was afraid it would come to this." Fisher tossed his cigarette down. Mindful of Jemma's concern about starting a fire, he crushed it out with his heel. "I hate using the Air Force computers. Maybe I can bribe somebody to do it for me."

"Andrew—"

"I'd ask you but I know you're busy."

"For the record, your clearance on this case is strictly limited. It doesn't cover the weapons system."

"Jemma, my clearance is higher than yours. You know, maybe you should put a little starch into your shirt. Get rid of the wrinkles. They dock you for that, right? Demerits or something? Take away your cigarette privileges."

Kowalski was heading the section reviewing the personnel records, which was, as Fisher predicted, using Air Force computers. The DIA agent took one look at him and shook his head as he entered the room. Fisher ignored him, walking toward the side of the large room where the coffee was sequestered.

"What'd you find in Canada?" Kowalski asked.

"Who the hell's making the coffee here? You?" Fisher held up the pot. About half-full, it was as thick as Texas honey.

"I'll send out if you tell me what's going on in Canada," said the DIA agent. "We're just reading electrons here."

"Found a part of an airplane."

"And?"

"And it was obviously planted there. So whose bank account just grew by a billion bucks?"

"Fisher."

"Come on. You've had enough time to dig up some dirt by now. A bank foreclosure, at least."

Kowalski glanced at the sergeant who had accompanied Fisher into the room. "I'm afraid Sergeant Johnson shouldn't be in on this discussion. Personnel matters are private."

"Sean's not going to talk, right? Besides, he doesn't speak English."

The sergeant gave a little smirk.

"Seriously, we can't talk about this in front of anyone who's not part of the investigation."

"Maybe I might find something to eat," said the sergeant. "Down the hall."

"See, now you hurt his feelings," said Fisher after the sergeant left. "Who's our perp?"

"What happened in Canada?" asked Kowalski.

"Piece of the wing from the 767 that has some sort of serial number on it. Looked to me like it was dropped from five feet off the ground."

"The engineers assessed it already?"

"No, but you know what they're going to say: 'No definable parameters' or some such bullshit. They might get something from looking at the side—the metal has a shear I don't think could've happened if it just ripped off. Anyway, it's definitely there as a red herring. The F/A-22V was over here about a hundred and, what, fifty miles?" He diagrammed it in the air. "Bonham went up there to check it out."

"Bonham went there himself?"

"Yeah, my kind of guy. Except he don't smoke. Can't be perfect." Fisher took a sip of the coffee, which was starting to grow on him: It was now merely undrinkable, as opposed to hideously undrinkable. "Slip a couple of lead plates in here and you could start a car," he told Kowalski.

"That far north, huh?"

"That's what I'm thinking. How the hell did it get way the hell out there, huh? Modelers screw up?"

Kowalski shrugged. "I had this A-10A case once. It flew for something like two hours before it pancaked in. Incredible."

"Yeah, but our plane missed some serious mountains."

"Talk to the experts," said the DIA agent. "Don't talk to me."

"So what I'm thinking, then, is if the Velociraptor could go that far, then the 767 could go even further, because it has a clearer path and it's higher. Right?"

"Presumably."

Fisher took another sip of coffee. He must've hit a good spot in the cup before: It was back to being hideously undrinkable. "So, who's the prime suspect if the planes were stolen? York?"

"No way," said the DIA agent. "All the crew people are clean. This could be an NSA operation, with all the background checks they put these people through. They didn't trust the DSS backgrounds. Special checks were done by an FBI unit after the DSS's came back clean."

"Oh, that fills me with a lot of confidence," said Fisher.

The DSS was the Defense Security Service, whose checks included not only searches of data records but visits to former neighborhoods. The FBI checks would have been similar but in theory more in-depth.

The FBI agent walked over to the two long tables at the center of the room where Kowalski and the people helping him had set up several computers. Two had hardware keys—actually, special circuits that acted as encryption devices—enabling them to directly access a government top-secret intelligence network known as Intelink. The network worked like a highly secure Internet; hypertext links connected to several sources on different subjects. There were limits: Intelink information did not extend to Sensitive Compartmented Information, ultrasecret data available on a very restricted basis. Cyclops, for example, would not be found in a query there. Nor could the computers access SpyNet, which was another top-level network used more for strategic security information.

Special authorization was needed to get into the personnel files Kowalski was using, and Fisher had to go through the biometrics ID routine twice, squinting into what looked like a set of stationary binoculars.

"Who are you interested in?" Kowalski asked.

"York."

"Why?"

" 'Cause she's not here. I only talk about people behind their backs."

"Weren't you saying a couple of hours ago that Williams was the prime suspect?"

"Sounded like me."

Kowalski snorted.

"See, that's why it's got to be York," said Fisher. "What do you figure the odds are of me being wrong twice in a row?"

"Astronomical," said Kowalski.

7

McIntyre took some pleasure in seeing Clayton T. "I'm More Connected and Twenty Times More Powerful Than You'll Ever Be" Bonham squirm as he tried to explain why the Cyclops aircraft had not yet been located.

Some pleasure. He was, after all, in Montana, not Hawaii.

"Colonel Gorman is in charge of the investigation and the search assets," said Bonham, gesturing toward the large grid map at the front of the Test Situation Room, which had been commandeered to coordinate the search operation. "The Air Force took over the search a few hours after the accident."

"What'd you do in the meantime?" said McIntyre.

Bonham glared at him, but said nothing. Calling NADT its own empire was an understatement; the ex-general had more power than Napoleon and was answerable only to a board of directors that met once every millennium. The board members were, for the most part, low-key, old-line big shots with massive stakes in various defense companies. On the other hand, even McIntyre had to admit that NADT had an excellent track record making things work; even with the accident, Cyclops and the Velociraptor were impressive war machines.

Gorman was conferring with one of the search coordinators in the front of the room, which looked a great deal like the mission control facility that tracked Shuttle missions. Three long banks of workstations arranged stadium-style in a backward semicircle out from the front wall, where a large multiuse projection panel was framed by a number of small displays, each of which could be slaved to different input systems.

McIntyre took a few steps toward the center of the room, looking at the main map as he oriented himself. The F/A-22V had been found well north in Canada. They now expected that the 767 would be found there as well.

Gorman came over and McIntyre, who'd never met her before, introduced himself. She was a bit abrupt, clearly not happy that someone from the NSC had been sent to look over her shoulder.

Not that he blamed her.

As Gorman explained why the earlier parameters had been wrong—the complicated explanation actually made it seem as if they were right and the plane simply got up and walked northward—McIntyre's eyes strayed toward one of the young officers in the front row. She was Air Force, a lieutenant with short, dirty-blond hair and military breasts. Feigning interest in the map, McIntyre began walking toward her, nodding as Gorman continued. The young officer looked up and smiled at him as he approached.

Dinner, a movie, a motel. Something with a hot tub—a little class for the woman in uniform, or out of uniform, as the case may be.

McIntyre was about three stations away when one of his cell phones rang. Unfortunately, it was the only one he absolutely had to answer.

"I have to take this," he said, looking first at the lieutenant and then back at Bonham. "Someplace secure?"

Bonham's office was austere, its furniture made of metal and the seats covered with what looked and felt like indoor-outdoor carpet. It was a sharp contrast to NADT's Washington-area office, and in fact quite a bit plainer than really necessary; no one would have begrudged the former general leather upholstery and cherry accents.

Obviously intended to impress visiting congressmen.

McIntyre clicked on his phone as soon as the door was closed.

"Hold for the professor," said Mozelle, Blitz's assistant.

Using *Professor* was a subtle warning: The national security advisor was not in a good mood. McIntyre had just enough time to take a breath before he came on the line.

"Mac. I need you in Asia."

"Asia?"

"India, to be exact."

"But—" Hawaii then Montana, then New Delhi. Antarctica would be next.

"I want you to assess the readiness situation at as many frontline bases as you can imagine."

"That's a military function," said McIntyre, though he knew it was hopeless. "Parsons would be—"

"Check the C option and report back."

C option was shorthand for the possibility that India would launch a preemptive attack on the Pakistani military. While American spy satellites covered the area, their flight paths were well known and there was ample opportunity to work around them. McIntyre was being told to confer with embassy officials—in most cases undercover CIA agents—and work off a checklist of indicators, some subtle, some not, to supplement the satellite snaps and intercepts. While the CIA would prepare its own report, Blitz liked the idea of having a person in country he could rely on.

Such as it was.

"Sniff around," continued the NSC head. "See if you can get to any of the Kashmir bases."

"Oh God, Kashmir. All the way up there?"

McIntyre turned around in the seat. He could guess at what Blitz was thinking: Probably the conflict would all blow over, but he'd get a firsthand look at what the Indians' capability was.

"You have a problem with that?" asked Blitz.

"All right," he said. His plans regarding the lieutenant changed abruptly: He'd bag the movie and go straight for the motel, maybe even settle for his quarters. "I'll grab the first flight in the morning."

"There's one already en route. I'm told it's about ten minutes from landing."

CHAPTER

8

When he finally reached his quarters, Bonham pulled off his shirt and pants and booted the computer before going to take a quick shower. His suite here was hardly that—two nearly bare rooms and a bathroom with a stand-up shower—and he bumped his elbow hard on the wall as he toweled off. Feeling a little less dusty, he went over to the computer and brought up the Internet interface; two clicks later he had ESPN.com on the screen.

The Red Sox had beaten the Yankees with a walk-off home run in the bottom of the ninth. Hallelujah.

Spirits buoyed, Bonham clicked over to CNN, making sure, God forbid, that nothing had been reported beyond his early bland release on the accident. It hadn't; the newspeople were concerned with the augmented-ABM tests, which had just been postponed another day due to technical problems with the monitoring network.

Bonham scrolled around in vain trying to find out what that meant. The reporters hadn't been told, and it was impossible to divine from the statements they'd been given what was really going on. Delays had a tendency to mushroom, throwing everything off. The tests should have been concluded by now; every sixty minutes' worth of delay added that many more problems for everyone.

But he had his own things to worry about. Fisher, for one, who had all the symptoms of a class-one troublemaker. This wasn't an FBI case—the Bureau had sent only one man, not the dozens or even hundreds it would detail for a blowout job—but Fisher was just the sort of bee buzzing in someone's bonnet to screw up everything.

Bonham leaned back in his chair. He could find out about the agent easily enough with a few phone calls. But that was a tricky thing: People might interpret it as paranoia, or worse. Better to suffer through the slings and arrows of outrageous behavior. Besides, Fisher was probably more of a problem for Gorman than for him.

Served the stubborn bitch right.

Someone knocked on the door.

"General Bonham?"

"Tom, come on in," he said, recognizing Colonel Howe's voice.

"Door's locked," said Howe.

"Oh, sorry. Thought I'd be sleeping already," said Bonham. He killed the computer and got up to open the door. "Checking the Red Sox. Beat the Yankees with a ninth-inning home run."

Howe nodded. He wasn't much of a baseball fan.

He also wasn't much of a late-night visitor.

"Come on in," said Bonham. "Drink?"

Bonham walked to the small bookcase where he kept a bottle of Scotch.

"No, thanks. I'm flying tomorrow."

"You're flying?"

"That's why I came over," said Howe. "The engineers want to put Bird One through its paces, and I'm going to do it."

Bonham poured two fingers' worth of Scotch into a tumbler, then went to the small refrigerator he kept in the corner of the room. The tiny ice tray in the unit's freezer was about three-quarters full; he popped out two cubes and put it back.

"Have a seat, Tom. Take a load off."

The sides of the small, foam-cushioned chair seemed to pop out as Howe sat on it, as if it were a balloon. Howe shifted uncomfortably, right leg over left, then left over right, then back. Bonham thought to himself that he would not have wanted to trade places with the colonel, who until a few days ago seemed to be riding the career rocket to a general's star and beyond.

Bonham liked Howe. He was a good, competent officer, and while more than a bit impatient with the bureaucratic side of the job—almost a given for anyone with the flying background Howe had—he made up for it by delegating those responsibilities to people who could handle them.

A little unimaginative. But that could be a useful flaw. Bonham would see that his career wasn't screwed by this. A few bumps, admittedly—Gorman was just the start— but with patience it could be overcome.

Hard for Howe to know that now, though. Surely he had no reason to be optimistic.

"Tough to lose a wingmate," Bonham offered.

"Yeah," said Howe.

"And Ms. York. I know you two were close." Bonham swirled his Scotch, then took a long sip. Either because of the drink or the hangdog look on Howe's face, he suddenly felt paternal. "We get through the inquiry stage, people are going to understand that what we do here is loaded with danger. Tragedy, people will understand. This isn't a normal situation," said Bonham. "It'll be taken into account. You'll probably be commended for saving the plane."

Howe gave him a wan smile, surely not believing him.

"You know, when I was a young buck, we lost a Phantom over Alaska," said Bonham, playing the old soldier who's seen everything. "Didn't find it until two years later. Person who found it, flying one of those old Otters or whatever the hell it was they call those things. Utter accident."

The story wasn't completely apocryphal; there had indeed been a crash in Alaska, though not while Bonham was there, and not by a Phantom. It had, however, taken considerable time to find, and Bonham knew enough details to use the story to make his point. And the Scotch warmed his mouth and throat in a way that he really, truly wanted to cheer the colonel up.

"Thing is, it can take forever in that wilderness to find a crash. We will eventually," said Bonham.

"It's odd that there was no satellite coverage," said Howe.

The statement seemed particularly pointed. Bonham got up and refilled his drink.

"I guess they took that one out for repair or whatever," said Bonham. "There are satellites, though. With the weather, where you were operating, they couldn't see anything. From what Colonel Gorman told me, they have ample assets for the search. We'll find it eventually. It takes time."

"Has Fisher spoken to you?"

"The FBI agent?"

"He asked me if Williams needed money."

Bonham laughed. "What, did he think he crashed on purpose?"

He shook his head as he drank the Scotch. A real bee, that FBI bastard.

"Listen, Tom, I wouldn't worry about the investigators, especially the FBI and CID people. They run around, kick over chairs, stir up dust, see what happens. This Fisher— he's probably just trying to rile you."

Howe rose. "Well, I just wanted to give you the heads-up."

"I appreciate it. You take care tomorrow."

"Yes, sir. Thank you."

After he locked the door, Bonham poured himself another drink, this one about halfway up the glass.

They put Fisher and the rest of the investigators up in what passed for VIP quarters in a building near the base of the mountain, reachable via a road obviously built for a donkey cart. *VIP* here apparently meant you were entitled to running water—cold and colder—in the bathroom. There was a personal coffeemaker on the bureau; its carafe looked like a shot glass with handles. The coffee itself was World War I surplus; if he'd had the equipment, Fisher would have ground up the furniture's cardboard drawers to add to the aroma.

The only thing that ticked him off, though, was the lack of a brew-and-pour device on the coffeemaker. The FBI agent was as much a traditionalist as anyone, but there were some pieces of technology that you just couldn't live without. A Mr. Coffee without brew-and-pour was not only anachronistic, it was practically a torture device.

Fortunately, Fisher was adept at dealing with such problems, managing a shuffle with two paper coffee cups that caught most of the dribbling liquid. What missed the cup added a nicely burnt aroma to the room's musty odor.

Coffee depleted, Fisher ambled out of the room into the long, dimly lit hall, where he was immediately assailed by Kowalski.

"Not going to be fashionably late?" asked the DIA agent.

"I try not to miss breakfast," said Fisher.

"No, for the briefing. Gorman didn't call you?"

"I have a policy against answering phones in VIP suites," said Fisher. "And I was probably in the shower."

"You don't smell it."

"You're getting funnier, Kowalski. Be joining the circus any day now." Fisher lit a cigarette as they approached the steel doors leading outside. A pair of Humvees were waiting at the dust that passed for a curb in front of the building. As soon as they reached the entrance to the underground complex, the strong scent of burnt caffeine tickled his nostrils, pulling him in the direction of the conference room.

Two large coffee rigs had been set up outside the room. The sight and smell restored Fisher's faith in the Air Force; finally a grouchy chief master sergeant had arrived and taken things in hand. His opinion was confirmed by the lavalike liquid that spewed from the urn. Fisher filled three cups, tripling them to keep from burning his fingers, then brought them into the small lecture room. Unfortunately, all the good seats were taken, and he wound up sitting in the front row.

"Glad you could join us," sniped Gorman as she strode across the room.

"Your health," saluted Fisher as he sipped the coffee. Its temperature had now dropped to five hundred degrees kelvin, just where he liked it.

"You have anything new?" she asked Fisher. She was in good form for such an early hour; her voice sounded like a cross between a snake and an injured lion.

"Found a few hot porn sites on the Internet. All amateurs."

Gorman gave him one of her middling frowns. "You're not being helpful."

"I'm trying."

"Would you be willing to interface with the Mounties, flesh out reports about low-flying planes?"

"I don't speak Canadian," he told her.

Gorman shook her head, then walked to the podium and began her meeting. She ran through the usual administrative diddly, then briefly summarized the present status of the search. As the team leaders gave their own updates, she stuck her nose into her notes.

"Hey, guest speaker coming up," whispered Kowalski, who'd managed to find a second-row seat almost directly behind him.

"How do you know?" said Fisher.

"She always checks her notes for pronunciation before mangling somebody's name."

Sure enough, Gorman did have a guest, whom she introduced when everyone else was through. "For those of you who don't know him, Stephen Klose is from the NSA. He doesn't have a job title."

That was obviously meant as a joke, since all of the Air Force people whose evaluations she could affect laughed. Klose came forward with an ultra-serious face, launching into the usual NSA bullshit about what he was going to say being "VSK"—*very secret knowledge* was the actual term the crypto-dweebs used at their dark castle in Maryland. *VSK* must not be used in any way that a normal human being might actually use it, and had to be permanently erased from the listeners' brain cells upon the end of its period of usefulness, which by definition had already passed.

Klose then launched into a fairly technical ramble, which meandered through various alphanumerics before his tongue stumbled on the words *a code variant common in high-level VPO connection communications.*

"Whoa fuck," said Kowalski with more than his usual eloquence. "You're telling us the Russians stole the plane?"

"No. There was, uh, uh spying operation, and the transmissions came from them," stuttered Klose amid gasps from the service people and titters from everyone else. "We'd have to decrypt the transmissions to be sure. We're working on that. But given previous patterns, we're reasonably sure."

Klose rambled on about possible Russian motivations, clicking different maps and pictures onto the large screen.

The spy plane's route had been tracked: It was nearly a thousand miles away.

"It's picking up telemetry with a towed antenna probe," said Klose.

"Can it?" asked someone from the safety of the back row.

Klose shrugged. "Not effectively. But maybe. Definitely maybe. The capabilities—"

"So, basically, you're just pulling our puds here," said Fisher.

"*Mister Fisher.*" Gorman's hiss was so perfectly snake-like, Fisher expected her tongue to poke him in the eyes. That hideous thought sent him back to his coffee, which, though considerably cool, was still pleasantly acidic.

Klose added a few technical details about the probable strength of the radio that had transmitted the signals, an explanation that involved sine curves and something about amplitude. The bottom line was that the Russians were probably aware that something had happened, but thus far there was no evidence that they had had anything to do with it. A thousand miles was, after all, a thousand miles.

"Fits with your stolen-plane scenario," Kowalski told Fisher out in the hall when they broke for coffee.

"Nah," said Fisher.

"The Dragon Lady thinks so," said Kowalski. "Didn't you see her eyes glowing when Klose started talking about the intercepts?"

"What Dragon Lady?" said Jemma, coming up behind them.

"Colonel Gorman," said Kowalski, "I think you mis-heard."

"I'm sure I didn't." Her glare drove the DIA agent away. "Andy, if we start looking in those lakes, can you head the team?" she asked.

"What lakes?"

"Bonham is pushing the theory that the plane is in one of the lakes. He wants to start close to the base, then work north."

"He's in charge?" said Fisher.

After he got the frown he expected, he added, "How does it fit with the Russian theory?"

"What Russian theory?"

"Klose's."

"That wasn't a theory," said Gorman. "The Russians were monitoring the flight. It's just information."

"You think they caused the malfunction?" asked Fisher.

The idea actually seemed not to have occurred to her. "I don't know."

"Well, I don't think so," Fisher said.

"Andy, don't do that."

"What?"

"You float out an idea and then clam up. I can't tell if it's serious or not."

Fisher shrugged. "Neither can I."

CHAPTER

10

Howe applied full military power, rocking the F/A-22V upward as the first phase of the check flight was completed. The readouts were green and glowing; the engine absolutely purred and the jet seemed eager to erase any doubt that she was fit. He rode the monster thrust from the P&Ws through thirty thousand feet, roaring toward the stars with an acceleration that would have made an Atlas-series rocket envious. He started to level off as the HUD laddered through 35,000, still burning a healthy share of dinosaurs and still nailing every indicator to its sweet spot.

The techies on the ground gave him a verbal thumbs-up as the Velociraptor's thick shark's skin brushed off a stream of turbulence at 43,000 feet. Howe slid into an orbit over the Montana wilderness, keeping the base in the center of his circle. Sweeping his eyes across the multiuse displays that flanked his tactical screen, he carefully examined each digit.

There were now about a dozen theories for the flake-out. Most involved some as yet unexplained energy spike through the shared radar-avionics system that somehow took out the main flight computers. But no simulation had been able to duplicate the problem.

Strip away the high-tech jargon and arcane formulas, and what the eggheads were saying came down to: *Damned if I know.*

Howe's own opinion was that something in the telemetry exchange unit freaked out when the Cyclops weapon cycled up. The engineers, of course, said this was impossible—but they would find out for sure in a few minutes, when they cycled up the unit in Cyclops Two, sitting safely on the ground on the ramp in front of its bunker.

Howe pushed his head down, stretching the muscles in his upper back. His right shoulder had started to cramp; he could use a good back rub.

Megan's fingers, sliding across his shoulder blade, diving into the pressure points.

"Bird Dog One, you're looking good," said Robert Jerome. The Air Force major was in the knockdown tower, monitoring the test flight visually, while most of the technical people were in the bunker control room. "You still got your chops, Rock."

"Roger that," replied Howe. Few people used his old nickname, but Jerome had flown with Howe early in his career; they'd even teamed up in a Strike Eagle squadron over Iraq.

Like many call signs, "Rock" had not initially been a compliment. It came from one of his early flight instructors, who'd described his maneuvers during a flight and what they had done to the plane's flying characteristics. Inevitably, it stuck with his mates, but had gradually become something of an honorific.

The mission boss gave him his new course heading and altitude, duplicating the leg of the Cyclops test where the problem had occurred. Howe's shoulder spasmed; he pushed his head around slowly, trying to relieve it, mad at his body for tensing up. He hit his marks perfectly, but the knot in his shoulder had grown to the size of a boulder, and his hands were wet and jittering.

He was nervous—beyond nervous. He was having trouble breathing right.

Howe had flown over two dozen combat missions, shot down two planes and had a hand in a third, and this had never happened to him. But those engagements had been so quick, almost literally bang-bang, that he hadn't had time to think.

Now thinking was all he could do.

"Not a peep of a problem," said Jerome. He sounded a little disappointed.

"Yeah, roger that."

"All right, we want to go around again. Use the synthetic view hologram this time," said Matt Firenze, one of the scientists in the control room. He was asking Howe to switch the HUD into the synthesized view so they could run an additional suite of tests.

Howe traded some data verbally with the ground people, duping what the sensors were telling them as he pulled the big aircraft back around. One of the women on the ground somehow reminded him of his ex-wife, Carmen, with her sharp rasp. He thought of her now, her pouty frown, her cigarette hanging out of her mouth in the hotel room they'd had their honeymoon down in New Orleans.

He hadn't thought of Carmen in quite a while. She was a bona fide nutcase, manic-depressive with borderline and narcissistic personality disorders: She had the diagnosis from not one but two different shrinks, their agreement apparently some sort of milestone of psychoanalysis.

The relationship had quickly disintegrated into a cycle of wild verbal fights, heartfelt apologies, and great sex—followed by weird accusations, wild verbal fights, heartfelt apologies, and even better sex. Howe had stuck it out sixteen months, but the marriage lasted that long only because he'd been overseas for much of the time.

He started to laugh, remembering her another morning sitting at their tiny kitchen table, hungover, breasts falling out of a gauzy, see-through nightshirt, arranging her tarot cards while the coffee poured through the machine next to the sink. She was beautiful in moments like that, unconsciously beautiful.

Very different from Megan.

Howe's hands were so wet with sweat he pulled off his flight gloves, even though he habitually wore them when he flew.

He'd miss them if he had to eject. Involuntarily, his eyes hunted the yellow handle near the seat.

His marriage hadn't thrown him off women completely. Sexwise, he'd had his share. He was far from a stud. Some guys could just walk into a bar and they'd be knee-deep in women. Howe wasn't like that; he'd never been like that. But he had seen women since Carmen—plenty of women—gone to bed with them, made love.

No one like Megan, though. She was beautiful, drop-dead beautiful. Her breasts a little small, if you were unbiased about it, as she herself used to say.

She talked about different things. She told him about a painting by Matisse; who the hell was Matisse? he'd wondered, and had to find out so he didn't look like a total schmuck.

What card had Carmen used to tell his fortune? King of Swords?

"Telemetry is ready on our side," said Firenze.

Howe had to punch a two-button combination on the right side of his instrument panel to change the HUD mode and initiate the test. He checked his speed and altitude first, gave the other flight instruments a quick read—went back over them more slowly, comprehending the numbers this time—and reached for the buttons.

The King of Swords wasn't a good fit. Too airy, she said, too flighty. Fiery. Prone to crash.

Prone to crash.

Carmen's eyes as she said that—accusing him of betrayal.

"I see a confused future," she said.

"We're ready for you, Colonel," prompted the ground controller. Howe's fingers still hovered over the buttons. His muscles had suddenly tightened to the point it hurt to move his fingers.

Jesus, what's happening to me? he thought. *I'm freaking.*

He saw Megan's body on the bed, then pushed the buttons.

Matt Firenze watched the numbers pop onto the second screen, raw assembler code blossoming before him. The functions were being translated in the first screen, and an array of monitors to his right were actually summarizing the data and its effect (or noneffect) on the aircraft. But Matt's job was there on the twenty-one-inch cathode ray tube. Hexadecimals—the computer used a base-16 integer number system, corresponding to the physical registers—sloshed across the screen. Firenze had preprogrammed the computer to alert him to a difference from the expected sequence: The green numbers would turn red.

Green. Green. Green.

He kept staring.

Howe's breath physically lifted the mask off his face. His arms and legs were moving—he was still flying the plane—but his head felt as if it were beneath a heavy blanket. His tongue sat dry at the bottom of his mouth.

This was the point where she'd gone out. She'd been flying to his left; it was his left, wasn't it? If he looked in that direction now, if he dared it, would he see her vanishing into the clouds again?

Her perfume lingered in his head.

As he regained control he'd come up there—and the plane loomed right before him.

How was that possible?

Its engines were working. Definitely working.

He'd trade places if he could. Surely he'd trade with her; let her live.

Carmen held the card out. Death: the grim reaper in a boat.

"Not death—change," she said. "Big change, but not death in a literal sense. Psychic change. Like love."

"Looking very good down here," said Firenze. "Can we run over it again? Just the way you did it originally, turning the HUD back to standard setting at the right point."

"Roger that," Howe told them. "Coming around for take two."

CHAPTER 11

When he was six, Amma Jalil had seen his mother set on fire by a Muslim madman.

He had been playing at the other end of the dirt-strewn street in the small northern India town where he lived. He happened to look down the block as the man ran into the neighbor's house where his mother was visiting. A second later something billowed from the window; at first it seemed to be an oversized red sheet inflated by the wind. As he stared, the edges of the sheet turned yellow and climbed upward along the roof.

A figure encircled by a red robe, ran from the house. By the time he realized it was a person, she was rolling on the street. Even before he started to run toward her, he knew it was his mother. She jerked upright, then fell back like a sack of rice collapsing.

In the twenty years since that day, Amma Jalil had run the thirty meters to his mother many times in his imagination. Never had he managed to arrive in time to hear her last words or receive her blessings.

The Muslim died in the house, as did the neighbor and her two babies. Supposedly the terrorist had set it on fire because the land had once been in the shadow of a now long-gone Islamic temple, but such reasons were often given to justify groundless murder.

The next day Amma Jalil's father and many neighbors burned down a block of Muslim houses. Amma Jalil watched them burn. He was puzzled afterward. He thought from something that he had heard that his mother would reappear after these new houses were burned, but she did not.

Several times since her death, he tried to feel the joy of revenge; perhaps it would come today.

Captain Jalil sat on a web bench a few feet from the rear door of the Mil Mi-26 assault helicopter, hurtling through the mountains near India's Kashmir border. The helicopter and its sister ship ran six or seven feet over the ground at nearly 290 kilometers an hour, rushing toward a concentration of vans and radar dishes parked beyond a mountain rift on a narrow plain about ten kilometers ahead.

Each Russian-made helicopter carried seventy-three men armed with an array of weapons. But from Jalil's point of view, the only important ones were Euromissile MILANs, man-carried antitank and bunker missiles that could take out a hardened target at three thousand meters. Six two-man teams carried the large, updated bazookas in each helicopter. The rest were simply there to make sure they found their targets.

"Five klicks from LZ," the pilot told Jalil, communicating through a wired headset with the assault team leader. They were a minute from touchdown. "I have the pathfinders."

"Yes," said Jalil. He nodded almost imperceptibly to his senior NCO, sitting across from him. In the next ten seconds everyone in the helicopter seemed to catch on. The nervous rustling that had begun shortly after they boarded the helicopter at the base north of Srinagar ended. As the helicopter began to slow, every member of the assault team leaned forward in his seat.

This was the most difficult moment of the mission. The eight massive blades that propelled the helicopters kicked up an enormous amount of dust, even at a hard-packed landing strip. Their LZ was a camel trail in the middle of a narrow wasteland filled with grit and pebbles. Send too much debris into the Lotarev D-136 engines and the mission would have to be scrubbed. Jalil's instructions were very clear: If he could not take the target precisely on time, he must send word that he had failed. Even though he did not like that particular order, he would dutifully follow it.

The helicopter landed roughly. The pilot said something over the intercom circuit—good luck, maybe—as the ramp door opened. Jalil jumped forward, one of the first men out.

The invaders quickly split themselves into three groups. Jalil went with Corps One, which would take the central approach to the target while the others came in from the flanks. They were running slightly behind schedule; he tapped at his watch as the corps leaders quickly checked their men and then set out. Each corps was subdivided into smaller teams, generally of six or eight men; one member within each team had a night optical device, or NOD, either an infrared or starscope viewer, usually the former. They needed them: It was exceedingly dark tonight, with an uncharacteristic full bank of clouds beneath the moonless sky and the desert.

It took nearly a half hour for them to walk the first kilometer. This was far too long. They had only an hour left to get into position to launch the attack.

Jalil worried that their weeks of training were now going against them; perhaps the men were too tired tonight to face the task before them. He went to each squad leader and urged him to move faster, waving silently with his hand. They made somewhat better time, reaching the midpoint to the assault within another half hour.

Jalil had the option of attacking the radars from long range with the MILANs; he had a good chance of taking out the dishes from two kilometers and in fact could see the outlines of one now through his infrared NOD. But he had planned a full-scale attack, with its much higher probability of success, and he intended on carrying that plan out. He checked with the other corps leaders; they, too, were making poor progress.

"Run," he told one of his lieutenants, jogging next to him.

Without answering, the man began to double-time and then lope forward. The others in his squad followed. As Jalil moved to issue the command to another of his men, that squad also broke into a trot.

They reached their final staging area thirty seconds late. Jalil thought it prudent to rest them all an additional five minutes before passing the word to begin.

Eight groups of men began moving forward, two holding back in reserve. The two squads in the middle stopped after they had gone about a hundred meters; their targets loomed before them, less than a half-kilometer away. Jalil stayed with these men until he was sure that their missiles were properly prepared and aimed, with each of the two radar dishes and its attendant operator van zeroed in by not one but two missiles. When he was satisfied, Jalil radioed the other groups. Corps Two on his right was just getting into position, but Corps Three was still at least ten minutes from its launch point, and probably more. That was a bad sign: It was the only one of the three groups that had Highway Five in sight, and thus the only one that could stop or even spot potential reinforcements. More important, it was tasked with cutting one of the two land lines from the complex.

Jalil urged the lieutenant in charge to move faster, then handed the radio handset to his communications specialist and turned his attention back to his own men, waiting in the shadows a few hundred meters ahead.

The attack had to be launched in twelve minutes. The plans, carefully coordinated with the Indian Air Force, provided exactly a two-minute window to take out both radar dishes, the transmission towers, and the land lines, isolating the early-warning facility. At the end of that window, the first wave of attack jets would pass overhead, spreading out through the radarless corridor Jalil and his men had provided to launch a preemptive strike against Pakistan's nuclear force.

The planes were undoubtedly already en route. The lives of their pilots counted on his success.

The men tasked to blow up the transmission towers reported in. There was no one guarding the approach; the charges would be prepared shortly.

No one guarding them?

Suspicion jabbed Jalil. Their intelligence people had predicted lax security—the Pakistanis were famously lazy—but this seemed unbelievable.

Unbelievable!

Jalil's communications specialist tugged his sleeve. Jalil saw one of his sergeants pointing in the distance, then heard the truck he was alerting him to.

A patrol, heading in their direction.

Jalil pulled up his night glasses. It was an American Humvee, undoubtedly one of the vehicles left to the Muslim devils when they had deceived the superpower into thinking they would fight against the terrorists in Afghanistan. There was a weapon on the back; an antitank gun, he assumed.

They would have night-vision gear as well, though they probably lacked the IQs to use it properly.

The Hummer passed by his team and continued onward, oblivious.

Jalil gave the order for the attack to begin. Two of the three radio towers crumbled simultaneously, the explosions sounding like a stack of chairs falling in a banquet hall. The third fell a second later, but the sound was drowned out by the short screech of a banshee as the first MILAN missile plowed into one of the radar vans.

Then hell opened her mouth and fire spit into the desert. The great god Shiva, the destroyer, hurled his bolts into the Muslims' early-warning system, obliterating it. Two heavy machine guns, lugged from the helicopter, began cutting down the three Pakistanis foolish enough to emerge from one of the personnel trailers.

A second later the trailer caught fire. Jalil put down his night device and watched as a pair of tiny flames emerged from the larger ones, spit falling from a mouth. They ran a few feet and then collapsed. He thought again of his mother and remained unsatisfied.

"Send the word to the planes," he told his communications man. "Destroyer has struck. The path is clear."

"Done," said the como specialist.

Jalil relaxed. The live-fire simulation was over. They could rest now. The next time they did this, it would be for real.

CHAPTER

12

Fisher watched the video again, studying the white lines. The lines were virtual contrails—computer-generated plots of changes in the atmospheric temperature and composition of the air due to aircraft engines. Below each was a green data log indicating what aircraft had made the track.

There were a few dotted lines—places where the radar had temporarily lost the input or, more likely, the expert explained, places where the records had gotten blurred for various reasons. The storm system had greatly complicated the process; the team responsible for the data—Air Force personnel and two satellite-radar experts from Raytheon—kept cautioning that they had only a 95 percent degree of certainty that they had everything. But everything they had was accounted for.

Fisher scrolled the display upward to the area covering the territory where the Russian spy plane had been tracked. "He's there before the test?"

"Absolutely," said the scientist at the keyboard, Tom Peters. He'd brought his CD-ROMs to one of the ancillary labs to go over the data with Fisher; they were the only ones there. "Flying those loops."

Fisher nodded. The NSA data showed that the spy plane flights had been going on for several weeks on an irregular pattern, not always coinciding with the tests at North Lake.

The techies told him there was no way the Russians could have caused the malfunction. Fisher was inclined to believe them, except that they couldn't come up with a reasonable explanation for the malfunction.

But one conundrum at a time. He scrolled back to the area where the accident had occurred.

"So, if there was another plane here, like really close to these guys while they're in the test area, we'd see it?" Fisher asked Peters.

"Well, like I said, a ninety-five percent—"

"Yeah, yeah, I know: If this were a baseball game, five times out of a hundred you'd lose. Otherwise, it's a team of Babe Ruths at every position."

"Yup," said Peters. He'd used the baseball metaphor earlier. "See, the satellite isn't really designed to track contrails per se. What we're doing is throwing the data through a program analyzing aerosols and—"

"Gotcha," Fisher told the scientist. "Go back to the event, okay?"

The scientist clicked his keys and then popped up the test area. The lines here were all dotted.

"Storm. We had to extrapolate," said Peters.

"So the storm screws it all up. Technically speaking."

"You could put it that way."

"Would other people know that?"

"What other people?"

Fisher shrugged. "You totally lose the airplanes?"

"Well, we know where they end up."

"We know where two of them end up," said Fisher. He pointed to the dotted line showing Cyclops heading north over the point where the plane part was found. "Do we know this?"

"Well, within—"

"Hang loose a second, Doc. Stay in the batter's box, okay? The thing is, your dotted line could go anywhere."

"No. It could only go in areas where the atmospheric conditions match the proper parameters, and of course it's starting with a certain vector, course, thrust—"

"Which can give the wrong results, as the location of crashed Velociraptor showed." Fisher folded his arms. "Where's the five percent?"

"The likely place for the error?"

"Yeah."

Peters scratched the top of his head. "Well, first of all, you have to think of this as three-dimensional, not a straight line. It's following a certain— It would have to be under a kind of river in the sky, if you want to think of it that way."

Peters's voice trailed into wolflike growling noises.

"Problem, Doc?" asked Fisher.

"Thinking." Peters began pounding the keyboard, his growls escalating. "Yeah, okay, here."

The screen showed a wide ridge of thick clouds running roughly north to south, about seventy-miles wide and then widening as it followed the storm.

"If we didn't know where it had started from, you could guess anywhere in here," said Peters. "More or less. I mean, if you want the real analysis—"

"This'll do," said Fisher. "This kind of an unusual weather pattern?"

"I'm an atmospheric scientist, not a meteorologist," said Peters.

"Yeah, but you can do that weatherman stuff with your eyes closed, right?" said Fisher, realizing the Ph.D. had been offended.

"Very common," said Peters. "I can tell you we deal with this pattern all the time. And anytime you'd have the tests they set up for here, to get this sort of heavy weather. You'd have it. See, the cold front—"

"Thanks, Doc. Listen, if you come up with a formula on who's going to win the World Series, let me know."

CHAPTER
13

He had very big hands. They folded over hers the way her father's had, and that memory made her vulnerable. Memory was a weakness, just as emotions were.

She longed for him now, even though she knew he'd been a mistake, a last-minute indulgence.

Not an indulgence. A temptation, a suggestion of what might have been had her fate been different.

Megan York spun her head around the cockpit quickly, checking on the crew.

"IP in two miles," warned the copilot. The IP was the initial point for their run, similar to the point an attack plane would use when calculating a bombing mission. It signaled the ingress into the actual target area, generally the most dangerous part of the mission and necessitating a series of precise maneuvers so the bomb or missile could be launched. In this case, the IP was 309 nautical miles from the actual target, and the maneuvers were mind-numbingly simple: The plane had to fly around a three-mile track at precisely 34,322 feet.

"We're there," said the copilot.

"Starting turn," said Megan, tugging gently on the controls. She executed a very shallow bank, coming south about twenty degrees.

"Two F/A-18s," said the weapons officer, whose screen interpreted passive intercepts from the radar warning receiver or RWR as it compiled target data.

"They have us?"

"Negative. Well out of range; they're headed east."

"Gun up," said Megan.

"Gun up," he said.

I'm ready now, she thought to herself. *We're ready.* The delays had caused considerable complications, but they weren't a factor now. Others would deal with them; she wouldn't. Her job was here.

"We have target data," said the laser operator. He exchanged a few words with his assistant, who was sitting next to him.

"On course," said the copilot.

Megan took one last look at her instrument readings. She had to turn the aircraft over to the computer while the weapon was fired.

"Engines are in the green," said the copilot. "We're on beam."

"Turning control over to the computer in zero-five," said Megan. "Counting down."

If it weren't for the tone in her headset, she wouldn't even have known that the computer had taken the plane. Megan leaned back, a spectator now on the most important flight of her life.

Second most important, maybe. The first had been the one when she'd stolen Cyclops One.

"Tracking target. . . . Calculated firing time is ten seconds," said the laser operator.

Megan looked at the target screen as the seconds drained off. When the timer hit zero, a tone sounded in her earphones. It cut off about half a second later, replaced by a tinny static and then utter silence.

"We have a hit," said the laser operator jubilantly.

"Yeah!" shouted the copilot.

"My control," said Megan calmly, taking the helm back from the computer.

"Target destroyed!" The laser operator's voice had gone up two octaves.

"Oh yeah," said the copilot.

"Coming to course," said Megan. "We have a long way to fly, gentlemen, and considerably more to do. I suggest you postpone your celebrations until we land."

PART TWO
Complications

CHAPTER

1

Blitz put his head back on the couch, jostling the headset as the conference call continued. He'd been on the phone since boarding the 747 in Hawaii two hours ago, discussing the Indian-Pakistan situation with various analysts. Things had moved so fast, he wasn't completely confident the two countries wouldn't be at war by the time he touched down.

He was fairly certain of one thing, however: If they did go to war, it would be extremely nasty.

If the CIA and NSA were interpreting the most recent Orion Elint intercepts correctly, a unit of Indian paratroopers had just practiced blowing up a mock radar site several hours ago. The exercise had included live ammunition, helicopters, and aircraft.

In and of itself, the exercise wasn't particularly interesting; everybody conducted live-fire exercises now and again to keep the snake-eaters tuned up. Nor was it more than simply alarming that the site had been set up to look like a specific Pakistani early-warning radar—one that the analysts said covered a key alley or path to Pakistan's two suspected nuclear-missile launching sites in the far north-eastern corner of the country.

What was truly ominous was the fact that the unit conducting the exercises could not be identified within the Indian chain of command. And that several Indian Air Force units had "disappeared" from their normal bases in the south and were believed to be in Kashmir.

Given political developments over the past few weeks, Blitz concluded that a small group of Indian military officers had decided to plan a preemptive strike against Pakistan's nuclear forces. It was undoubtedly seen as a way to prevent the increasingly belligerent forces in the Pakistani military from trying to take advantage of the deteriorating political situation in India. The plan was a solid one: The special forces would take out the radar; Indian jets would come across the border a few minutes later. Within twenty minutes they would be at their targets—just before the missiles could be launched if a warning was received.

There was only one problem: The Pakistanis had secretly relocated two missiles to a base deeper in the country. Augmented by a booster shipped from China three weeks before, the missiles could obliterate any part of India.

The Indians obviously hadn't picked up on it yet. Their preemptive strike would do just the opposite of what was intended: ignite a nuclear exchange, not head one off.

Blitz had just debated with the secretaries of state and defense what to do. State wanted to find some way to warn the Indians off. Defense wanted to do the same for Pakistan. Blitz argued that there was no way to do either without both compromising future intelligence-gathering operations and making the situation even more unstable.

They had to come up with something. The military analysts examining the plan believed it had been set up for a moonless night, the first of which was five days away.

"Professor?" Mozelle ducked her head around the partition across from the couch. "You wanted General Bonham. He's on two."

The other major headache.

"All right," said Blitz. "Could you get me some water?"

"No coffee?"

"I think I'm going to give up caffeine."

Mozelle rolled her eyes. Blitz went off coffee about once a month.

His earphones clicked, and General Bonham's basso came on the line.

"Dr. Blitz, this is Bonham."

"General, thanks, I know you must be busy. Where are we?"

"Still no change."

"The President is asking about this," said Blitz. "He wants a resolution."

"I believe one's in sight, sir. Colonel Gorman is optimistic. It is, technically, her ball game."

Mozelle reappeared with a bottle of Pellegrino and a glass. She mouthed the words *All I could find,* then set the glass down on the table at his side. There were small indentations to hold the glass and bottle during turbulence.

"I understand that there's a theory that the aircraft was stolen by the Russians," said Blitz.

"There's little to support that theory," said Bonham. To his credit, his voice was remarkably even.

"The crash is still unexplained?"

"I'm afraid so. My technical people, and everyone who's been sent here—we're working on it around the clock. You can assure the President of that."

"I'll try," said Blitz. Mozelle was once more at the partition. "I'd appreciate it if you'd keep me informed."

Blitz killed the connection.

"McIntyre on one. And the President wants to know when you'll be back in D.C."

"Better ask the pilot." Blitz took a sip of the water. It reminded him of being on vacation—which reminded him he hadn't taken a vacation in three years. "McIntyre?"

"Professor, this place is hell."

"I'm not interested in cosmology, McIntyre. How close are these people to war?"

"Couldn't tell you. I just got into Delhi. You know what the temperature is?"

"You're whining an awful lot."

"I am, yes."

"Did you start on those bases?"

"Well, no. Not yet."

"Get an update at the embassy, then get moving. There's an Indian general who's offered you a plane. Take advantage of it."

"How did the tests go?" McIntyre asked, tacitly surrendering.

"Jolice hit a home run. Then we had bad weather and canceled the other two shots."

"Really?" said McIntyre.

"There were so many delays, it was agreed to scrap them. Only the Jolice people were upset," said Blitz. "We've rescheduled the tests for a week and a half from now. We're moving them up to Test Area D, south of the Aleutians. I don't want a vendor circus ever again."

"Is Jolice going to take part?"

"Absolutely," said Blitz. "I want to make sure their hit wasn't a freak shot."

"Did they complain?"

"Oh yes."

"They've come out of nowhere, missile-wise," said McIntyre.

"You think they screwed with the tests?" asked Blitz.

"I don't see how. But I'm with you about rerunning the tests."

Until now Jolice's claim to fame was manufacturing very small parts in rocket motors. Some of the other partners were fairly major players: Ferrone Radiavonics, for example, had done a great deal of work on Cyclops. But Jolice and the rest were newcomers in the ABM field.

"A minor problem, compared to India," Blitz told him. "Keep me informed. I want you to check in six hours from now."

"But it's four in the morning here," managed McIntyre before Blitz clicked off the line.

The national security advisor picked up his glass of water and took another sip. Three more lines were lit with waiting calls.

"Line two is your friend from New York, Kevin Smith, wondering about that ball game next Monday," said Mozelle. "The Yankees?"

Blitz grimaced. Smith had field box seats right behind the dugout. But there was no way he'd get a chance to get to New York with everything that was going on.

"Better tell him we'll reschedule," said Blitz. "Who's on two?"

CHAPTER

2

The northern Wyoming airport had been a military base back in the sixties. All that remained were a few low-slung hangars dating from the forties or fifties. Even from the distance, it was clear that weeds had overgrown the runway—though the expert on forward air fields Fisher had persuaded to accompany him explained that wouldn't be a real problem. The pavement itself was in good condition, clear of debris and not even dusty, as if it had been swept recently.

Which Fisher thought very possible.

"You could put a C-17 down on this," said the sergeant, walking along the cement with him. The Air Force Special Tactics or Special Forces squadron member was trained in combat control tactics, or landing aircraft in hostile or potentially hostile areas near the front lines. A lanky Texan with a scar on his cheek, Sergeant Bowman preferred Marlboros to Camels but didn't turn down freebies. "You might even get a loaded C-5A off. Nice long runway. Good shape."

"You think it's been used lately?" asked Fisher as they walked toward what had once been a hangar area.

"Well, something's been in and out: We know that just from what the sheriff was telling you," said Sergeant Bowman. "But uh, pinpointing it to a 767—that all's detective stuff."

"Where we going to find one of those?" said Fisher. He bent down to examine a spot on the pavement.

The local sheriff had told him that the strip had been used by pot smugglers during the nineties. The sheriff claimed he'd put a stop to it; Fisher figured that meant his price had started eating too far into the overhead.

There had been two reports of low-flying jets in the general area called in to the dispatcher three nights before, which would be the night after Cyclops's disappearance. They'd actually sent a car out but of course found nothing.

"Fuel truck was there," said the sergeant. He walked to a stained spot near the cement about twenty feet away.

"When?" asked Fisher.

Sergeant Bowman got down on the pavement. "Recent. Real recent."

"Well, don't taste it." Fisher walked to the edge of the pad, then around toward the wall of the large building that sat at the corner of the ramp. The weeds weren't all that high and a few were brushed back, but whether a truck had driven over them recently was anybody's guess.

Fisher took a fresh cigarette out and lit up. The main entrance to the base was up a road to his left. They'd seen another service road farther south when they'd been in the air. There were all sorts of tracks running across a spot at the north side: ATVs, it looked like.

The next-door neighbors were a good twenty or thirty miles away. They had to be interviewed, even though it was unlikely as hell they knew anything.

The sheriff had offered his help. That'd be a laugh, almost as big as the one he'd get when he called the local Bureau office, surely undermanned, for help.

Fisher studied the tip of his cigarette. Was the dry air affecting it, or were his Indian friends doing something to make them burn faster?

The large hangar in front of him had no doors, but its roof was intact. Fisher walked to it and went inside.

The floor was so clean, it could have been vacuumed. Undoubtedly was.

"Pilot wants to know how we're doing," said Bowman, who was wearing a radio headset.

"Tell him we're ready to go," said Fisher. "And ask him if he saw a good place for a burger."

"Are you part of the investigation or what?" demanded Gorman as Fisher got off the helicopter back at North Lake.

"Both," he told her.

"You can't just go around commandeering helicopters, Andy. You're part of a team. There's a procedure."

"Yeah, well, listen, Jemma, I found out where our plane's been, or was, for a couple of days. Bitch of it is, I was about three days too late."

"What the hell are you talking about?"

"Maybe more—hard to tell. I'm thinking we can get those guys to do that thing with the contrails and radars again, only change the area. Then we backcheck that against the legitimate flights, because this was probably camouflaged as a legitimate flight."

"What the hell are you talking about, Andy?"

"Buy me some coffee, Jemma. You owe me big-time."

CHAPTER
3

Sitting in the second row in the control room, Howe watched the instrument readouts change on the big screen at the front as the technical people reviewed the data from his flight yet again. They'd been over it so much by now, Howe suspected they had every bit of computer code memorized, and still they hadn't figured out what the problem was. According to the data, there was no problem.

The Velociraptor pilot who'd been bumped from the original test, Timmy "Blaze" Robinson, had come down to the control room to kibitz. He was perched on the back of the seat next to Howe, sipping a cola. In the row in front of them, Firenze—the head of the team that had developed the shared avionics system and its related interfaces, and one of the most important scientists on the F/A-22V project—stood over one of the displays, his finger jabbing at the data flow like an old-West gunman using his revolver.

"Copacetic," said Firenze finally. "Perfectly copacetic."

"What's that mean?" asked Timmy.

Firenze looked up and blinked at him. "Means I can't find a problem."

"Maybe there isn't one," said Timmy.

"Mass hallucination," said Firenze. The other scientists were knocking off to get some refreshments, soda mostly. "Kinda like the song on that new Weezer."

"Haven't heard it," said Timmy.

There were talking about a CD by a rock group. The two men were roughly the same age, and while Howe didn't see that they had much else in common, they apparently shared the same musical tastes.

"Mind if I borrow it? You're going to be tied up, huh?"

"Go ahead," said Firenze. "It's up in the lab."

"You're a guy, Doc." Timmy turned to Howe. "Hey, boss. Lunch?"

"Sounds good," said Howe. "What do you think, Matt?"

"Very fuggled," said Firenze. "We're going to have to get into the bizarre theories next."

"How bizarre?"

"UFOs," said the scientist, who didn't appear to be kidding.

"Hungry?" Howe asked.

"Nah. Thanks. Thinking to do."

Howe caught up with Timmy in the hall. They went up a level to the NADT Lounge, a plush cafeteria that was one of the serious benies of working with a "private" contractor rather than the regular Air Force. Even the best military chow paled in comparison to the offerings at the Lounge.

Not that the pilots selected from the gourmet side of the menu. Timmy ordered a sausage-and-pepper grinder and insisted on extra garlic. Howe ordered a hamburger with melted blue cheese. It filled the plate, and the spiced fries were sharp and golden.

Megan used to love them, though she'd only eat a few.

"Too many make me fart," she said.

It seemed impossible that the word had come from her mouth.

"They're really grinding on the avionics system," said Timmy. "They keep running it back and forth."

"I don't think they have a clue." Howe picked up a fry. He'd been eating one the first time he met Megan; she'd walked in wearing jeans and a pair of T-shirts, looking like one of the kids working the food line.

He'd give anything for that moment—anything.

"Hey, boss, what's your flight level?" said Timmy.

"Huh?"

"You're up in the sky somewhere," said the other pilot. "Still running through the tests?"

"Yeah, I guess."

"I talked to Williams's dad last night. Nice guy."

Howe nodded. He'd spoken to the father as well, making the arrangements.

"Hell of a looker."

Howe jerked his head up, vaguely aware that Timmy had continued talking but unsure of what he had said. Had he been talking about Megan?

"What?" asked Howe.

"I said I met Williams's sister once. She was a hell of a looker."

"Oh."

The two men continued eating in silence.

"You liked her, huh?"

Howe stared at him. The younger pilot wasn't trying to be insulting, not at all.

"Megan York," prompted Timmy.

"Yeah. I did," said Howe.

"Sucks. She was pretty nice."

Howe nodded. He didn't want sympathy; there really wasn't much call for any.

"I know you didn't publicize it," said Timmy. "But, uh, she, uh, she was pretty nice."

Howe smiled, both appreciating the attempted delicacy and amused by it. "She was nice," he said.

More than nice, but he'd only known her—slept with her, he meant—for four weeks. He really shouldn't be feeling like he'd been kicked in the ribs, should he?

If he'd known it was going to be that short, would he have done things differently?

Like . . .

. . . talk her out of taking that flight?

Why had she frowned at him that morning? What was she thinking?

He'd make sure they gave her a hell of a funeral.

And then?

Then he'd feel like shit for the rest of his life, his one real chance at true love blown all to shit in the Canadian Rockies.

"Yeah, sucks," said Timmy. He smiled, back to his old self. "You think Firenze really believes in UFOs?"

CHAPTER

4

General Vladimir Luksha stood with his legs spread slightly and his arms straight out, bent at the elbows so that his fingers touched the sides of his head. He twisted slowly at the waist as he exhaled, moving first in one direction, then the other, practicing a yoga routine he had learned years and years ago as a young lieutenant on assignment to India. It was the only thing of value that had come from that brief tour as a foreign advisor; his three months there did not help his army career, and surely the Indians learned nothing of value from him.

He felt the joints at his neck crack, temporarily releasing the tension there. He went back to the desk in the bunker office he had borrowed for his operation, putting on his sweater as well as his jacket. It was an unusually hot summer day outside; that meant it might be approaching fifty, about as balmy as the Russian Far East ever got.

The temperature in the bunker itself never varied more than two degrees from 72° Fahrenheit; nonetheless, Luksha had felt cold the moment he flew over the Urals from Moscow two months before, and from the moment he arrived at the base ten miles from Petropavlovsk-

Kamchakiy on Kamchatka he had worn a sweater as well as his jacket. If any of the others in the borrowed facilities at the former naval base thought this eccentric, they didn't share their comments with the general.

Luksha's long-range spy planes were confined to the far quarter of the facility, guarded and serviced by a special detachment of men who lived behind two rows of barbed-wire fence. Luksha's intelligence analysts—mostly language and telemetry experts, though he had an assortment of scientists, photo interpreters, and aeronautical engineers—lived in the compound as well. It was a large family with its own rules and entertainments; for the most part, the men got along without problems.

They had to. Unless one could prove extreme family hardship—and had the proper political connections in Moscow—he knew he would stay behind the barbed wire until the operation was over.

The buzzer on Luksha's desk signaled that his appointment had arrived. The general pushed the button to acknowledge the call; he had no secretary, and his visitor knew from experience that the fact the intercom buzzed back meant he could enter.

Luksha waited as Laci Chapeav came into the room. The former KGB specialist shifted his eyes nervously about, as if looking for a bugging device; he headed Luksha's analysis division, and so paranoia was nothing but an occupational hazard. Chapeav's long frame had been thin, almost gaunt when Luksha met him many years before. Now he had a potbelly and large bags beneath his eyes like drooping golf balls, but his mind remained sharp.

"The Americans have lost their aircraft," said Chapeav. "It's the only logical conclusion."

"So you said two days ago. Where is it?"

Chapeav's right hand began to shake, a by-product of a neurological disorder, not nervousness. Chapeav did not get nervous, at least not when dealing with his area of expertise.

"The Geofizia data has been reanalyzed," he told Luksha. "We are confident that the target aircraft crashed in the mountains, roughly where they are looking. All transmissions ceased. It's the only possible explanation."

"Then why can't they find it? Are they really looking, or is it a ruse?"

Unlike many of his colleagues, Luksha did not overestimate the Americans' capabilities. Nonetheless, he felt it almost unthinkable that they would simply lose one of their most valuable weapons systems in a common air accident.

"There is a coordinate of doubt," admitted Chapeav. "But the transmissions that the Geofizia picked up and that we have culled from the satellites are consistent with American SAR procedures. If they are merely going through the motions, they are doing an excellent job."

Luksha nodded. Their high-altitude spy plane—a Myasishchev M-55 dubbed the Geofizia, because its "cover" mission was as an environmental tester—had been a thousand miles from the actual test area, using its long-range sensor array to gather electric transmissions from the Americans as they tested their aircraft. With the exception of a few rather incidental voice communications, the telemetry from the test craft was coded and essentially indecipherable. Nonetheless, it gave experienced analysts considerable information about the types of systems involved and some of the procedures for using them. Coupled with the spy satellites, Luksha knew enough about the American system to know it represented a turning point in airborne warfare.

He had suspected from the first that the accident was actually part of a deception campaign, though if so, he couldn't explain where they might be thinking of using it. Perhaps it was merely a ruse to pretend that the weapon was not ready and thus hide its actual deployment.

Possible. But why go to the trouble given the secrecy surrounding the project.

They must know they were being spied upon.

Of course they did.

"General?"

Luksha looked up at Chapeav.

"We will need more resources," said the general.

CHAPTER

5

Bonham cocked his head to the side, listening as Colonel Gorman outlined her latest theory on what had happened to the Cyclops 767. She was obviously tired, and her voice barely carried to where he was sitting in the second row of the control room. The bags beneath her eyes seemed to grow as she spoke.

"It's incontrovertible that an aircraft was at the Wyoming site," she said. She nodded to the airman sitting at the computer station near her, who put a screen capture showing a radar plot up on the video projector. She flashed her laser pointer at a small blip in the right corner. "This anomaly is unexplained. We think it was the airplane taking off."

"Twelve hours after the event?" asked Colonel Howe, who was sitting in the front row.

"Yes."

Matt Firenze began asking questions about how far the plane would have been able to travel. Gorman turned the questions over to one of the technical people. The Cyclops planes were 300ER versions of the versatile airframe, which gave them a published range of 7,400 miles (with their Pratt & Whitney engines unmodified); the actual range varied according to a large number of factors, starting with how much fuel had been loaded into the plane.

The discussion segued into the difficulties of using the weather-mapping radar to coordinate with the other flight data. Bonham didn't feel he should object to the technical points—he saw no point in speaking at all—and so waited impatiently for them to move off the technical points to the real problem: where Gorman and her people thought the plane had gone.

The FBI agent, Fisher, had taken a seat at the end of the back row, slouching behind a cup of coffee. Bonham watched him from the corner of his eye; it seemed to him that Fisher was studying him as well.

"What you guys are basically saying is that you have no idea where the plane went, and that it could have gone very far," said Howe. "But you also don't have any real evidence that it was at this base."

"Something was there. We're positive of that." Gorman glanced up in Fisher's direction—he'd been the one who found the plane—as if she were expecting him to say something, but he didn't.

"I can't believe that Megan York would have stolen it," said Howe. "That's treason. She wouldn't do that."

"Maybe she didn't," offered Fisher.

Everyone turned around and looked at him, but he didn't add anything.

"Anyone aboard that plane who objected to what was going on could have used the radio," said Gorman. "The pilot especially. Flying the big plane through those mountains would have taken two people."

"Not necessarily," said Howe. He felt his cheeks burning. Why wasn't anyone else standing up for Megan?

"At this point we have to work on the assumption that everyone aboard was in on it," said Gorman.

Howe turned to the FBI agent. "What do you think happened?"

Fisher shrugged, then looked over at Bonham as he spoke. "I don't know. I'd like to look at some of those lakes in the Canadian Rockies."

"Which lakes?" asked Howe.

"The ones General Bonham suggested."

Bonham cleared his throat. "I don't believe I suggested that."

"My mistake," said Fisher.

"I may have said something that maybe we should search in that area," said Bonham, retreating under the agent's stare. "Obviously I was wrong."

"Our best theory is that the plane was here," said Gorman, retaking the initiative with a sharp tone. "And, coupled with the NSA data regarding the Russian spy operation—"

Bonham saw his chance. "What Russian spy operation?"

"We briefed that the other day," said Gorman.

"Maybe you could go over it again," he said.

Gorman began talking about transmission intercepts and a high-level Russian operation based in the Far East.

"We want to get a close-up look at that operation as well as other bases they may have in the interior of the country. I'm asking for more people," she added. "I may set up a new option; I have to talk with my superiors."

"What kind of option?" Howe asked.

Gorman hemmed a bit. Bonham realized that her original orders had included not merely investigating the incident but recovering the plane. She was thinking about a logical extension: an operation in Russia, if she could find it there.

Logical?

Good God, what a cowboy. What was it about women officers, anyway? Why did they always try to out-macho the men.

Bonham looked at Howe, who was fidgeting in his seat, obviously agitated by the possibility that Megan York and the others aboard Cyclops One were traitors. Poor dumb bastard.

Gorman asked for questions.

"I want to volunteer," said Howe.

"Volunteer for what?" Gorman asked him.

"I want to make sure I'm involved," said Howe.

Gorman looked over at Bonham, as if to suggest he say something, but Bonham realized there was little use: Howe wouldn't listen to logic right now. This was one of those times when a manager did best by doing nothing; Gorman eventually realized it and wrapped up the meeting.

"I'd still like to look at those lakes," said Fisher as Bonham passed him on his way to the door. "What do you think, General?"

Bonham shrugged. "I guess that's up to you. Your boss lady seems to think the plane's not there."

"Do you?"

Bonham looked at him a second, unsure whether the FBI agent thought he was being sly or suspected Bonham was just psychotic. Unable to decide, he finally shrugged and left the room without saying anything else.

CHAPTER

6

The copilot, Abe Rogers, had been the most problematic choice for the project from the start. He was the only one of the three who was active Air Force, as opposed to an NADT hire, and yet he was by far the most greedy. Megan didn't mind greed as a motivator: It was powerful and relatively predictable. But the blatant money lust annoyed her, if only because it reminded her that others involved with Jolice, Ferrone, El-Def, and all the related companies were also primarily interested in money, not the ideals that motivated her.

Her uncle would have pointed out that it didn't matter. Greed and corruption were always there; even some of the people around Washington and the other Founding Fathers were greedy and corrupt. What mattered was the end goal, and your own purity.

"We were supposed to be done," he said, standing beneath the overhang that led to the hangar facilities.

"I'm not in charge of the test schedule," she told him.

"What are you in charge of?" Rogers's tone was close to a taunt; he pushed his chest forward as if he were an ape trying to intimidate her.

Let the bastard try something, she thought to herself. *I'd only like the chance to cut him down.*

She didn't need a copilot.

"I want more money," he demanded.

"I'll pass the request along."

"Do that."

He spun and walked toward the access door. Megan was angry enough to go out from under the artificial rock outcropping and walk up the path toward the shore. Technically she shouldn't; the satellite would be in range relatively soon.

They'd been cooped up here too long. The last-minute changes in the ABM testing schedule had made everything more difficult. She could only guess what was going on at North Lake.

The complications had begun with the Velociraptors. She knew that Williams had died. The blackout should have lasted only a few seconds—a blip, really—just enough to sever the connections and let Cyclops One get away.

But events always took their own course.

Like Howe. He was an accident.

Worse: confusion. Still, if he'd been the one killed and not Williams, what would she have felt now?

The waves lapped at the rocks below. Megan listened for a while, then, mindful of the approaching satellite, went back below.

CHAPTER

7

Howe couldn't stand or sit still, could hardly walk instead of run. He couldn't go anywhere, or couldn't decide: He had to do something, had to what?

Punch something.

It was bad enough when he thought Megan was dead. He wandered through the underground complex, jogging up the stairs rather than taking the elevator, going to the hangar bunkers and lab areas. He moved quickly, warding off conversation, pausing only for the card checks and retina scans. He wanted to be alone, and yet, he walked nowhere that he could be alone. His mind spun like the turbine in an engine cut loose from its controls. He couldn't believe she was a traitor; he couldn't believe she'd used him.

Was this what that look on the runway had meant? Had she been laughing at him all along?

He'd kill her himself.

Maybe it was Rogers, the copilot. Maybe he'd gotten up from his seat, strangled her or poisoned them all somehow, killed them and taken the plane himself.

Gorman was wrong, wrong, wrong.

But that look—what had it meant?

Howe found himself standing in the hallway near Bonham's office, waiting for Bonham to get off the phone. As soon as he heard him hang up, he walked in, knocking on the doorframe.

"Whatever it takes, I want to help track them down," he said as he walked in.

Bonham squinted, as if there were words on Howe's face he couldn't read.

"We're all involved," said Bonham finally. "There's no question about that."

"No—I want to be on the front lines. Every asset we have, including the Velociraptors, ought to be involved. I want to be there. I deserve to be."

Bonham got up abruptly and went to his outer office door, closing it as well as the inside one. When he came back, the expression on his face was even more pained than before. He seemed to have to push the words from his mouth.

"Your concern's going to be appreciated. It's understandable. Totally. Completely," Bonham said. "But . . . well, I'm not in the chain of command, so what I say . . . it's just based on my . . . my experience and sense of things. Careerwise, your best bet—the thing you should do right now . . . I'd hang back. Let events take their course. No one's going to blame you if the plane was . . . if it turns up somewhere else."

The lie seemed to embarrass Bonham, and he stopped speaking. If the plane had been stolen, Bonham's head would be the first chopped off—God knew what would happen to NADT itself—but Howe's would surely tumble soon afterward. If the accident hadn't already killed his career, this had.

"I want to be on the front lines," insisted Howe.

"It's not my call."

"I ought to be involved in recovering the aircraft," said Howe. "It's my project. I want to stick with it to the end."

"It's *our* project, Tom. *Ours. We* are involved. Whether we like it or not. But we can't do every single thing. You know that. Besides, recovering the plane, if there were an operation . . . it wouldn't really be our assignment. You know?"

"I want to be. You have the pull."

Bonham pursed his lips together but said nothing. Howe's energy had finally run out. He nodded, then rose and left the office.

8

Dr. Blitz shifted uneasily in the secure videoconference room. The national security advisor's private facility in the sub-basement of the Old Executive Office Building was only a few weeks old and the environmental controls still hadn't been fine-tuned. Given a choice between freezing and sweating, Blitz had opted for freezing. His fingers were now nearly frozen into position.

There were advantages to using this room, however. The conference coordinator sat across from him, separated by the sort of glass window that would be used in a radio DJ booth. Blitz sat in front of a panel that allowed him immediate access to several different secure networks and his own personal computer files. He could talk to his staff, either via secure text IMs or vocally over the phone while the mike was on mute. Two other stations could be occupied, and it was up to him to decide whether to put them on the air or not. The system allowed him to get real work done while pretending to listen.

Not that he needed that capability today. All his attention was directed toward the others on the line as they discussed the disappearance of Cyclops One.

It wasn't bad enough that India and Pakistan were about to start lobbing nukes at each other. The Air Force colonel assigned to investigate the Cyclops accident had just come up with a bomb of her own: a theory that the Russians had stolen the aircraft and its weapon.

An incredibly plausible theory, as the silence of everyone else on the circuit—the CIA director, the defense secretary, the head of the Air Force, and the Joint Chiefs of Staff (JCS) chairman—attested.

"We start by surveying the Russian base," said Colonel Gorman, her square chin firm despite the shaking video feed. "I've asked Special Operations Command for input on an attack option."

"Slow down, Colonel," said the defense secretary, Myron Pierce. "You're talking about an act of war in a foreign country—a member of NATO, I might add."

"Stealing our plane wasn't an act of war?" snapped Gorman, adding belatedly, "With respect, sir."

"They're not going to keep it in the open if they *did* take it," said the CIA director, Jack Anthony. "And I doubt they'd have it at that base where the spy planes are. The satellite review hasn't turned it up."

"The interpreters are reworking that," said Gorman. "Obviously we don't have twenty-four-hour coverage of that base. It's possible it stopped there, refueled, and moved on."

"What else would the attack option include, Colonel?" asked General Grant Richards, JCS chairman. It was a softball question with an almost solicitous tone; Blitz realized Gorman had already briefed him.

Smart.

"In the best-case scenario, I'd like to use Cyclops Two," she said. "It would neutralize anything we came up against."

"Cyclops Two?" said Blitz. "I thought the aircraft on the project were grounded."

"That would be unnecessary if Cyclops One were located, proving there was no malfunction," said Gorman. "I would note that aside from some minor technical points, everyone from the scientists to the maintainers at North Lake has failed to find a problem. This explains why, frankly."

"What about the Velociraptors?" said Blitz.

"I wasn't asking for them, sir," said Gorman. "But I'd certainly take them."

"They also have a clean bill of health," said General Richards.

Blitz realized that the Air Force was going to push strongly to get the plane back, not just because it was their asset, but because doing so would put them in an excellent position to get rid of NADT and regain the initiative on their own development programs.

He was sympathetic to that. And there was a certain symmetry to using the weapon that had gotten them into the problem.

Still, this was one of the few times he actually agreed with the defense secretary: They were getting ahead of themselves.

Gorman detailed a preliminary order of battle that involved a good hunk of the forces available to the Pacific Command. Simply mobilizing that large a force would surely tip off the Russians.

Assuming, of course, that they had stolen the plane.

"I think we're getting ahead of ourselves," said Blitz. "Far, far ahead."

"Sir, I was authorized to retrieve the aircraft," said Gorman. "My orders were explicit. They went beyond investigating the circumstances."

"Your orders were issued under a different set of circumstances," said Blitz. "In any event, we have to find it first."

He glanced at the wall clock. He was due upstairs to talk with the President about India and Pakistan in five minutes. He'd bring this up as well—recommend a search without the strike option.

"I intend to find the aircraft, sir," said Gorman. "But when I do, wouldn't it make sense to be in a position to retrieve it immediately?"

"What about a smaller task force?" said General Richards.

"We would prefer overwhelming force," said Gorman. "In case of any contingency. On the other hand, a small strike force, operating with Cyclops Two, could be used for a pinpoint operation."

"We haven't heard from the FBI," said Anthony. "What does Andy Fisher think of all this?"

"Mr. Fisher was the one who figured out where the airplane had been taken," said Gorman.

"Oh? Let's hear him, then."

"I'm afraid he's not available," said Gorman. "Mr. Fisher tends to work according to his own schedule."

"Speaking of schedules, I'm afraid the sand has run out of my egg timer," said Blitz. "I think we should press ahead with the search but hold any attack option in reserve."

"I think Cyclops Two and the Velociraptors should be prepared for a mission," said General Richards. "We'll formally take the aircraft over this afternoon from NADT."

The others murmured agreement. Blitz saw no point in objecting.

"I'm meeting with the President in a few minutes," he told the others. "I'll bring it up with him."

CHAPTER

9

Out of other options, Fisher resorted to a tactic he had learned from an old hand on his first week as an FBI field agent: guile. He phrased his request for a helicopter in such a way as to make the request sound as if he wanted to retrace the probable path from the test area to the abandoned base, something not even Jemma Gorman could object to. But as soon as the MH-60 Blackhawk got over the Canadian border, Fisher leaned forward into the cockpit area with his red-lined topo map.

"What we really want to do," he said over the headset they'd given him, "is head up north, to the point where they found that plane part, and work up from there. I want to look at this wedge here, these lakes especially."

"That's not our flight plan," said the pilot.

"Yeah, I know. You allowed to smoke in here?"

"Not really."

"Even if I open the windows?"

A half hour later the helicopter passed over the plateau where the 767's part had been found. The area was marked out with small triangular flags but was no longer guarded.

"So what exactly are we looking for?" asked the pilot as they flew along the western leg of the triangle Fisher had marked out.

"Damned if I know," said Fisher over the interphone circuit. "But I'll tell you if I see it."

"Pretty country," said the crew chief, standing near him at the side door.

"Yeah," said Fisher.

"You know, some of this area has been gone over quite a bit," said the crew chief. "We went over it ourselves."

"Yeah," repeated Fisher. "I want to get further north, though. How deep you think that lake is?"

"Couple hundred feet, I bet. Real deep."

"What I think I'm looking for is something very deep with a deserted road nearby for access."

"You looking for a hunting lodge?"

"Maybe," said Fisher. "Actually, an abandoned place would be perfect. Road doesn't have to be much. Enough to get a couple of trucks in."

"Hmmm," said the chief.

"That mean you remember something like that?"

"Means I could use a smoke too."

There were two reasonable candidates, both at least fifty miles farther north than the search grid, but both on line with where the part had been found. One sat in a crevice between two rocky peaks and had a paved road around the bottom quarter. But there were cabins a few miles south with a view of the road, so Fisher opted for the other site. A flat area emptied out of a road and on the lake at the southeast; they put the helicopter down there.

Fisher got out of the chopper and walked up the road, which looked like a logging trail cut through the woods. There were a few stacks of brush alongside it; the cuts looked weathered, though none of the people in the helicopter had been Boy Scouts and so they couldn't tell how old they were. The trail ran a hundred yards to a macadam road.

Fisher stood at the turnoff, smoking a Camel pensively. There were tire tracks at the edge of the road. He paced off the width, deciding the trail was roughly twenty feet wide—more than enough to get a flatbed down.

But if there was anything in the water, it was fairly deep. And there was no debris on the shoreline.

Back by the lake, the crew members were sitting on the rocks, dangling their feet in the water. The pilot stood gazing over the surface.

"So?" he asked Fisher when he returned.

"Could be," said Fisher.

"Could be what?"

"Nothing or something. Hard to tell."

"If the plane crashed in the lake, wouldn't there be debris on the surface?" asked the chief.

"I did see a candy wrapper," said Fisher. "But then again, Canada's always coddled litterbugs."

CHAPTER

10

Dr. Blitz had nearly reached his office in the West Wing when one of his secure cell phones rang. Glancing at the number, he saw it was McIntyre. He took the phone out and stood against the wall, deciding he would go straight to the President's office when he finished the call.

"Blitz."

"McIntyre. Something's definitely up."

It took considerable fortitude not to use any of the dozen or so sarcastic responses that occurred to the national security advisor. "Like what?"

"I don't know. I wangled an invitation to some bases up in Kashmir. I'm leaving in ten minutes."

"Good," said Blitz.

"The army's on high alert. Everybody's antsy. You want a rundown from the embassy people?"

"What I want is more information than I can get from CNN," said Blitz.

McIntyre started to protest.

"I understand it's a difficult situation. I have to go," said Blitz as someone came down the hall. He snapped off the phone, then smiled at Wordsworth Cook, the secretary of state. A small horde of Cook's aides clogged the hallway, going over some last-minute items with the secretary as Blitz slipped into the Oval Office.

Jack D'Amici was standing at one side of the desk, hitting small golf balls into a practice putting device. The balls snapped into one side of the chute and then were spit back across the thick, regal carpet. His chief of staff stood nearby, watching.

"Professor."

"Mr. President."

Blitz took a spot next to the putting range, careful to position his feet in the rough.

Ordinarily, D'Amici would chat as he putted, but today he concentrated on his shots.

A very bad sign, Blitz thought.

The chief of staff excused himself as Cook came in. The two men, one blue-collar striver and the other drenched in old money, couldn't stand each other and barely exchanged nods.

The President continued to work on his golf after the door was closed.

"India is going to strike Pakistan," said D'Amici finally, sinking the last ball in his line in the hole, "because they're convinced Pakistan will hit them. How do we stop them?"

"Bump their heads together," said Blitz.

Neither the President nor the secretary of state laughed.

"I think if we permit a nuclear war to proceed, we'll have committed almost as grave a *sin* as those who start it," said the President. "And I use the word *sin* on purpose."

D'Amici put up his hand to keep Blitz from interrupting. "I think that we have to do everything we can to prevent India from attacking Pakistan," he continued. "Clearly, if they strike the missiles, the Pakistanis will have no option but to respond."

"Nothing we can do will prevent them from attacking," said Blitz. "Even if we shared intelligence, they'd simply change their plans."

"We could also tell the Pakistanis they're coming," suggested Cook.

"Then how do we guarantee they wouldn't launch a preemptive strike?" said Blitz. "If we were in that position, I would."

"As would I," said D'Amici.

No one said anything as the President lined up his golf balls for a fresh round. Blitz couldn't help but think about the augmented ABM system; what would this conversation be like ten years from now? Would the President simply call both sides and tell them they wouldn't be allowed to fight?

It would be more complicated, surely, but at a minimum they could prevent a nuclear exchange.

Ten years from now. Not now.

Maybe simple rhetoric would scare them off now. Hints, rather than hard facts—get them to realize what was at stake.

"I spoke to Howard McIntyre earlier," said Blitz, trying to move the conversation forward. "He's sure they're close to action. Maybe a strongly worded speech on national television, getting the entire world's attention; it might get them to pause."

"If this was simply the government, that might work," said Cook. "But this is clearly a splinter group. And as for Pakistani reaction . . ."

He let his voice trail off. Blitz generally had a hard time reading the secretary of state; he seemed to be something of a pacifist, yet had served in the Defense Department and came from a family that had contributed a number of generals to the Army. A onetime senator, before returning to government he had been on the board of several defense contractors.

"Assuming I appeal to both sides and that doesn't work," said D'Amici, "what do we do next?"

Blitz glanced at Cook, who glanced at him.

"Can we stop the Indian attack on the radar site?" asked D'Amici. He smacked his golf ball so hard it scooted nearly to the opposite wall. He walked over and retrieved it.

"That would be quite an operation," said Blitz. "To get aircraft that deep in Pakistan——we can do it, but the Pakistanis, and probably the Indians, would see us."

"What if we used Cyclops?" asked the President.

Blitz thought many things at once. Striking a helicopter would be fairly easy for the weapon, which had already proven it could do so in trials. It could operate out of Afghanistan and fly either over that country or just over the border. And, if successful, it would have a tremendous impact on both countries, impressing them with American resolve to prevent nuclear war.

On the other hand, it was filled with risk. American lives would be at stake; worse, if it failed and word got out about the attempt, American prestige would suffer.

What was prestige next to millions of lives? If they stopped this war, wouldn't that prevent others? Wouldn't it help deter attacks against America itself?

"The laser system itself may work," said Cook. "But the plane crashed, didn't it?"

"We have another one," said D'Amici. "What do you think, Professor?"

"How can we trust it when the other malfunctioned?" interrupted Cook.

"There have been new developments," Blitz said. The report on Gorman's latest findings—and, just as important, what she wanted to do about them—would come over from the JCS. But, given the circumstances, the President would not be happy if Blitz didn't tell him about it now. D'Amici stopped putting and stood with his golf club in his arms as Blitz summarized the latest theory and recommendations.

"I can't believe the Russians would steal the aircraft," said the President finally.

"Nor can I," said Cook.

"There are questions that are worth investigating," said Blitz.

"We can't just invade Russia," said Cook. "That's what Gorman's talking about here."

"They want to use Cyclops Two?" said the President.

"I think the idea is that it would be able to neutralize anything the Russians had," said Blitz, uncomfortable at carrying water for a plan that hadn't been finalized and wasn't his to begin with. "But it may have been added because the people at North Lake are pretty adamant about wanting to be involved."

"If the Air Force is thinking of using Cyclops in an operation, obviously they believe it's ready to be used," said the President. "And if that's the case, then we should use it in India, if all else fails."

No one spoke for a moment. Blitz looked at a picture on the wall behind the President that showed Dwight Eisenhower taking the oath of office. D'Amici admired Ike for many reasons. Like Ike, he was in favor of a strong military, yet suspicious of the industrial complex necessary to equip it. Eisenhower had taken a proactive role in several conflicts; would he do so here?

"I'd like to see what a plan involving Cyclops looked like," said D'Amici. "Can you take care of that, Professor?"

"Yes, sir," said Blitz.

CHAPTER

11

Captain Jalil stretched his legs as he walked up the ramp to the headquarters building, fighting against the urge to run. He could think of only one reason his colonel had summoned him. The attack date had been set.

The regiment's forward base consisted of a short airstrip and a collection of tents scattered around two L-shaped buildings, both of which appeared to date from the British occupation, if not before. Made of large clay blocks covered with more than a century's worth of paint, the buildings had large windows along their sides; they were more like arboretums than military offices. The morning was still cool in the valley northeast of Sutak in Kashmir, and Jalil felt a chill as he walked down the long hallway. Perhaps it was energy and anticipation: He had waited so long for this that he couldn't hope to hold himself back, now that the moment had arrived.

Jalil turned the corner to his commander's office, entering the wide doorway and snapping to attention. His commander continued to work over something on his desk, not offering the slightest hint of acknowledgment. The commando captain stood at stiff attention the entire time; it was relaxing in a way, allowing his muscles and bones to ease into a perfect posture.

"Captain, we have a slight difficulty to deal with," said the colonel finally before looking up.

Jalil didn't answer. He felt disappointment—worry, really—that the plan had been canceled. But he kept his body motionless.

"Due to the nature of our arrangements, not everyone is aware of our commitments." The colonel frowned. Only a small portion of the army and air force were involved in the plan to make the country safe from the terrorists across the border; while they knew they would be supported after the fact, success depended on maintained secrecy, even from those superiors not privy to the plan.

"We are receiving a visitor in the next day or two who must be handled very carefully," the colonel continued. "He is an American—a spy, really—though of course he won't admit that. I believe he was allowed to come here because the base seemed the most innocuous place for him to be: far from the front line and nearly unoccupied."

Jalil resisted the temptation to grin at the irony. "What if the visitor is here when the order comes?" he asked.

"Then I suppose it would be useful for him to meet with an accident. While on patrol with us, perhaps," said the colonel. "Demonstrating the audacity of our enemy. I would prefer that it did not come to that, but if it did, a suitable script could be arranged."

Jalil nodded. His colonel grimaced a second, then turned his attention back to his desk, jotting something on a pad. The captain waited nearly a full minute, still at attention, before leaving the office.

12

"We're not dredging the lake," said Gorman.

"I don't want to dredge it," said Fisher. He reached into his pocket for a cigarette, even though they were inside the North Lake control room. "I want to look in it. All I need is some sort of sonar to run across the bottom."

"And what exactly do you think you'll find?"

"Maybe nothing. Maybe a big hunk of an airplane with something big enough to identify it."

"It's a waste of resources."

Fisher shrugged.

"The plane wouldn't have just disappeared in the lake," Gorman said. "No. We're not wasting our time. Don't smoke that cigarette in here or I'll have you arrested."

Fisher tapped the cigarette on the table. "You're not going to make me have the Canadians do it, are you?"

Gorman didn't answer.

"They were setting it up to look like a crash, but something went wrong," said Fisher. "That's what I think."

"We flew over that area several times during the search."

"Not that far north."

"We did go over it."

"It's beyond your grid. And a lot of that shoreline would be covered by trees from above. That may have been part of the idea."

"You're way off base, Andy."

"Here's your chance to prove it."

Gorman said nothing.

"You wanted me to interface with the Canadians, right?" said Fisher. "Consider this taking you up on your offer."

"As a matter of fact, Andy, why don't you just go search the lake yourself. Jump in it, as a matter of fact."

Fisher stuck the cigarette in his mouth. "Sarcasm isn't your thing," he said, leaving.

Firenze squeezed his eyes so hard, the eyeballs hurt. The recycled air of the protected research facilities was triple-filtered and adjusted for humidity as well as temperature, but something in it nonetheless aggravated his sinuses and seemed to drain all the moisture from his body.

Even if Colonel Gorman's theory was true and Cyclops One had been hijacked or stolen, he still couldn't explain what had happened to the F/A-22Vs. While it seemed logical that some sort of kill command had been sent from Cyclops One to the Velociraptors, there was no evidence in the telemetry data. Not one integer was out of place or unaccounted for.

They'd looked at everything, even the radar altimeter. There was no way the accident had occurred. No way.

The scientist slid his chair back. Fatigued, his brain no longer functioning properly, he decided there was only one thing to do: He pulled out his laptop and fired up Free Cell.

Firenze had gotten through one deal when he was interrupted by a loud *garrumph*. A lanky government-type stood in front of him, a foam coffee cup in one hand and a Pepsi in the other.

Fisher, the FBI agent.

"You look like a Pepsi guy," said Fisher, handing him the can.

"Thanks. Hey."

"Hey yourself. Got a minute?"

"Sure."

"You want to finish the game first?"

Firenze killed the game without saving it. "Just helps me think, you know?"

"Cigarettes are less frustrating," said the agent.

"More expensive, though." Firenze laughed.

"You know what happened to the Velociraptor yet?"

"I've been working on it. What happened was impossible. It was like snapping off a power switch. Except that it came back on."

"Maybe there was a loose wire somewhere and Howe just hit it hard enough to get it to reconnect," said Fisher. He pulled over a chair and sat on the back, his feet balancing it on the floor. "Used to have a TV like that. You had to slam the top a couple of times to get the colors right."

Firenze laughed again, though they'd actually checked into a more sophisticated version of the agent's theory.

"You think Howe faked it?"

"Faked it?"

"Like he didn't really have a malfunction."

Firenze shook his head.

"You didn't think of that, did you?" The FBI agent took a long sip from his coffee.

"No, I didn't. But Colonel Howe would never be involved in something like this. Never."

Fisher nodded slowly. "What about Megan York?"

"I don't think she would, either."

"Other people on the plane?"

"I don't know. I don't think so."

"Tractor beam," said Fisher suddenly.

"Tractor beam?"

"Sure. That Russian spy plane—has a giant tractor beam. Flashes through the air, tows Cyclops One back to base." Fisher smiled. "I talked this thing over with one of my guys back at the Bureau. Hope you don't mind. He knows a lot about computers and stuff. Not too good at Free Cell, though."

"Why would I mind?"

"He thought it had to be one of two things," said the agent. "One, it didn't really happen to Howe. Or two, there's a command in your computer that erased itself."

"The code couldn't have erased itself. We can see all the commands," explained Firenze.

"You can see the commands you're set up to see."

"Well, yeah. That's everything."

Fisher looked at him for a minute, then shrugged and stood.

The environmental system, thought Firenze: the circuit that controlled the heater and the air conditioner.

No way.

But they hadn't checked it.

Fisher dug into one of his pockets. "This cell phone— you can get me anywhere, anytime. Works all over the place. Unless you call from my boss's phone. That's blocked out." He unfolded a bent business card from his other pocket and gave it to Firenze. "You get something, give me a call, okay?"

"Okay."

"Really okay?"

"Really okay," said Firenze.

"I think you're right about Howe," Fisher said. "For what it's worth."

CHAPTER

13

Bonham considered not picking up the phone, since he'd already told his assistant that he was leaving, but then habit got the better of him. He picked up the handset and then practically barked into the mouthpiece, intent on scaring off anyone who wanted to waste his time.

"Bonham."

"General, this is Dr. Blitz. I have a request. I realize it's unconventional, and I want you to speak candidly and without prejudice in response."

Bonham sat down in the chair and listened as Blitz briefly outlined the situation in India and Pakistan. The bastards were really going to kill themselves, Bonham thought.

"Could Cyclops Two be positioned to strike the helicopters before they attacked?" asked the national security advisor.

"Of course." The words slipped out of Bonham's mouth automatically, without any consideration whatsoever. Blitz obviously realized that and asked the question again.

This time Bonham thought about the problem more carefully. It wasn't simply a matter of sending the airplane halfway around the world. Its entire support team had to go as well.

But it could do it. One of the early simulations as well as a war game exercise had outlined almost exactly the same mission.

For a brief moment Bonham returned to the Air Force careerist he'd once been, aware not only of the importance of the mission but the difficulties involved in getting the job done. Above everything else was a strong desire to succeed, to accomplish the job; logic came after the emotion, a plan to succeed.

And then came something darker and deeper—something that had been part of his makeup as an officer but suppressed.

Bonham saw that he had an opportunity that could not be thrown away. He didn't have a plan yet—he was far from a plan—but he sensed there would be one.

"We can do it."

"Actually," said Blitz, "it will be an Air Force operation, not NADT's. That's why I'm asking for your assessment."

"War Game Bosnia 2," said Bonham, naming the exercise. "We took out a SpecOps helicopter team. You'd want the Velociraptors as backups, just in case, but it's doable. Very, very doable."

The war game had taken place during the previous administration, but Blitz was no doubt aware of the outcome. He murmured vaguely.

"We can have Cyclops Two ready. It *is* ready. And the Velociraptors," said Bonham. "We've been scrambling the team for Colonel Gorman; this just involves shifting priorities."

"It's not going to be your operation," said Blitz again.

"I understand that."

"I'd like to speak to Colonel Howe."

"Of course. It will take some time to locate him," said Bonham.

"Our discussions—this doesn't represent a final decision," said Blitz.

"Of course not," said Bonham, his mind seeking ways to make sure it was.

CHAPTER

14

Howe watched from the sidelines as Gorman and her people refined their plans to find Cyclops One. It was impressive, a veritable air and sea armada that could cover several thousand square miles of the Russian Far East. If her plan had been approved, fully half of the available assets—and a good portion of the unavailable ones—in the northern Pacific, Hawaii, and on the West Coast would have been thrown into the project.

Twice, the people at the Pentagon sent her back to the drawing boards. Through it all, Cyclops Two and the three F/A-22Vs remained out of the mission plan, apparently because of objections from the top. Only the Cyclops test monitor aircraft, an RC-135 whose test equipment could presumably be modified to help detect the laser plane, was in the mix.

Howe would accept that. He could fly aboard the plane as an advisor to the task group. It wasn't what he wanted—he wanted to be in the Velociraptor, he wanted to nail Meagan himself—but he could accept it.

The memories that had haunted him over the past few days had retreated now behind the flames of a burning house. He saw his anger at being betrayed as a physical thing, something consuming the past and leaving it in ashes. He would get her; he would bring her back.

And yet, for all his rage and hatred, part of him didn't believe it could be true. Part of him thought she would never ever do this—never give up her country. Rogers, maybe, or even one of the weapons people, but not Megan. Part of him thought they must have killed her to do this.

Megan was rich enough to do anything she wanted, but she had become a pilot and gone to NADT because she believed she could contribute something. She wanted to make the world safer; she saw Cyclops as exactly that kind of program, something with far-reaching implications.

Had her whole spiel been bull?

The lasers were one-of-a-kind products, hand-built, worth hundreds of millions of dollars. The two they had had taken more than twenty-four months to construct, and there weren't any others in the pipeline.

He'd get her.

As finally approved by the Pentagon, Gorman's plan called for a Special Forces unit to stand by while a pair of Rivet Joint ELINT gatherers and U-2s conducted off-shore surveys of the Russian Far East, concentrating on the area where the Mystic Bs were operating from. Additional satellite assets were being ordered into place over that part of Russia, and two fresh teams of interpreters were being assigned to help look for clues about the planes. The NSA was reviewing intercepts from the area over the period to hunt for clues to the plane's disappearance; a Navy spy vessel that worked with the agency was being directed into the area.

"Make love to me," she said. "Make love to me."

After Gorman's plan was finally settled, Howe went about checking on the myriad administrative tasks associated with Cyclops. Crisis or no crisis, there were innumerable details to be checked, initials to be scribbled, E-mails to be acknowledged. His mind squared his emotions off into the corner, and while he felt as if he were missing part of himself, he managed nonetheless to go about the routine business with what he at least thought was a veneer of reasonable calm.

Howe worked his way over to the Testing Lab 2, where a team had begun working on the modifications necessary for the monitoring aircraft. Firenze and a knot of scientists huddled at the far end over some hastily arranged tables; a row of workstations duplicated part of the RC-135's readouts, allowing them to test their changes.

Firenze, though the youngest in the group, was by no means the strangest; that honor went to one of the two experts in digital compression and communication techniques used by the shared avionics system. The two engineers were both about 350 pounds and dyed their close-cropped hair matching shades that varied according to some scheme Howe had never managed to decipher.

Firenze put up his hand as Howe came in. Howe waited while he finished whatever business he was going over with the others. When he came over, he seemed to shy away a little, as if he were a kid apprehensive about being punished for something he'd done.

"We're looking at a tough timetable on the Monitor," Howe told the scientist, using the RC-135's nickname. "I just wanted to make sure the technical people are going to be ready. Just see if there's anything that needs to be done."

"Sure." Firenze pulled out a PDA and popped up a scheduling screen, which took several different Gantt charts and compiled them into a hieroglyphic decipherable only by the scientist. He went through the different major tasks, assuring Howe that the aircraft and personnel would be ready shortly.

"What about Cyclops Two?" Howe asked.

"I didn't think it was part of the operation," said Firenze.

"It's not. I'm just wondering, if the aircraft were needed, if it would be ready. And the Velociraptors."

"You have to talk to the maintainers," said Firenze. "But there's no technical reason on my side to keep Cyclops Two on the ground." The scientist gave him a funny look. "Bird One, though—that's still mine. Until we figure out what was wrong with it."

"I thought it was cleared following the tests the other day," said Howe.

"I have some ideas I want to check out." Firenze's phone began to play the "Battle Hymn of the Republic." The scientist grabbed it from his belt. "Gotta get this call," he said, retreating to the other side of the long lab room.

Howe's own beeper went off a few seconds later, with the code showing that Bonham wanted to talk to him. Rather than finding a phone, he went back across the base and down into the main bunker. He ran into Bonham as he was walking toward the control room.

"There you are. Good," said Bonham, abruptly turning around and heading back toward his office.

Howe felt a little uneasy as he trailed behind; the former general was walking faster than he ordinarily did, frenetic energy practically oozing from him.

Megan had betrayed Bonham as well. He presented a calm exterior, but inside he'd be roiling.

Howe wanted to pound her. Pound her.

Unless she was a victim. Unless she hadn't been lying to him.

How could she have lied? She hadn't felt as though she'd been lying.

"We have a chance," said Bonham, ushering him through the outer office.

"What chance?" asked Howe. "What about?"

"The national security advisor is going to talk to you about an operation involving Cyclops Two in India."

Howe reached for the seat in front of the desk, listening as Bonham told him of the situation in southern Asia. As Bonham laid it out, the mission itself sounded very similar to one of the scenarios in their early trials.

"It's a chance to redeem the program," said Bonham. "If we can pull this through . . . any fallout from these Russians, or whatever the hell happened to Cyclops One . . . it won't touch us. Your career will be saved. Don't tell me you're not thinking about that, Tom. I know you are."

His career was so far from his thoughts that Howe didn't answer.

"I don't know the operational details," said Bonham. "I'm not sure there are any. They're going to keep me out of the loop, I'm sure, because I'm not—because NADT is strictly development. I understand that. But could the Velociraptors fly shotgun with Cyclops Two? What's their status?"

Almost against his will, the details of what Howe would have to do to undertake such a mission began turning through his mind. He started a list of whom he'd need—an intelligence officer first thing. Weapons people . . .

The main people were already in place on the Cyclops side, and the Velociraptors.

Support—tankers, AWACS, patrols for them. Reconnaissance. He'd need a lot of backup.

SAR.

"Tom, call Dr. Blitz," said Bonham, turning the phone toward him, then reaching over and punching the numbers. "Here, I'll get the connection."

Three different checkpoints blocked the road off the mountain base. Bonham made a point of lingering at each one, stopping and chatting with the guards as if he didn't have a care in the world. He'd changed into jeans and nondescript clothes, which was standard procedure for anyone leaving the base via the highway. He was also driving a civilian pickup with Montana plates, also standard procedure. It was not unheard-of for him to go off base while he was out here; he usually took off a few hours every visit, loading fishing gear into the back of the pickup. The gear was there now, and if anyone had asked he would have mentioned a stream about fifty miles from where the base road met the highway, a stream where he often fished.

No one asked. And no one followed when he turned off the highway and onto the dirt road leading to the stream. He got out, put on his waders, and then went into the water. The first sting of the creek brought a rush of blood to his chest and upper body; he walked upstream ten or twelve yards, then set out a cast.

If casts were only measured by distance, it would have been perfect; his fly sailed in a long, high arc for what seemed like forever. But it plopped hard into the water, too dead to fool a fish, too loud to be anything but a piece of bait. He might just as well put a cut-up rubber worm on the hook.

No matter. Bonham reeled in slowly and cast again. The fly went even farther this time and landed even harder. He tried again, arms jittery, his mind too filled with other things, too distracted to relax.

Bonham stayed in the stream near the deep part of the channel for more than a half hour, listening to the water and the stillness around him. Several times he thought he heard someone coming up the road behind him, but it was only the thumping of his heart.

Finally he strode out of the water and went back to the truck. He packed away his gear slowly, then opened the small case where he kept his flies. He touched each specimen carefully, hoping the ritual might relax him.

It did not.

Back on the road, Bonham turned left instead of right, heading toward a McDonald's about five miles away. He stopped and went in, using the rest room. When he came out, he paused at the public telephone booth. As if acting on impulse, he squeezed in and threw a quarter down the slot. Then he punched an 800 number.

It took a while for the number to connect. When it did, he said firmly, "I have a new plan. It has to be followed precisely and quickly. It's not perfect, but it will divert attention. Things can be left open-ended."

The person on the other end of the line said nothing as Bonham continued to talk. There was a simple acknowledgment when he was done. Then Bonham hung up and went to buy a Big Mac before returning to the base.

CHAPTER

15

What was presented to Megan wasn't so much a plan as an idea, and a difficult one at that. To pull it off she'd have to fly her aircraft to the very edge of its endurance limit. There was a single field available for her to refuel at, and while the foreigners there would be well paid to forget her presence, there would be no way of controlling any future complications.

On the other hand, she recognized the dilemma.

This would not only draw attention away; it would allow her to complete her mission despite the delays and fresh demands.

Was that still important?

The augmented ABM system was. It was part of her goal, her real goal, and she would do anything to make it a reality.

The first time her uncle told her his story about flying over Tokyo during World War II—*how old was she? nine? and by then he was in his seventies*—from the moment that he told her that story, her purpose had crystallized.

We can end war.

Not naïvely, not by putting your head in the sand or throwing away your guns, as the Quakers would urge. Her father's father had made that mistake, and where had it led?

To three hundred feet over Tokyo, flying through clouds of acrid smoke, flesh and bricks on fire below, the roar of your engines not loud enough to drown out the babies' cries.

Because of weakness. Had Hoover challenged Japan in the beginning, in China, the outcome would have been different.

Her father saw that, and her uncle. They even agreed that if Congress had acquiesced to Roosevelt's rearmament—had they gone beyond his requests—the Japanese never would have dared.

But give her uncle and the others credit: The American bomber crews in World War II did what had to be done. She would too.

"What are we doing?" demanded Rogers.

Megan hit the Delete button and confirmed, then looked up from her computer terminal.

"Why are you in my room?" she demanded.

"I want to know what was going on."

One thing she had to give him: He didn't try to make himself attractive.

"We're going to plan a new mission," she said. "It will eliminate the complications."

"Will I get paid?"

"Of course," she said, oddly comforted by his avarice. "Extra. Help me plan."

CHAPTER

16

Fisher had almost made it to the helicopter when the evil sibyl's gaze fell upon him. The landscape turned purple and a hideous howl filled his ears. The earth would lie fallow for seven years.

"Mr. Fisher!"

A curse formed on his lips but went unuttered; he didn't want to lose the grip on his freshly lit cigarette. Instead, Fisher pretended he hadn't heard anything and continued toward the waiting airplane.

It was no use. Gorman had the angle and appeared in front of him with twenty yards to go. Fisher threw on the brakes lest he touch her and melt.

"Hey, what's up, Captain Bligh?" Fisher asked. "Tahiti in sight already?"

"Where are you going?"

"That plane over there."

"Who authorized your flight?" she asked.

"You color-blind, Jemma?"

"Huh?"

"This isn't a blue suit I'm wearing. I'm outside of your chain of command. Plane's got a seat and I'm taking it."

He took a step toward the plane but she put her hand up.

"Whatever you paid for the manicure, you got ripped off," Fisher told her.

"Andy, you can't leave."

"Why not?"

"We're in the middle of an investigation."

"That's why I'm getting on the plane," said Fisher.

"But if the Russians took Cyclops One—"

"Which they didn't."

"Damn it, listen to me."

Jemma's face flushed, probably with embarrassment that she had used a four-letter word. Fisher smiled and took a long drag on his cigarette. "Mom's gonna wash your mouth out, probably with lye soap."

"Listen, if the Russians—whoever—took the plane, then they had to have inside help."

"Makes sense."

"We have to figure out who it is and build a case. That's FBI territory."

"You think? I pegged it for CID or DIA or something," said Fisher. "Jeez, Jemma, when you roll your eyes like that, how come they don't pop out?"

"Are you serious?"

"Yeah, really, they look like they're going to drop on the ground."

"Are you going to help or what?"

"I *am* helping."

"By leaving?"

"Didn't you make that suggestion yourself the day I got here?"

She drew back, her face turning red. Fisher would have enjoyed the performance immensely, but he was concerned about missing the flight. It was the only plane headed eastward for several hours. "Andy. Listen. Do you know who was helping here? Beyond the crew? Was Howe involved?"

"I haven't a clue," said Fisher. "Probably not Howe."

"Why do you pull my chain like that?"

" 'Cause it's so easy."

"Do you think there was a conspiracy here to steal the plane?" she demanded.

"Makes sense." Fisher shrugged. "But I'll tell you more when I get back."

"Andy . . . I . . . we need someone here who knows what they're doing," she said.

"Leaves me out," said Fisher. He took a step forward.

"I'm asking nicely."

"Can I get a sonar up to look in those lakes?"

She looked exasperated. "No. That's . . . to get permission to do that, and then get the gear . . . given the other evidence now . . . You're nuts. Why are you obsessed with the lakes?"

"Bonham's the one who's obsessed."

"He only suggested it."

"You don't think that's interesting?"

Gorman's sigh sounded like the mating call of a horse. "I don't understand you. You figure out that the plane has been taken, then you come up with a crazy theory one hundred and eighty degrees in the other direction: that it crashed in the lakes."

"Who says that's my theory?"

Gorman stamped her feet, a gesture that reinforced Fisher's suspicion that she had equine blood in her. "I'm going to put Kowalski in charge."

"It is kind of nice to see you grovel," admitted Fisher, seeing the crewmen starting to button up the plane. "But I gotta get going."

PART THREE
World War III

CHAPTER

1

Howe shut down his aircraft, slowly working himself out of the restraints, moving with great deliberation as if he were reluctant to leave the plane. He'd flown nonstop to Kabul, Afghanistan, refueling by air along the way. Ten thousand miles, give or take; it was a serious haul, even in the pilot-friendly Velociraptor, coming on top of several hours of intensive planning and then hustling to leave. By all rights and normal flight rules, he was owed some major sack time, but nothing about this operation could be called "normal."

There was no way he could go to bed until he made sure the operation was under control; a slew of details had to be attended to if they were going to be ready to take off tomorrow night, the analysts' best guess about when the Indians would launch their attack.

Howe extended his arms and stretched his back, twisting his muscles. Deciding he had officially caught a second wind, he pulled himself out of the cockpit and onto the ladder that the ground crew had brought over. The men had been waiting for some hours for his arrival and were already swarming like ants on a jelly sandwich. The Velociraptors' "home" team was due to arrive in another few hours from North Lake, but the crew here—residents and others gathered as the ad hoc operation was pulled together—gave up nothing to them in terms of skill, speed, and precision. With a wide range of experience in various aircraft, the maintainers could probably have rebuilt the aircraft from the ground up if necessary.

It wasn't. The Velociraptor and its sister, now being secured by Timmy a short distance away, had performed perfectly. If he hadn't been there, Howe would almost have doubted that the glitch that killed the controls on his original aircraft had even happened.

"Man, do I have to take a leak!" yelled Timmy by way of greeting as he climbed down from the plane. "Piddlepack's full up, and I had my legs crossed the last thousand miles."

Howe shook his head and began walking toward a pair of Humvees waiting nearby. By the time he had ascertained that they'd been sent to bring him over to the base commander, Timmy had joined him.

Part of the air base had been given over to the operation, in effect quarantined from the rest of the world. A two-star general had come over from CentCom to take charge of the operation and was waiting for Howe in a suite down the hall from the base commander's headquarters. Eight F-15Cs and a KC-135 tanker were tasked to the group, along with Cyclops Two and the Velociraptors. An AWACS and its escorts were due in shortly from Saudi Arabia, along with an E-3 upgraded Rivet Joint aircraft code-named Cobra Two, which could provide real-time intelligence from intercepted electronic transmissions, including radio and telemetry. There were two different SAR packages already here, manned by troops from Special Forces Command and including not only Air Force PJs or pararescuers but Army SF troopers as well.

The packages were built around a pair of MH-60s, modified Blackhawks used for long-range missions; within a few hours they were expecting a long-range MC-130 that could be used for long-distance operations as well.

Compared to the way the military ordinarily did things, the operation was thrown together. But the force it was able to project was, pound for pound, one of the most potent ever assembled, short of a nuclear-strike team. The warfighters were relying on not dozens but hundreds of highly skilled personnel backing them up: aircraft mechanics, survival shop specialists, weapons orderlies, fuel handlers, cooks, clerks, security people, communications whizzes, drivers, and gofers. The pilots might get any glory that was handed out, but in reality they were a very small piece of the pie.

Major General Alec Liu had been briefed on the mission by the planners who had helped Howe outline it back in the States, as well as by the Pentagon and even Dr. Blitz. According to the latest estimates, the Indians would hit the radar site within the next twenty-four to forty-eight hours. The attack would be made at night, but as yet it had been impossible to get a better idea of when. That meant a twelve-hour patrol, on top of the time it would take to prep the mission and get into position.

Liu, an Air Force officer, realized how far that would push the flight crews and kept shaking his head as they traced the expected flight area on the map. There was no way to provide proper relief crews for the main elements of the mission: Howe, Timmy, and the crew of Cyclops Two were going to have to fight through their fatigue for the marathon mission.

Liu's borrowed command center had been a recreation room twenty-four hours before; the general and Howe stood over a large Ping-Pong table as they reviewed the tasking order and other data relating to the mission. Other officers gradually filtered in, and what had started as an informal brief took on a more comprehensive tone, complete with a weather report from one of the general's staffers. Liu, shorter than Howe and a bit pudgy, was a roll-up-the-sleeves kind of guy, and gave the impression he could run out on the tarmac and drive the fuel truck himself if the ground crew turned up a man short.

Captain Atta Habib, the commander of Cyclops Two, arrived just as the briefing was breaking up. He'd left some hours ahead of Howe, but his slower aircraft naturally had taken longer to arrive.

Habib looked as if he'd run the entire way. His eyes drooped and he seemed to be tottering on his legs. Howe didn't even bother recapping the latest intelligence reports; he told Atta to go and hit the sack.

"That sounds like a good idea," Liu added over Howe's shoulder. "As a matter of fact, I think it should be an order for all flight personnel."

"I wanted to check on the weapons for the Velociraptors," said Howe.

"Taken care of, Colonel. Go get some rest. Now. We have just under twenty-four hours before this thing goes off."

CHAPTER

2

At some point in every investigation, it became necessary to journey to the heart of enemy territory, to brave destruction in the quest for the truth. You could gird your loins with body armor, arm yourself with all manner of weapons, but in the end, it came down to two things: luck, and timing. Luck could not be controlled. Timing, however, could be managed. Fisher, relying both on precedent and clandestine reconnaissance, adjusted his plan accordingly and plunged into the abyss, also known as FBIHQ.

Thanks to his careful preparation—and luck—he made it over to his destination in the great bowels of the enemy camp without incident. In the deepest, dankest basement corridor, in an area once reserved for industrial waste—or worse—he found his quest: Betty McDonald, a true believer, pure of soul and smoky of lungs.

"Cut the bullshit, Andy," said Betty, who headed a forensic accounting team that worked on national security projects but was actually assigned to the government crimes section of the Criminal Investigation Division, probably because someone had hit the Tab button incorrectly when preparing the last organizational chart. Betty had helped Fisher several times in the past and apparently didn't have the pull to be permanently unassigned from such duty.

That or she'd lost the paperwork in the pile that flowed from various portions of her desk.

"Just tell me what you want," she said as he closed the door to her office, battling a bag filled with shredded paper. The remains inside the clear bag looked suspiciously like candy wrappers.

"I'll take a cigarette for starters," said Fisher.

"You can't buy your own cigarettes?"

"On what they pay me?"

Betty's laugh sounded something like the snort of a hippopotamus.

In a good way.

She rose from her desk and went to the lateral filing cabinets, where a large air-filtration machine sat. She poked the side and the smoke-eater began to whirl.

"You don't really think that does any good, do you?" asked Fisher, taking a cigarette from her.

"Keeps the boss happy," she said, sitting back at the desk. She opened the top drawer after she lit up, taking out a bag of Tootsie Rolls, which she habitually chewed while smoking. The combination kept her teeth a healthy black.

"Did you get those financial profiles?" Fisher asked.

"No."

"Didn't DOD send over those authorizations?"

"I got the data you asked about, Andy. They're not financial profiles. They're barely disclosure statements. Do you have any idea of what we do down here?"

"Besides the orgies?"

Another hippo snort. "If you're looking for bribes, you want to go over to U-Rent and get a metal detector," she told him. "You'll have better luck digging up coffee cans in their backyards."

"You're getting funnier, Betty. You really are."

"It's the nicotine talking." She reached down into the nether regions of her desk, digging out a file she had had prepared for him. NADT mandated annual security checks for all its personnel, and the checks routinely included credit reports as well as asset listings. A member of Betty's team had gone over the data.

"If they know their accounts are being checked, they're unlikely to hide any money there," said Betty, handing over the information. "We did comparison sheets where the records were deep enough. Three years."

"Boring as hell, huh?"

"Your missing pilot's rich. I'd like to be in her will."

"So I hear. These are the same forms they had out at North Lake?"

"You've seen them already?" Betty's tongue nearly got tangled in her candy. "God damn it, Andy, you know how short-staffed I am?"

"So, how rich is York, anyway?"

Betty began rattling numbers through the smoke rings, calming somewhat. The family was among the top thousand in the country, depending on how their holdings were valued. On the one hand, she had no close relatives—her parents were dead and she had no sisters—

but on the other hand her "real" money was parked in trusts.

"You can't even tell how rich these people are from the statements," said Betty. "That's my point. They're basically the same bullshit forms Congress uses, and you know how revealing *they* are."

"Like your shirt."

While Betty inspected her clothes, Fisher looked at the sheets, which—contrary to what he had insinuated—were somewhat more detailed than the data available at North Lake. York's included a long list of trusts that she had an interest in.

"Can you find out what these trusts hold?" he asked.

"After you get the subpoenas and double my personnel line, sure." Betty popped another Tootsie Roll. "Overtime pay would be nice too."

Fisher leaned forward. There was a cup of coffee at the edge. Something appeared to be growing in it; otherwise, he might have taken a sip.

"I have this other idea," he said. "But it's a long shot."

"What idea of yours isn't?"

Fisher reached into his jacket pocket and pulled out a three-page list of names. "These are the companies that are involved in Cyclops," he told her. "Just the weapons part. I was wondering if we could get an idea of any relationships they have."

"What are you, a marriage counselor?"

"Watching Jay Leno is really paying off for you, Betty."

She took the list and immediately started to frown. "Are these *all* private companies?"

"I don't know. What's the difference?"

"Well, for starters, it's as hard getting information on private companies as it is for individuals."

"So, it'll be a snap, huh?" Fisher took a long draw on the cigarette. Betty smoked no-name cigarettes, and this particular one reminded him of horse dung. But insulting her would not be particularly productive. "There may be paperwork over at DOD that lets us look at their financial records."

"Did you ask?"

"Not directly."

"Have you talked to GSA to see if there have been any audits?"

"See, that's why you're the expert. I didn't even think of that."

"Do we have grounds to look at their books?"

Fisher shrugged.

"That means no. This is a lot of work, Andy. Even without going in and looking at their books."

"I'd also be interested in whatever else they're doing, what other project they're tied into. Also, I'm looking for real estate records. I've hit a dead end on that side."

She tried to hand the paper back to him. "This isn't really accounting, Fisher. This is something you should be doing yourself."

"You know me and numbers," said Fisher.

Betty turned aside to one of the three computers lined up on the side of her desk—she had a laptop and a PDA on the desk itself—and pressed a few buttons.

"Hmmmm," she said.

"See. I knew you could do it."

"It's going to take longer than I thought. No way."

"Great," said Fisher, jumping up. "Call me, okay?"

"Andy. Andy!"

In retrospect, Fisher realized that he had made a tactical mistake in managing his exit, for undoubtedly Betty's rather sonorous voice had set off some sort of deep vibration within the Bureau's clandestine internal security system. Nonetheless, he almost succeeded in escaping completely from the complex—but then, *almost* only counts in horseshoes and grenades.

Actually, the latter would have been an appropriate metaphor.

"Andrew Fisher!"

When faced with a difficult situation, Fisher knew, there were only two possible ways of dealing with it. The first was to face it bravely. The second—infinitely preferable—was to run away as fast as you could.

Given that his way down the hall was barred by several security types, Fisher chose the former.

"Hey, boss," he said, swirling around. "What's happening?"

Jack Hunter's red face glowed in the corridor, his mouth open while his brain worked to string together a sentence of passable coherence. Hunter was executive assistant director for National Security—Special Projects, a kingdom that had been carved out of Counterintelligence when no one was looking. It was often said that Hunter was old-school Bureau, though no one could figure exactly what school that might have been. In any event, he was among the most deliberate speakers in Washington; several field agents believed that talking to Hunter was the best way to prepare for a lifetime as a Zen Buddhist monk.

Fisher, for one, had never put much store in Eastern religion and believed that patience was overrated. Still, with no avenue of escape open, he waited for his boss to get to the point.

"A camel, Fisher? A camel?" said Hunter finally.

"Yeah, bit me," said Fisher. "Ain't that a bitch?"

"It should have bitten your head off. And what was this about water?"

"Hey, Egypt's in the middle of a desert. Had to buy water."

"Five trainloads of water?"

"I think it was only four. You better send somebody over to check that one out."

Hunter's face shaded even redder. "Why does Colonel Gorman want to talk to me?"

"Sounds like a personal matter," said Fisher. The way was now clear, and so he hustled toward it.

"Fisher! Stop this instant."

Fisher obeyed, but only because he could no longer afford to waste time discussing Bureau finances. He pulled his cigarettes out.

"You can't smoke in here. It's a federal building!"

"Right, chief," he said, turning and heading toward the doors.

"Fisher!"

"I'm going, I'm going."

CHAPTER

3

The transmission clearly belonged to a Russian aircraft. Even Luksha, no expert, could see from the graph how the query to the Russian satellite for its position matched the pattern of a dozen other aircraft, including his own. Luksha could also see that the geopositioning gear that made the query had once been in a Tu-160; this match was also perfect.

But according to the three intelligence people fidgeting before him, no Tu-160 had been flying to make the query. The few currently operating with Voyenno-Vozdushnyye Sily's Long-Range or Frontal Aviation units—officially there were six of the aircraft the Americans dubbed the Blackjack, but in reality only two had actually flown in the past six months—had both been grounded when the query was made.

"So is this a Tu-160, or just the GPS system?" asked the general.

"It is impossible to know for certain, of course." Chapeav nestled his hands on his potbelly. "Several Tu-160s from the Ukraine were sold for parts some years ago. It is likely that this came from that lot. Some airframes were sold in those transactions, but given the location over the Pacific, we rule this out as an actual Tu-160. It's simply a GPS unit, and perhaps related avionics, that's been placed in another aircraft."

"We rule it out because it's not the answer we're seeking," said Luksha, as usual becoming impatient with Chapeav's know-it-all manner.

It was possible that one of the Russian military's development commands or even an aircraft factory was operating a Tu-160 for test purposes or covert missions that his people were not privy to. The bomber, though oldish, was a large, relatively stable platform that was quite usable if kept in good repair. But Chapeav dismissed this with a wave of his hand, claiming that his impeccable sources would have made it clear already if this were the case.

"It is possible that one of the Middle Eastern governments—Iran, I would think—has refurbished an aircraft or two and is conducting long-range testing over the Pacific," conceded Chapeav, almost as an afterthought. "But our inquiries have not lent support to that theory. That is why we believe the GPS unit itself is all that is involved."

"Why would the Americans use our satellites?" asked Luksha.

"Assuming it *is* the Americans, it would make it harder to detect or defeat."

"By them, not us."

Chapeav smiled faintly, then turned to the short bearded man on the right, a specialist who had worked for the PVO. The man reached into a folder and laid out a set of satellite images showing a bare island near the water.

"Among the islands included in the agreement with Japan for oil exploitation in the Kuril'skije Ostrova was one once intended as a relief base," said Chapeav. His right hand began to shake; it occurred to Luksha that were it not for this physical disability, the intelligence expert would be intolerable. But the disease softened his hard opinion of him.

"This is a photo of the island," added Chapeav, pushing the picture at the far right of the series in front of the general, "taken within the past week. And this one is from an aircraft before the leases to the private companies, some years ago."

As Luksha compared the two photos, Chapeav spoke of the island. It had been used during the 1950's and sixties as a base for spy flights over Japan and the Pacific, gradually falling out of use during the 1970's. A brief round of activity in the 1980's brought improvements to the base under a plan to operate long-range bombers with cruise missiles in answer to the American deployment of the B-1B. The bunkered hangar, cut into the rock, could hold six aircraft, and the access was angled in such a way as to avoid exposure to American satellites then in use—an advantage, Chapeav noted, that continued to this day.

There were obvious differences in the photos Luksha was examining. The older one was black-and-white, and taken at a slightly different angle. A rectangular patch of metal and machinery, which appeared to be an oil rig, sat at the right side of the island in the new photo. But Luksha could not see anything else of significance. He put them down and held out his hands. "The oil derrick?"

"They have reactivated the hangar," said the intelligence expert triumphantly.

"How can you see that?"

The photo interpreter proceeded to explain, pointing to a thin line at the lower right of both photos. The field itself was camouflaged by shadows that appeared to be rock outcroppings. The line, a reflection of the closed hangar blast door, was not present in the middle series of photos.

"It is not part of the oil-drilling process, which, as you can see, was abandoned," added Chapeav. "I would believe they timed the work according to the satellite coverage, possibly using the oil derrick as a cover. The small boats that came in and out at that time—they would all have appeared to be part of the oil project, which stopped six months ago."

"But the base is now in use?" Luksha asked.

"We believe so."

"By the Japanese?"

"There are no indications that the Japanese Self-Defense Force is involved, but they cannot be ruled out."

"You're telling me that whatever used the Tu-160 GPS flew from this island," said Luksha, "and that it was the 767 aircraft that housed the laser weapon."

"No," said Chapeav. "We have not made that connection . . . but it is an interesting guess."

His tone was triumphant, as if they were playing some parlor game. Clearly the intelligence expert had made that guess himself: The GPS reads began only twenty-four hours after the laser plane had disappeared.

An interesting coincidence, but no more.

"Can that airfield be used by an airplane as big as the 767?" asked Luksha.

"Yes, though it is not as easy as it seems," said the third expert, who until now had not spoken. His area was aeronautics; he proceeded to explain how difficult it would be for a plane to take off and land on the strip. The bomber, though heavy, had the advantage of variable-geometry wings. But he ended the discussion of impossibilities by saying it could be done.

"Who owns the lease?" said Luksha.

"We are examining that," said Chapeav. "It is under Japanese authority by treaty, which makes the information slower to obtain. According to their official records, it is abandoned."

Luksha leaned back in his seat, considering all that he had been told. In order to do anything further, he would have to travel to Moscow personally to ask permission and gather additional resources.

"It would be useful to visit the island," he said finally, knowing it would elicit another parlor-game smile from Chapeav. "I will begin preparing the arrangements."

CHAPTER

4

Blitz sat down at the small metal table across from the large stove in the White House kitchen. It was nighttime, and he could see both his reflection and the President's in the window next to the refrigerator as D'Amici fixed himself a cup of herbal tea. He could, of course, have gotten an aide to do it; Blitz imagined most presidents would have. D'Amici not only liked to do things himself, he liked places like the kitchen—places normally out of bounds for the chief executive. They reminded him, he said, of the real people he was working for.

Corny, but Blitz had known him since he was a governor, and knew he meant it.

The dark window showed there were deep lines in the President's face; the mirrored view showed none of its usual confidence and self-assurance. Earlier, D'Amici had spoken to the leaders of both India and Pakistan, strongly hinting that he knew they were at the brink of war. Neither had done more than mouth a few platitudes, and intelligence reports since indicated his calls had accomplished nothing.

The Cyclops Two battle group was in Afghanistan, awaiting the President's final, personal call to proceed.

Or not.

"So, do we go through with it?" asked D'Amici, bringing his cup of tea back to the small table.

"I think we should, yes."

Blitz could smell the strong mint of the tea as D'Amici held the steaming cup to his face. He put the cup down; it was too hot to drink.

"If it goes sour, we'll lose people," said D'Amici.

"The weapon and the F/A-22Vs," said Blitz.

"I don't really care about the machinery," said D'Amici. "I care about the lives."

Blitz understood, even though the equation was lopsided: A dozen or two dozen Americans against the possibility of a million, many millions, of Pakistanis and Indians.

"I think we should do it," he told the President. "I think we have the potential—it could change a number of things."

"The end of war," said D'Amici. His tone was somewhere between tired and gently mocking. "You're starting to sound like a brochure for the augmented ABM system."

"I don't think it's the end of war," said Blitz. "I'm not naïve. And I'm not pushing a weapons system. But I do think it's a chance. It'll show people we're determined. It could have an enormous impact."

D'Amici got up and began pacing through the room. "I think about Lincoln sometimes, walking upstairs the night his son was dying. He had all those men in uniform on the battlefield. Roosevelt, pushing himself along in a wheelchair, or being pushed. And Ike, ordering the overflights of Russia, even as they kept taking shots at his planes. They all faced difficult decisions."

"Thank God they made the right ones," said Blitz.

"Sometimes they didn't. That's the point." The President picked up his cup, blowing into it to cool it. "You remember during the campaign, the first time you briefed me on India? You predicted this."

"I predicted difficulties," said Blitz. "Not this specifically."

D'Amici sipped his tea, then put the cup down. "Come on," said the President, starting back upstairs. "I have to get the order out now if it's to do any good."

CHAPTER

5

Captain Atta Habib completed a fresh round of checks with his copilot, then undid his restraints. His neck had stiffened under the weight of his helmet. He took it off as he rose, stowing it in his seat before stretching his legs on the flight deck. While the 767 could—and usually was—flown in shirtsleeves, the accident that had claimed Cyclops One had reinforced the importance of survival gear. Unlike "normal" 767s, the Cyclops aircraft were fitted with special ejection seats, specifically designed adaptations of the ACES II model standard in fighters like the F-15. The seats ejected upward through large hatchlike cutouts in the roof of the plane. The metal pins, along with tags to manually blow the hatches if the automated system didn't work, were visible above each seat.

Atta wondered if York and her crew had thought about the ejection mechanism too. He remained convinced that they had been lost in an accident: He didn't buy the hijacked plane theory at all; no one who knew Megan could.

Atta felt his vertebrae crack as he leaned backward, all of the muscles stretching. The flight decks on the Cyclops warplanes were more spacious than their civilian counterparts, thanks to the modifications necessary to carry the weapon. Originally designed for a three-person crew, the two-man cockpit in production 767s was a comfortable executive office; in Cyclops it was a veritable suite. Behind the pilot's and copilot's chairs were four crew stations for the laser, two apiece facing consoles along the wall. The configuration allowed for decent walking space to the back galley. The walking space covered the access points and one of the wire tunnels for the laser gear, but these were covered by a carpet, and the crew joked that there was enough room for a regulation bowling alley, an exaggeration that nonetheless hinted at its spaciousness. The galley included a rest room and a small kitchen area complete with a microwave and a thermos coffeemaker supposedly rated to stay inside its fitting at negative 10 g's. Future versions of the aircraft would probably include a second crew compartment, where a reserve team could catch a snooze on a long mission.

The Boeing people hadn't planned on making a revolutionary warplane when they drew up the 767; they were looking for an economical way of moving people around the globe. But just as they had done with the venerable 707, their fundamental engineering values had created a versatile airframe capable of going far beyond even the visionary's dreams. The engineers and contractors working for NADT had a good basis to work on, and credited the original designers for most of their success. Habib had taken this airframe through a stress test—ostensibly for the laser nose—that included a barrel roll and an air-show loop. Granted, it wasn't a sleek F/A-22V or a teen-series fighter, but the big jet was surprisingly nimble and extremely well behaved, even at the far edge of its advertised design limitations. Habib felt confident it would perform today.

He thought the same of his crew. The four of them together had over fifty years in the service and had spent the last year on the Cyclops project.

The same things could have been said of everyone on Cyclops One.

Atta paused behind the designating station. While the pilot actually made the shot, the designating specialist—

Technical Sergeant May Peters, in this case—guided the computer as it worked with the various inputs and prioritized potential hits.

Had she been male, Atta would have given her a good-natured slap on the side or back. But he worried about doing that with a woman—worried it might be misinterpreted or, worse, that he might actually hurt her. Even though he knew Peters rather well—had met her husband and even had dinner with them once or twice—he remained formal.

"Good work, Sergeant," he told her.

"Thank you, sir," she said, her tone not quite as rigid as his but still well shaded toward formality.

Atta went over to the other station, which was manned by another tech sergeant, Joe Fernandez. Feeling he had to treat Fernandez the same as Peters, he repeated the same words and received precisely the same response. Satisfied, he looked over his domain one more time, pausing before returning. He had thought of making a little speech as a morale booster. Colonel Howe had given one on the tarmac earlier and he'd been impressed. But Atta wasn't that good a speaker in front of crowds, even tiny ones; he felt something growing in his throat and decided not to chance it.

He thought of saying a prayer but worried that might be taken the wrong way: He was a Muslim, and maybe Christians would think he was imposing his beliefs on them. So instead he stretched one more time and went back to his seat.

"We're looking good," he told them over the interphone after he slipped his helmet back on. "Looking real good."

CHAPTER

6

Airborne and on course, Howe worked his eyes across the dimming purple sky, scanning for enemies. The integrated sensors in his aircraft would surely alert him to another plane well before he could see it, but there was no way in the world he would feel secure, no way he could fly, without using his eyes. Part of him believed, truly believed, that they'd see something the radar and infrared would miss; part of him was convinced that even the powerful radars in the AWACS and Cyclops Two were no replacement for his own Mark One eyeballs. Howe was not so superstitious—or foolish—about this that he wouldn't trust the display on his gee-whiz tactical screen, much less forgo the very real benefits of technology. Both of his kills had come from beyond visual distance; he hadn't seen either target before launching. But still, his eyes hunted the darkening space around him, a miner's pan sifting for danger.

The overall plan was laid out almost exactly as the exercise dubbed Bosnia 2 had been over a year ago, allowing for differences in geography. As the Velociraptors worked over the Pakistani border near Indian Kashmir, they would feed data back to Cyclops Two, which would remain in Afghan airspace. Their low-probability-of-intercept radars could not be detected by the gear believed to be aboard the helicopters or the front-line Indian aircraft that the planners thought would be nearby; at the same time, the F/A-22Vs would be able to slide through the rough terrain, overcoming the clutter that shadowed part of the likely approach. The laser aboard Cyclops Two would make the hit, but the two Velociraptors would be close enough to strike the helicopters if it missed.

The radar in the F/A-22Vs had been developed from the original APG-77 perfected by Northrop Grumman and Raytheon, the first active-array antenna radar fitted into a fighter aircraft, but the Velociraptor version was nearly as far from its ancestor as the APG-77 had been from its own predecessors. Unlike old-fashioned radar "dishes," the radar signals were sent and received through nearly two thousand short antennas carefully arranged around the aircraft's hull. The embedded array allowed the radar to operate in a variety of modes at once, essentially giving complete and instantaneous coverage while still employing low-probability-of-intercept tactics. In an older radar the sweep of the beam and spikes in the energy levels provided easy detection points for a careful enemy. The F/A-22V—and even the "stock" F/A-22—could use its active radar and still not be detected by most interceptors until it had already fired air-to-air missiles—in other words, until it was far, far too late. The aircraft's eighteen different modes were capable of working together so that a long-range target might be found, identified, and targeted seemingly instantaneously. The targets were passed along immediately through the intraflight data link (IFDL) to Cyclops, which would then use the information to nail them.

The tough thing, the almost impossible thing, was the length of the mission. The planners were convinced the attack would go off as soon as it was completely dark, which would be roughly an hour from now. But there were no guarantees, and even the long-legged F/A-22Vs would eventually get thirsty. Howe and Timmy had worked out a plan to swap off on refuels several hours into the flight; the complicated fuel matrixes were stored in the Velociraptors' computers, and the flight computer had a preset panel that would show their fuel profiles throughout the mission.

Maybe it wouldn't come off at all. The diplomats were supposedly burning their own dinosaurs on the ground, trying to cool things down.

"Bird Two to One," snapped Timmy. "Hey, boss man, how's it looking?"

"We're clean," Howe told his wingman. "Eight minutes to border."

"Roger that."

Timmy was flying at a five thousand feet offset a mile off his right wing at 38,000 feet. Once over the border, they were going to run one circuit through the mountainous area together to get their bearings, then split up to cover more territory, in case the analysts' guesses were off the mark. The automatic ground modes on their radars would hunt for any hidden bases, allowing the Cyclops Two operators to rule out—or in—possible surprises.

The AWACS checked in, relaying a report from one of the Navy surveillance craft helping to monitor the peninsula that the Indians were launching one of their Russian Beriev A-50 "Mainstay" radar aircraft from a base to the southeast, near the coast. The Mainstay was more than five hundred miles from their patrol area, and its radar range was less than two hundred miles. Unless it got considerably closer, it was unlikely to pinpoint the stealthy F/A-22Vs, and still less likely to be able to vector anything toward them.

Even so, Howe felt himself leaning forward on the seat. He edged his thumb along the top of the sidestick, watching the computer count down the time to the border in the course module above his left multiuse display. Howe checked the aircraft data, took a slow breath, and flexed fingers on the throttle. It was getting fairly dark now, and so he push-buttoned the HUD into synthetic view, the hologram rendering the outside world at a one-on-one scale/first person. The fishbowl before him duplicated what he would have seen if it were a perfectly clear day. He stared at it a second, mentally orienting his eyes and brain to accept the synthetic data, then flicked into one-on-ten, which felt a little like watching an O-scale train layout instantly downsize to HO. He enabled verbal commands, then had the Velociraptor's computer pencil in some geography and flight plan data. He could see the border etched out on the virtual ground ahead.

Megan wasn't gone from his memory, but she'd been pushed back, his anger and other feelings corralled.

Corralled, not eliminated.

"Bird Two, we have thirty seconds. You ready, partner?"

"Piece of cake," said Timmy.

Howe counted down the last few seconds, then goosed the engine. The two F/A-22Vs rocketed over the Indian coast, knifing through the darkness.

Two minutes later the radar detector in Howe's plane began to bleat. The system identified and located the radar, an early-warning ground station southeast of Charsadda, rendered as a purple dish icon in the far reaches of the hologram's dusty 3-D hills. The radar was attached to a Crotale 2000 surface-to-air missile system, a relatively short-range mobile SAM intended primarily for point defense of airfields and other strategic targets. The radar could not see the Velociraptors, nor would the missiles it guided present much of a challenge to the aircraft's ECM suite if it came to that. Nonetheless, the avionics system made note of them, opening a file and storing the data for the pilot's reference. If Howe wished, he could direct the computer to present him with a list of options for eliminating the radar and its missiles; one button and one verbal command later, a small-diameter GPS-guided bomb would spit from the Velociraptor's belly and the radar would be history.

If Howe wished.

"Bird One, this is Big Eyes," said the AWACS controller. "Be advised, Indra is airborne."

Indra was the code name they'd settled on for India's northern-based Phalcon AEW aircraft, arguably the only serious threat to the mission. The 767's multisensor radars could provide early-warning and tracking data, serving in a somewhat similar capacity as an AWACS. While not the equal of American systems, it was still impressive—and in theory capable of finding the F/A-22Vs, or at least their radar transmissions. Indra flew regularly, and its launch was not unexpected—in fact, just the opposite. Howe took it as confirmation that the mission was a go. The AWACS would keep tabs on the aircraft, which presently was several hundred miles to the south of Howe's flight path.

"Bird One," acknowledged Howe.

CHAPTER

7

McIntyre unfolded himself from the helicopter seat and walked unsteadily across the cabin. The damn thing shook like a washing machine, and the metal was so thin he worried he'd put his hand through the side as he steadied himself before stepping out onto the tarmac with his bag. If it wasn't the oldest helicopter in the Indian inventory, it had to be in the running. As he stepped out, grit flit into his eye; he walked forward blindly, half expecting to be decapitated by the rotors even though he was bent forward.

The helicopter fanned the air behind him, rushing away in the dusk. The mountains cast an odd green-purple glow over everything as night fell; the dim light made him feel even more tired, and McIntyre was glad this was his last stop for the night. He'd been to several bases over the course of the day, each one duller than the rest. Hopefully the CIA guys were gathering better information.

A figure in brown stood to the right, blurring into the dusk. McIntyre worked his thumb against the corner of his eye, trying to clear it.

"Damn dirt has glue in it," he said, trying to make a joke.

The blur didn't speak. McIntyre finally pushed his eyelids apart, trying to bring the blur into focus. All he could see was the man's frown.

"Name's McIntyre," he said, letting go of his eye and holding out his right hand to shake. The man, a captain, didn't take it.

"I'm to show you around," said the officer.

"Let's start with the john, then," said McIntyre. He grabbed his bag and waited for the blur to move. By now his eye was tearing uncontrollably; McIntyre realized that he ought to just let the tears clear out the grit, but it was difficult to avoid the urge to rub. Finally the Indian captain began to move toward a gray cloud on the right. McIntyre followed, gradually gaining his sight as he went.

He'd been kept from the bases where the Su-27s and Su-30s were, and hadn't seen a MiG. When he'd come as an assistant to a congressional party a year before, the Indians had eagerly shown off the aircraft. Admittedly, they'd emphasized their defensive abilities, and talked quite a bit about how much easier life would be if they could only purchase F-15s, but still, the difference now was obvious. He'd asked to see one of their Israeli-built Phalcon radar planes but had been told that the aircraft were out of service for maintenance, a fact that he knew was a lie.

This place—a landing strip with no helicopters and no access roads. They were obviously parking him here for the duration.

McIntyre followed his laconic captain toward the low cloud, which soon came into focus as a building. He was not unsympathetic to the Indians; they had their own priorities and concerns, he knew, and in some ways their fierce attitude toward their northern neighbors were justified by history, both recent and ancient. But sympathy wasn't why he was here.

He was a little late calling Blitz. He hoped his minder would leave him alone in the john so he could make the call.

Captain Jalil had made his decision as soon as the American stumbled from the helicopter. The colonel had left the option up to him, saying any contingency could be covered.

The man's ineptness, however, seemed too much an opportunity to let pass. The Americans would be sympathetic when they learned that one of their own men was killed during an inspection of the border area; it would prove to them finally where the danger really lay.

The buzz of the helicopters approaching removed any doubts that Jalil might have had. The captain stopped in front of the empty barracks room and pushed the door open. "You will leave your bag here," he told McIntyre.

"Looks like a monastery," said the American. No longer rubbing his eye, he sauntered inside, walking the way all Americans walked: as if he were a great prince visiting part of a far-flung empire. "No locks, huh?"

"There are no need for locks here," said Jalil. "Come."

"You know what, I think I'm going to take a nap before dinner, if that's okay," said McIntyre. "And I still have to hit the john."

"No," said Jalil.

"No?"

Jalil smiled at the American's surprise. They were not used to being contradicted.

"I believe you'd like to see the helicopters that are arriving," he told him.

"Maybe later."

Jalil reached to his holster and pulled out his gun. "Now would be a much better time, Mr. McIntyre."

CHAPTER

8

Timmy double-checked his position as they came over the border, accelerating to stay on the dotted line the computer provided. The flight indicators were all in the green; every system aboard the aircraft was working the way the manuals said it should. Timmy's aircraft could have been used to benchmark the fleet.

Which meant everything was boring as shit. Timmy had no doubt they'd nail those suckers if they came up, but he did seriously doubt they'd make their play. The intel people were always—always—overaggressive. They never saw one threat where they could imagine three or four.

More than likely, they'd be orbiting up here for twelve hours straight, back and forth, twiddling their thumbs. He was already feeling a little tired.

Wait until tomorrow, he thought. He kicked himself for not bringing the MP3 jukebox. He'd left it on the bench when Howe saw it and frowned. Mandatory flight equipment from now on.

The colonel had always been the serious type. He was a good pilot, a good leader—a warfighter with scalps on his belt. But serious, very serious.

Losing Cyclops One and Bird Two had hit him pretty hard. He'd been hung up on York; that was obvious.

Pretty quiet about it. Timmy didn't figure she was a traitor—they'd probably find her and the others smacked against a mountain any day now—but it still was a lot of shit to take.

Keep him awake, though. The pilot clicked the computer to look at his fuel matrix, then put his eyes back on the synthetic view hologram, set at max magnification.

* * *

Howe was just reaching the end of the patrol area when the radar picked up two contacts coming hot out of the north, about 122 miles away. Relatively small and moving fast, the two aircraft were either F-16s or Super-7s. Built with Chinese help, the S-7s were multipurpose fighters roughly comparable to early-model F-16s.

The computer placed the two contacts in the far end of the outer circle in the main tactical display, too far away to show on the HUD hologram. There were three circles, which represented a hierarchy of threats: Anything in the outer ring could be tracked by the F/A-22V, but was not yet close enough to be targeted; the middle ring represented aircraft that could be targeted without detection; the inner ring or bull's-eye represented aircraft whose sensors were definitely capable of seeing the F/A-22V, though of course combat conditions (and active and passive jammers) might prevent the enemy from actually acquiring or locking on the plane.

"Bogeys," Howe told his wingman.

"Yeah," said Timmy. The contacts had been shared through the IFDL and appeared simultaneously on the displays of both aircraft. Nonetheless, standard procedure called for the pilots to alert each other to the new contacts, maintaining situation awareness.

"Turning," said Howe.

"Two," acknowledged Timmy.

The Pakistani planes were still flying in a straight line south toward the border. It was possible they were intending to cross over and take out the Indian AEW plane, though much more likely they were meant either as an answer to its launch or were even oblivious to it and flying a training mission.

The Velociraptor's sensors sniffed out a burst of energy that matched the signature of a Phazotron radar from the airplanes. That allowed the system to positively ID the planes as S-7s and gave the artificial intelligence-based tactics section something to work with as it presented its pilot with a variety of options for attack.

They were roughly fifteen minutes away from an intercept, unless they went to afterburners, and even then they probably wouldn't be able to find the F/A-22Vs unless they had a way to home in on the radars.

"They don't see us," said Timmy.

"No, they don't."

"What do we do if they find the helicopters?"

"Let them shoot them down," said Howe. His orders had been explicit on that point. It was far better for the Pakistanis to do the heavy lifting on their own, without U.S. help.

"I'm getting a contact south," said Timmy, "in grid alpha-alpha-two. Fighters. MiG-29s. Four of them."

"I see it," said Howe.

"Four more aircraft. This may be it."

"No, it's a diversion," said Howe. "It's out of the target area. Stay on track."

"Looks real to me: Sukhoi-30s, four of them—eight! Attack package, and these motherfuckers are *moving*."

CHAPTER

9

There was a bright side to all of this, McIntyre thought to himself as the helicopter hurled itself through the looming shadows of the mountains: He had done his job very, very well. He now knew exactly what the Indians were up to.

Well, not exactly. He assumed they were going after a radar site, though there were any number of other possibilities. He guessed he'd find out fairly soon, however.

Unless they decided to dump him out the door of the helicopter before they got to where they were going. That might not even be such a terrible option, since they weren't all that high—maybe only six or seven feet over the ground. If they threw him out now, it would be more like falling from a train than an airplane.

Assuming the train was moving at two hundred miles an hour.

The captain had taken his phones, but what galled him was having to hand over his wallet. What the hell—did the bastard plan on stopping at an ATM along the way?

The Russian-made Mil Mi-26 tilted on its axis. McIntyre slid on the bench, grabbing for the metal at the bottom of his seat to steady himself. The helicopter was relatively large. The two dozen troops inside it filled only about half of the bench seats. The other helicopter looked to have roughly the same number of men.

McIntyre glanced sideways toward the captain who had forced him aboard. He'd strangle the bastard with his bare hands, then kick his face black and blue.

Next lifetime, maybe.

CHAPTER
10

Howe put the HUD hologram to max mag to watch the Pakistani S-7s as they altered their course and began tracking toward the Indian MiGs. There was no way they could have seen the aircraft with their own radars; if they knew they were there, the planes must have been picked up by one of the ground-based early-warning units farther west.

That told him this had to be a diversion.

He was tempted, sorely tempted, to radio the Pakistani fighters and tell them what was going on.

Two more fighters took off from a base near Lahore, these ID'd by the AWACS as F-16s. Their flight path ran in a direct line toward Howe's.

Ground defense radars were spiking up all across Pakistan. The Indian MiGs, meanwhile, kept coming north, though they were still a good distance from the border.

Howe reminded himself the helicopters were the real prize. This was a diversion: It was going to happen soon.

"Indian MiGs are ten minutes from the border," said Timmy.

"They're not the story."

"Roger that."

"Eyes, those Pakistani F-16s—do they have a target?" Howe asked the AWACS.

"Negative as far as we can tell here."

"They don't know about the MiGs?"

"Not sure, Colonel," answered the controller. "Uh, we're— Hold on: fresh contacts."

The controller gave Howe fresh data: A pair of Mirage IIIs were taking off from a base farther north and coming south.

"Hell of a picnic," said Timmy. "Are they putting everything they have in the air, or what?"

"Colonel, be advised, the Pakistani flights may be following routine patrol patterns," said the AWACS supervisor, stepping in. "They tweak each other regularly."

Howe acknowledged.

"What do we do if those MiGs don't turn back?" asked Timmy.

"You're going to have to follow them while I concentrate on the helicopter," said Howe. While the Indian planes were out of range to attack Cyclops Two, they could in theory get much closer by juicing their afterburners. There were four F-15s guarding the laser plane, but Howe wasn't about to lose it.

"PAF aircraft don't seem to be going after the Indians," said Timmy. "What's up with that?"

Howe guessed that the various aircraft were playing chicken. If the Indians went over the border and used their weapons, the Pakistani Air Force planes would as well.

"Hold on: MiGs, all Indian planes, are turning," said Timmy. "They were just looking for attention."

The S-7s remained on course for a minute longer, turning away just shy of the Indian border. So did the F-16s.

This all fit, Howe realized. The Indians had launched a flight that was sure to be picked up. That would not only decoy the Pakistanis but get them used to the idea that the crazy Indians always did this if they happened to find the real attack package a little while later. At the same time they probably knew what the Pakistanis had as reserves: He guessed there would be a window of opportunity as these planes returned to base; the PAF simply wasn't big enough to keep launching aircraft all night.

If he was right, the helicopters ought to be closing in.

So where were they?

There, right there: 122 miles south, just coming north near the border area east of Gurais.

"Bird One to Cyclops. I have your target approaching the southeast corner of box alpha-alpha-three. Advise me whether you can arrange a shot."

"Cyclops Two acknowledges contacts," answered the pilot. "They're about two minutes from our target area at their present course and speed." There was a pause. "We're moving in to set up a better shot."

Howe hesitated before acknowledging. The closer Cyclops got to the border area, the more vulnerable it became.

The F-15s, not wanting to attract attention, were flying to the northwest but could close the gap in a heartbeat. So could he, for that matter.

One SAM missile—one freak shot from a Pakistani aircraft that thought the lumbering American 767 was an attacker—and he'd have lost his third jet.

Cyclops Two could fend for itself. Nothing could touch it. Nothing.

"Go for it," he said finally.

Timmy had just turned back east to close the gap between him and Howe when the audible warning on his radar alerted him to fresh contacts: four MiG-27s, much lower to the ground and flying out of the south. They were slewing into a combat trail; this must be the attack package the helicopter attack was going to prepare the way for.

"Bird One, we have four—whoa, wait up, six, eight aircraft. Looks like they're saddling up for an attack, probably going to follow that helo strike in," Timmy told Howe.

"One."

"I can take them down, boss," Timmy added.

"Negative," replied Howe. "Keep track of them. If they get close to the border and it looks like they'll make it through, then we'll let Cyclops Two nail 'em."

"Two. Just saying I'm ready if things don't go according to plan." Timmy adjusted his course slightly, edging a little southward so that when they swung back to the west, he'd still have the MiGs close enough to take in a quick dash.

It'd be over in about thirty seconds. The basic MiG-27 design dated to the 1960's; it was essentially a ground-attack version of the MiG-23. The Indians had upgraded the design with avionics that allowed for night and all-weather attacks; they'd also improved the power plant. But it was still a relatively slow aircraft with limited radar—easy pickings for the Velociraptor.

The radar continued to track the eight aircraft, watching them as they slipped into a mountain pass. The HUD hologram had them as small dots that shone through the hulking mountains, as if the plane had X-ray eyes and could see through the rocks. The helicopters, meanwhile, were hugging the valley, approaching the border, and just now entering range for the laser weapon nearly three hundred miles away.

"Stand by for Cyclops firing," warned Howe.

As Timmy pressed the mike button to acknowledge, a new contact blipped onto the far edge of his tactical screen, a green-hued cluster of mismatched pixels. The computer tagged it as a large, unknown aircraft flying at 45,000 feet, identity unknown. Too slow for a bomber, the plane's profile was similar to that of the AEW aircraft India had launched earlier—except that it seemed to be flying in from the coast.

"Somebody's coming to watch the show," he told Howe. "That one of ours?"

"Unknown," said Howe. "Probably an airliner."

They'd briefed the scheduled airliners and routes, and Timmy knew without looking that it wasn't on the sheet.

"Eyes on the prize," added Howe before he could point that out. "Cyclops is thirty seconds to target point."

Howe checked his position, waiting now for the crew on the laser plane to confirm they were ready to fire. It was exactly like the war game exercise they'd run a year ago—except that time was with Megan.

The bitch. He'd strangle her.

Unless she was already dead. Then he'd simply mourn her forever.

"Cyclops Two to Mission Leader," said the laser plane's pilot, contacting Howe. "Permission to engage."

"Engage," said Howe.

11

Captain Jalil checked his watch. They were within five seconds of their schedule—nearly perfect. The operation was moving along as easily as any of the practice runs.

Ideally, he'd find a Pakistani weapon to kill the American with, then take the body back. The story would be easily concocted: They were on a routine patrol, showing the American the dangers, when firing began.

The man would end up being a hero to his people. The irony brought a smile to Jalil's lips.

Would he feel good when he shot the first Muslim?

Yes. It would feel very, very good.

McIntyre coughed, then worked his tongue toward the back of his mouth. It felt as if something were lodged there, or as if the junction of his throat and mouth had been lined with cardboard—disintegrating cardboard. He coughed again, shook his head.

"Could I have some water?" he asked, looking toward the Indian captain.

He coughed again. The captain hadn't heard him over the whine of the engines.

"Water?" asked McIntyre, getting up. He had to put his tied hands up against the racks at the top of the cabin area to keep his balance in the helicopter, which danced left and right as it moved through the rugged terrain.

"Water?" he said to Jalil. He tried to clear his throat, holding his Adam's apple with his fingers.

Jalil looked up at him as if he didn't understand.

"Water," said McIntyre. As he let go of the rack to gesture with his hands, he felt his anger building up suddenly. He fought an urge to start pummeling the bastard.

Then he thought to himself: Why not? He's going to kill me anyway.

"Water," he said.

Something cracked at the top of the helicopter. McIntyre was thrown sideways as something long and hard smacked the side of his right calf. There was an explosion and a shout behind him, and in the next instant he felt himself tumbling into purgatory.

For one bewildering second, Captain Jalil thought he was six years old again, a child in his village, back on the day when his mother was killed.

Except that this time he was in the house, and the flames were grabbing for his clothes. He tried to beat them back with his hands, fight them off, but they were too fierce.

Escape! he screamed at himself. _Escape!_

Then he realized he was not six years old. Anger sprang from the center of his chest. He would avenge himself against the Muslim bastards. He would have the full revenge he was entitled to.

"Yes," whispered a voice in his ear. He recognized it as his mother's.

Jalil turned to see her but found only blackness.

CHAPTER

12

"They've fired," the weapons operator reported. "Two targets down."

"Are they still tracking?" Megan asked.

"The radars are all active."

She pushed her eyes across the instrument panel, forcing her thoughts away from Tom. He'd be out there, thinking about her.

That should have been her, firing the weapon.

She saw him now: the way he looked at her on the access ramp outside the aircraft, puzzled. Why was that what she thought about—not their date rock climbing, or the time she'd had him take her to an opera.

Some opera. It was a traveling company in a gymnasium. He'd hated it—just about fallen asleep—but pretended to be interested when she started talking about it later, nodding in all the right places.

She was right, and she had done the right thing. This proved it, didn't it?

Others wouldn't see it that way. Tom wouldn't. He couldn't.

"ETA to the target area is now five minutes," said the weapons operator.

"Yes," she said, still struggling to focus.

CHAPTER

13

"Only a partial hit on target two," reported Cyclops as Howe swung his aircraft toward the shootdown. Both helicopters had disappeared from the screen seconds after the indicators flashed on Howe's screen, indicating the weapon had discharged. "They're definitely down, though."

"I'm going to take a look," Howe told them, slapping the throttle into afterburner. The flood of fuel into the rear chamber—tweaked and perfected after literally thousands of man-hours of fuss—ignited with a smooth, incredibly powerful ripple that nearly doubled the aircraft's speed. The nozzle at the front of the engine was wide open, changing the world's most efficient-at-speed jet engine into the world's fastest jet-fueled power plant. The F/A-

22V covered over thirty miles a minute, a proud cheetah running down her prey on the Africa savanna.

Howe's heart beat lackadaisically, keeping time like the bass drum in a band, its cadence lazy enough for the hottest summer day. But his stomach felt the brief burst of acceleration—his stomach and the muscles in his arms, the tendons at his knees, his ribs, his joints, the small fibers of hair below his ear. They felt the acceleration and they thrilled to it. This was flying, moving through the air as fast as a Greek god, the leading edge of sheer thought. The aircraft strapped on his back was one of the best—*the best*—pieces of machinery ever perfected by man, attached through an electronic umbilical cord to a weapon as powerful as Zeus's lightning bolts.

And it had just been used to avert World War III.

Thomas Howe, and the nearly thousand men and women connected to the mission, had just saved several million lives.

The idea was as intoxicating as the speed.

"Doesn't that sound like a worthy thing to do? It's something I'd die for. Truly."

Howe pushed Megan's voice back into the rush of the jet as he eased back on the gas, swooping to give the radar's ground mode a good look at the wreckage. They needed to make sure the helicopters truly were down.

Timmy checked in, updating him on the attack package that was following the helicopters toward the border. The lead plane was now about twenty minutes from Pakistani airspace; they'd planned the attack very closely, giving the ground people ten minutes to take their targets.

Would they go ahead with the attack if the radars were still working?

No one knew. If they did, Cyclops Two and the Velociraptors would take them out.

"I have the lead plane," said Timmy.

"Stick to the game plan," Howe told him. "We've got plenty of time."

He tucked his wing and plunged toward earth, flicking off the holographic HUD projection. The night was dark but clear, and he could see a pinpoint of fire at about ten o'clock in his windscreen, one of the targets burning after it had crashed.

"Splash one, definite," reported Howe.

He was moving too fast and still too high to see much, even if it had been daytime. He went back to the synthetic view as he slid around the valley. The radar hunted the ground as if it were in its free-form attack mode, developed to help the next-generation attack planes turn up Scud missiles in tinhorn dictators' palaces. The ground radar that the Indians had been targeting was only a few miles ahead; his RWR noted that it was active and hunting through the sky, though the Velociraptor had not yet been detected.

Push a button, and he could take it out himself.

Howe slapped the side stick, banking away. He hadn't found the wreckage of the second helicopter, but he also hadn't found it flying, either.

"Those MiGs are coming hard," warned Timmy. "Eight of 'em."

"We have them all," said the Cyclops pilot.

"Hold on," said Howe. "Wait until they're at the border."

"Hey, Colonel, you see that contact Unk-2?" said Timmy, referring to the computer tag on the large unknown aircraft flying northward near the Indian coast. "What's his game, you figure?"

"Has to be a spy plane," suggested Howe, just as he had earlier.

"Not Indian, though. Came off the ocean."

"Could be the Russians." They were a bit too far away to get good information about the aircraft, but its size and speed made it fairly obvious that it wasn't part of the attack package.

Advising them, maybe, though one of Howe's own ELINT aircraft ought to be picking up signals in that case. Cobra Two reported that the Indian forces were still flying silent com. The Pakistanis, meanwhile, did not seem to know anything was amiss.

"Lead MiG will be in range of the Pak radar in zero three," said Timmy. "I don't know. . . . He's pretty low; he might just get through."

"We wait until he's committed to crossing the border," said Howe. He'd begun to climb now, swinging around the coverage area of the radar site. All of the Pakistani flights had returned to their bases; the only thing that the PAF had in the air were two Mirage IIIs back near Lahore. Besides the attack package closing in on the Kashmir border, the Indians had their 767 radar plane and its escorts flying near the border to the west, giving them coverage just about to Afghanistan.

Howe suspected that the Indians had other groups of planes airborne to the south, out of his task force's detection range; they'd be preparing a follow-on strike once the first group of planes took out the sites. At the moment, though, they were too far off to see or worry about.

"One minute to border," said Timmy. The two Velociraptors had separated about fifteen miles, Howe to the northeast and Timmy to the southwest of the lead MiG. They could divvy it up between them if they had to.

"Cyclops is tracking. We're ready anytime, Colonel."

"Bird One."

"MiGs are slowing—turning! Shit," said Timmy.

"Don't sound too disappointed, my friend," said Howe. "This just means we did our job."

"Yeah, well, figures they'd wimp out," said the wingman.

Howe laughed. His joints cracked; he hadn't realized how tense he'd become.

"Bird One, be advised the strike force you've been tracking has used the word *abort*," radioed Cobra Two.

"Bird One acknowledges. Well done, team. Kick-ass job, everybody," said Howe. "How we looking out there, Timmy?"

"All I see is fannies with tails between their legs, scurrying home," replied the wingman. "Our UFO's still coming north, though. Sucker's going to be at the border in, like, zero-five."

"Yeah, I see," said Howe.

"Maybe we ought to check him out," suggested Timmy.

"Negative," said Howe. "Cyclops, you're cleared to head back to the barn."

"That would be cave," said Atta, the Cyclops pilot.

"Just don't run into Ulysses," said Howe.

Cyclops banked north, heading for its temporary Afghanistan base. The other aircraft checked in; Howe listened to the AWACS escorts working out a tank with Budweiser, the KC-135 assigned to make sure they didn't go dry.

"Hey, that unknown contact is hitting the gas," said Timmy. "They should be on Pakistani radar by now."

"Bird Leader, be advised Mirage flight is being vectored south," said Eyes.

"Confirming that," said the AWACS controller. "Not sure what they're doing. Could be heading for that unidentified contact, R2."

The Pakistani airplanes would be picked up by the Indian radar plane quickly.

"Shit!" yelled Timmy. "MiGs are turning back."

For a second, panic surged through Howe: the irrational fear he'd felt in the wake of the accident.

Then it was gone. He squeezed his hand on the stick, felt himself relaxing ever so slightly, giving himself over to the plane.

"MiG flight is receiving new orders," said Cobra Two. "They're being told to proceed. . . . They're proceeding!"

"Understood," said Howe. "Cyclops, give me status."

CHAPTER

14

NADT's headquarters was not marked from the highway, although Fisher surmised he was in the right place by the strategic rock formations that sheltered video cameras along the driveway. A half-mile in from the road, a row of closely spaced trees partially hid a picket fence extending around the property; the pickets themselves half camouflaged a grid of wires, probably electrically charged.

A guard post sat where the fence and one-lane access road met. Two security officers in nondescript uniforms stepped out to flag Fisher's car down.

His Bureau credentials did not work their usual magic, but the guards did grudgingly admit him after calling for instructions. Fisher drove through the gate, over a bridge, and past a moat with geese that looked as if it had been stolen from a Disney movie; he almost expected to find Snow White and the Seven Dwarfs waiting for him at the front door.

Close. A woman in a black business suit, her skirt cut so high it had less material than a napkin, flagged him down near a long concrete apron punctuated by cement barriers.

"Mr. Fisher?" She leaned into his car, filling it with so much perfume, Fisher would have gone for a gas mask if he'd carried one. The top of her shirt was strategically arranged to highlight the natural skin tones of her chest; NADT obviously didn't fool around.

"I was this morning," said Fisher from his car.

"Very good, sir. Will you follow me?" Her tone was somewhere between officious and luscious. "Someone will come for the car."

"Why not?" Fisher got out and followed Snow White to the one-story black glass building. The dwarfs were nowhere to be seen.

A single security desk stood in the exact center of the vast space; there was no other furniture, not even a potted plant on the first floor. Fisher's guide smiled at the guard—he looked to be at least eighty and very possibly was the evil queen in butch disguise—then turned abruptly toward a ramp that opened in the floor nearby.

"You won't want to smoke in here," warned the woman as they strode down the ramp toward a single elevator. "Sets off alarms. Nasty things come down from the sprinklers."

"Water?"

"Some sort of gas," she said.

Fisher was tempted to test the system but held off, worried that the gas might be an even stronger version of her perfume. There were no buttons in the elevator, and no floor indicators. The car moved smoothly downward for about thirty seconds, then stopped.

Still no dwarfs. Snow White led him down a long hallway to a large reception area, where another young woman in an equally short skirt sat at a glass-topped table, her nipples poking rivet holes through her blouse. Fisher began to wonder if he had somehow made a wrong turn and ended at a brothel.

"General Bonham is not here, Mr. Fisher," said the woman at the desk.

"I can wait."

"You really should have called ahead." She traded a smile with Snow White. Fisher realized that his knowledge of Disney films was severely lacking; he couldn't figure out who she was supposed to be.

Figaro, maybe? But that would make him Pinocchio. Ouch.

"I'm afraid you'll be waiting a long time," said the woman. "I believe he's in Montana."

"Is he?" Fisher had already checked: Bonham was in fact en route to D.C. Not that he actually wanted to talk to him. "Maybe you could check for me."

"I'm never wrong," said the woman.

Fisher spotted a pot of coffee on a credenza nearby. "Can I have a cup?"

"I'm sorry—the coffee is cold," said the woman.

"I drink it cold."

She smiled indulgently.

"Actually, I'm looking for Justin Pierce," said Fisher. "I understand he's the titular head of the agency."

The word came out smoothly, despite the innuendo.

"Mr. Pierce is never in," said the woman.

Fisher scratched the side of his head, emphasizing his confusion.

"Lice?" asked the woman.

"I think they're gone, actually," said Fisher. "Shampoo worked wonders. I want to talk to Megan York's boss. I believe that would be the head of the technical support team. His name was Lee, I think."

"Her name is Sylvia Lee, and she is in Hawaii for a conference."

"ABM tests?"

"I wouldn't know."

"Personnel records?"

The woman curled her lips. Now he remembered who she was supposed to be: Cruella, the dog-hater in *101 Dalmations*.

"Our personnel records are confidential. Unless you have a court order, of course. That's the law."

"Yeah, the law's a funny thing," said Fisher. "Who deals with the contractors, Miss—"

"That would be Ms."

"You deal with them?"

"Only the general."

"Your accounting office is which way?" said Fisher.

"Accounting is handled by an independent firm," said the woman.

"Organizational chart?"

"It's being redone. Anything else?"

"If you let me take a shot at that coffee," said Fisher, "I'll bark for you."

The halls of the Rayburn Building were proportioned in such a way as to impress mere mortals as they walked down them, and not even Fisher was immune to their spell. He felt imbibed in the spirit of democracy as he found Congressman Matt Taft's office; though a poor government worker himself, Fisher understood the inherent importance of his role as public servant.

That and the fact that he had a slight caffeine buzz on, due to the consumption of not one but two Dunkin' Donuts Big Gulps on the way over from NADT. Cruella had denied him her own blend, even after he'd demonstrated a howl pro bono.

Besides drinking the coffee, Fisher had used the trip to bone up on who exactly Congressman Taft was, besides being Megan York's cousin. His briefing came courtesy of a newspaper reporter at *The Washington Times* who owed him a few favors and thirty bucks from a Super Bowl bet gone bad. Fisher had frankly expressed his ignorance, which for some reason never failed to impress newspaper reporters, and had received a detailed description of the congressman's career, only partially condensed from the newspaper's computer morgue.

This had taken all of two minutes. Several janitors at the Capitol Building had higher profiles than Megan York's cousin. The twenty-ninth ranking minority member on the House Armed Services Committee, his name had appeared in exactly two stories over the past twelve months, and one was about rolling eggs on the White House lawn.

The congressman was not in his office, which wasn't particularly surprising. His legislative assistant, a short, gnomelike man with a beard that reached to his chest, agreed to see him after growling at the receptionist, who reacted by cracking her gum somewhat louder than before. Fisher took one look at the gnome's brown-stained hands and reached into his pocket.

"Why don't we go outside?" he said, holding up his cigarettes.

The legislative assistant nearly bolted through the door. They were barely on the steps before he reached back and took a cigarette from the agent's pack, jabbing it into his lighter.

"Been trying to quit," said the gnome.

"Gee, and you struck me as a reasonable guy," said Fisher. He followed the gnome down the steps, watching as the man's entire body underwent a transformation. Five minutes ago he had been an exploited career bureaucrat; now he was a maker of men.

"No way I'm quitting," said the assistant.

Whatever else happened that day, Andy Fisher had saved another soul.

"This about Megan?"

"In a way," said Fisher.

"They found her body?"

"Nah," said Fisher. "You think she's dead, huh?"

"After all this time? You don't really think she's still alive, do you?"

Fisher shrugged.

"Look, Matt's in an awkward position," said the gnome. "Obviously he wants her, uh, recovered. But he can't put pressure on a top-secret project. Technically he probably isn't supposed to know about it, since he's not part of the intelligence committee."

"Do *they* know about it?" asked Fisher.

"I don't know."

"What about his calls to NADT?" said Fisher.

"Which calls to NADT?"

"He didn't try to get General Bonham?"

"He knows Bonham, of course; maybe he called and I didn't know."

"How does he know Bonham?" asked Fisher.

The gnome's eyes opened a bit wider, then slunk back in their sockets as if retreating into a cave. "They've known each other for a while. But from where, I don't know."

"Does the congressman vote on appropriations for NADT?"

The gnome did a very interesting eye-rolling thing where his eyes seemed to disappear in the back of his head, then reappear at the bottom of his feet. The effect made it seem as if his eyeballs had traveled all around his body, a not unimpressive skill and certainly one that would be appreciated in Washington, where eyes had to be rolled several times a day, at least.

"His business interests are in blind trusts, if that's what you're getting at," said the gnome. "The Tafts and Yorks and Rythes—the family owns a lot of high-tech stuff. Yeah, they're connected. But they're big in consumer goods and oil, energy: You'd expect it."

"That's what I figured," said Fisher. "What board was he on, Ferris or something?"

"Ferrone? Nah, he resigned that."

"You have a list of his family holdings?"

"Have to talk to the trustee."

Fisher nodded. "He doesn't like Megan, does he?"

The gnome shrugged, then drew his cigarette down to the nub. "Sure he does. She was close to his father, General Taft."

Fisher shoveled out another cigarette. "Who was Taft? Like, the same guy who was president?"

The eye roll again. Fisher thought it was a real winner. "Fill me in," he prompted, giving the aide another cigarette.

General Taft—part of the same family as William Howard Taft, president and jurist, but well removed—had been a bomber pilot in World War II and had actually written a book about his experiences—self-published, of course. He and his brother-in-law, Megan's father, made a fortune adapting early computers so they could be used in targeting devices. That alone would have made them rich, if they hadn't been rich already.

"So they struggled through the Depression all right?" said Fisher.

"Struggled? Ever hear of the Rubber Trust?"

"Prophylactics?"

The eyes again. "*Rubber* rubber. Before synthetics, it was as big as oil. Bigger. The family was hooked in. Great-great-grandfather of the congressman made a killing supplying Germany and France in World War I. When Wilson declared war, they stopped selling to everybody except the U.S."

"How can Megan York be the daughter of somebody who fought in World War II?"

The gnome's smile wasn't nearly as interesting as his eye roll, and it had the unfortunate effect of ejecting an even greater than normal whiff of his bad breath.

"She's a third-tier baby—you know, third wife. And it was the brother who fought in World War II. Megan's father was younger, and that was a different marriage, which is why the names are different."

"This is a close family?"

"Depends on your definition of *close*."

"What's the book called?"

"*Flying through Fire*. I'll lend you a copy: We got tons of 'em. Came out ten years ago and we can't give 'em away, even on the campaign trail. Too big to stuff in people's mailboxes."

Fisher nearly passed on the book, expecting it to be a rambling self-congratulatory rumination on a life spent making a killing by selling weapons of destruction. Part of it may in fact have been that, but the opening chapter was anything but. In fact, it was a rather moving account of what it was like to fly the low-level incendiary bombing raids over Japan, knowing that the acrid smoke choking you was coming from things that ought never be burnt.

Taft spent considerable time talking about the effect on the victims, eloquently talking about how badly their lives must have been ruined. At the end of the chapter he wrote that he understood the raids had been ordered as part of an overall war effort. He did not regret his role in them, but at the same time he admitted they had killed hundreds of thousands of innocent lives. This was the face of battle, he said, a condition of modern warfare where the lines between civilian and combatant were no longer clearly drawn. It was the reason, he said, that America must be strong to deter future wars and that, eventually, war must be made obsolete.

Four chapters from the end of the book, he explained how this would be done with a variety of weapons, including an ABM system.

Fisher, who'd started reading the book while standing on line for a burger and was now sitting alone at a table eating, flipped to the notes at the back. There was a section thanking everyone who had helped, including a long list of scientists and military consultants.

Bonham was on the list—as a colonel.

So was Megan, who got her own sentence: "One of the few who truly understands and is dedicated to the future."

Unable to figure out exactly what that might mean, the agent tucked the book under his arm and went to work on the burger.

15

In the space of ninety seconds, everything had gone from perfect to seriously fucked up. Not only had the Indian MiGs resumed their course northward, but another group of planes—a mixture of MiG-29s and Su-27s, obviously an attack package with escorts—had just come into the large outer circle of Timmy's tactical display. And the Pakistanis weren't sitting on their hands either: The AWACS was reporting F-16s taking off from the base near Lahore, and four S-7s mustering over Islamabad, the capital.

Radars were coming up all across the subcontinent. The Velociraptor's audible warning system sounded like a frenetic synthesizer, bleating out tones: A missile battery had just come to life about two miles south of Timmy. The computer ID'd it as an SA-8, a Russian-made mobile SAM with a range to about 42,500 feet and approximately ten miles. It hadn't been briefed: There had been *no* mention of SA-8s in the Indian inventory. Nothing had locked on the slippery F/A-22V, but he wasn't feeling particularly warm and fuzzy.

Timmy slid the Velociraptor eastward, pushing to get into an attack position to hit the MiGs at the end of the formation. They'd bunched as they came back north, but were now stringing out into the loose trail they'd flown before. The targets were easy to pick, but the sheer number of planes complicated the attack.

Not for Cyclops. The laser plane's pilot gave a warning and the oversexed flashlight in its nose went to work. Timmy flexed his fingers on the side stick as Cyclops picked off the members of the flight one by one, taking them at precise fifteen-second intervals. The laser's operator used his ultrasophisticated targeting gear to create a hot spot in the planes' wings where their fuel tanks were; it was like putting a balloon against a thousand-watt light-bulb.

A kerosene-filled balloon. Even at fifteen miles away, Timmy could see the fireballs as the first planes in the formation popped. The third plane began to turn; that bought it perhaps ten seconds. Timmy looked at his tactical screen as the aircraft began to separate, aware now that they were in deep, unprecedented shit.

He had five octagonal targets in the middle circle. The MiG closest to him—twelve miles ahead on a direct line from his right wing root—blinked in the screen, then disappeared as the laser firing indicator lit. The other planes ducked east and west; one disappeared, apparently running into a mountain as it tried to escape.

Timmy pulled the Velociraptor south with a sharp bank and roll, acrobatically sliding around to follow the farthest plane if it got out of Cyclops's range. It was unnecessary; he'd barely gotten his wings back level when the last Indian exploded. Poor fucking bastard.

It had taken just under three minutes to eliminate eight aircraft. Captain Robinson, who would objectively rank no lower than the top five percent of fighter pilots in the world and who was flying unarguably the world's most advanced jet, would have taken at least twice as long to shoot down half that number from close range—and even then would have had to consider himself incredibly lucky, and his opponents incredibly stupid.

I'm surplus war material, he thought to himself. *Washed up at twenty-five.*

Howe steadied the Velociraptor at 35,000 feet, quickly reviewing everyone's position as Cyclops finished off the Indian attack force. It had been easier than any of the tests they'd conducted over the past several months.

There wasn't time to gloat, much less analyze it all: Both the Indians and the Pakistanis were filling the air with attack planes. Lucy—an American Compass Call electronic jammer that was also controlling a number of remote jamming drones—came south from Afghanistan to fill the air with electronic fuzz, making it difficult for the combatants' radios and radars to work; they'd thought it a necessary precaution if things started to get out of hand, since it helped shield the easily seen Cyclops Two. But there was a definite downside, as both the Indian and Pakistani air forces interpreted the jamming as hostile acts by the other side. The jammers, meanwhile, degraded Howe's ability to communicate with some of the far-flung members of his task force, though he had full secure communications with Timmy and Cyclops.

The question now was: What next?

His orders covered this contingency: If both sides went crazy, he was supposed to stand back and let them go at each other.

"Missiles in the air!" warned the AWACS operator. The Indians had detected and were targeting one of the ECM drones as it flew south over their border.

Losing the UAV was no big deal, but sooner or later his real aircraft were going to be in danger. At least two dozen Indian aircraft were now headed north; the Pakistanis had almost as many coming south.

They'd been so damn close. One radar blip, one general's decision to rush ahead, one chance move somewhere, too subtle to be tracked down, had turned the MiGs around and started World War III.

There was still a chance. If he took out the Indians' radar plane, the Indians would be blind. They'd have to pull back.

Hitting the plane would be exceeding his orders.

"Bird Two, you have EW1?" he asked Timmy, using the computer's reference for the Indian radar plane.

"Roger that. I have him at about a hundred and fifty miles, coming north. He's trying to vector their fighters. For escorts, Su-27s."

"We're going to take him out."

"Now you're talking."

Howe told Cyclops Two what was going on, telling them to remain in their patrol pattern over Afghanistan and to let the two sides go at it. As they were talking, the Indian SAM struck the drone, destroying it.

"Should we take out Unk-2?" asked Timmy, referring to the unidentified contact.

The plane was now in a two-mile orbit over the Himalayas. Still unidentified, it seemed to be hugging the Chinese border, which to Howe meant that's who was probably operating it.

"Negative," he said. "They're not a factor."

"I think that's what the Paks were reacting to."

"If so, that's because they're clueless," said Howe. He laid out his course and plan of attack to take the Indian AWACS. There was no need to be fancy; he and Timmy could take it straight at the Indian plane, which, despite its high-tech gear, probably wouldn't detect them until they were about fifty miles away. At that point it would be within AMRAAM range, though he'd want to launch from inside forty miles to guarantee a hit.

"You want fat boy or the guard dogs?" Timmy asked.

"I'll take the radar plane," said Howe. "Target the closest interceptors, but don't take them out unless they get hostile."

"Guard dogs are mine." Timmy's tone guaranteed the planes would end up being considered hostile.

At their present course and speed, they'd be in range to fire in just under five minutes. The two American fighters streaked through the sky, their dagger-shaped wings cutting through the thin, icy air. Far below, millions of people slept through the night, completely unaware that their fates were being decided while they dreamed. Pakistan had twelve nuclear-tipped missiles and a single air-dropped bomb; India had twice as many. The analysts who had briefed Howe had made a point of noting that it was very possible not all of the weapons would work if used. Both sides had had problems constructing and testing their weapons, and J.D. Powers wasn't around to help improve quality control. But even if only half the weapons worked half as well as advertised, several million people would still die.

When he closed within seventy-five miles of EW1, the radar receiver caught the power spikes from the Sukhoi radars and painted them in the outer circle on Howe's tactical scope, confident of their location. The radar in the big plane, meanwhile, continued to grope the sky unsuccessfully, its long fingers not quite sticky enough to grab him.

At sixty seconds to firing range, the computer had the attack completely mapped out for him; all he had to do was choose the option and push the button.

"I have something," warned Timmy. "Shit—I'm spiked."

"ECMs," said Howe.

A ground unit had just come on to the west. It wasn't an ordinary radar: Working with a microwave transmitter, it had managed to find Timmy's stealthy profile. The electronic countermeasures quickly snapped the invisible chain that was trying to latch on to his wingman's plane, but the damage had been done; the Indians knew they were under attack.

Not that it would do any good. He was thirty seconds from firing range.

"Guard dogs are coming for us," warned his wingman.

"Yours," said Howe. "Fire at will."

* * *

Timmy tucked his wing down, angling toward the Sukhois as they separated from their mothership. They were roughly seventy miles away, each plane a mile right and left from his wings. He figured they'd go for some sort of bracket once he made it clear which plane he was going to attack; that pilot would move to engage while the wingman swung out, ready to pounce when the other broke. If Timmy kept coming down the middle—something they'd have to figure he might try, given the juicy target behind them—they could simply turn and have at him as he came past, confident that their Lyulka AL-31F turbofans would allow them to catch up in the unlikely event that they misjudged his speed; the Russian-built jets had an awesome capability to accelerate, matched by only one or two airplanes in the world, and exceeded by only one.

Which happened to be the plane they were going against. The fact that the Indian pilots apparently thought they were facing a lone Pakistani F-16 gave Timmy a tremendous advantage, as did their likely weapons set: The Indians were not known to have the most advanced Russian R-77 or AA-12 missiles, and while their R-27 Alamos were very potent, all of the radar versions were well known and could be knocked off by the Velociraptor's ECMs. IR missiles, of course, were a different story—even the most obsolete heat-seeker could be a pesky PIA under the right circumstances—but Timmy didn't intend to get close enough for the Sukhois to launch any.

He made a cut south, purposely taking the fighters away from his flight leader. That put him temporarily on the nose of the plane on his right, which didn't react. The radar locked both bandits tight and the Velociraptor prompted him to fire. Timmy waited a few more seconds, riding in so he'd be positioned better to hunt the other planes.

"Fire one, fire two," he said finally. The interceptor seemed to grunt its approval: The AMRAAM vertical ejector launcher spit the missiles from the ventral bay with a force of roughly 40 g's. Timmy didn't make the traditional radio call warning that he had fired; the shared radar and weapons system took care of that for him, giving Howe an audible tone as well as designating the targets and showing the missile tracks on his screen.

As soon as the missiles were away, Timmy hit the throttle and accelerated, his focus now on the two Sukhois that had hung back with the AEW plane. He knew they'd be somewhere between the 767 and him, but he wasn't exactly sure where: ECMs, apparently aboard the big plane, had managed to significantly degrade his sensors.

Something for the tech guys to work on.

The radar plane was about ten degrees to the southeast with its gas pedal to the floor and descending. He guessed the other Sukhois would be near its tail. He checked Howe's position—running in from the east, no more than ten seconds from firing—then decided that he would just hold his course for a bit until his targets turned up.

The Velociraptor gave him a buzz. His first missile had hit home. Target one was history.

Something had gone wrong with the second shot, however. The Sukhoi was turning and accelerating, trying to solve the mathematical equation that would give it a shot on his tail. Timmy's RWR went ape shit: The Sukhoi fired a pair of Alamos from twenty miles. Timmy threw the Velociraptor into a set of hard zigs, chaff exploding behind him to confuse the radars in the missiles' noses. He lost one almost immediately, but the second was working with super glue: It hung on his back even though he was taking nearly 8 g's with his evasive maneuver.

Timmy felt his heart smack against his ribs: *This* was what he liked about flying. He jabbed at the ECM controls, even though the fuzzbuster was already singing songs in fifty different languages at once. A hard turn west, more chaff, a flick on the stick and he came clear, the missile detonating itself about two and a half miles from his right wingtip.

There wasn't any time to celebrate—the RWR called out a new warning: A pair of SA-2A SAM missiles had just been launched five miles ahead, and damned if one of the Sukhois he'd been looking for hadn't chosen this moment to turn up—three miles behind his butt.

Smack in the middle of heat-seeker range, a point which the Indian pilot underlined by launching two missiles, then following up with two more.

Howe waited until Timmy had engaged the Sukhois to make his move. The Indian AEW aircraft wasn't particularly difficult to follow. As he closed to twenty miles Howe's holographic HUD caged the target with a rectangular "fire" cue, showing that it was now in easy range for the AMRAAMs. He waited a second longer, making sure the gear wasn't being overly optimistic, then dished out a pair of AMRAAMs; within seconds the missiles were galloping forward at Mach 4.

Howe turned his attention to his wingman, who was drawing a lot of interest to the southwest. One of the two fighters Timmy had engaged had dodged his missiles and was sweeping around from the north, angling for a rear-quarter attack. The RWR lit with fresh contacts, this time from ground-based radars; the Indians were throwing everything into this one, launching SA-2As, their best long-range anti-aircraft missiles. Timmy danced in the right corner of Howe's screen, another Su-27 behind him.

"Two, your six!" warned Howe. "Break!"

"Yeah, I see the asshole," replied Timmy. "Fucker's dead meat."

Howe wasn't too sure of that, but he was too far away to help his wingman with that pursuer. Instead he went for the throttle, aiming to keep the northern Sukhoi off. With his momentum down he didn't quite have a shot; he had to build more closure or momentum toward the enemy or his arrow would be shrugged off at long range.

And where the hell was the other Sukhoi?

Howe's AMRAAMs struck the radar plane in quick succession. One of the warheads ignited fumes in the plane's fuel tank, and the explosion broke the aircraft into several pieces, five of which were big enough for Howe's radar to track as they disintegrated. Howe barely noticed, however, focusing on the northern Sukhoi as he tried to decide whether the Indian was running away or angling for an attack. He didn't want to waste a missile on someone who was already out of the game.

The HUD's rectangular piper jammed the Sukhoi into its sweet spot. Howe fired, figuring better safe than sorry; as the missile shot away he got a fresh warning on the SA-2s, one of which had managed to sniff out his airframe and was heading in his general direction. As Howe jinked left, the F/A-22V's radar gave the AMRAAM a fresh update on the targeted Sukhoi, still flying a perfect intercept, apparently unaware that it had already been caught in the crosshairs.

The SA-2B was an ancient weapon; early versions had been targeted at B-52s over Vietnam, and it was an SA-2 that had taken out Gary Powers' U-2 in 1960 at the height of the Cold War. That had all happened an awful long time ago, and while the missile—code-named Guideline by NATO—had been updated, it was thoroughly understood by the people who had put the Velociraptors' ECM suite together. Even so, it had to be respected: With a warhead that weighed just under three hundred pounds and a velocity that could top Mach 3.5, its boom could definitely lengthen a pilot's day.

Howe pushed back south as his aircraft's electronic warfare suite played with the missile's mind. It told the missile it was beautiful and sleek, the most powerful thing spinning through the universe. Then it pointed down the block, claiming that it had set up a date with the fattest, juiciest target it had ever seen, a veritable Daddy Warbucks that would make a perfect match. It slapped the missile in the rear end and told it to go have some fun; by the time the missile realized it had been had, it was at nearly sixty thousand feet and several miles from its intended target. It wailed in frustration, so distraught that it immolated itself, its remains trailing to the ground like the shreds of a funeral shroud.

Howe, meanwhile, struggled to sort the cacophony and chaos around him into a coherent map of the battle. The graphical representations of the battle on the HUD and tactical screen showed that Timmy had not only broken the enemy's attack but was now launching his own; the cockpit pulsed with the shot warning. And here was the Sukhoi that had managed to hide earlier—five miles south of Howe, headed back east.

With the Indian taking himself out of the fight, Howe started to turn toward his wingman. Before he could tell him he was coming, a transmission from Cyclops interrupted him.

"Bird One, be advised missiles are in the air. We're taking evasive action."

Cyclops was under attack.

CHAPTER
16

The launch indicator flashed. The Pakistanis had obviously mistaken the 767 for a Chinese spy plane and were determined to take it down.

Megan looked at the large tactical screen next to her, waiting for Cyclops Two to target and destroy the four missiles. They were early-model American HAWKS—easily handled.

So why the hell weren't they firing at them?

They had to see it. They had to.

They had to fire quickly. The missile spread increased the difficulty of aiming, and at this short range they had a relatively short window of opportunity.

She could take it out herself. But she, too, had only a limited opportunity.

The plan was to wait until they couldn't be intercepted, then to simply fire once. But they hadn't foreseen this; they hadn't thought the Indians and Pakistanis would go this far.

She should get into the mix now. This was exactly the situation Cyclops had been invented for, the sort of future she'd foreseen.

And yet, she'd be risking it all if she did.

Risking what? Only herself.

The ABM shield as well. Everything.

Was that more important than saving the lives of her friends?

They weren't her friends anymore.

If it were Tom, would she hesitate?

Megan put her index finger on the touch screen, designating the rising missile. But just as she opened her mouth to give the verbal confirmation to fire, Cyclops Two obliterated the missile on its own.

"Thank God," she said to herself.

CHAPTER
17

Perhaps it was a premonition, or maybe his brain just worked out the logic on its own. But even as Cyclops took out the last of the HAWK missiles that had been aimed at it, Howe found himself putting the throttle out to the firewall and clicking in a warning to Cyclops without stopping to think exactly what he was doing.

"They're going to launch ballistic missiles," he said. "Stand by for ballistic missiles. Take out anything that's flying."

Howe slapped his radar out of dogfight mode and into the wide-range tactical feed for Cyclops.

"Timmy, we need to be north," he said tersely.

"Roger that," acknowledged his wingman.

"Bird One, be advised we have missiles launched, Indian missiles launched," warned the Cyclops Two pilot.

He didn't have to say ballistic missiles.

"Take them out," said Howe.

"Not in range."

"Come south. This is it. Get everything you can get." Howe told the F-15s to accompany the plane and pulled two more off the AWACS. Not only did he expect the Pakistanis to take another shot at Cyclops, he expected them to launch their ballistic missiles as well.

Good God, what suicidal idiots.

A flight of MiG-29s headed toward the Pakistani border to his north. They were low and hot, probably in fighter-bomber mode.

He fired two AMRAAMs at them, reserving his last one. The missiles sped toward the first and second aircraft in the formation, which were apparently unaware they'd been chalked up on his screen.

"North, Timmy, north," he radioed, a basketball coach barking at a forward to get back and guard the basket. "The Indians are launching a nuclear attack, and the Paks are sure to retaliate. Cyclops has the missiles."

"Two."

The first AMRAAM hit the lead MiG, but the second missile missed its target. The planes kept coming.

No way in the world could Howe's team prevent every aircraft from crossing the border. They were playing Russian roulette: If one got through with a nuke, what then?

The intelligence people had said confidently that most of the two countries' nukes were in missiles. "Only one or at most two," they felt, were likely to have been made into bombs, which were harder to deliver and easy to defend against.

What if they were wrong? Cyclops Two carried only enough laser fuel for roughly thirty shots, depending on the duration of the blasts.

The Pakistanis were most likely to use a bomb; he'd look for an F-16 flight.

The AWACS warned of one flying south out of Islamabad, a two-ship formation streaking due south. As Howe got it on the wide screen with its shared data, Cyclops started plucking Indian IRBMs out of the sky.

"North Two, get north."

"I'm on your six."

CHAPTER
18

Atta looked down from the heads-up screen to the more detailed target list at the left side of his glass panel. There were six live targets, two of them SAMs and the rest ballistic missiles. The computer—with Sergeant Peters's approval—ranked the SAMs first. But the ballistic missiles were higher and farther away, which meant they were much more complicated shots.

And more critical. Besides, the SAMs were ID'd as early-model Crotales, which had a maximum effective altitude about twenty thousand feet below where he was flying.

"Override one, override two," he told the computer, punching the screen quickly to confirm the shots. "Acquire."

The computer buzzed its acceptance. Atta could feel the laser turret whirling in the nose ahead of him, trying to lock on the new target. A second tone sounded and the triangle in his HUD blinked green, showing he had a lock.

"Fire," he said, though this was superfluous: His finger had already pushed the button at the top of his grip, and in combat mode the computer accepted either command.

The laser shot was practically instantaneous. The beam tracked with the rising target for an infinitesimally small time, a highly focused blowtorch rubbing the skin of the missile. The beam heated part of the fuel tank in the second stage of the Indian Agni rocket, expanding it so quickly that it exploded in the space of half a second. The computer cycled up the target list, once more putting the SAMs on top; Atta quickly reprioritized them and took his shot at another ballistic missile. This was a harder shot; the laser caught the solid propellant first-stage motor but failed to destroy it immediately, sending the rocket off course but leaving it intact. Atta had to verbally order a fresh shot, since the computer was programmed to accept sending a missile off target as a hit.

"We're locked and being tracked," said the copilot. "Pak SA-2 battery."

Unlike the Crotales, this missile was fully capable of reaching the Cyclops aircraft, especially since it had to fly a predictable path for the laser. But Atta held off ordering the ECMs, fearing that they would degrade the radars helping him target. By the time he fired and destroyed the third target—another Agni—the Pakistanis had fired two missiles at them.

They probably saw this as a holy war against the infidels. Idiots.

The computer moved the missiles to the top of the list. Atta hesitated a second, then approved the selection of the first one.

"More Crotales—where the hell did the bastards get all these missiles?" the copilot asked.

The first SAM went down easy. The second SA-2, however, tracked off its expected course, and the computer seemed to take forever to get a lock. Atta felt his cheeks puffing out with his breaths as he finally fired and took it out.

More SAMS, various contacts; the adrenaline buzzing in Atta's brain started to shake his concentration. He felt confused, fatigue overwhelming him.

The target list offered an SA-2 climbing through five hundred feet.

Another Agni had just launched.

Atta overrode, took out the ballistic missile.

"Captain!" His copilot's voice went up an octave.

The pipper was yellow: no shot.

"ECMs," said Atta. He took the yoke from the computer and swung around much tighter than the automated pilot would have allowed, pulling 6 g's to get back in the firing track. Stabilizing, he went back into firing mode, allowing the electronic brain to hold the plane steady. The piper went red and he fired—a good hit on the first blast. The missile imploded.

Atta heard a popping sound that seemed to come from behind him. At the same time the left engine whined and the plane seemed to fall into his hands.

"We're hit—shrapnel in the left engine," said the copilot.

Unlike before, his voice was extremely calm. Atta interpreted that as a bad sign.

CHAPTER

19

Timmy angled westward, following Howe back toward the border. The AWACS operator screamed out contacts, Cyclops Two chopped down missiles, the radio crackled with talk from the F-15s. The chaotic jumble was music to Timmy's ears.

Howe had sorted through the confusion and come up with a coherent plan. A pair of F-16s were charging toward the Indian border well to the west.

"We're going to take those planes out," the lead pilot told him. "They're the only aircraft on the board that may have nukes. I have the plane on the right."

"Two."

The F-16s were just over two hundred miles away, streaking perhaps fifty feet off the ground as they approached the Thar or Great Indian Desert in the center of the border area. The gear aboard the Velociraptor not only allowed the aircraft to "see" them—incredible in itself—but gave hints on how to best counter them.

Not that Timmy thought he needed the hints.

The F-16s were moving at over six hundred knots, and the gap between them closed at something over thirty-three miles a minute. But they might just as well have been moving backward as far as he was concerned.

"Your man is turning," warned Howe as the Falcon cut to the east.

"On him."

Timmy nudged his stick, pushing to his right to stay with the F-16. It wasn't clear whether the Pakistani was merely changing his position behind his leader or striking out on his own course. The planes were now roughly a hundred miles ahead, a bit over a minute and a half from firing range, depending on what happened in the next thirty seconds.

The HUD painted in its holographic display, a yellow dagger at about eight o'clock, relative to his position. The tactics section shaded an intercept attack point at his request, helpfully plotting a turn that would bring him onto the bandit's tailpipe.

And then the F-16 disappeared.

Was it lost in the ground clutter, simply obscured by irregular terrain or jumbled returns or some anomaly in the coverage area, which was being cobbled together from three different inputs? Or had the pilot flown a bit too low and bought it in the darkness?

Timmy stayed on the course the computer had plotted, figuring it was by far his best option. Two Indian MiGs were in the vicinity, but he did his best to ignore them. Howe said something over the radio that he didn't quite catch; Timmy leaned forward and started to rock gently, willing the F-16 back into the sky.

When it finally appeared, they were separated by less than twenty miles. The Pakistani pilot had managed to get down below ten feet, a mark of either superior flying ability or tremendous stupidity—maybe both. The piper's boxed fist closed around the Pakistani plane and held it there as the AMRAAM popped out from the Velociraptor's belly and flashed toward its target.

Timmy was only vaguely aware of the Velociraptor's applause when the missile rammed home. He was too busy ducking two Indian MiGs that had been vectored into the area to find the F-16 but found him instead. The MiGs launched homers; he countered with tinsel and laid on the revs, spooling the turbos to max power and escaping north.

Howe, meanwhile, had taken out his F-16 and was running back toward Cyclops. As they crossed the Pakistani border, a pair of Mirages turned out of the northwest, coming to meet them. They were at twenty-seven and thirty thousand feet, below Howe but above Timmy; their turn took them between the two aircraft—and right into Timmy's screen.

"I got 'em," he told his leader. The computer had already brought up the weapons bar indicating the AIM-

9M all-aspect Sidewinders were ready to fire. The audible indicator growled, telling him it was ready to fire; Timmy push-buttoned the first Mirage to death, the missile slapping out of the F/A-22V's side. The second Mirage slid to the right as the first one blew apart; Timmy couldn't find it and decided to leave it be; he was low enough on fuel to dial up the bingo matrix on the variable-use screen. As he started to look down toward his dash, his eyes caught the glow from several fires on the ground.

"Looks like World War III down there," said Timmy, laughing a little.

"Hopefully not. Cyclops is hit."

Howe's voice sobered him. He found his leader's wing and scanned for bogeys.

CHAPTER

20

Whatever had nailed the 767's left engine had torn through the housing and wrecked the blades but left the wing itself undamaged. There hadn't been a fire, either; in many ways they'd been incredibly lucky.

Atta and his copilot worked to compensate for the loss of the engine, trimming Cyclops Two and taking it lower. They ran quickly through the rest of their systems, making sure they hadn't sustained any other damage. While undoubtedly there were more pockmarks in the skin of the aircraft, all their systems were functioning properly.

The plane retained considerable maneuverability with just one engine, and Atta and his copilot routinely practiced handling exactly this sort of situation, both in a simulator and in the aircraft. What they hadn't done was use the laser with only one engine; standard procedure called for a stricken plane to return to base ASAP.

But standard procedure didn't take into account a fresh volley of ballistic missiles, this time from the Pakistanis.

"Two missiles," said Sergeant Peters as Atta finished his controlled descent to 25,000 feet.

"Yes," said Atta, glancing at the target priority screen. The missiles were the only items on the board.

"Captain, we're on one engine," said the copilot.

The few words describing the obvious fact represented a novel's worth of meaning: Not only was Atta being reminded that they were in serious danger, but his judgment was being questioned. He might have barked at his subordinate or ignored him, but he was a mild man, and confident besides.

"We're all right," he said, pushing the button to laser the target.

The lower altitude made the plane more stable, but it also made them an easier target for interceptors and missiles. More important, it cut down on the laser's range. Atta got the second missile, but just barely; he turned southward, pushing on a direct line toward Islamabad as the radars caught two more probably ballistic missiles coming up off the ground. One of the pilots in the F-15s escorting them barked something into his ears; Atta was too busy trying to get the shot lined up to make sense of it, let alone respond.

He had to get these missiles now. He had to take them all out. Miss one, and he might as well have missed them all.

"SAMs up," warned the copilot.

Atta pushed southward, setting up a new firing track. He turned the airplane over to the computer and then fired. He caught the first missile at five thousand feet; the second was nearly level with the plane when the laser finally destroyed it.

Two Pakistani interceptors had been scrambled to try and take them down. The F-15s were responding.

"SAMs are launching," said his copilot. There was another barrage of missiles from the Indians, unidentified by the sensors: probably more ballistic missiles.

Six of them.

They were going to run out of fuel for the weapon soon.

Atta started to override the target selection, then froze. There were too many targets, spread over too wide an area.

He glanced back at the HUD, fired—a mistake, since he hadn't locked. The blast missed.

Atta took a breath and waited for the laser to recycle and position itself. He fired, taking out the first SAM. But the second was coming hard, and he didn't have a firing solution: It was locked on one of the Eagles.

I should let it go, he thought to himself. *The nukes are more important.*

But he didn't. He banked the 767 hard, momentarily forgetting that the plane was flying on only one engine. He recovered quickly, but the craft shook violently and it took precious seconds to stabilize before he could set it to fire. The cursor went red and he nailed the warhead about twenty seconds away from impact.

Atta put the plane on its wing, a bit more gently this time, hoping to hold an angle that would cover a wide arc of the sky. But the computer wouldn't keep the plane like that: The programming insisted on straight and level on one engine. He wasted time going back, and then even more overriding the weapon system's insistence that he give up helm before firing. He had six missiles but time to take out only four.

The first two were easy. His hands began trembling on the third, and by the fourth he had to give the plane back to the computer to make the shot. They took out the missile just before the second stage separated—the last possible moment.

It was too late for the others. Atta, now deep into Pakistan, turned to go north, cursing himself. He looked at the targeting screen to see if there were more targets.

The screen was blank. So was the missile-tracking radar.

"What happened to the other two missiles?" Atta asked Peters.

"Five and six are gone," said Peters.

"Were they decoys?"

"I don't know," replied the sergeant. "I have secondary strike indications; did you shoot at them?"

She knew the answer as well as he did, but Atta said no anyway.

CHAPTER
21

Howe pushed northward, running toward the laser plane. The contact screen was now completely blank; they were the only aircraft left in the sky. In fact, except for a few stray bubbles of flak, they were the only *anything* left in the sky. Cyclops had taken out all of the nukes.

"How you looking, Bird Two?" he asked his wingman.

"Disappointed. I got a missile left."

He didn't sound like he was kidding.

"I assume that means you're in one piece," answered Howe.

"Oh yeah."

The Velociraptors were now way low on fuel, and Howe checked with the tanker to make sure they could catch a refill.

The AWACS and the eavesdropping aircraft assured him that both sides had called it quits. They had also shot their wads: Both had used all of their nuclear weapons.

"Good work, Cyclops Two," Howe told Atta as he closed on the plane ahead. "We just saved a couple of million lives."

"Thank you, Colonel," snapped Atta. "One thing: Uh, we lost two of the contacts in the last box. And that unidentified spy plane—that's gone too. We're going to have to sort it out on the ground," he added. "But we're pretty sure the contacts we lost were ballistic missiles."

"They hit the spy plane?"

"Negative. They were separated by about a hundred miles. Here's the thing: When those missiles disappeared, our gear recorded laser strikes, just like ours."

PART FOUR
Recovery

CHAPTER

1

There was no part of his body that didn't hurt. His right knee felt as if it had been turned inside out; a jagged numbness ran diagonally across his back to the left side of his neck, where it plunged through his chest and came out at his breastbone. His temples felt as if daggers were pressing against them.

McIntyre lay on his stomach in the darkness for an hour or more, gradually growing colder and colder. Images fluttered before his eyes, some real, some imaginary.

He saw a dozen girls he should have laid but hadn't.

That was how he knew he wasn't going to die. If he'd been about to buy it, he'd have seen a shadowy figure standing in front of a long tunnel, just as all those near-death books and movies claimed.

That, or a babe with serious knockers leading him to hell.

McIntyre pushed with his arms and legs, trying to lift the metal from around him. He pushed through the darkness, working his way in the path of least resistance. He began to feel cold. Several times the blackness closed around him and his head floated away from his arms and legs. At some point he realized he was on the ground outside of the wreckage.

His legs and arms felt stiff, and his neck buzzed with whatever he'd done to it. But he was free, he could move; he pushed over and sat up.

There was a rifle near him, a Russian Kalashnikov.

He reached for it. His hand moved in slow motion. When he finally touched it the metal seemed on fire. He pulled the gun toward him, used it as a crutch to get to his feet.

The helicopter lay a few yards away, nose-first against the side of the hill. There were people outside, near the door: bodies, none moving. He took a step forward, saw a man next to him: Captain Jalil.

The bastard who had kidnapped him.

McIntyre swung the rifle up and crashed it down on Jalil's head. The Indian fell straight down. McIntyre swung again, hitting the back of his skull so hard that he felt something crack inside it. Surprised at his strength and the ferocity of his anger, he knelt over the captain. Blood streamed from his ears and mouth; the man was dead.

Something moved near the helicopter. McIntyre heard a shout. He grabbed the rifle right-side up, pulled it to his side and fired into the thick of the shadow as he turned around.

The shadow fell away. But rather than going over to make sure the soldier was dead—rather than getting up and seeing if any of the others were alive—McIntyre sat next to Jalil's lifeless body.

"Why did you want to kill me?" he asked. "Why? Why kill anyone?"

Then he collapsed, unconscious, his chest landing on the motionless remains of his enemy.

McIntyre's body transformed itself in the dazed nightmare of his troubled sleep. His arms became long icicles, and the back of his head swelled larger and larger until it lifted him up from the valley, sending him soaring through the darkness. He saw himself, then saw women—beautiful, gorgeous women in an endless parade, traveling through the rift in the mountains.

A gust of wind took him and spun him around; he woke to find himself sitting against part of the damaged helicopter's tail. It was now mid-morning.

His first thought was: *I'm in real shit.*

His second thought was: *Damn it's cold.*

His third: *I have to take the world's biggest leak.*

McIntyre could do something only about the last. He rose, unbending unsteadily, then walked a few yards away. He remembered bashing his captor's head and body; had it been part of the dream?

His hands were covered with blood, so he knew it had to have been real. Still, he couldn't quite prepare himself for what he saw when he went back. He pushed it over, avoided looking at the battered face as he searched for his satellite phone.

He found a photo in one of the pockets. McIntyre threw it aside without looking.

Someone groaned from inside the helicopter. McIntyre steeled himself, continued searching. There were papers, a very small pistol; the phone had been tucked into the Indian's hip pocket and was still warm.

There was another moan. Worried that some of the men might be alive, he took the phone and jammed it into his back pocket. An assault rifle sat on the ground; McIntyre stooped to pick it up. Blood rushed from his head; dizzy, he put his hand out and dropped the phone into the dirt.

The helicopter's cockpit had been crushed, but the rear compartment was more or less intact. The side door had been torn off and there was a long, narrow hole running back from it, as if it were a seam that had split. Five or six bodies lay nearby. One moved, then another.

McIntyre saw another rifle and two clips lying close to it. He grabbed them, then whirled, sensing someone was watching him. Once more the blood fled from his brain.

One of the Indian soldiers sat upright on the ground, propped against the helicopter, eyes open. McIntyre stared at him, not sure whether he was alive or not. He started forward, thinking of poking him with the gun. As he took a step something seized him—not fear, and not precisely anger, either, but something he couldn't have defined. It made him press the trigger. Three bullets burst from the gun. One glanced off the helicopter near the man's shoulder and the others completely missed, McIntyre's aim thrown off by the recoil. But though he hadn't been hit, the man slumped over and fell to the side. He'd already been dead.

McIntyre stripped off the soldier's bulletproof vest. There were grenades in it, two hooked into small pockets in the front and two more clipped on the top. The tops were taped so they wouldn't accidentally explode. There were several clips of ammunition for the rifle as well.

Someone started talking inside the helicopter. It wasn't a moan or a plea; McIntyre couldn't make out the words or even the language, but the words had a calm, logical sound.

McIntyre took one of the grenades in his hand and held it. He started to push off the tape, thinking he'd blow up the helicopter, killing the men inside.

He'd expelled his anger, though. He didn't want to kill; he just wanted to live.

He couldn't think. He started to reel back and throw the grenade into the helicopter, then turned and threw it toward the rocks. His legs seemed to disintegrate; he pushed his body forward, sprawling and belatedly covering his head with his hands.

There was no explosion. He hadn't set the grenade.

He had to get out of here.

McIntyre staggered, the rifles dragging over his shoulders as he began picking his way across and then down the slope, not sure which way he was going, only that he was moving.

CHAPTER

2

They were beyond tired, all of them, but Howe needed to get it all sorted out. He rubbed his eyes, hunching over the map as Atta and the crew members of Cyclops Two slowly—painfully slowly—worked through the cockpit gear and replotted each strike on the paper map. The map was so large that it draped over the small folding table they were using; they had to push it up to get the last of their plots in. They'd taken out a total of thirteen Indian ballistic missiles and six Pakistani IRBMs, as well as two SAMs.

"This hit," said Atta, pointing to the far side of the map, "was definitely not ours."

"We're assuming it's a missile, not a shadow contact," said Howe. "Or a dummy warhead." He leaned back against the frame of the weapons operator's seat, slightly hunched over despite the ample clearance on the flight deck.

"The other may be," said Atta, "but this here is definitely a live warhead. And the strike pattern on the target is exactly like ours: tracking laser, then the hit."

It had to be Cyclops One. The AWACS radar contacts were consistent with a 767. They had tracked the contact's flight north, then lost it in the mountains east of Jammu. There had been a series of Indian SAM launches; it appeared that the plane had been shot down by a Trishul missile, though the data was inconclusive. It was possible that the NSA would be able to supply more data about that in a few hours, pending their own analysis of the battle.

Had the Chinese stolen the plane, then used it to help Pakistan? Or had the Pakistanis stolen it themselves, only to lose it in battle?

Or was Megan responsible somehow on her own?

"There are several other contacts that we can't completely account for," said Atta. "Once the AWACS people review everything and compile it with the other data, they may be able to sort it out."

Howe glanced at his watch. He was supposed to brief the Pentagon in five minutes over a secure video hookup in the headquarters building; it would take at least ten to get there. He looked around at the small knot of people crowded into the 767.

"All right. Anything else?"

Atta shook his head. The rest stared, more or less blankly.

"You guys, everybody, get some rest," Howe told them. "Sleep. Good job. We did a good job. Better than anyone could've asked for."

Outside, engine specialists and a veritable army of maintenance experts were busy dissecting the damaged engine and wing. A new power plant had been located and was en route. Howe nodded at the few men who seemed to notice him—most were absorbed in their jobs—and then walked toward the Hummer that had been assigned to transport him over to the base commander's suite. His legs felt as though they had lead inserts at the knees, and the rims of his eyes seemed to vibrate with a metallic fuzz.

What would have happened if they hadn't been here? Ten million, twenty million people dead? Fifty million injured?

If the other plane was Cyclops One, then Megan had been flying it. She had taken down the other two missiles.

She might have been ready to take down others.

His anger toward her seemed to have faded into confusion. He got into the truck and rubbed his eyes, bracing himself as the driver raced across the base. Inside the general's temporary command post, the secure conference had already begun.

"Good job, Colonel," said Dr. Blitz on the screen at the side of the room as Howe entered. "Beyond expectations. Very, very good job. The President is proud of you and your people."

The screen changed; the feed showed the "tank," the secure conference room in the basement of the Pentagon. The head of the Joint Chiefs of Staff repeated Blitz's congratulations. Several other military people chimed in, then the defense secretary told him they'd just made history.

Howe ran down the tally. They'd heard the initial reports, but this probably seemed more solemn, more official. He concentrated on the missiles, adding the F-16 and its probable nuke almost as an afterthought.

Someone at the Pentagon mentioned that the CIA analyst thought the plane had been carrying a five- or eight-megaton bomb.

"We believe the Indians have two missiles left," said Blitz. "That's our best guess. Both sides have agreed to a cease-fire. The UN Security Council is going to meet in a few hours in emergency session. You're a hero, Colonel Howe. You and your people." He seemed almost choked with emotion.

"Hear, hear," said someone at the Pentagon.

"The President is going to address the nation in a few minutes to let them know what happened," said Blitz. "He will mention you and your team."

"There's one thing we have to talk about," said Howe.

"Two of the hits that were made—we believe they came from another laser. It had to be Cyclops One."

CHAPTER

3

Luksha had flown all night and his eyes felt as if they were on fire. He stared through the window as the car sped down Pereulok Sivtsev Vrazhek in the Arbatskaya section of Moscow just outside the Kremlin. Once something of a bohemian quarter and now a tourist favorite, the area included several new government buildings carefully concealed behind old facades. The one Luksha's military driver was taking him to, in fact, had only been occupied a few months before; this was Luksha's first visit, and he did not quite know what to expect.

The car stopped in the middle of the street, in front of a four-story yellow building whose exterior dated from the late eighteenth century. A single guard in a black suit stood at the doorway, eyeing Luksha suspiciously as he walked up the steps. The man touched his ear—there was an ear bud for a communications system there—then nodded to Luksha, who nodded back and pulled open the thick door. Two guards, these in paratrooper uniforms, stood inside the long but narrow vestibule. The men had AK-74s equipped with laser-dot sights; their fingers rested on the triggers. They neither moved nor said anything as the general walked past. His boots slid slightly on the polished marble floors; the lighting was so dim that he could not have read a newspaper. A large abstract painting by Kandinsky hung at the far end of the hall, which formed an alcove for a short flight of stairs to the left. Luksha walked down the stairs and there was met by two more paratroopers, who snapped sharply to attention and stood silently while a petite woman in an army uniform strode forward.

"General, please," she said, waiting for his nod before turning on her heel and leading him to a waiting elevator.

As soon as Luksha was inside, the doors slid shut and it started downward, picking up speed as it went. The young woman stared at the door as it descended; Luksha felt his ears pop.

The door opened on a corridor of polished granite. The rug on the floor was so thick Luksha felt as if he would trip as he walked. They turned right; two men in civilian dress passed, saying nothing, eyes studiously avoiding both Luksha and his attractive guide.

Two short corridors later the young woman deposited the general in the office of his commander, Andrev Orda, who besides being a major general was a member of parliament. As was his habit, Orda played the fussy old maid welcoming a long-lost relative, ushering Luksha in and offering him a vodka, which could not be turned down. Luksha felt himself sinking into the leather chair in front of Orda's pristine glass desk, his tired bones precariously close to sleep.

Two toasts later Orda's hospitality evaporated into the more comfortable—for Luksha—abruptness of a former army field general.

"The American weapon was used over India," said Orda. "You told me it was not operational."

"On the contrary," said Luksha. "My last communication not only noted that the remaining plane and its escorts had left the base but spoke of the possibility that the weapon might be used."

"The Americans are celebrating already. Their president has gone on television and declared war obsolete."

Luksha said nothing. He could not blame the Americans for celebrating, though in his opinion their claims for the weapon were overblown. It would make war more efficient, not obsolete.

"What happened to the plane that crashed?" asked Orda. "Or was that intended as some manner of ruse?"

"That is why I am here," said Luksha. As succinctly as he could, the general laid out what his people had found and what they had surmised. He made it clear that he could not explain why the weapon would have been flown under such conditions from its development base; he was not, he admitted, certain that the aircraft had not crashed, since the American actions were consistent with an all-out search. But the hints of activity at the supposedly abandoned island in the Kurils, added now to telemetry that seemed military in nature and records of a fuel delivery some eight months before, seemed "provocative."

Luksha used the word deliberately; it was one Orda relished.

Two flyovers by his Geofizia, outfitted with a photo reconaissance pod, had proven inconclusive; a ground inspection was necessary.

"I can answer many questions simply by going there," said Luksha. "Four or five destroyers, a battalion of paratroopers . . . We quarantine the island, take it over, capture the weapon."

Orda's face, reddened by the vodka earlier, turned nearly white.

"This is Japanese territory," said the general.

"The presence of a military installation would violate the treaty and return the land to us," said Luksha. He had been prepared for the objections—legitimate, surely—and now played his trump card. "Given that we have detected signals from a Tu-160 device, we could say that we were searching for such an aircraft that was reported missing."

Orda remained silent, staring at him as if he were an unfamiliar man who'd burst into the room with an incredible plan to go to war against America. Luksha began to feel less sure of himself.

"The Americans have occasionally used private companies as fronts for the CIA," he said, repeating a theory Chapeav had raised. "It is possible they are planning to do something against the North Koreans, if not ourselves."

Luksha waited, trying not to wince under the force of Orda's stare. General Orda had the authority to grant permission for the operation, but if he didn't, should Luksha go over his head?

He would have to speak to the premier himself. Just getting on his calendar would take days if not weeks.

"The Japanese would view this as an attack," said Orda finally. "If there are troops there, they would resist."

"There are no defense forces that are using standard communications equipment on the island," said Luksha. "The Japanese have not been on the island as far as we can tell for at least six months. We would approach peacefully, with no intent to harm anyone, unless we were fired upon.

"A reconaissance is hardly an attack," he added quickly. "Looking for our aircraft, we find another. If a weapon happens to be aboard it—in violation of an international agreement—then surely it would be our right to examine in detail."

Orda stared at him. There was no doubt about the laser's capabilities; the Americans had just proven all of the scientists' speculation. If it truly was this close to them, it had to be examined—if not destroyed.

"A large-scale operation would be out of the question," said Orda finally. "But a reconaissance in force, conducted at a time when the island was not monitored by the Japanese or the Americans, proceeding carefully as you've outlined . . . What is the minimal force you would need, if such a group were under your direct, personal command?"

CHAPTER

4

"Define *venti*."

The skinny young man with half a goatee blinked.

"*Venti?*" repeated Fisher.

The thick aroma of ground caffeine in the upscale coffee shop had obviously intoxicated the clerk's delicate senses. Fisher sympathized, but not to the point of being patient.

"How about I hop over the counter and get the coffee myself?" he asked the clerk, who had a tag on his shirt declaring he wasn't a clerk at all but something in an obscure Romance language that seemed to mean lawgiver.

"*Venti* would be, uh, bigger than *grande*," said the clerk. He pronounced the last *e* with an exaggerated swagger, as if the accent might somehow make him European.

"So there's *grande* and extra *grande*, which is large and extra large, except that large is what used to be regular, but you can charge more by calling it large. So *venti* is large, and I want extra large, so I guess I want extra *venti*." Fisher took out a cigarette. "What would that be? *Vento?*"

"Um—"

"Because it sounds kind of Latin, you know what I mean? It's not Latin, but it's close." He lit the cigarette. "*Venti, vento, ventanimous*—I came, I saw, I coffeed. Works for me."

"You can't smoke in here," said the clerk.

"Yeah, I know," said Fisher. "So you gonna get me the *ventanimous* or what?"

The clerk stared at the cigarette. "Mocha?"

"Just regular coffee. Straight."

The young man took cover behind the dessert display, whispering to one of his coworkers. Fisher surveyed the counter, looking for something to put his ashes in. A display near the register was filled with CDs "celebrating the organic music of the Rain Forest." Next to it was a small glossy photo of the man who had actually picked the coffee being prepared today; it seemed likely the company had spent more on the glossy photo than on the beans. A legend below the photo declared that the coffee had been harvested with integrity, which Fisher agreed was a good thing: You couldn't have too much integrity in a hot beverage, as far as he was concerned.

On the other hand, Fisher wasn't sure about organic music. Possibly it was the song they sang when they tore the trees down to panel the interior of the store.

The clerk with the pseudo-Latin job title sent a braver, skinnier coworker forward with the coffee. Fisher paid for it—the price represented a month's car payment—and then sat along the wall. Several people stared, eyeing his cigarette with obvious envy.

He'd taken only two sips from the coffee—while admittedly on the strong side, it lacked the metallic, burned aftertaste so highly prized by true connoisseurs of java— when a gentleman clad in the dark blue favored by officers of the law approached his table. Fisher reached into his jacket for his Bureau ID, expecting the cop to riff a variation of "license and registration" on him. Instead he touched his holster, unsnapping the gun restraint at the top.

"FBI," said Fisher. "Relax."

"Put it down slowly," said the cop.

Fisher pulled out his ID and laid it on the table.

"I meant the cigarette," said the policeman.

Fisher's cell phone began to vibrate.

"How about I take it outside?" he suggested, figuring the heavy lacquer of the walls would interfere with his reception.

"Good idea," said the policeman, whose hand remained poised near his weapon as the FBI agent walked out. The small concrete patio near the sidewalk was crowded with smoking refugees, but Fisher found an unoccupied table near the Dumpster, where the refreshing aroma of spent coffee beans mixed with more earthly scents.

"Fisher."

"McDonald."

"Betty, how are you?" he asked, starting to sip the coffee. "Did the GSA help?"

"About as much as Congressman Taft," she said.

"Good," said Fisher. It was best not to acknowledge sarcasm in an amateur.

She sighed. Fisher recognized the sound of a Tootsie Roll being unwrapped.

"We persevered despite your help. There are some interesting intersections," she said between chews. "Ferrone Radiavonics, which according to your papers worked on the F/A-22V's radar."

"Yup?"

"They're owned by a company which is owned by another company which is part of a trust controlled by the people who control El-Def."

"This is going somewhere, right?"

"Megan York's family and friends have an important interest in about half a dozen defense projects besides Cyclops," she told him.

"Controlling interests?"

"Big interests."

"Like which ones?"

"God, Fisher, do you do anything besides drink coffee and smoke cigarettes all day?"

"Nope."

"The augmented-ABM project is the biggest. The connection's rather convoluted."

"Bonham's involved?"

"He has stock in some of the companies. His stake is unclear. There are others." Betty ran down a list that included an unmanned submarine project and a satellite network. "Awful lot of stock to own, given his supposed net worth. Get this: He claims his condo cost under two-fifty. Can't possibly be, not near the Beltway. No way."

As she talked the call-waiting feature beeped Fisher's line with another call.

"Gotta get going, Betty. Keep digging."

"Digging for what?"

He clicked onto the other line and immediately regretted doing so.

"Where the hell have you been?"

"Why, Jemma, hello to you. Actually, I am in a coffee emporium in downtown central north Alexandria. I think it's downtown. Hard to tell."

"I need you to get on a plane right away. You have to go to Afghanistan. Did you catch the President's speech?"

"The President?"

"Fisher, I don't have any time for your bullshit."

"Such language. I bet there's an ordinance against it here."

"Fisher—I'm going to give you twenty minutes to get over to Andrews. There's a plane waiting."

"A big one, I hope."

CHAPTER

5

Blitz had expected some of the criticism. It was mostly knee-jerk anti-Americanism, the kind that would interpret a cure for cancer as somehow part of a plot to bring a McDonald's restaurant to every intersection in the world. A few of the sources were surprising, or at least ironic: A German newspaper accused the U.S. of trying to enforce its "ethos" on the world, as if eliminating all life-forms from several hundred thousand square miles was a lifestyle choice.

But there were a few nuanced opinions—he couldn't call them criticisms exactly—that did disturb him. One, recognizing that mankind now stood at the precipice of a new age, went on to warn that the shape of this age was not so clear-cut:

> One of the lessons that seems not to be understood about the use of the atomic bombs against Japan was that they helped end the war precisely because they were weapons of indiscriminate annihilation. They made possible the erasing of an entire people—not simply the removal of combatants, but of all people. World War II to a great degree erased the line between combatant and noncombatant. The Allied powers involved in the fight understood—though they could not admit it publicly—that the only real way to win the war was to combine military victory with severe crippling of the civilian population. The atomic bombs were the culmination of that, a step further along the line that led from Dresden to the firebombing of Tokyo. There would have been no final victory without these mass destructions, just more in the cycle of engagements that had wracked the world for one hundred, two hundred years.
>
> And so, when the possibility of complete destruction is removed, what then? Does it lead to more stability—to no more war, as the President declared in his forceful speech last night? Or does it lead paradoxically to an era of more instability? If a country can only be defeated in war by total annihilation—

the lesson of World War II—what happens when that possibility is removed? Is the answer truly peace? Or is the result more cycles of violence? Low-grade violence compared to world wars, certainly, but inevitable and intractable nonetheless.

The American action against Iraq in the first Gulf War is a case in point. By limiting their objectives in the war, America and its allies inadvertently set the stage for years of continued conflict and great suffering, necessitating actions in 2003 which even now we do not fully understand the ramifications of. Would the result have been so much different if Saddam Hussein—or, better, a successor who rose to power by assassinating the despised leader— swore off weapons of mass destruction? Would the Kurds have been freed, the Shiite majority unchained? The Cyclops weapon—along with the ABM and augmented ABM system currently envisioned—can eliminate nuclear war. But will they make the world safer? And in pursuing this safety— admittedly a seemingly glorious goal—are we actually making ourselves less secure? . . .

Not only did Blitz disagree with some of the essay's conclusions; it bothered him considerably that the essay had been written by one of his mentors, Donald Byrd, who had preceded him at Harvard and in his estimation remained his teacher. In essence, his friend was saying he had done the opposite of what he had intended.

But what was the alternative? What would he have said if they let the war go on?

"Lost in thought?" asked the President as he entered the East Sitting Room on the second floor of the White House. The President pulled one of the ornate wooden chairs from the table where one of the aides had stacked the newspapers and printouts. A silver coffee service sat on the floor; D'Amici bent over and helped himself. "So?" he said finally. "What's the verdict?"

"Mostly positive," said Blitz.

"I don't mean the press reaction," said D'Amici. He waved his hand dismissively. "Will the cease-fire hold or not?"

"I think it will," said Blitz. "They sound scared."

"What about the other plane? Was it Cyclops?"

D'Amici hadn't slept—Blitz knew this for a fact, since he hadn't himself—but he looked as if were rested and ready to go bicycling or on a picnic. The doubt he'd seen the other night was gone. He'd made the right decision, and his people had executed it perfectly.

"We're still going through the satellite photos," said Blitz. "Colonel Howe should be conducting the search by now."

"Howe's still in Afghanistan?"

"Yes, sir. The Pentagon . . . His aircraft have the most advanced gear available. And he volunteered."

"He's got a future." The President smiled in a way that suggested he might consider adopting the colonel—or placing him on the ticket as vice president for the next election.

"We're a little worried about Chinese reaction," added Blitz.

D'Amici shrugged. "If they're the ones who have the plane, their reaction is irrelevant. And if they don't, well, we'll deal with that down the line. You don't think this is parallel Chinese technology?"

The CIA had raised that possibility yesterday, claiming that their review of the strikes showed differences in the weaponry. Bonham's experts had snickered, and Blitz sided with them.

"Doubtful. And it's definitely not Russian. They're clearly years behind."

"So the Pakistanis stole it?"

"I just don't see that," said Blitz. The Pakistani theory—that they had stolen the plane to protect themselves from just such an attack—was popular at the Pentagon but had no evidence to back it up, especially given the plane's flight path from the time it was spotted off the Indian coast. A task force of intel experts was trying to piece together the plane's flight path prior to that, but had made little progress.

"Someone took it. I doubt the original crew hijacked it for Greenpeace," he said sarcastically.

"I agree," said Blitz. "Maybe the Russians."

"Then why aren't they talking about the shootdown, or the fact that they lost the aircraft?" The President was referring to intercepted communications, not public announcements, since saying anything would implicate their guilt in taking it.

"They know we can read them."

D'Amici bent to the floor and poured himself another cup of coffee. "Congress is going to approve the augmented-ABM funding, as long as next week's tests go well. We're riding a wave, Professor. Riding a wave. The end of war as we know it." He picked up a folded newspaper from the floor, holding open the editorial page. The lead editorial, congratulating him, bore that title: "The end of war as we know it."

Blitz looked up as a familiar set of footsteps echoed through the second-floor hallway. Mozelle appeared from behind a pair of Secret Service agents. She greeted the President first, then looked at Blitz, tacitly asking whether she should speak. But there was really no option: D'Amici didn't like secrets, especially ones so obvious.

"McIntyre is missing," she said. "We're not sure yet, but it looks like he was at one of the Indian bases in Kashmir. No one's heard from him since the exchange."

6

Pure oxygen was a tried-and-true hangover cure, and while Howe didn't have a hangover, the O_2 worked wonders, clearing his foggy head and wiping away much of his fatigue as he and Timmy began their search for the downed aircraft believed to be Cyclops One.

A day and a half's worth of analysis had yielded a five-hundred-square-mile box where Unk-2—still not positively ID'd as Cyclops One—had apparently been hit by an Indian SAM before going down. The area, which Howe and Timmy were just entering, included a small portion of Pakistan and India as well as China and Nepal. The peaks rose over six thousand meters—eighteen thousand feet.

What would he do if he found her—if Megan were down there in the snow or worse, crumpled in the rocks?

Kick her in the face?

No, he couldn't. He'd bend down, ask her why.

Why?

It wouldn't be like that. He'd be in the plane, and if there were a body rather than leg or mangled bit of burnt flesh . . . Howe took a slow, deep breath, forcing himself to concentrate on flying the aircraft. The ground-scanning mode of the radar had been tweaked by one of the engineers, allowing the AI tactics module to assist in the search. In effect, it was like having a backseater with a magnifying glass going over the readout.

"It thinks it's looking for a squished Scud," the technical expert had explained.

"You don't know who T. S. Eliot was?" Meagan asked.

"No."

"T. S. Eliot was only the most famous poet of the twentieth century. Chr-ist." She smiled at him.

"What'd he write? 'Tyger! Tyger! Burning bright'?"

*"Blake. That was Blake. T. S. Eliot wrote 'The Love Song of
J. Alfred Prufrock,' The Waste Land, Four Quartets."*

"Big hits."

*"The biggest. You really never, ever heard of them? In school
or anywhere?"*

He shrugged again now, remembering, reliving the
conversation.

"How do you live in an age where death is constant?" she
asked.

"Is that a serious question?"

"The Waste Land is about rebirth," she told him. *"You
have to find a way beyond the cycle."*

"How?"

*"If I knew, the poem would be boring. But I'll tell you this:
Fear death by water."*

"Huh?"

Her laughter dissolved the memory. It was a joke, a reference to a line in the poem, as she'd explained later by
reading it to him. It was an interesting, kaleidoscopic
poem—not that he knew much about or, to be honest,
cared about poems. But they were as real to her as airplanes, and that intrigued him. It was different; it was one
of the things that was interesting about her beyond her
eyes, beyond the smooth curve of her hips.

Yet, he still hated her for being a traitor.

"What are we doing, Bird One?" asked Timmy, bringing him back to the present.

"Two, we're going to start the sweeps as we planned,"
he told his wingman. "Anything on Guard?"

"Negativo."

"Let's do it."

The two delta-shaped aircraft plunged downward,
arrowheads hurled by a god toward the snowy mountains below. There were no clouds today; under other circumstances this might have seemed a purely majestic
view.

"Don't even see any mountain goats down there," said Timmy in Bird Two.

Howe let his speed bleed off gradually, coming below three hundred knots as he banked into the next search track. He lifted his right wing slightly, concentrating on the view ahead. They took a circuit and then another one, reaching the edge of their search box, then pulled around and began again, retracing their steps backward.

The climate and terrain combined to make this a very difficult place to live, yet settlements dotted the valleys and roads ran around the steepest mountains.

Resourceful species, humans.

"Got a couple of aircraft at long distance," said Timmy. "Shenyang F-8s, pretty far off—two hundred miles."

The Chinese F-8MII interceptors were double-engined interceptors that could be viewed as outgrowths of the MiG-21 family. In contrast to their forebears, they were not particularly maneuverable, but they could go relatively fast. Howe thought of them as a poor man's updated MiG-25; equipped with radar missiles, they could be a severe annoyance.

Not today. The planes soon passed out of range to the east. Howe kept making his tracks, varying his path and trying to keep his memories of Megan at bay.

Something caught his eye when he reached the southeast corner of their search area for the fourth time. The sun had flashed off something a few miles farther into China—or maybe not, because when he stared in that direction he saw nothing.

The tactical screen was clear, and the computer hadn't said boo to him about seeing anything.

Still, it was worth checking out.

"Two, follow me."

"Got something?"

"Just hang with me."

"On your butt, boss. Smells like aftershave—now *that's* a story."

Howe pushed down in the direction of the glint. There was a peak there, a mountain 6,570 meters high—just under twenty-thousand feet above sea level. That was a decent altitude in an airplane, and beyond the rated ceiling of many helicopters—an important factor if a rescue mission was launched.

Forget that. She's not going to be standing down there waving her arms at you.

"Got something?" asked Timmy as they crisscrossed around the peak and the nearby ridges.

"Negative." Howe looked at the ground through the canopy and then back at the tactical screen, back and forth.

The AWACS working with them back near the Afghan border reported that an unknown aircraft was taking off from Lop, a small airfield in the Xinjiang Uygur region to the north. The contact, probably a small commercial transport, headed east.

Howe checked his fuel state, deciding that a brief break from the search would help. And it did—sort of. As he looked back at the large display, he saw a double triangle in yellow at the right. Magnification made it look like a rock with a hatchet on it.

He tracked back, practically climbing out of the cockpit to get a better view. It was just a pile of rocks.

But there was something dark about a half-mile away, on the side of the slope facing India.

Dark and gray—the color of Cyclops One.

The computer bleeped a target tone.

"Two, I think I've found it," he said, changing his course.

7

Special Forces Captain Dale "Duke" Wallace didn't know exactly what to make of Fisher. The first thing the FBI agent had done on boarding the C-17A in Bahrain was to ask if there was a smoking section. The next thing he'd done was ask if they were jumping out.

He seemed equally disappointed to hear that the answer was no on both counts.

The C-17A Globemaster III had been designed as a combat-area transport, able to move people and gear great distances at a moment's notice. Its interior measured two inches beyond sixty-eight feet (counting the ramp); six Marine Corps LAVs could be loaded inside with room left over for a company mascot or two. In this case, Duke and his team of SF troopers from the Army's 56th SFG (A) were the only cargo. They sat along fold-down seats at the side of the aircraft, Alice packs and mission gear nearby, mostly dozing. Two of the men had stretched mats on the steel floor and were sleeping there.

Fisher, on the other hand, was alternating slugs between two massive thermoses of coffee, which he'd somehow managed to obtain on the tarmac as he walked—walked, not ran—from the E-3 that had delivered him from the States.

Fisher glanced up and saw him staring. "Want some?" he asked.

Duke shook his head, then went over and sat next to him.

"We'll be landing in Afghanistan in an hour or so," Duke told him.

"Sounds good."

"We want to take right off."

"Makes sense," said Fisher.

"We have a transport en route, an MV-22. It's going to meet us on the tarmac and fly us right to the wreckage they've spotted. Assuming that's the wreckage. But I guess that's why you're here, right? You're the expert."

"MV-22," said Fisher. He took a long sip from the thermos bottle. "That's the airplane that thinks it's a helicopter, right?"

"The Osprey, yes, sir. The MV-22 is a Special Forces version. Equipped with a chain gun in the nose, ports for mini-guns and additional weapons. Whatever we need we can get. We'll get you in and out, no sweat."

"I investigated a crash of one of those three years ago, looking for sabotage," said Fisher. "Wasn't sabotage."

"Uh-huh?"

"I investigated another one of those two years ago. That wasn't sabotage, either."

"Are you making a point, Mr. Fisher?"

"You sure I can't smoke in here?"

Some hours later, Andy Fisher stepped out of the MV-22 into six inches of snow, surveying the wreckage of what had until very recently been a 767. He'd seen one of the engines as they'd flown in, and that would be enough to definitively ID the plane. Which was a good thing, because the rest of the aircraft had disintegrated beyond recognition.

Airplanes could do funny things when they crashed, but usually what they did fell into general patterns. Fisher wasn't a crash expert per se: The real experts got off on analyzing the way metal twisted, and could look at a burn pattern on a piece of cloth and tell you what the pilot had for lunch. Still, Fisher had seen enough to know that this plane had been wracked by something more than an anti-air missile before it exploded.

Interestingly enough, the revolving turret where the laser had fired from was only beaten to shit as opposed to disintegrated beyond recognition. So it was easy to cinch the identification.

"Our plane?" asked Duke.

"Not a doubt," said Fisher. "When do we get the forensics team in?"

"We're in China, Mr. Fisher. You aren't getting any forensics people in here. There's bound to be some sort of Chinese army patrol sooner or later. My orders are to assist you making an ID, then blow the remains up into little pieces."

"Be a hell of a lot better if we had a forensics team."

"Be a hell of a lot better if we were sitting on a beach, catchin' rays," said the SF captain.

"Good point," said Fisher. "We want to take samples so we can check for explosives. Something helped the plane go boom besides a bad attitude."

"Hey, down here!" shouted one of the soldiers from a ravine about fifty feet away.

Fisher tagged after Duke, sliding down the rocks to a relatively flat plain about twenty feet wide. The soldier was standing over a twisted black blob of gear that looked as if it were covered with tar.

"It's a boot," said Fisher.

"How the hell can you tell?"

Fisher knelt down near it. "Believe me. That's what it is." He picked it up and looked at it. The bottom half had been burned by high heat; Fisher guessed it would help the lab people recreate the fire and explosion. A bit of sock was evident in the mass, so even if there wasn't any flesh in the blob there, they'd have a shot at DNA.

Maybe. Of course, if the blob included bones or even just burnt flesh, that'd be even better.

The FBI agent held it out to one of the soldiers, who suddenly looked a little pale. "Evidence."

"Don't you want to, uh, put it in a bag or something?"

"Nah," said Fisher. "By the way, the foot's not in it."

"How do you know?"

"Just guessing," Fisher admitted. "But if I told you it was, you wouldn't take it, right?"

"How can it be empty?" said the trooper, still hesitating.

"Boot probably got blown right off while the foot and leg were burning to a crisp along with the rest of the body. Lab guys'll get off on this."

The soldier took the boot without further comment.

Fisher walked down another slope, surveying more of the scattered bits and pieces. A piece of green cloth lay tangled against a few rocks about twenty feet to the right, tangled with a long piece of burnt metal. Fisher bent down and saw that it was a collar from a flight suit—or at least might have been. He folded it and put it in a paper envelope from his jacket.

"Watcha got?" asked Duke, tramping down the slope.

"Cloth. We'll look for DNA."

"Yeah? Will that work?"

"Gives the lab something to do," said Fisher.

"The pilots have a good read on some more pieces west," said Duke, who'd been talking to them on his radio. "There's some good hunks out there."

Fisher took a long drag on his cigarette.

"I need as many pieces of metal as we can get to test for explosives."

"Which pieces?"

"The ones where the bomb was," said Fisher, throwing his cigarette butt away and walking back up the hill.

8

Clayton Bonham had always believed that you could tell a great deal about a man by what he ordered at an expensive restaurant. In his particular case, the filet mignon—medium rare, with a pepper sauce and oyster mushrooms—meant that he was a solid, conservative man who appreciated the finer things in life, but nonetheless eschewed flamboyance.

The choices of his guests fell in line with his theory. Congressman Taft had chosen a nondescript chicken and pasta dish from the lite side of the menu, an attempt not only to demonstrate that he was watching his weight but also that he was not a spendthrift; the dish was nearly the least expensive entrée, though *least expensive* was a relative term on M Street. Jeff Segrest, by contrast, had ordered a grilled salmon soup with foie gras mousse floating on a black corn taco—a bizarre though thoughtlessly flamboyant mélange that looked about as appetizing as the napkin covering the wrought-silver bread basket.

The restaurant, named James after its owner and executive chef, ranked comfortably in the top tier of Washington power eateries, a fact that Bonham kept firmly in mind as he ate, since it meant that their conversation had to be circumscribed. This was not necessarily a bad thing, however; while he found Taft inoffensive, Segrest was a serial blowhard, and only the possibility that he would be overheard kept his boasts within somewhat reasonable bounds.

It also meant that he was semidiscreet regarding Cyclops, which was what both men wanted to talk about.

"Revolutionary," said Segrest. "That was the President's word."

"Yes," said Bonham. Things in India had gone remarkably well—much better, in fact, than he could have hoped. Incredibly better. The intelligence agencies were closing in on the wreckage, with the early reports indicating that an Indian SAM had taken out the plane. Depending on what theory they began to favor about the aircraft's theft, evidence would be supplied—nothing firm, of course, just hints and suggestions. A money transfer, a name on a visitors' list, a credit card transaction—the sort of things the sleuth Fisher would eat up.

The bastard had sniffed out the lake plan somehow, even though they hadn't gone through with it. Bonham still hoped Fisher might manage to convince someone to have the damn thing drained. Serve the idiot right.

"Do you think this is the end of war, General?" asked Taft.

Bonham smiled. The President had used that phrase, and a number of commentators had picked it.

"I think it's a bit premature," said Bonham.

"My cousin thought the augmented ABM system more critical," said Taft.

Bonham smiled again, though this time much more tightly. Though anyone who really mattered would surely know who the men and their relationships were, Bonham nonetheless would have preferred that Megan's name not be mentioned. She surely would have preferred that herself.

"The antimissile system is critical," said Segrest. "And when we get the contract, it will be a windfall."

More than a windfall, you greedy bastard, thought Bonham, sipping his wine. Segrest controlled a considerable portion of the Jolice and related portfolios, and so he had to be dealt with very carefully. Still, Bonham fantasized about the day when he would tell the fat pomposity to get out of his office.

His White House office.

"Don't be premature," Bonham said mildly.

"We'll score well in the next round of tests," said Segrest. He looked at Taft. "The congressman agrees."

Bonham realized belatedly that Segrest wasn't merely boasting: He was demanding that the weapon be used in the next round of tests.

"The tests will show what the tests show," said Bonham. He could feel his throat starting to close. "Anything can happen. Whatever the results, Jolice should be funded. An argument is there."

"More than an argument when the results of the first test are duplicated."

He was ordering it. Ridiculous!

Bonham picked up the napkin from his lap and daubed at the sides of his mouth, surreptitiously glancing around the room to make sure no one was listening.

The plan was to dismantle the weapon and the base, and to leave. Anything else was far too risky—for him especially. He'd gone to great lengths to cover their tracks.

And why, really? Because of greed. Because Jolice and its backers stood to gain billions if the augmented ABM system was built. Never mind that it might not work. Never mind that companies much better suited to build it—Lockheed and Boeing, for example—were being flim-flammed out of the competition.

Meagan York's motives were pure, but no one else's were, not even his. He wanted power, not money; at least he had the wisdom to realize when they'd gone too far.

"I believe the weather in the Pacific is very tempestu-ous," Bonham said, as close to a hint as he dared.

"Nonsense," said Segrest. "The weather there has never been better. Don't you agree, Congressman?"

"Oh yes," said Taft.

"We have to move along the course I've outlined," said Bonham. He kept his voice low; still, he worried about being overheard.

"No. That's far too cautious. You're conservative, General, a conservative by nature." Segrest's voice was so loud, it could have been a toast. Bonham pushed his teeth together, sure that others were staring. "The future—imagine the possibilities."

"Yes," said Bonham.

"Very rich possibilities," said Segrest, signaling to the waiter for more wine.

CHAPTER

9

The first day after the crash, McIntyre managed to walk only a few hundred yards beyond the ravine where the helicopter had gone down. He lost his strength somewhere after midday and, lying down to rest, fell fast asleep. When he woke it was dark; he went back to sleep and didn't open his eyes until the sun forced them open. He got up and began walking. After a while he realized the aches and stiffness he'd felt had melted into a gnawing hole in his stomach, something he thought must be hunger, though it felt slightly different than that, as if his stomach had been emptied and then twisted in his body.

McIntyre came to a hillside so sheer that the only way was to slide on his butt. He couldn't find a comfortable way to hold the guns and finally decided to loop the straps around his neck. As he started to push down he changed his mind, thinking it would be better to crawl on his belly, but it was too late: Unable to stop himself, he slid sideways, then rolled and kept going until he slammed against some rocks. The gray hands that had climbed over his eyes pressed in and he lost consciousness.

He was out for an hour, maybe more. Then the ground in front of his face turned blue. He opened his eyes and saw that he was about fifty feet above a trail through a valley. Bushes began to rise in the terrain about twenty yards to his right, gradually becoming thicker until the entire valley was covered in lush green.

McIntyre picked up the guns from his chest and got to his feet. He slid a few yards, walked a bit, then gave way to his momentum and began trotting down the hill. For a second his aches, pains, and bruises disappeared. He reached the bottom of the hill and caught his breath, hyperventilating slightly. His head remained clear.

The blood on his clothes had dried into stiff patches that felt like pieces of wood. He wasn't hungry, but his mouth was dry.

His butt hurt, as though the bone in his rear end had been broken.

He had his phone there. He'd put his phone there yesterday, then completely forgotten, blacked out before he could use it.

McIntyre began to laugh. He laughed so hard he rolled over, face in the dirt. *All I've got to do,* he thought, *is just call someone and tell them to pick me up. Send a taxi. Send a friggin' taxi!*

The laughter caught in his throat and he began to spit. His phlegm came out in red gobs. When he stopped, McIntyre reached back for the phone. Had he tried it yesterday? He didn't think he had, but yesterday was a jumble, the crash was a jumble. He remembered hitting the Indian captain who had kidnapped him, and walking, but nothing else.

McIntyre put his thumb on the Power button and held it down. When he let it off, the display flashed green, then faded; he couldn't tell in the direct sunlight whether the phone was working or not.

At first he thought it was dead. His chest rippled and tears erupted from his eyes. He dropped the phone and hunched over his knees, weeping in despair. He saw himself from the distance; he sneered at the miserable wretch who was so pathetic.

He hadn't cried since he was a little boy, six or seven years old. Crying was a thing sissies did, and girls, and he was neither.

Shaking, he tried the phone again. Holding it sideways this time to avoid the sun's glare, he realized that it was in fact working. The battery was only at half power, but the phone was working.

He thumbed the menu up, got the main switchboard, hit Send.

McIntyre put the phone to his ear.

He heard nothing.

"NSC."

"Hello?"

"Hello? I'm having trouble hearing you."

"This is McIntyre," he said. "I'm in India, I think. There was a crash."

The operator didn't say anything, and for a long moment McIntyre thought he had lost the connection. Then there was another voice on the line, a louder voice, male, vaguely familiar.

"Mac . . . this is James Brott. Where the hell are you?"

Brott was one of the intelligence liaisons, a CIA officer over on assignment.

"I'm in India."

"Are you all right? We're starting to track the call and get a location. Do you know where you are? Do you have a GPS?"

"No." McIntyre spoke softly, as if someone were nearby. The crying jag had taken his anxiety away; he wanted to tell Brott everything and yet he felt calm, or almost calm. "We were flying near the Pakistani border, west of a base called Pekdelle. I'm not sure I'm pronouncing it right. They took me on the attack. I guess they were going to either throw me out of the helicopter or make it look like the Pakistani soldiers killed me."

"Where are you, Mac? Describe it."

McIntyre looked around, then began to describe what he saw. Mountains rose in the distance—mountains rose everywhere, actually—and the nearest one had a green circle on it that looked like a fist.

As he spoke he heard a truck somewhere nearby. He got to his feet, looking for the road.

"There's something coming," he said. "I'm going to flag it down."

"No, McIntyre. No!" Brott shouted. "They're at war, Pakistan and India. Stay hidden."

"Hidden?"

"Mac, there are guerrillas fighting all over Kashmir, even though there's a cease-fire. You have to try to hide. We'll send someone; we'll find someone we can trust to rescue you. Stay hidden."

The road was across the hill, to the right. McIntyre walked sideways across the grade, peeking down toward it. A large, open transport rounded the tar-paved road. White rocks were piled alongside the road where the shoulders should have been, funneling the pavement over the sharp terrain. The truck continued past, then downshifted as it went downward. He looked across the way and realized that the road ran around the opposite rise; he was exposed here.

"How safe are you?" Brott asked.

"Safe?"

"Are you in shelter or out in the open?"

"The open. Listen, my battery is weak. I have maybe an hour of talk time left."

"All right. You're going to have to assume—we have to assume—that anyone you see right now is the enemy. *Anyone.* We're going to try to get your location; I think we're going to be able to get it. The NSA has been looking for your signal, so I'm sure we're going to get it; I just haven't been able to get them yet. I don't want your battery to die, though. Can you get somewhere safe—somewhere we could send in a team and find you?"

"I don't know. Yeah, I have to. Yeah."

"A good-sized field, someplace in the open, but with a place you could hide. . . ."

McIntyre started to laugh. "I'll just check the Michelin guide."

Brott started to apologize, but McIntyre held the phone down; he heard the truck downshift again, the motor revving as it started up opposite him.

"Look, I don't think this is a good place. I'm going to move," he told him.

"Don't hang up yet," said Brott. "I want to make sure I have the location."

"I have to save the battery," McIntyre told him. If they had been looking for him, the NSA had more than enough to find him now. "I'll call in an hour."

"McIntyre, listen—"

He hit the End button, then got up and began running toward a low thicket he'd seen to his left.

CHAPTER

10

Fisher sat on the long canvas bench, staring at the pile of retrieved aircraft remains in the center of the Osprey and wondering if the odds of finding a trace of an explosive could be measured in the billions or simply the millions.

Millions, he decided. But it was also likely that whoever had worked this out had probably also been smart enough to set it up in a way that would be hard to pin down, maybe making the fuel do most of the work.

He had the boot and the cloth sample, which appeared to contain a hair. Could they trust a DNA sample?

His cell phone began vibrating. Fisher took it out of his pocket.

"Fisher."

"Mr. Fisher, this is Matt Firenze."

"Hey, Doc, whatcha got?"

"Well, we took apart the environmental control system, and there it was."

"Back up. What are we talking about?"

"It's like a Trojan Horse virus. Actually, we didn't find the code, but we found that something had erased something, and we figure that's where it has to be. We couldn't duplicate it on the bench units. It had to be there. We have a model—"

Fisher let the boy genius explain how he thought a rogue program could have caused a power surge in the circuitry connected to the shared radar sections and at the same time knocked out the controls. It was rather convoluted, but the agent knew better than to cut off a scientist mid-theorem.

"It's just a spike, a temporary hit," concluded Firenze, "and that fits with what happened."

"Who developed that system?"

"It was purpose-built for this model of the plane," said Firenze. "I think Carie Electro Controls. But it could have been Jolice too."

"Jolice?"

"They have a lot of little divisions and things. It's hard sometimes to keep them straight."

"They owned by Ferrone?"

"No, it's the other way around, I think," said the scientist. "I think Jolice is the bigger company."

"Why don't you work for them?" Fisher asked Firenze, whom the records had shown was working on the project under a special contract with the Air Force.

"Jolice, NADT, all those people—they make you rich, but then they figure they own you," said Firenze.

"I know how that goes," said Fisher. "Except for the rich part."

CHAPTER

11

McIntyre watched the wheels of the truck bounce up the trail. He could tell it was something small and relatively old, but he was too afraid to rise and get a good view of it. When he was sure it had passed, he sat up and tried to take stock of his situation.

They'd be working on finding him. The NSA would have the location of his transmission by now. But could they do anything about it? He was half a world away.

There'd be Navy units in the Indian Ocean. Somebody could come up and get him.

It might mean staying another night at least. He'd have to find a place to hide.

Something to eat would be good too. And drink.

McIntyre rose and shouldered his guns, then began walking toward the road, going in the direction the truck had come from. It took only a few minutes to reach the nearest curve, which made its way across a notch on the side of a series of hills. There was a switchback in the distance, but he couldn't tell if the one-and-a-half-lane pressed-chip-and-tar road led to it or not.

He began to walk. Two or three minutes later he heard a vehicle coming up behind him. There were some trees a short distance away and he managed to get to them before the truck passed. It was a pickup, and it moved at a pretty good clip. Just as he started out from behind the tree he heard another truck. He slid down, watching a military vehicle speed past. It was a Russian-made KAMAZ 6x4, or possibly an Indian knockoff. The six-wheeled truck had a canvas backing, the kind that might be used for light cargo or soldiers, but what it was loaded with or even if it was loaded at all he couldn't see.

Was it even Indian? He might actually be over the line in Pakistan. The border in Kashmir wasn't very well defined, and now there might not be a line at all.

McIntyre walked for a long while, his head gradually stooping closer to the ground. Finally he heard noises. Thinking it was another truck, he climbed over the stones at the side of the road and hid in a small depression a short distance away. Minutes passed without anything appearing, and he finally realized the sound wasn't getting any louder. It seemed to be an engine of some sort, but it was standing still.

A large boulder stood on the slope across the road from him. Thinking it might give him a vantage to see ahead, he slipped back across the road and clambered up the slope. But the rock was higher than he'd thought, and tired and battered as he was, he couldn't get to the top, not even when he put down the rifles. He settled for sidestepping across the slope below it, pushing through the bushes to see.

Something orange flashed in the distance.

A tiger.

He reached for a rifle, realizing belatedly that he had left them on the ground. He took a step and then the tiger sprang forward, charging him from the distance.

McIntyre tried to run but quickly lost his balance and slid down the rocks. He covered his head, cowering against the dirt and scrubby vegetation, waiting to be torn apart.

Except that he wasn't; the tiger had stayed where it was.

It wasn't a tiger. There were no tigers here, or other large cats; even the snow leopards had long ago fled, leaving man as the only predator. The orange was a piece of cloth, and as he walked toward it he realized it wasn't even orange but yellow. It was draped over a bush, and it wasn't moving.

McIntyre looked past the cloth and saw a building in the distance, set back near a clearing. This, he thought, might be a good place to arrange the pickup, though he'd have to scout it first, see if there were people nearby. He checked his watch: He had a half hour left before he was supposed to call.

The bushes in the back didn't provide much cover, but the building looked run-down and possibly abandoned. McIntyre gathered his courage and walked down a shallow slope toward what seemed to be the back or a side wall, studying two large metal housings on the roof. There was no sound, and he could see no vehicles nearby. The highway swung around somewhere ahead, passing in front of the building.

The door must be on that side. Here there were only windows, one boarded, the other's glass covered with a thick layer of grime.

McIntyre edged to the left side of the structure. There were two windows. A car or truck passed; he crouched before it came into view and couldn't see it.

He tried to come up with a plan, but his brain wouldn't supply one. What would the occupants do if a man with a rifle—two rifles—appeared at the front door, his clothes torn and covered with blood?

Shoot him, or run for their lives.

But then again, if no one was here, it would be a perfect place to stay and wait for a rescue.

McIntyre hunched on his knees, thinking. Finally he pushed up from the crouch, walking toward the building with the guns still in his hands.

When he was about twenty feet away, he tried to run. After a single step his right thigh muscle began to spasm. He managed to reach the wall and hurled himself against the blocks, catching his breath before edging toward the front corner.

A metal door was set into the front wall about a third of the way down. The road was visible through some trees to his left.

McIntyre steadied the rifle in his right hand, glancing at his finger on the trigger. Then he knocked on the door with his left hand as hard as he could manage, and stepped back.

No one answered. He tried again, stepped back farther this time. The third time he used the butt end of the rifle, the other gun swinging awkwardly off his shoulder. When no one answered, he reached for the handle.

The door was heavy and opened toward him rather than inward. Slapping his side against the door to hold it open, he stood against the darkness, anger inexplicably mixing with his fear and exhaustion; with a rush he went forward into the building, not so much ready for anything as resigned to it.

There was no one inside.

The building housed some sort of machine shop. A pair of desks sat in the front, separated from the work area by some filing cabinets and open space.

There were phones on both desks. McIntyre went over and picked one up.

A dial tone.

A dial tone! He wouldn't have to rely on the satellite phone and the draining battery.

But didn't the fact that the dial tone worked mean the building wasn't abandoned?

Was it a trap? Was someone watching him?

McIntyre put the phone back down and walked through the rest of the building. There was a washroom in the back. He opened the tap and put his face under the faucet. The warm water tasted metallic and moldy at the same time, but he was so thirsty he gulped it down.

When his thirst was quenched, he realized he was a few minutes late for his phone call. He went back to the front and took out the satellite phone.

Brott picked up before the first ring ended.

"We think we know where you are," he told him. "We're going to arrange a rescue, but it's not easy. It's chaos over there. There've been several riots."

"Get someone here," said McIntyre. He sat down on the floor against the desk. "Get somebody here."

"We're working on it. You have to relax."

As McIntyre struggled to control his response, the door began to open.

CHAPTER

12

Blitz had the answer ready, but Byrd would not call on him. The others were droning on about terrorist threats, the need for force on the ground, the fool's gold of technology. Finally he could stand it no more: He stood up from the desk and found himself in the middle of the circle. The others were dressed as he had known them in college, in jeans mostly, but he was in the suit he'd been wearing in the White House a few hours before. Instantly he was self-conscious. Byrd looked at him, waiting.

And so he started.

"Nation-on-nation violence can be halted. We've done so for the first time," he said. The words sounded strange in his ears, as if he were talking through a tube. "Terrorism remains a difficult problem, but the impact there also will be great, with more pinpoint attacks. Imagine fighting the *Intifada* with the ability to eliminate individual bomb-making facilities with absolute certainty. Imagine the 1996 attack on the Al Qaeda camp in Afghanistan with Cyclops rather than cruise missiles. The attack on the World Trade Center never would have occurred."

Byrd nodded, then asked, "What does that mean for those who possess the weapon?"

Blitz had thought of this at some length, mostly from the perspective of what they should do if an enemy obtained its own version. But for some reason his brain refused to formulate an answer.

"Does the selectivity mean the weapon will be used more often, or less?" asked Byrd. "And is either beneficial?"

Again, Blitz had thought of this; the answer, he thought was obvious: the weapon did not need to be used to be effective, but its use must be as carefully controlled as the nuclear bombs had been. But he couldn't speak.

"Well, Dr. Blitz?"

What was the alternative, he wanted to know. Do nothing? They had been right in India: Millions of people owed their lives to that gamble. That good could be measured unambiguously.

Blitz began to stutter.

"Dr. Blitz?"

Blitz pushed his head upward from the desk as the classroom disappeared. He was in his office; he'd fallen asleep, exhausted, waiting for word about McIntyre.

One of the military liaisons was standing at the door.

"Dr. Blitz?"

"Go ahead. I'm sorry, I was dozing."

The aide nodded. It was a little past three in the morning.

"Mr. McIntyre just called again. We have a good location. The Pentagon people are trying to contact the task force working with Colonel Howe."

"Good." He rose, stretching some of the fatigue away. "I'll go over to the Tank as soon as I can."

CHAPTER

13

Howe and Timmy climbed through thirty thousand feet, circling upward over Chinese territory as the MV-22 finished collecting the last member of its team and set course back to Afghanistan. It would stay low for a little under two hundred miles, threading its way through the mountains and valleys to avoid any possible detection by radar. At that point it would climb and skirt into eastern Pakistan and then over into Afghanistan.

Though much faster than a helicopter, the Osprey was still a propeller-driven aircraft, and flying low through the unforgiving terrain was not something that could be rushed. It would take close to an hour to reach the relative safety of the Pakistani border.

Timmy proposed to fill that time with a song.

"What sort of song?"

"I was thinking something by Limp Bizkit," joked the wingman.

"If you try that, I'm going to order silent com," said Howe.

"Don't you think there ought to be an M3 hookup in these?" asked Timmy. "Actually, a karaoke rig. That's what we need. I'm going to talk to Firenze about that when we get back."

Laughing in spite of himself, Howe was just about to suggest that Timmy sing "Old MacDonald" when the

AWACS supervisor radioed, requesting that he switch to a new frequency. The moment he keyed in, an Army lieutenant colonel at the Pentagon introduced himself by saying they had found their man.

"Which man are we talking about?"

"An NSC staffer was in the helicopter your plane shot down at the start of the Indian operation," said the colonel, who was transmitting from the Tank through a satellite hookup. "He's alive on the ground nearby."

"How nearby?"

Howe listened as the colonel explained the situation. The location was very close to where they had taken out the helicopters in the Kashmir border area, reachable via a short though significant detour from their planned flight path.

"That's not a pretty place," said Howe. "My briefers this morning were talking about guerrilla conflicts all through that region."

"That's why we need him located and rescued ASAP," said the Army colonel. "He's a valuable commodity."

So are we all, thought Howe, though he didn't say it.

CHAPTER

14

McIntyre stared at the door as it cracked open slowly. The guns were next to him on the desk, but he made no move to get them. He just stared as the door opened.

A teenager took a step inside. He swung a bucket before him, setting it down on the floor and starting to reach back for something outside before seeing McIntyre across from him in front of the desk.

He froze, and for a second they stared at each other, neither able to react.

It was the Indian who moved first. He fell backward out of the building, scrambling away as the door closed. McIntyre followed, still holding the phone in one hand. He cracked open the door, crouching at first, worried that there would be more people outside.

The boy had disappeared. No one else was there as he gradually opened the door wider and wider.

"McIntyre—what the hell's going on?" Brott was asking when McIntyre closed the door and brought the phone back up to his ear.

When he told Brott about the kid, the aide said he should have shot him.

"Yeah," answered McIntyre. "Do you know where I am?"

"Listen, you're going to have to go somewhere else now. Do you understand? Is there a place back where you were that you can hide, near the first place you called from?"

"No," said McIntyre.

"Can you leave the phone on?"

"I'm worried about the battery," he said, glancing at it.

"Get to a safe place and call again," said Brott. "We have assets en route, but it's going to take a while. It may take a long while."

A safe place. McIntyre wanted to laugh. Instead he just looked at the phone.

He couldn't kill a kid who had nothing to do with him, who was just coming to wash the floor or the windows, for chrissakes.

"Yeah, I'll call," he said abruptly, then pushed the End button, got his guns, and went outside.

15

Howe spotted the wreckage of the helicopter strewn across the side of a slope, then began arcing north-westward in the direction of the GPS coordinates he'd been given. He needed to strike a balance: go slow and low enough to be seen by McIntyre, and yet somehow not be slow and low enough to be nailed by some joker with a shoulder-launched SAM.

Couldn't be done. He had to risk a good portion of his butt to save McIntyre's.

Not that he wasn't willing to make the trade. He just wanted to understand the equation.

"One, yeah, I see the debris," said Timmy. "Uh, you got maybe two feet over that ridge, boss."

"Come on, now, I have five at least," said Howe, who was actually close to a thousand feet over the peak that rose two miles off to his left. Howe pushed toward a black-topped road that wound up one of the hillsides, trying to compare it with what the Pentagon colonel had described, which of course was itself second- or thirdhand.

"Got a couple of army vehicles back here," said Timmy. "Uh, two transports, armored car or something in front—near that city."

"That's a city?" asked Howe. He began banking to get lower and take a closer look, putting his nose up slightly to make sure he didn't run into anything while his attention was directed toward the ground.

"Not all of us were born in New York, you know."

"Timmy, that's not even a city in North Dakota."

The radar synthesized a small downtown area of a dozen buildings. The three vehicles Timmy had spotted were moving northward on the road, parallel to the border. Howe looked down through the canopy as he passed, but he was roughly five thousand feet above them and moving close to four hundred knots; he could tell they were vehicles, and thought the lead one had a gun at the top, but there was no way he was reading license plates from here. He took the Velociraptor along the road, looking for more activity. Timmy, studying the passive IR plot from the sensor suite, nudged to his left when he got a flare of something.

"Fire, I think," explained the wingman.

As they turned and started a fresh track, the Pakistani radar over the border—the one that had been targeted by the Indians to start all this—turned itself on.

"Somebody's watching," said Timmy.

"Roger that," said Howe.

"Yeah, but I'd like to go pee on him anyway."

"Eyes on the prize." None of the radars associated with SAMs had come up. The Pakistanis had given the Pentagon a blanket assurance yesterday that no U.S. planes would be targeted, though for security reasons they had not been alerted to the Cyclops One search. The Indians had not agreed to permit "spy flights" over their territory.

The Osprey checked in; they were now thirty minutes away at top speed. He went over his game plan with Howe: If their pickup didn't make his call back on time, they were going to try to drop the SF team near the last phone-in point so they could have a look around. They'd play it by ear from there. An MC-130 was being launched to stand by to refuel the Osprey if things took too long; a second assault team was being rounded up in Kabul, though launching it would take at least two or three hours.

Howe and Timmy would have to start thinking about a refuel soon as well.

"Couple of, uh, Land Rovers maybe," said Timmy. "You got 'em?"

Howe glanced at his tactical screen, where Timmy had cursored them for him. They were moving across an east–west roadway into a village at the southwest, ten miles away from the crashed helicopter.

"You sure those are military?" Howe asked.

"No."

"I'm going to get down there and get close," he told his wingman. "Hang tough."

"Only way to go. Got your six."

Howe dipped his wing. He came over the road at three thousand feet—not counting the nine thousand or so holding the tar up in the mountains.

There were definitely troops in the back of the trucks. As Howe began to pull up he saw a glint of something. He went immediately for the defensive flares, accelerating away.

"They shoot at you?" Timmy's voice was practically a shout.

"You tell me," said Howe.

"Didn't see anything."

"Getting jumpy." He pulled around to his left, angling in the direction of the road, trying to see where the troops were going. A puff of smoke erupted near a cluster of buildings that sat before a bend; the buildings looked like storefronts, with large colorful signs at the top. A pinprick of smoke fluttered across the other side of the bend, near a building. Howe saw movement, people running. Bingo.

"Have some action here," he told Timmy.

"Is it ours?"

"Good question. I'm going to get back with the Pentagon people, see if they can get the Indians and Pakistanis to stop shooting up here."

"Part the Red Sea next," said Timmy.

CHAPTER

16

Duke went over the map with the copilot, trying to figure out the area where their pickup would most likely be. McIntyre's last call had been made from a building on the outskirts of a small town, but he'd been spotted and had to move. He hadn't called back yet.

The pilots in the Velociraptors reported fighting nearby. Whether it had to do with McIntyre wasn't clear.

Duke moved to the back and laid it out for his guys. As he expected, they nodded and threw in a few positive suggestions. Not one of them pointed out that finding the American alive was a serious long shot.

The FBI agent had a pained expression on his face.

"Something up?" the captain asked, plopping into the seat next to him.

"Yeah," said the agent. "I should've brought more coffee. Two thermoses just don't cut it overseas."

"You think we're going to find him?" Duke asked.

"Question is probably whether you'll find him dead," answered Fisher. "But you're kinda stuck, right?"

"If things got tough, could you handle a weapon?"

"Depends," said Fisher. "The place we're landing, that a nonsmoking area?"

Duke started to laugh. "Smoking."

"Then I'll lead the charge."

CHAPTER

17

McIntyre felt the dryness in his mouth, his thirst returning, as he started toward the road. A low fence cut off some of the view to the right; he heard a truck coming and trotted toward the fence for cover, huffing and wheezing as he slid in. An empty flatbed passed a half-second later.

When it was gone he started to the left, walking roughly westward as he cut a diagonal toward the road. There was a ravine and then a rise on the opposite side, but there were some scrub bushes he might use for cover on the left if someone was coming.

As he reached the road he looked down it to his right. It curved sharply northward; he could see the edges and roofs of buildings beyond.

A figure appeared just taking the turn about two hundred yards away. Dressed in grayish white, the man wore a headband and carried a rifle.

Another figure appeared behind him.

McIntyre took a step back toward the building, then realized they'd look for him there. He ran instead along the road as he'd intended, holding the rifles in his hands. He heard gunfire, trucks, aircraft maybe; he sensed that the commotion wasn't about him, but knew that if he stopped he'd be caught in it.

Fear overcame his exhaustion, and he ran at a decent pace for perhaps ten minutes, running at the side of the road as it curved first left and then right. A stone wall started abruptly at the right side of the road about ten feet past the second curve. The wall, chest-high, was made of pure-white stones that all seemed the same size. His breath finally failing, McIntyre ran behind it and collapsed to the ground, unable to move.

When his will returned, he saw that there was a house a short distance away. The whitewashed brick facade was punctuated by oversize windows with elaborate wooden frames, as if the glass were part of a shrine. A mountain rose several hundred yards behind the property, its bluish-black flank punctuated by the brown scar of a road.

McIntyre got up, making sure he hadn't been followed, then began walking to the back of the house. A metal shed sat at the edge of the yard, collapsed on the ground, its roof and walls a bright mélange of rust and white paint. McIntyre went to the shed and examined it: If he had trouble in the house he could retreat there and hold off anyone who came out. He put one of the rifles down, propping it at the back so it would be easy to grab. He hesitated. The gun was easily seen and, if taken, might be used against him. McIntyre hid it under a loose piece of metal siding at the back of the ruins, then went to the house.

There was no door in the back but there were two large windows. Long drapes or curtains blocked off his view of the inside. He went to the one on the left and pushed; it gave way easily.

He stepped inside, heart pounding.

It took a moment for his eyes to adjust, and another for him to figure out that he was in a bedroom. There were two thick mats at the side on the floor, blankets; with a start he realized there was an infant tucked on one side of the bedclothes. Maybe two or three months old, it stared at him with one eye, following as he walked as quietly as he could to the doorway.

Not a baby: a doll. He realized that as he put his hand to the slatted door.

Before he could touch the doorknob, it pushed inward. He stepped back as a woman entered. She saw McIntyre and froze.

She had an infant against her chest. He'd already leveled the gun at her.

"Are you alone?" he said.

She didn't answer. It wasn't clear whether she understood or not. Her face had paled, and her eyes wore the glaze of a death mask.

Somehow her terror terrified him as well, though he was the cause of it. For a moment, he couldn't speak.

"Alone?" he managed, voice cracking.

The woman nodded. He pointed with his other hand, motioning for her to back up. She took a step out into what he thought was a hallway but turned out to be a large common room. There was a TV and some upholstered chairs on one side, an old sewing machine, a pile of fabric, something that looked like a shrine on the right. Beads covered another doorway to the front of the house. A slatted wooden door similar to the one to the room he'd come in through sat opposite it. Staring at it, he went to the door, looked at her; neither she nor the baby moved, or even seemed to breathe. McIntyre rapped on it, then reached down and turned the knob. He flung the light door open with his hand. It was another bedroom, this one with real mattresses, though they were all on the floor. He couldn't see anyone in the tumble of clothes and sheets.

"All right," he told the woman. "I'm not going to hurt you." He reached into his pocket and took out his phone.

The woman's cheeks seemed to implode as the baby began to wail. Tears streamed from the mother's eyes. McIntyre pushed her to the floor; he tried to be gentle but she collapsed in a tumble. He went back to the front room. There was a table there, a washing machine, a stove, an old refrigerator.

Something had happened to his phone. He couldn't connect.

He went to the window, tried again.

Nothing.

Cursing, he punched the Power button twice, staring at the corner of the screen where the battery icon would appear. It had about a third of a charge left; it should work.

There were sounds outside. McIntyre turned and saw something moving by the window, then realized there was someone coming through the doorway. He spun around and pressed the trigger on his gun.

A small child, a boy of four or five, had come out from hiding near the closet where McIntyre had missed him earlier. By the time McIntyre realized what he had shot, the boy's neck had been cut nearly in half by his bullets. In the next moment the child's mother ran into the room, screaming, a knife in one hand and the little baby in the other. He took a step to the side as if he were a matador, pushing her slight body to the floor with his left hand. She rolled to the floor, the knife clattering away as she collapsed in a convulsing heap over the baby.

Blood from the dead child flooded around her. McIntyre took a step back, his head pounding. The whole house seemed to shake.

It *was* shaking: A helicopter was flying nearby.

CHAPTER

18

Duke trailed along the south side of the road just a few yards behind the man who had the point. Their man had called from a point about a mile up the trail, near what passed for a highway here—right in the path of Indian troops pursuing a small band of Muslim guerrillas.

Poor bastard's luck was holding.

He hadn't called back yet, a bad sign. They had the building where he'd called from pinpointed about a quarter of a mile away. There was a village along the highway to the right; to the left the road switched back and forth like a snake, gradually making its way up a mountainside beyond. There were a few small houses in that direction;

they'd check them after the building, then take stock
before reconning the village.

Assuming the Indians and Pak guerrillas hadn't started
taking shots at them yet. The Osprey had let them off a
quarter of a mile behind in a sloping field, then taken off.
Duke had left one of his men and Fisher aboard to play
cavalry if needed.

Duke came to the edge of the field behind the building.
McIntyre had picked a good spot: It would have been easy
to make a pickup here.

Poor dumb bastard. Just had horseshit luck.

"Let's take a look," he told his point man. But before
they could approach the building, two figures dressed in
dark brown clothes emerged from the opposite side of the
field and ran toward the highway. Duke and his trooper
ducked down, watching as the men—obviously guerrillas—checked the road and then crossed. Two others
appeared from near the building, running up near the
road and setting up a position there.

Trucks were coming down the road.

CHAPTER
19

McIntyre fled in the direction of the helicopter,
running toward the building he'd been in earlier. He got
maybe a hundred yards before his lungs started giving out
and he felt stitches in his side like knives. He stopped, then
abruptly fell to his knees. Bright dots of red covered his
knees; he stared at them, thinking for a moment that they
were paint.

Then his stomach started to turn. He felt as if a fist had
taken hold of his insides, punching upward. Vomit spewed
from his mouth; for a minute, maybe more, he retched
uncontrollably, only vaguely aware of his surroundings.

Deep instinct took hold of him then, made him wipe his mouth on his shoulder, forced him back to his feet. He left the idea—the absolute knowledge—that he was a murderer in the pool of puke and began walking toward the road. His legs shook; he was far past his limits of endurance. But the instinct that had picked him up would not let him stop. He walked to the stone wall, paralleling it for a short distance, tripping in the loose dirt and vegetation. Realizing that he could make better time on the road, he put his hand on the wall and went to hop over. He didn't have the strength nor the balance; his legs landed awkwardly, but he managed to get both on the ground and, though stumbling, kept himself going.

Sounds were jumbled in his ears: vehicles—tanks, maybe—and gunfire. He walked a bit farther, maybe twenty feet, then realized something else was coming up the road from behind him. He climbed back over the stone wall and hunkered down, waiting for what seemed like an eternity. As he waited he realized he'd left the other gun behind at the wrecked shack; for a moment he actually considered running back to get it.

Instead he decided to try the phone again. He turned it on, waiting this time as the small screen flashed.

He thumbed the menu, selected, hit Send.

Nothing.

CHAPTER
20

One of the guerrillas fired a bazookalike weapon at the lead truck as it rounded the corner. The missile plowed into the engine and exploded, but most if not all of the men in the back managed to get out before the fire really got going. In the meantime other troops surged up from behind, fanning out in pursuit of the guerrillas.

Duke's communications specialist, who was maintaining contact with the Osprey and F/A-22Vs, slid over to the captain and told him that two Indian helicopters had been reported about twenty minutes away. They were being escorted by fighters. Meanwhile an armored vehicle was making its way up the road from the west; it would reach their position in another few minutes.

It was possible McIntyre was still in the industrial building, but if they were going to check it out, they were going to have to do it now.

"Tell the Osprey and the Velociraptors to stay close," Duke told the como specialist. "As soon as we check that building, we'll bug out."

CHAPTER
21

McIntyre stared at the phone. It was ringing.

It was *ringing*.

He pushed the Talk button and held it to his ear. "Yes?"

"McIntyre, our guys are looking for you," said Brott. "Are you in the building?"

"No," he said. "I—I'm up the road about a mile. There's a house—Wait."

He heard something coming behind him, something big.

"Something's coming for me."

"We're tracking you down," said Brott. "Keep talking. We're very close to you. I have somebody who's connecting with the ground people now. You're looking for a guy named Duke."

"You're breaking up," said McIntyre. "My battery is dying."

"Leave the phone on. Just—"

Brott said something else, but it was garbled. The tank was close now, very close.

McIntyre threw himself down. The heavy stutter of the diesel shocked the ground. He concentrated all of his energy on wishing it away, wishing it past him. As the sound began to fade he turned his head up just enough to see that there were soldiers walking behind it.

One of them shouted.

McIntyre jerked up, drew the gun to his side, and began firing. The dozen or so soldiers in the road dropped down, unsure at first how large the enemy force was.

CHAPTER
22

Timmy had his cursor zeroed in on the armored personnel carrier, waiting for a decision.

"What we doing, Bird One?" he asked Howe over the short-range radio, checking his speed and altitude.

"We're hanging tight," replied Howe. "They're checking the building now. They want to see if he's inside."

A moment later Brott's excited voice, filtered by static as it was relayed across the globe, broke into his helmet.

"There's a tank—something—men firing at him. He's a mile up from the building. He said there was a house."

"I have a BMP," Timmy said, referring to the infantry fighting vehicle leading the attack. Its turret and tracks made it look like a tank. "I'm going to take it out. Tell our guy to kiss dirt."

Howe started talking to Brott, trying to get better details on the location. The Osprey chimed in, but Timmy was so intent on the target, the babble of voices didn't register as one of the mini-bombs slid out from the belly. Guided by a GPS steering package, the bomb's warhead struck within an inch and a half of the center of the BMP's turret. Though the bomb weighed roughly half what an old Mark 82 did, the combination of its shaped high explosives and precision accuracy made it arguably as effective as a thousand-pound bomb, possibly even more.

In any event, such fine points were lost on the truck's crew. The bomb blew through the thin armor skin as if it were the top of a tuna can, incinerating the men. Fragments from the shell of the personnel carrier flew into the squad of men who'd gathered behind it for protection, downing them all. Timmy had no idea of the casualty count; he just saw that he didn't have a substantial target.

"Osprey, I see you," he said, running over the road. He saw a lot of bodies down on the road, and a man running to the left. "Hot down there. Hold off!"

The MV-22 appeared over a ridge as he banked, the rotors on its long arms already pointing upward as it slapped down for a landing. The chain gun began spitting slugs in the direction of the flattened BMP.

Must be an Air Force pilot, Timmy thought to himself. *Doesn't like to take orders.*

CHAPTER

23

The aircraft appeared in front of him, its two arms held up in the sky as if it were descending a ladder. There was a gun at the chin, moving.

An Osprey.

His rescuers.

McIntyre threw down his rifle and held up the cell phone, desperate to make them see that he was on their side. But the gun blinked anyway, its roar so loud that he lost his balance.

He was dead, he knew he was dead.

Gradually he realized that the bullets were landing well behind him, back at the road. The gunfire stopped abruptly, the Osprey whipping around overhead, now behind him, now on the side, once more in front. McIntyre, his eyes filled with dust and his whole body vibrating, got to his feet. The plane stuttered in the air in front of him, then dipped forward.

Shit, the bastards got him! Shit!

McIntyre felt himself pulled forward. He was running; the aircraft was there, intact and unharmed. One of the crewmen was alongside, someone helped him in, they were moving, moving, whipping upward into a surreal swirl, his mind and body twisting in a frenetic mélange.

For a while he seemed to lose consciousness. Not that he blacked out—his brain just couldn't process information. Then McIntyre found himself sitting along the wall of the aircraft, next to a man in a wrinkled business suit.

"I'd give you a cigarette," said the man, "but this is the nonsmoking section."

McIntyre blinked. He knew the man, though the part of his brain that would have connected his face to his name was temporarily out of order.

Andy Fisher.

"So, what do you know about Jolice Missile Systems, anyway?" asked Fisher, smiling and giving him a cigarette despite what he'd said earlier.

CHAPTER

24

Howe took a pass over the road as the Osprey cleared. The SF contingent was already set for a pickup near the building. The Indians, somewhat confused about what was going on, were rushing down the road toward the BMP Timmy had splashed, bypassing the building.

Howe cleared through the pass, then circled back as the MV-22 rendezvoused with the ground team.

Two more Indian troop trucks were coming out from the village. Howe saw them stopping, men pouring from the back.

The lead truck was in the middle of his tactical screen. He hesitated for a second, but it was no contest: A shoulder-launched missile from there could easily splash the Osprey, and even an automatic rifle could do enough damage to take it down.

The small-diameter bomb spun out from his belly, zooming toward the truck. He dished a second one into the other vehicle, at the same time telling the Osprey what was going on. The MV-22 pilot thanked him; ten seconds after the second one exploded, he was airborne.

The Pakistani radar had turned itself off.

"Do we take out the MiGs?" asked Timmy, referring to the Indian planes coming north to help in what they thought was a firefight with Pakistani guerrillas.

"They're not a threat. Hold off," said Howe.

"Damn."

"I love you, Timmy, but sometimes you're a bit much," said Howe, snapping his Talk button off.

Heroes
and Villains

PART FIVE

Heroes
and Villains

CHAPTER

1

Howe listened to the windshield wipers slap as the driver made his way through the security checkpoint at the entrance to the Pentagon. The rain came in wind-driven sheets, as if it were pieces of plywood thrown down from the clouds. Like everything else around him for the last forty-eight hours, it seemed completely surreal.

The cease-fire that had been declared between India and Pakistan was holding, and both countries had corralled, at least temporarily, the radical elements that had driven them to the brink of nuclear winter. India's army had booted out what the spokesmen called "a parcel of radicals"; Pakistan was talking about elections. Meanwhile a committee of diplomats from both sides was discussing Kashmir.

That was just the start. Israel and the Palestinians had scheduled a conference to focus on Jerusalem's future, and there were rumors that the president of South Korea was planning a visit to North Korea to discuss unification.

To hear the talking heads on TV speak—and Howe had spent yesterday in a hotel room doing almost nothing but—the world was entering a new reality, a place where permanent peace was possible. America had stopped a war. That had never happened before. There was awe in people's voices, deservedly so.

Howe, who'd been there—who'd not merely seen the results but actually was responsible for them—couldn't quite process it. He thought of Megan, dead in Cyclops One: Why hadn't she shot down the missile targeting her? It would have been child's play, an easy shot.

Easy, maybe, if you weren't there.

Why had she taken the plane in the first place? Why was she a traitor, a liar?

The questions were a numbness now; he didn't really ask them, didn't ponder them. At the moment no one was really sure she'd even been in the wreck; DNA analyses of the recovered remains had not been finished.

The car stopped. There were umbrellas outside. Howe saw the umbrellas but not the men holding them. He got out of the car; people were smiling at him, congratulating him. He started to walk with them. He forced himself to smile, laughed at a joke about being escorted into the Pentagon, not out. An admiral met him just inside the door, began pumping his hand. Howe fell into place, walking down the corridor. He'd been in the building many times before, but this was different, very, very different; it was almost like being plucked from the stands of a football game, hustled down to the locker room, and suited up to play quarterback.

Or rather, it was as though he'd already done that, and thrown the game-winning pass. He was a hero.

Hero. People actually used that word. Real people, not giddy girls. Admirals and generals and captains and majors and real people.

To Howe, a hero was somebody who jumped out of a foxhole and ran through a jungle as machine guns were firing and mortars exploding, picked up a guy on the ground, and hunkered back to the lines with him. A hero was a Marine, or a grunt, or maybe one of the Air Force Special Tactics guys, or the SF soldiers who'd snatched McIntyre from the ground fight.

A pilot who shot down ten or twelve or even one or two fighters, or went down against enemy ground fire to save a bunch of guys pinned down—who held his breath and his bowels while all hell broke loose—those guys were heroes.

He'd done that, he reminded himself.

"I want to thank you again, Colonel, for saving me."

Howe smiled at the man standing before him, then belatedly realized that it was McIntyre.

Somehow, in new clothes and smelling like he'd just stepped from the shower, the NSC official seemed in worse shape than when they'd reached the base. He seemed to have shrunk, and clearly he'd lost weight, considerable weight, just in the past two days.

"You doing all right?" Howe asked.

McIntyre barely moved his head as he nodded, and pulled his arms tight to his body, forearms pitched outward as if they were the tucked wings of a bird. "Hard to get sleep."

"Yeah, I know what you mean."

Others pressed in behind McIntyre, trying to say hello, trying to add their personal congratulations.

"I'm glad we got you out," said Howe.

"If I can do anything for you, I will," said McIntyre.

Howe watched him recede into the background of the room as the knot of people swelled. They began moving from the reception to a small auditorium.

Megan would have eaten this sort of thing up in her sleek black dress, with her VIP smile. She was used to dealing with these kinds of people, movers and shakers. Why had she fallen in love with him, anyway? Just to use him?

No. He couldn't let himself believe that—couldn't let go of that last strand of respect maybe.

She did love him, even though she was a bitch and a traitor, and if that boot they'd found belonged to her, or if some of that charcoaled metal contained her remains, he'd spit on it.

Part of him would. The other part would just shake his head.

Belatedly, Howe realized everyone around him was rising. The President of the United States had come into the room and was approaching the podium.

Howe felt his face flushing, even before the President pointed him out in the front row. Then D'Amici launched into a short, punchy speech about how America had met the challenge and would continue to do so, thanks to the men and women in this building and the armed services beyond. It was a good, uplifting talk, punctuated by enthusiastic applause.

There was no mention of McIntyre: Doing so might embarrass the Indians at a delicate point. Nor, of course, was there any mention of Cyclops One.

There weren't even any medals. Those would come later, undoubtedly as part of another media event.

Timmy sat a few chairs away from him, beaming like a lightbulb. He was a good kid, a fine aviator—a better pilot than Howe, really, though only time would tell if he had the stomach it took to get into the upper command ranks. Howe thought he did; Timmy even joked with the President when he shook his hand. Good for him.

Howe just smiled and nodded, smiled and nodded.

When the President had left, Bonham came over like a long-lost uncle, congratulating Howe and introducing him to several two- and three-star generals and admirals. He shook maybe three dozen hands, smiled a lot, nodded even more.

"You're going to go far," Bonham told him. "Very, very far. I told you. I told you." The former general leaned close to him. "DNA preliminary result is in," he said in a whisper. "Megan York's on the flight jacket. Positive match."

Bonham pulled back. "You'll be head of the JCS one day. Maybe President."

"Great," was all Howe could think of answering.

CHAPTER
2

Some cases slammed shut, tight as a box, ten minutes after you looked at them.

Others had the look of a crumpled cellophane wrapper stomped on in the mud. They were like overpacked suitcases; no matter what you did to them, something always hung out.

As a general rule, Fisher's cases fell into the latter category. It was the nature of his assignments. Oh, there had been a few easily solved kidnappings back in his salad days, and the murder of a federal judge that had taken all of two cigarettes to close. But these days he could consume half the tobacco grown in Georgia and still have a twenty-three-sided rectangle.

Not that Jemma Gorman wasn't doing her best to lop off the extraneous corners.

"With the identification of the remains and a review of the intercepts, we can reach certain conclusions," said Gorman, holding forth via video from an Air Force base in Alaska. She'd gone there to coordinate the spy flights off the Russian Far East. Either the video reception was lousy or she had managed somehow to get a tan. " 'In a nutshell,' " she said, curling the first and middle fingers of her raised hands, " 'the plane was stolen by parties unknown, but undoubtedly linked to the Pakistani government. It was flown clandestinely to southern Asia, where it was intended to be used against the Indians. Unfortunately, it was shot down and its crew lost during the engagement.' "

"I have a question," said Fisher, pressing the garish green button on the mike in front of his place. He had to hit the green button, then wait for a yellow light on the mike console before pressing a purple button to speak. The gear looked as if it had originally been intended for a Sony PlayStation rig.

"Mr. Fisher?"

"How come you do that quote thing with your fingers when you say *in a nutshell?*"

"Are there any serious questions?" asked Gorman.

"Yup." Fisher pressed the button again. "Me again. Why would the original crew get involved?"

"Which?"

"Start with York."

"We've called your agency in to prepare psychological profiles," said Gorman. "Belatedly, I admit."

"Yeah, but they'll bullshit, don't you think? And, uh, no offense, Colonel, but the FBI's a bureau."

"Money's not a good enough motivator for you?" asked Kowalski, speaking from the Cyclops base.

"Oh, money's good. I like money," said Fisher. "I just haven't seen any evidence of it. And York's rich."

"You can't be too rich," said Kowalski.

"Or dead," said Fisher.

"Money is undoubtedly behind this. We'll find it," said Gorman. "We have forensic accountants hunting it down as we speak. Are there any real questions?"

Fisher took out a cigarette and lit it. Previous experience had shown that he could consume exactly 1.6 cigarettes in the secure videoconferencing center before setting off the alarm.

One of the CIA people asked about the Russian connection. Gorman handled it with her usual smooth aplomb: She changed the subject.

"There's still a great deal of work to do. I'd like to reconvene our working groups at the base in three days. Agreed?"

Fisher looked at his watch as one by one the task force members voiced no objections. He was supposed to see Betty McDonald by eleven, but he wondered if he could talk to some of the lab people before then.

"Mr. Fisher, can you be at the base in three days?" asked Gorman.

"Kinda depends," he said.

"Please try to make it."

"Please? Did you say *please?* What happened, somebody gave you a dictionary?"

"Good afternoon, Andy."

The screen went blank.

CHAPTER
3

Megan leaned against the side of the chair, reading the Web site news report on the computer screen. Still tired from the mission—she'd slept twelve hours straight after getting back—she felt a smug feeling of satisfaction curl around her as she thumbed through the reports.

Everything she'd believed, everything she'd envisioned, had been right.

Luck had played a hand—a large hand. If Cyclops One hadn't been there, two of the Indian missiles would have gotten through.

Luck . . . or maybe the Almighty.

You could think in those terms; it was possible, wasn't it, that God was playing a hand in all this? For surely he'd want the end of war.

There was still much further to go. The augmented ABM system. With or without Jolice, it would be built now.

Thanks to her, and thanks to the weapon. The development teams needed more time, just a little more time, which Congress and the other critics hadn't been willing to give. They didn't understand how weapons development, how research, worked. They weren't willing to give the developers the time they needed to make truly revolutionary systems.

Now they would, assuaged by the first test results and buoyed by the intervention in Pakistan and India. Which had been the point in the first place. Jolice or another consortium, it was all the same to her in the end. Megan knew that for most of the others—for all of them, really—money had been the motivating factor. She didn't care, though: Motives were not important; results were. Results.

Howe was getting a lot of play in the stories. He deserved it.

Maybe in ten years she'd see him again. In five?

In two, if she went ahead with the surgery. She hadn't decided yet. There was time for that. For now, they had to get ready to dismantle the operation; they'd stayed here much longer than they'd anticipated, running all sorts of extra risks.

Risks that had paid off handsomely.

Something clunked behind her. Megan turned slowly from the chair in her room and saw Rogers standing in the doorway. He'd done an admirable job flying Cyclops One by remote control, and yet, uncharacteristically he hadn't bragged about it.

Hope for him yet.

"What are you reading?" he asked.

"Just our reviews. We're a rave. Packed yet?"

Rogers moved his hand from his side. He had a PDA in it. "There's been a change in plans," he said, handing it to her.

There was an E-mail screen and a message from Bonham:

Need you at new test. Details will follow. Sorry.

"This is crazy," she said, thumbing back through it. "Why did he send it to you, not me?"

Rogers shrugged. "Maybe he thinks you'll disagree."

"It's too risky to use the weapon again, and there's no need." Megan felt her face flushing. "I can't believe it. We're set to leave. I already sent half the security team away."

"It's no big deal," he said, taking the PDA back.

"Screw you, it's not a big deal."

Rogers smiled as if he'd like to get the chance.

"I'm going to E-mail him myself," Megan told him.

"Fine with me."

"You think we can fly off here indefinitely?"

"I think if we haven't been seen yet, we won't be seen for a while. I wouldn't worry," Rogers added. "Segrest'll add some stock to keep us happy."

"How do you know that?"

"That's how he is." He put the handheld computer in his pants pocket and smiled.

Had the bastard talked to Segrest as well? There were no phones here, of course, but E-mail was a different story.

"You talked to Segrest?" she asked.

"No. But I know him."

She couldn't tell if this was just his usual blowhard BS or what. Maybe Bonham had told Segrest to pony up, anticipating there'd be a problem.

But why didn't he come to her?

"This isn't Segrest's call," said Megan.

"E-mail Bonham."

"I'm not doing it."

"You think you're the only one who can fly the Blackjack?"

"Rogers, be realistic. We're taking too much of a chance."

"Flying all the way to India wasn't too much of a chance? You wanted to do that, not me."

"We did that so we could get out of here without them hounding us for the rest of our lives."

"We didn't do it for humanity?"

She ignored his sneer.

"I'm sorry," said Rogers, suddenly contrite. "Listen, what's one more mission, more or less?"

"I'm going to contact Bonham," she said.

"Fine with me."

"How are we going to feed the rest of the people on the island?"

"We'll cash them out and tell them to leave once we take off. We blow the plane up with the hangar, just like we planned, and we leave. It's just a few days later than we thought, that's all," said Rogers. "A few days later, and a lot richer."

Megan shook her head. "You're too greedy, Abe. Too greedy."

"Listen, Megan, that's easy for you to say. You were born rich. I just gave everything I have up to do this. Yeah, I agree, the ABM system makes a hell of a lot of sense, but you know and I know that the real reason this got done was because the people behind Jolice stand to gain billions."

"Congress never would have voted to fund more development without the test," said Megan. "We had to have good results."

"I'm not disagreeing. I'm just saying that the motive for a lot of people happens to be money. I'm not arguing the results, but I don't want to be criticized by you because I'm taking my share."

Megan pressed her lips together. There was no arguing with that: Segrest and many of the others were going to profit. She would too. And Bonham—his motivation was political power. None of them were pure.

"I can fly the plane without you if I have to," said Rogers. "I've already talked to the others. They want the money."

"I'll bet." Megan sat in the chair, her eyes focused on the floor. The thing to do now was get out—out, out, out!

But Bonham must have thought the whole thing through. Rogers was probably right: It was highly unlikely they'd be spotted if they hadn't been already.

Still.

"I'm going to E-mail him," she said, spinning back in the chair.

"Be my guest. Let me know if the new plan comes in."

CHAPTER

4

So he was a hero. Now what?

Colonel Thomas Howe, in civilian clothes, sat at the end of the small bar in Alexandria, Virginia. In front of him was a beer that had been poured roughly an hour before, the glass still half full. To his left was a small bowl of stale popcorn. Every so often he'd reach into the bowl and take a single kernel—always a single kernel—examine it, then put it in his mouth and chew deliberately. There was a baseball game on the screen above the bar; Howe stared at it intently, as if he actually cared who won or even knew the score.

He'd wanted to eat dinner by himself, but in the end had been swept up by Bonham with one of the contractors on the laser project and taken to a restaurant somewhere in the Washington suburbs. The parking lot was filled with Mercedes and BMWs, the waiters wore stiff tuxedos, and there were no prices on the menu. Howe had steak. It was very, very good steak, though in truth he would have been fine with a hamburger back in his room at the hotel. He'd practically had to beg to be taken back there, rather than the parties Bonham had lined up.

He had gone inside intending to sleep, but the light was blinking on the phone when he got into the room, and he decided he was better off making himself scarce for the night. He didn't feel like talking any more today.

So he'd found his way here, a suburban bar with green felt paper on the walls and highly polished wood and flat-screen, wide-tube TVs, and beer that cost $7.50 a glass. The bartender, a woman in her mid-twenties with an hourglass figure, smiled in his direction every fifteen minutes or so, but otherwise left him alone. The place was about three-quarters full when he came in, but people had been slowly draining away; there were less than a dozen left now, including two parties in the leather-covered booths at the other end of the room.

He picked up another piece of popcorn.

"Orioles can't hit. They don't understand the value of taking pitches."

Howe turned to his left, surprised by the voice. It belonged to Andy Fisher. The FBI agent pulled out his cigarettes.

"You're a pretty good detective to figure out where I was," said Howe.

"Not really. You're driving a rental that uses a satellite locator." Fisher ordered a beer from the bartender. "Put a head on his while you're at it."

"No, thanks," said Howe.

"Want my theory?"

"On what? Baseball?"

"Cyclops One."

"Probably not." Howe picked up his glass and took a sip.

"You're still hooked on York?"

Howe turned to him, said nothing, then turned back.

"Well, for what it's worth, I think she's alive."

Howe laughed. "How do you fake DNA?"

"Oh, you can fake anything. Look at the bartender. Those aren't real."

Fisher took a long drag from his cigarette, held the smoke in his mouth, then exhaled slowly.

"They didn't have to fake the DNA. There was no flesh in that partial boot. The hair on the flight suit—that's real. Probably a bunch of those spread around. Plane's real too. But the laser's not there, not the inside works."

"You know that for a fact?" asked Howe.

"Not yet. There's going to be traces, just enough to convince us. Like the hair on the flight suit. Something else is going on. I'll bet there was another plane."

Howe's frustration and anger burst past the last restraints. He spun, ready to slug Fisher.

The agent stopped speaking, but only for a second. "Ever hear of Jolice Missile Systems?"

Howe looked down at his fingers, curled into a fist on the bar. His hand was bright red.

"What about Jolice?"

"I have a theory. You want to hear it before you hit me, or after?"

In outline, the theory was simple: The laser plane had to be stolen to help Jolice do well in the augmented-ABM tests. Jolice's performance there had been nothing short of amazing, especially considering that the company had never built an antimissile system before. There were all sorts of connections between the people who ran Jolice and Cyclops, Bonham being the focal point. One of the companies in the web of connections had purchased property in Canada six months before: an old hunter's lodge that just happened to include a lake north of the search area.

But once the FBI agent began talking about the details, things got considerably murkier. Anything close to Cyclops One would have been detected if it had been in the sky during either the ABM tests or the action over Pakistan.

"Unless," said Fisher, "it was something like your Velociraptor."

Howe laughed so loudly the bartender looked over. Fisher held up his glass for a refill.

Howe shook his head. "You don't know jack about Cyclops. The laser's as big as the plane."

"Can't shrink it?"

"Not much."

"What about another stealth plane? A B-2."

"Not going to fit in a B-2."

"No?" Fisher took out a fresh pack of cigarettes and pounded it into his palm. "Want one?"

"No."

"You're telling me it won't fit no way, no how?"

"Well, if you made about a million changes to it and the plane."

Fisher took a long drag on the cigarette. "A million changes? What about a B-1?"

"Still too short."

"Not by that much. In fact, Firenze says the manufacturer proposed a scaled-down version for a stealth aircraft that was only a few feet longer than a B-1."

Fisher put up his finger to quiet him as the bartender approached.

"There's no way," said Howe when she was gone. "You're telling me they stole a B-1?"

"If they could steal Cyclops One, which obviously they did, they could steal anything." Fisher sipped at the beer. "But I don't know. All the B-1s are accounted for."

"There goes your theory."

"No. There goes the easy solution, that's all."

"Why would Megan York be involved? She wouldn't be after the money."

"You sure?"

"She wouldn't be." Howe took a sip of his beer. It tasted stale and bitter in his mouth.

"What do you know about her uncle?" asked Fisher.

"Which uncle?"

"The guy who dropped bombs on Tokyo. The congressman's father."

Howe pushed back from the bar and turned toward Fisher, looking at him as if for the first time. "Let's get some coffee," he told him.

They found a diner not too far away. Fisher noted that it was too upscale to call itself a diner—the walls in the foyer were made of shiny vinyl and looked only moderately tacky—but was somewhat mollified by the coffee, which he said tasted as if it had been made in a garbage can four days before and boiled ever since.

In other words, perfect.

They also allowed smoking.

"Megan was involved in Cyclops and the laser program because she truly wanted to end war," Howe said. "I know it sounds strange, but I'm positive; she could have done anything she wanted. She didn't have to work—she was educated up the yin-yang—but she chose to do this because she believed it. Like a religion."

"You think a laser weapon's going to end war?"

"As part of a global defense system, sure." Howe stared into Fisher's face; he didn't react. "Look what we did in India."

Fisher still said nothing.

"I don't know. It can change things, strategies, make some weapons obsolete. Look, I'm not a peace freak, okay? I just think it'll change things. It already has. A lot of people owe their lives to it."

"What about the new ABM system?" asked Fisher. "What's the deal there?"

"Same thing. The whole system works together. You need a lot of interlocking layers. The augmented ABM system allows us to deal with things we don't have advance warning on. We could strike cruise missiles over the sea: You see, the standard ABM system, the one Congress already approved, can't hit cruise missiles. This is a big improvement." He sipped the coffee. "You don't think it will work, do you?"

"I think most of the things that happen in the world happen because of one of two things," said Fisher, pulling on his cigarette. "Greed and lust. Plenty of greed involved here, if the project goes through."

"Megan wasn't like that."

Fisher shrugged. "She didn't have to be." He picked up his coffee cup, debating whether to ask for another cup. When you found sewage swill like this, you really wanted to load up. But they were running a little late.

"What motivates Bonham?" he asked the pilot.

Howe shrugged. "I don't know. He buys into it, I guess. We don't really discuss philosophy."

"Not money?"

"He wants to be defense secretary someday," said Howe.

"What do you think about talking to him?"

"When? Now? It's after eleven."

"Yeah. If we're lucky we can catch him in his jammies."

CHAPTER

5

Bonham turned on the TV and flipped over to ESPN as he pulled off his jacket and tie. The swirl of parties and receptions over the past forty-eight hours—the whole hail-fellow-well-met routine—was an intoxicating diversion, but it was only that. Segrest and a number of the others were determined to use the weapon for the second stage of augmented-ABM tests, set to begin in a few days. They were trying to isolate him, maneuvering behind his back.

He'd sent Megan York a long, coded E-mail telling her to carry through with the dismantling of the weapon immediately. Her one-word acknowledgment had been uncharacteristically short. There was no way, however, to safely contact her or the others on the island.

ESPN cut to a commercial; he'd have to wait for the scores.

Bonham slipped off his shoes. His paranoia was starting to get the better of him. Things had gone incredibly well, and his idea to set up the Cyclops One crash in India had worked out even better than he had hoped. The satellites had been able to definitively identify the strike on the Indian missiles as a laser discharge, and the investigators would spend months if not years trying to somehow connect the Pakistanis to the theft. In the meantime NADT was getting all the credit for Cyclops Two's performance, and despite the tarnish of the theft Bonham's stock was rising proportionately.

He would have preferred burying the plane in the lake by remote control as planned. But this was the next best thing. The loss of the Velociraptor and the delays in the ABM tests had complicated everything.

Segrest was being greedy. They had achieved so much—why did some people always want even more?

ESPN SportsCenter came on, leading with a story Bonham didn't want to hear: The Red Sox had lost again. They now trailed the hated Yankees by two games.

The doorbell relieved his anguish.

At this hour the security people at the gate ordinarily would insist on a visitor calling ahead. But there were several people they knew well enough to send right through, and Bonham indulged in a brief fantasy that one had decided on delivering a midnight pick-me-up in person.

Colonel Howe's voice punctured the fantasy as Bonham reached the door.

"General Bonham, this is Tom Howe. I need to talk to you."

"Tom."

Bonham pulled open the door. Next to Howe was the annoying FBI agent, Andrew Fisher.

"Come in," Bonham said, trying to remain the gracious host. "Why didn't you call ahead?"

"We didn't want to wake you if you were sleeping," said Fisher.

A lie, obviously. But why?

Pain-in-the-ass Fisher—why hadn't he been reassigned yet?

Bonham led them back up to the den, killing the TV and offering drinks. They declined but he got a Scotch for himself, retrieving a few cubes of ice from the kitchen.

Howe sat ramrod straight in one of the chairs. Fisher sprawled against the corner of the sofa, his feet up on the table.

"Do you know where the Cyclops laser weapon is?" asked Fisher.

Bonham took a sip from his drink. "Is that a trick question?"

"Mr. Fisher's not convinced that the weapon from Cyclops One was destroyed in the crash," said Howe.

Bonham felt a twinge of panic. It was hard enough dealing with Fisher, who at least had a reputation as an eccentric and maverick. Howe not only was smart but had access to people who would listen to what he said. Bonham steadied himself with a sip of the Scotch, letting the bitterness sting at the insides of his mouth. He sat back down and closed his eyes momentarily, as if fighting off fatigue.

"As far as I know," said Bonham, "the preliminary findings from the task force assigned to the disappearance of the plane is going to reflect—well, it's going to say that it crashed in China after a fire aboard, which blew up the laser fuel."

"There's no evidence of that," said Fisher.

"No?" Bonham knew that there was—they had very carefully worked out what the crash would "look" like—but it was not difficult to act surprised. "Did the Chinese get there first? Or the Indians?"

"Maybe the laser wasn't there to begin with," said Fisher.

Bonham looked at Howe and smiled, as if they were in on the joke together. "Well, I guess the satellites and Cyclops Two's sensors were wrong, then."

Bonham walked over to the chair and sat down. The more he heard of Fisher's theory, the easier it would be to discredit it, though the agent had already given him more than enough ammunition.

"There was definitely another laser fired," said Howe. He looked at Fisher, who was still staring at Bonham.

"So, was there another plane?" asked Bonham. "Chinese? Russian? I guess Russian wouldn't work, because they're allies of the Indians. Unless they were being altruistic. Possible, I guess. *We* were."

Howe looked over at Fisher. Fisher, suddenly seeming very reluctant to talk, shrugged again.

Howe rose abruptly. He was angry, though characteristically he controlled his emotion so well that only someone like Bonham, who'd dealt with him for a while, recognized it. "I'm sorry we bothered you, General."

"No, no, listen, I want to hear what you think," said Bonham. "Have a drink."

"It's late," said Howe.

Fisher remained on the couch.

"Tell me your theory," Bonham told him. "Where is the laser if it didn't crash?"

The FBI agent pulled out a pack of cigarettes. "Mind if I smoke?"

Bonham hesitated, but only for a moment. He had clearly discredited Fisher in Howe's eyes, but it would still be useful to know what Fisher was thinking. He balanced that against his growing revulsion of the agent.

"Go ahead," he told him.

"Maybe I better not," said Fisher. He unfolded himself from the couch. "Probably bother your wife."

"I've been divorced from number two for five years," Bonham told him.

Howe was already at the hall to the door.

"He's got my ride," said Fisher. "But thanks anyway."

"Now listen, if you boys have something solid, I want to know what's going on. I know Jemma Gorman is competent, but maybe there's something that's been overlooked."

"I'll let you know," said Fisher, shambling out.

CHAPTER

6

Howe didn't talk until they were back in the car.

"What the hell was that about? We looked like a couple of assholes."

"Pretty much," said Fisher. "What do you figure a condo here goes for?"

"Maybe you like looking like an asshole," said Howe. "I don't."

"According to his financial disclosure, he spent under two-fifty on the place when he bought it two years ago. Just from what I saw, there had to be three bedrooms, I'm going to guess a formal dining room on the other side of that living room, the den we were in, at least two baths plus the master bath. Gated community, yada yada yada—what, million? Million and a half? Tall ceilings, though, so probably even more. TV setup, furniture, paintings, that Chinese vase in the corner? Wasn't Crate & Barrel."

"You blew smoke up my ass, didn't you?" said Howe. "Why did you want to see Bonham? Just to check his condo out?"

"Relax, Colonel. You're too high-strung. Wave at the guards and smile. They did us a favor."

Howe tightened his hands on the steering wheel as he passed out of the condo property.

"The general wouldn't have seen you if you had come alone, is that it?" Howe asked.

"Part of it."

"You should have just said that without bullshitting me about another plane, then. I don't like being bullshitted."

"I ain't bullshitting you, Howe. Unlike everybody else."

"Fuck you." The traffic light ahead was turning yellow. Howe stopped at the intersection and turned to Fisher, who was sitting slumped against the door, his thumb pressed against his lips watching him.

"What's the real story here? Was the laser destroyed or not?" asked Howe.

"Not," said Fisher. "I think."

"You *think?*"

"If I knew for sure, I wouldn't be here, Colonel. I'm sure Bonham has a lot to hide. Maybe just money, maybe more. Whether it's related or not, I don't know. Everybody hides things."

"You think he was paid off to steal the laser?"

"I think that would've come later, once he's involved. Or not: Maybe these guys just figure they can do whatever the fuck they want. Just from what I can see, they control a lot."

"They stole the laser so they could rig the ABM tests."

"Yup." Fisher squirmed in the seat. The light had turned green. "Listen, you didn't expect him to drop to his knees and confess, did you? Of course not. He wouldn't have gotten where he is, much less pulled this off, if he was like that. Hell, kid who breaks into a house isn't even like that. You got some cars back of you."

Howe stepped on the gas. "Why him?"

Fisher shrugged. "Had to be somebody pretty high up. I don't have York, I trust you, so that leaves Bonham."

"Why do you trust me?"

"There was a virus thing in your plane's environmental system that nearly caused you to crash. Firenze compared what was left of it to the system in the plane that crashed and it's identical. Doesn't totally let you off the hook, I know, but it's all I got to go on at the moment."

"There was a virus in my plane?"

"They have a more technical explanation." Fisher took out one of his cigarettes. "You think I operate by gut, huh? I look at you and decide you're honest?"

Howe felt so unsure of so many things now that he didn't know what to feel, much less to say. Bonham and Megan traitors?

"You go by your gut, bad chili dog can throw you off," said Fisher.

"Bonham wouldn't have fooled with that plane," said Howe.

"Not himself, no. May not have been meant to kill any-body; your wingman went a little lower than he was supposed to, and maybe that got him nailed." Fisher shrugged. "I may never know for sure, though. The people who did the controls won't talk to me, which is a hopeful sign."

The entrance ramp to the Beltway was just ahead. Howe put on his blinker, figuring he'd dump Fisher off and go back to the hotel and sleep, maybe for a month.

"I do have another idea," said Fisher, rolling down the window and throwing the cigarette away. "If you're interested."

CHAPTER

7

This time the kid was sitting on a park bench, waiting for him. McIntyre tried to stop himself from moving forward, but it was hopeless: He had as little power to change the dream as he had to change what had happened in Kashmir.

The sky began to change color, subtly shading from deep blue to a greenish gray. Tinges of red appeared near the horizon. McIntyre tried to concentrate on them but his eyes were inevitably drawn to the boy sitting on the bench.

A bell began to ring. At first he didn't know where it was coming from; he thought it was part of the dream. Then he realized it was the doorbell. He threw off the covers, grabbing anxiously for the light at the side of the bed. He wasn't fully awake, but he was thankful for the interruption, glad to be spared the nightmare.

By the time McIntyre pulled on his bathrobe and slippers, he was almost completely awake. The bell continued to sound at regular intervals. His relief faded as he glanced at the clock on the night table. It was just past two o'clock in the morning.

"Yes?" he said when he reached the door to the condo. "Who is it?"

"Colonel Howe," said the voice.

"Howe?" He hesitated for a second, not sure whether it might be some sort of gag or a trick or something. He unlocked the dead bolt but left the chain, pulling the door open a crack before reaching to turn on the light.

"McIntyre, we have to talk to you."

It was Howe. There was someone else with him, though McIntyre couldn't see who it was.

"Colonel . . . it's a little late."

"I know."

Had he heard about the kid and his mother? Maybe he was here to warn him.

McIntyre pushed the door closed, then undid the chain.

The FBI agent, Fisher, was with Howe.

They must know.

He nodded to them both without saying anything, then led them inside. They trailed him to the kitchen. The overhead fluorescents stung his eyes when he snapped them on.

"I'm going to make some coffee," said McIntyre. "Sit down."

"I know we're disturbing you," said Howe.

"That's all right." McIntyre measured out three scoops of Maxwell House into the filter.

"Hit it again," said Fisher.

McIntyre froze. It took a second to figure out that the FBI agent wanted him to make the coffee stronger.

"Mr. Fisher has a theory," said Howe.

McIntyre's fingers trembled and he dropped the scoop.

"Let me do that," said Fisher, getting up. "Have a seat."

McIntyre's robe fell open as he pulled out the chair. He fussed at it in slow motion, pulling it together, feeling suddenly cold in the room. Howe began to talk as he tightened it.

He was talking about the laser, about Cyclops One—not what had happened on the ground.

Fisher thought the laser had been put into another aircraft to be used during the augmented-ABM trials.

McIntyre couldn't believe that was why they were here. He hoped it was, though—he wanted it to be, wanted the boy back alive, back before him, breathing or even crying, but alive.

"It would take a lot of people to pull it off," said Howe.

"Just the right people," said Fisher.

He put the coffee down in front of McIntyre. It was stronger than he was used to; the aroma alone was enough to jar McIntyre's senses. It helped drive the dream away.

"There were traces of the chemicals used in the laser system at the site," McIntyre told them. "I was briefed on the preliminary findings by Gorman."

"Yeah." Fisher took a gulp of the coffee. "There's traces but no real volume. Lab people pointed that out. Unfortunately, we don't have anything to compare it to. I suggested we blow up the other plane but nobody went for that."

He didn't seem to be joking.

"I have another idea," said Fisher. "We watch the ABM test and see what happens."

"They'll know we're watching," said McIntyre. The coffee was good for his head, but what was it doing to his stomach?

"Yeah, you're right," said Fisher. "Probably it's just a wild goose chase."

"I think we ought to do it," said Howe.

McIntyre didn't know if the theory made any sense or not; he just knew he didn't want to be alone, fearing the nightmare might return.

"Tell me more about your theory," he said.

"There's not much more to it," said Fisher.

Howe glanced at him, frowning as if he knew he were lying, but the Air Force officer said nothing himself.

"Another time," said Fisher, getting up.

"Wait." McIntyre looked toward the doorway, as if he expected the child to appear. "It wouldn't be too hard to set up, but I'd have to talk to Dr. Blitz about it."

"Good," said Fisher. "Where's your phone?"

An hour and ten minutes after being woken by McIntyre's phone call, Dr. Blitz sat behind his desk in the West Wing of the White House, trying to run the fatigue from his eyes. McIntyre still looked shell-shocked from his experience in India, and Colonel Howe just looked exhausted. But the FBI agent, Andy Fisher, smirked in a way that suggested he didn't need the coffee he was chugging. His offhand manner was difficult to decipher; Blitz couldn't tell if he was trying to provoke a response or was just naturally a jerk.

"I don't believe any of this," Blitz told Fisher after he outlined his theory.

"Yeah, it is pretty far-fetched," said the FBI agent. "It's out there."

"So why are you here?"

Fisher leaned his face forward as if he were going to say something utterly profound. Instead he scratched his ear. "You came to D.C. from teaching, right?"

"What does that have to do with anything?" Blitz had the distinct impression that Fisher was examining him as he spoke, watching his reactions the way a miner panned through sediment, looking for gold.

"Nothing." Fisher leaned back against the chair, resuming his slump. Blitz knew the agent had been involved in high-level espionage and technology cases before, and assumed he wasn't the dummy he pretended to be.

And then suddenly he realized the import of the question he had just been asked.

"You think I'm involved, don't you?"

"Are you?" answered Fisher.

"I ought to throw you out of here."

"It's happened before."

Blitz locked his eyes with the FBI agent.

"Don't be a wiseass, Mr. Fisher." Blitz turned to McIntyre. "The launch-surveillance satellites can't pick up the laser discharge except under very specific circumstances."

"I'm aware of that," said McIntyre. "But we could use the test monitoring plane, the RC-135."

"It'll tip them off." He looked over toward Fisher.

"Probably," said the agent.

"It won't matter if they know," said McIntyre. "That's the point, isn't it? You want them to know you're watching, because you're hoping they'll do something you can trace. And if they don't and you're right, their missile will miss and that'll be evidence anyway."

Everybody looked at Fisher.

"Anybody mind if I smoke in here?" he asked.

CHAPTER

8

Bonham knew he had convinced Howe that Fisher was crazy, but that didn't completely eliminate the FBI agent as a threat. Before going to bed, he sent another E-mail to Megan emphasizing the importance of carrying out the dismantling program and in the morning picked up where he had left off in his campaign to reassure himself that the others weren't stepping around him. Bonham decided he could use Fisher to his advantage and discreetly mentioned the FBI agent's visit during several phone calls. He also decided he would have it out personally with Segrest, and so arranged to have lunch with him. Segrest suggested a Chinese restaurant well out of town; Bonham didn't particularly care for Chinese food but he decided to go there anyway, since the setting would give them freer rein to talk.

At twelve-thirty in the afternoon he left his office and drove farther out into rural Virginia, passing green hills divided into horse paddocks by thick, flat rails of white pine. If he hadn't been following the directions carefully, he would have missed the turn, and if he hadn't known about the restaurant, he never would have seen it. It was an old farmhouse marked only by a small wooden sign near the driveway.

Inside, the two-hundred-year-old structure had been gutted and given a sophisticated sheen. Wide chestnut planks with thick varnish greeted him in the foyer, along with a very short and thin Asian-American who bent nearly to the waist. The man led him into a large room whose far wall was now old brick; spotlights played on the empty fireplace, and two waiters stood in the corners, though there were no other guests at the small tables.

Bonham told him he was waiting for someone and opted for water rather than a drink.

Eric Hovanek walked in a few minutes later, towering over his host as he was shown to the table.

"Where's Segrest?" demanded Bonham.

"Relax, General. Something came up." Hovanek ordered a martini. "They don't have menus," he told Bonham. "You can ask for anything you want or just let them feed you."

"Why isn't Segrest here?" Bonham thought of leaving: Hovanek was just a sophisticated gofer, a former stockbroker whom Segrest had befriended. After a short stint as Segrest's personal "moneyman," he had taken on the role of clone, sitting on boards and attending meetings the wealthy young bastard was too lazy to attend.

"Something came up. You said the meeting was important, and so he sent me instead of canceling at the last minute."

Hovanek's cell phone rang before he could say anything, and Bonham found himself staring at the thick layers of cloth on the table, which alternated between white and mauve. The host soon returned with Hovanek's martini; Bonham asked for a Glenfiddich. Hovanek was still on the phone when a young waiter appeared with a dish of pickled sprouts.

"Cash flow problems," said Hovanek, his voice shaded toward an apology after he snapped the phone closed. He pointed to the sprouts.

The waiter appeared with a plate of noodles slathered in sesame sauce and topped by a row of shrimp and cucumbers.

"This is to get us in the mood," said Hovanek. He took his chopsticks and sampled the food. "Excellent."

"I want to talk about the FBI agent, Fisher," said Bonham.

"Why?"

The host appeared with the Scotch. Hovanek told the man to go ahead and feed them with whatever the chef decided they should have.

"You worry too much, General," said Hovanek. "Everything is fine. You yourself are doing well. I heard your name mentioned for assistant defense secretary the other day."

"Fisher wants them to watch the tests for a laser," said Bonham.

"Is that a fact?" Hovanek was neither surprised nor, from what Bonham could see, concerned in the least.

"All right," said Bonham. He pushed his seat away from the table. "Make sure everyone knows. My way or no way."

"General, you haven't eaten. You really should." Hovanek smiled up at him. "Mr. Young will think you don't like his food."

Bonham drove around for a while, trying to seperate his distaste for Hovanek from what the lackey had said. He hadn't actually said anything meaningful, Bonham finally decided, but whether that meant Segrest really was up to something or not, he couldn't tell. Exhausted and finally hungry, Bonham pulled off at a McDonald's around three to get something to eat. It was the last place anyone would look for him, but as soon as he stepped through the doors and approached the overlit front counter, he felt comfortable, a teenager again slipping away from high school to grab a burger after school.

Bonham ordered a Big Mac Meal, declined the super-size option, and walked with his tray to the back. He started to grab for a newspaper along the way, then thought better of it. He needed a break from everything for at least a few minutes more. He was getting too paranoid to function.

A young father was fussing over his four-year-old son in the next booth, dabbing his chin with a napkin. Bonham gave the guy a smile, watching the pair as he ate. The kid was reasonably cute, and the father was attentive; they would have made a decent commercial as they walked out the door hand in hand.

It was a bit pathetic that a grown man had to play baby-sitter in the middle of the day, Bonham thought. But what the hell.

The food put him in a better mood. Bonham listened to an old Johnny Cash CD on the way back to his office. Once there, he whipped through some paperwork BS and returned a few phone calls, including a backgrounder for a *Washington Post* reporter, who traded a bit of gossip about one of the senators on the Intelligence Committee. The bad taste of Hovanek gradually washed away, and by the time he walked into his condo a little after eight, Bonham was in an expansive mood. The Red Sox were on the tube: They had a 3–0 lead over Baltimore. Bonham jacked up the volume and pulled off his jacket and tie, walking to the bathroom. As he turned on the light, something moved behind him. Before he could react, the back portion of his skull seemed to implode.

CHAPTER

9

Fisher hated murder scenes, not because he didn't like looking at dead bodies, but because the forensics people went ape shit if you disturbed something, which in their eyes you did simply by breathing in the air. Poke your head inside wearing anything less than a hermetically sealed body bootie, and they ran out to their vans to plunge pins into their voodoo dolls.

Fisher put little stock in voodoo, and cared even less who he pissed off, but he did nonetheless strain to put himself on his best behavior, since getting a report without the usual red tape depended on it. The crime scene guys— state police, though he wouldn't hold that against them— working Bonham's condo were relatively low key, once he put out his cigarette. Still, they said flat out they wouldn't let him in the bathroom where Bonham had died until they finished their work there; at the rate they were going, that seemed likely to happen sometime next winter.

Fisher contented himself with booting the general's computer in the den, examining its browser and E-mail programs for anything of note.

The history folder was completely clean, and Fisher couldn't find anything in the trash folder, either. Bonham obviously had an industrial-strength scrubber program loaded. Fisher looked over the program list; there were two different baseball games, but otherwise nothing that didn't come stock on the machine, a relatively new Dell.

"What are you doing?" demanded one of the investigators as she walked in behind him.

"What the FBI always does," said Fisher, keying up the hidden directories. "Screwing up the crime scene."

"Well, I'm glad you admit it."

"Got a scrubber program in here I can't find. Probably want to send it over to our lab." Fisher leaned away from the machine, pointing to the screen.

"Who exactly are you?" asked the woman detective.

"Andy Fisher, FBI."

"Why are you here?"

"Oh." Fisher leaned back from his chair. "One of the uniform guys figured out who Bonham was and called us, and for some inexplicable reason the person who got the call actually knew how to follow the right procedure and tell me about it. Lightning has to strike somewhere, as improbable as it sounds."

"You're a wiseass."

"Yeah, actually, the guys in the field office are usually pretty sharp. It's when you get to headquarters that you get the lobotomy."

"I'm Susan Doar," said the woman, holding her hand out to him. She was in her mid-thirties, with just enough of a cynical smile to hint that this wasn't her first murder case, nor the first time she'd dealt with the FBI.

"Andy Fisher. Mind if I smoke?"

"You can't smoke in here."

"Everybody says that." Fisher got up. "Seriously, we want the computer. If you send it to the Secret Service or,

God forbid, the NSA, you'll never find out what's on it. Those guys are close to unbribable."

"Someone from the Defense Department is on his way over," said Doar.

"They're not so bad," said Fisher. "Except they tend to lose stuff. I think they actually end up using it for target practice."

"I'll use my own lab, thanks," said Doar.

"You got a time of death?"

"Autopsy hasn't been done."

"I never trusted those doctor types."

"Neighbor heard the TV blaring last night about eleven, called over to complain, banged on the door, got worried," said Doar.

"Nosy-neighbor type?"

"I think he was pissed off because he couldn't get to sleep," said Doar. "Left a nasty message. Then maybe he felt guilty."

"How did our hero die?" asked Fisher.

"Hit the back of his head in the bathroom. Slipped getting out of the tub."

"Can I take a look?"

"If they're done with the pictures. He's not wearing anything."

"I knew there was some reason I came."

"That's what I said."

The downstairs bathroom was bigger than Fisher's apartment. The general lay sprawled faceup on the floor, a trickle of blood coming from his ear. He seemed to have slipped coming out of the whirlpool bath, smacked his head on the side of the marble wall where the bath was recessed, then pirouetted down and smacked the back of his head again.

"We took hair and some skin off the wall," said Doar pointing. "Probably open and shut."

"Bathrooms are very dangerous places," said Fisher.

"Yeah."

Fisher knelt near the door. The scene was laid out perfectly, the distances precise, soap in the bottom of the tub, water almost but not quite turned off, a towel pulled cockeyed off the corner of the rack as if Bonham had started to grab for it.

He rose and went back into the den. They'd hit the mute on the TV, but otherwise had left it on, just as they'd found it. Fisher looked around, re-creating the scene from the other night when he and Howe had come over, comparing it to now. Bonham had thrown his jacket down, as though he'd just come in.

"Was he drinking?" Fisher asked.

"It's not obvious," said the investigator. "No glass or anything."

Fisher walked back to the bathroom. There was a small TV in the corner. It was off.

"What?" asked Doar as he started to leave.

"Open and shut," said Fisher.

CHAPTER

10

Howe heard about Bonham's death just as he was suiting up to fly out to Alaska. The lieutenant who brought the information had it third- or fourthhand and couldn't add anything beyond the simple fact that the general had died in an accident.

Howe didn't know what to feel or even think. Away from Fisher, he'd started to doubt the FBI agent's theory, though he couldn't really dismiss it. He nodded to the lieutenant, then continued getting ready; he had to be in Alaska by nightfall to help prepare the monitoring mission. He went out to the planes with Timmy feeling a little numb; he could focus on the plane and his job well enough, but could only manage a grunt or two as his wingman made his usual jokes about anything and everything.

They were finished with the preflights and about to strap in when a Humvee flew around the corner and nearly crashed into one of the small tractors standing on the apron. The lieutenant who had told Howe about Bonham jumped from the truck, running toward the planes and waving his arms like a madman. Howe leaned over the side of the aircraft; the lieutenant spotted him and began gesturing madly that he should come down. He produced a cell phone from his pocket, holding it up toward Howe.

"FBI wants you," said the lieutenant when he reached the tarmac.

"FBI?" asked Howe as he took the phone. "Fisher?"

"Last time I checked," answered the agent.

"This better be important."

"Tell me something: How big a sports fan was Bonham?"

CHAPTER

11

"The whole idea of offshore banks, Andy, is that they make it almost impossible to get access."

"Yeah, but not for you, Betty." Fisher fed another cigarette into the forensic accountant's fat fingers.

Betty lit the new cigarette off the one in her other hand. "You're right about that condo. Worth a hell of a lot more than he said. But the transactions are there to back up the price."

"Have to be offshore accounts."

"I need account numbers. At least banks."

"They're not on the computer, not according to the state police lab guys. I sent Bartolomo over to help them."

"Oh, that was smart."

"Hey, for a computer geek, he's almost human," said Fisher. "I had this other brainstorm while I was talking to him."

"Spare me."

"He says you can track whether inquiries are made on bank accounts from ATMs and phones and things, because their networks log all the contacts."

"What's the point?"

"Well, see, if the four people who were supposed to have died in Cyclops One aren't dead, then they're probably checking their bank accounts. We just look at the statements, right?"

"I don't know if we can come up with those kinds of records," said Betty. "Besides, not everybody's as paranoid about their money as you, Andy."

"I'm not paranoid about money."

"Excuse me. *Cheap* was the word I was looking for. You have the companies laid out." Betty suddenly put on her motherly voice, the one she usually used before telling Fisher to hit the road. "Put some pressure on the officers and board members, things will start to open up."

"Or maybe a few more people will slip in their bathrooms," said Fisher. He rose.

"We'll do what we can," she told him. "No promises."

"Thanks, babe. Get ahold of me if you think of something else, okay? I'm counting on you to break this sucker open."

"Where you going?"

"Alaska. I hear it's almost warm this time of year."

★　★　★

Fisher got about halfway to Dulles Airport when he realized he was being followed. It was the sort of break you couldn't pray for, but the agent managed to contain his glee, unholstering his revolver—the two hideaways were small automatics—and putting it on his lap. He got off the highway and drove a bit farther; when he was sure he hadn't succumbed to wishful thinking, he started hunting for a bank. Finally he spotted one on the wrong side of the highway; he veered across traffic and pulled into the ATM lane around the back.

His pursuer was obviously driving his own car, because rather than chancing the traffic he drove down the road, turned, and then came back, pulling in front as if he intended to use a teller inside. Fisher, about three vehicles from the machine, jumped out of his car, cell phone in one hand, gun in the other.

He had to dial with his finger through the trigger guard. Doar picked up on the second ring.

"Listen, Doar, this is Andy Fisher, FBI."

"Mr. Fisher—"

"I have your murder suspect in view, parking lot of FirstWay Bank out here in Taylorville."

"Murder suspect? Who?"

"Bonham was a Boston Red Sox nut. If he was having a bath, he would have had the TV on in the bathroom and probably been drinking a Scotch. And don't buy the justifiable-homicide play."

"But—"

"Gotta go."

Fisher threw himself down maybe a half of a half of a half-second before the bullet hit the side of the bank where he'd been peering through the window toward the front. The next three shots chipped the sidewalk, sending chips ricocheting everywhere but not actually hitting him. He rolled to his feet, gun in hand, but whoever had fired at him had already retreated. Fisher scooped up his phone and gave a little wave at an old lady staring at him from her car.

Doar was gasping on the other end of the line.

"Yeah, I'm okay," said Fisher. He walked over to the wall, looking to see if he could find a bullet. "I'm thinking the idea was more to get my attention than to hit me, but they wouldn't have cried about that, either."

Fisher walked over to where the gunman had fired from, stooping down to see if he could find any shells. He could hear sirens in the distance.

"Tell me why Bonham is a homicide," said Doar.

"I told you, he didn't have the Red Sox on in the bathroom," Fisher told her. "I checked: They were on national TV that night until after midnight because the game went fifteen innings. I have a plate number I need you to run. You might want to tell the uniform guys about it too."

"But—"

"Yeah, a pro wouldn't have been so inept, so the idea is probably just to divert attention for a while. Shame, though: Nobody's really tried to kill me in must be at least six months, and that was just my boss."

PART SIX
Unforgiven

CHAPTER

1

Of all the people Howe might have expected to greet him in the dimming light as he stepped down from the F/A-22V after arriving in Alaska, Jemma Gorman rated close to the last.

"Colonel Howe."

"Colonel Gorman."

"You can call me Jemma."

"Yeah," said Howe.

"I need to talk to you."

"Okay."

"Privately."

Howe looked around. The nearest person, one of the airman tasked to look after the jet, was a good fifty feet away and wearing ear protection besides. But Gorman was already walking down the ramp.

Elmendorf, the large air base near Anchorage that served as the home drome for the 3rd Wing, was overflowing with units associated with the tests. Because of that, Howe, Timmy, and the RC-135 had been sent farther north to a somewhat sparser base that once prepared spy planes for flights near—and in a few cases over—the old Soviet Union. The base now housed a hearty squadron of F-16s, A-10As, and assorted support and reconnaissance craft, as well as accommodated a variety of transients and the occasional stray. It didn't seem particularly busy at the moment, and in fact most of its resident aircraft were off participating in an exercise with RAF and Canadian aircraft.

Though it was summer, the air temperature was dropping through the forties; even seventy would have been a severe shock after Florida. Howe followed Gorman along the edge of the tarmac, curling his arms in front of his chest as the chill started to eat through his flight suit.

"The plane that went down in China, during the Indian-Pakistani exchange. I don't believe it had the Cyclops weapon in it," said Gorman.

"Fisher said that."

"Yes, well, even Mr. Fisher is occasionally correct." Gorman continued to walk. "I know you've been assigned to look for laser emissions during the ABM tests," said Gorman finally. "I want to work with you. We're not technically part of the ABM tests, but I want to make sure that the laser plane doesn't show up—or, rather, if it does, that we know about it."

"That's not up to me," said Howe.

"That's true," said Gorman. She stopped, seeming to find something in the distance interesting. "I still think it's likely the Russians took the airplane. But we have no evidence, and while Mr. Fisher's conspiracy theory appears to be yet another of his wild goose chases, I have to admit that it cannot be easily dismissed."

Her words could be interpreted as trying to talk him out of the theory that Fisher had: that the laser had been stolen by an "inside" group. Then again, they weren't necessarily wrong. It still made more sense to Howe that a "traditional" enemy had taken the weapon: China if not Russia, even Pakistan or India, someone with considerable resources. He knew from McIntyre that the CIA people also still thought that.

"My mission is to recover the weapon, wherever it is," said Gorman. "It doesn't matter to me where it is or who took it. I want to get it back."

"Me too."

Her hands bounced as she emphasized her point. "I have broad authorization to carry out my mission. I can shoot down the plane if I see it, or do what I have to to capture it. I can go anywhere—*anywhere*—to get that done. I can call on just about the entire military if I have to."

"Uh-huh," said Howe.

"I want you to work with me voluntarily," she added.

"Doing what?"

"Coordinating your search. I'll have support assets, fighters, whatever else we need."

"The plane probably isn't going to show," said Howe.

"We can't take a chance."

Howe could see her breath in the cold air. Her face behind it was blocky, not attractive in the least. She was very different from Megan.

If this was a guy standing in front of him, would Howe consider how ugly he was?

No. He wouldn't be thinking about Megan, either.

"Look, Tom, we want the same thing here. Andy—Mr. Fisher—he comes up with these conspiracy theories all the time. He goes off on a tangent, gets burned, comes back. Occasionally he's right, but more often he's wrong. In the meantime he wastes a lot of time and resources."

"I'm going ahead with the monitoring during the test," said Howe. "I have orders."

"Yes, I agree." Gorman pitched the top half of her body forward. "Some people might interpret what you and Mr.

Fisher did in Washington as an end run around me—around my task force and my authority. A political move."

"I'm not interested in politics."

"Everybody's interested in politics."

"I'm not."

Gorman studied his face. "Okay. I'm going to be part of the operation."

"It's not my call," said Howe.

"That's right. Look, we can do more than just sound the alarm if the light goes on in the dark. I want to make sure you have the resources to get the job done," she told him.

"Usually when somebody talks to me about resources, my budget lines get cut."

"I want to plan the operation together."

Howe shrugged.

"All right. Have it your way. I can play hardball too."

CHAPTER

2

Brooklyn, New York, was in many respects exactly the same as Alaska: It had a colorful cast of exotic animals, the natives were eccentric though in general tolerant, and the scenery could be breathtaking.

"So you got on the wrong plane?" said Karl Grinberg. The special agent was an expert on the Russian Mafia and, in times gone past, the KGB. "I would've thought the taxis gave it away."

"They have taxis in Alaska," said Fisher. "It's just their drivers actually speak English."

"Old joke, Fisher. If you really do have to catch a plane, get to the point." Grinberg glanced up at the waitress, motioning for more of the muddy dregs they claimed was coffee. "I for one have to get some work done today."

"Here's the thing—you figure Borg would miss?" asked Fisher.

"Never."

"You think he would work for the Russian government?"

Grinberg started to laugh.

"That's funny?"

"Well, Borg *would* kill anybody if there was money in it."

"So he would?"

"No fuckin' way. He hates the Russians."

Borg was, of course, Russian. He was also one of the top four or five contract killers in the country, and he'd been tracked as the probable shooter in Fisher's bank parking lot. Through a rental car, no less.

"How about if it were a renegade group, old-line commies or something?"

"Only thing he hates worse than the Russian government are Russian commies."

Fisher leaned back in the seat as the waitress poured the coffee into his cup. He reached into his pocket and took out the digital photo from the bank's surveillance camera, which Doar had politely faxed to him.

"That him, you think?"

"Jeez, Fisher, if you can even ID this as a human being you get points."

"I don't think it was really Borg."

"Not if he missed."

"Well, he might have been paid to miss. Thing is, I don't have much time, and I want to track him down."

"You're out of your mind. He'll chew you up."

"You have an address?"

"I can give you a couple of hangouts. Fisher, seriously, Borg'll have you for lunch."

"Hope the food's better than here."

★　★　★

Rostislav had been a duke of Moravia in the ninth century, but why he had given his name to a social club in Brooklyn was unknown, even to Grinberg. Nor had the FBI special agent supplied Fisher with much information about the club itself, except for the obvious.

Then again, Fisher would have gone in through the kitchen anyway, especially when he saw the only thing between him and the open doorway was a barbed-wire fence. He scaled it, flashed a laser pointer at the video surveillance camera to blind it, and then walked in, nodding at a man in checked chef pants who was sipping a drink near the burners. A kid with some kitchen garbage and a large knife turned near the door but froze as soon as he caught sight of Fisher's Bureau ID, which he was holding out in his hand.

That, or the pistol in his other hand.

The kitchen opened into a dining room on the left and a hallway to the right. Fisher went to the right, pushing open the second door on the left and entering the bar. There he found himself eye to eye with a six-foot-six bartender who had a blackjack in his left hand.

"Magnum," said Fisher, holding the .44 Ruger under the man's nose. "I'm just here to talk."

The bartender said something in Russian regarding Fisher's ancestry.

"Actually, I was adopted," said Fisher. "Borg, I need a word."

A dozen eyes in the dimly lit room were blinking at him. For a second Fisher feared his Hollywood entrance had been totally wasted on a collection of Mob honchos.

"*Da.* Who the fuck are you?"

"Guy you tried to kill." Fisher stepped past the bartender, his pistol still aimed at the man's head. That probably didn't bother Borg much, but the hit man wouldn't kill Fisher without giving him a chance to clear up the slur on his reputation.

Then, of course, he'd kill him.

"No one I try to kill lives," said Borg. He was short, five six or eight at the most, and looked more like an out-of-work accountant than a paid killer, undoubtedly one reason he was so successful.

Fisher pulled out the photo of his would-be assassin. "This son of a bitch wants me to think he's you. He used one of your pseudonyms and a credit card from a job you did to rent a car. That's the license plate. You can run down the paperwork yourself."

Fisher slid the paper along the bar.

"There was another hit a few days back near D.C., not quite your style," said Fisher. "I thought you might have some ideas about who did it."

"Why?"

"For one thing, I think it was probably this asshole," said Fisher. "And for another, I hear you're a nice guy who always cooperates with federal agents."

Borg snorted.

"Looked like an accident," said Fisher. "Like a guy got out of a tub and slipped. But it was definitely a hit."

"Don't know him."

"Dead man's name was Bonham. Mean anything?"

"*Nyet,*" said Borg.

"Accident thing remind you of anybody?"

Borg shook his head.

"Well, all right," said Fisher. "I'd like to stay for lunch, but I have to get going."

As Fisher was talking, the bartender had started side-stepping toward the end of the bar. He was now about two feet from the door.

"You know, the thing that pisses me off is the paperwork involved if I shoot this thing," said Fisher leveling the pistol. "I mean, I shoot one bullet, I empty the gun, just about the same amount of work. I shoot you or I shoot everybody, I still have to fill out a fistful of paper. Kind of pisses me off, you know what I'm talking about? At least the bullets make nice big holes."

The bartender stopped. Fisher pushed up the panel at the far end and walked toward the door at the front of the room that led to the street.

"You decide you know who that is, let me know. My number's on the paper," he said. "Thanks are not necessary."

CHAPTER
3

Within two hours of their conversation, Jemma Gorman had managed to tug her connections hard enough to get a terse directive sent directly to Howe, designated for his eyes only: COOPERATE w/TSK GP.

It was signed by the head of the Air Force.

Was Gorman just protecting her turf? Or something else?

Bonham's death, Megan, Gorman pulling strings . . . Who could Howe trust?

Himself. Timmy.

Fisher?

Not necessarily, but maybe.

Not Gorman, certainly.

McIntyre?

Maybe McIntyre. Although it might be possible that the shoot-down and rescue had all been set up.

It was a snake maze, one question suggesting a dozen others.

Howe tried to push away the questions and doubts, concentrating on planning the mission. With the tests now roughly twenty-four hours away, he presided over a briefing session to go over the basic layout of his plan with

Gorman and her team leaders. The main furniture in his borrowed office consisted of a pair of desks that seemed to date from the discovery of aluminum as a workable metal; he pushed them together as a crude map table and had the others crowd around while he outlined his skeletal game plan. Gorman, flanked by two stone-faced intelligence officers, stared at the map impassively, listening as he went over the main points of the mission.

One thing he had to give Gorman: She had serious resources at her beck and call. All of the assets she'd amassed for the surveillance around Russia were available for the mission. That meant not only a radar plane and a full squadron of F-15s but three air tankers and assorted support personnel. She also had Army Special Forces units ready for any contingency.

Definitely a first-team operation, though whether it was on his side or not was an open question.

They set up the mission carefully. The RC-135 and F/A-22Vs, along with any support craft detailed to them, would be part of the overall test operation, though their actual role was "covered" by a story that they were conducting tests of the F/A-22V radar systems in conjunction with the missile firings, not looking for lasers. The cover was unlikely to fool anyone who knew much about the aircraft, or what was going on, but given the fact that Cyclops One had not even been officially "found" in China yet—or Canada, for that matter—it would at least give a spokesman something to tell the press if asked.

In summary, the plan was extremely simple: The RC-135 with its monitoring gear would fly a figure-eight pattern around an arc at the northwest side of the test area, which Howe had concluded would be the most likely place for a laser plane to fly, given the location of the Navy ships launching the cruise missile targets and monitoring the tests. Gorman's two telemetry gathering aircraft would also be airborne, positioned to cover a northern approach to the test site.

"I want a Special Forces strike team in the air with you, ready to follow the aircraft," said Gorman when he finished going through the highlights. "The laser plane has to land somewhere. We take it as soon as it lands."

"What if it goes back to Russia? Or China?"

"Then we'll take it there."

"It's not going to be in Russia. Or China."

Howe looked up from the table. Andy Fisher had arrived and was standing at the door with one of Gorman's security policemen, looking as if he'd just wet his pants.

"Tell my buddy here he's not getting detention, Jemma," said Fisher.

Gorman nodded and the man retreated.

"You don't have to worry about Russia or China," said Fisher, coming over to the map.

"So where should we be?" Gorman asked sarcastically.

"Jeez, Jemma, you want me to do everything for you? Hey, Colonel," Fisher said to Howe. "Sorry I couldn't answer your phone calls—I was too busy getting shot at. Crimped my schedule."

"Another satisfied ex-lover," said Gorman, "or just someone who objected to you smoking?"

"Act still needs some polish, Jemma, but you're getting there."

Fisher bent over the map, putting his nose so close to the paper he could have sniffed it. He studied it for a long time, then looked up. "That dotted line there is you?" he asked Howe.

"Yes."

"Long flight, no?"

"It is," said Howe.

Fisher snapped back up straight so fast, Howe thought he'd get a nosebleed.

"You're going to fly around out there the whole time?" Fisher asked.

"Pretty much."

Without saying anything else, the FBI agent left the room.

Of the many human activities Fisher did not fully comprehend, the insertion of polished steel into cork surely rated among the most mysterious. The preliminaries themselves were relatively transparent: One wound up the body with appropriate consumption of alcohol. But the unleashing of the steel—what was this, some primitive throwback to prehistoric hunting?

As a trained detective, Fisher knew only one way to discover the secret of this arcane art: He went to the dart line in the base club and asked one of the participants to explain.

After getting his attention by tapping his back.

"Shit, you made me miss the dartboard completely," said the man, a Special Forces captain named Kenal Tyler.

"Guess I owe you a beer," said Fisher. "Come on and I'll pay up."

"Damn it," Tyler groused as the Air Force major he'd been playing retrieved the darts and went to the line. He nonetheless walked over toward the bar, where Fisher was catching the attention of the airman who served as barkeep.

"Make it a pitcher," said Tyler. "I have to keep my boys happy."

"Not a problem," Fisher told him. "I'm Andy Fisher. FBI."

"So?"

"You're leading one of the assault teams tomorrow. I want to come with you."

"What?"

The bartender came over with the glasses of beer Fisher had ordered, then went back to get the pitcher.

Tyler's "boys"—all sergeants who looked to be in their thirties and older than the captain—drifted over to see what was going on.

"I was looking at the way they plotted out the mission, and you guys are going to make the arrest," said Fisher. "So I want to be there."

The captain gave him a dubious look, then left to take his turn at darts. One of the sergeants—a tall, skinny black guy with a Midwestern accent named Daku—asked if Fisher was *the* Fisher.

"Probably," said Fisher. "You here to subpoena me?"

"You were with Duke and his team," said the sergeant. "Right? In Kashmir?"

"My summer vacation."

The sergeant started laughing, then told the others that Fisher had been involved in the rescue of McIntyre. "He got a truckload of Dunkin' Donuts coffee flown into Afghanistan. Met them on the tarmac," added the sergeant.

"If you're going to have coffee, go for the best," said Fisher.

"Did you get doughnuts too?" asked one of the soldiers.

"Boston Cremes. I thought they weren't stale enough," said Fisher. "But you know, war zone, you make sacrifices."

"Hey, Captain, is Fisher riding with us?" asked Daku when Tyler came back.

"We don't need no FBI guy watching over us," said the captain. "Aren't you supposed to be on Colonel Gorman's plane?"

"Do I look like a masochist?"

"This guy's all right," said the sergeant, who proceeded to give a thumbnail account of Fisher's Kashmir adventure.

"This true?" Tyler asked. "You worked with Duke?"

"Duke's all right," said Fisher. "For a guy who doesn't smoke."

"How do you know where the action's going to be?" asked Tyler.

"I used one of those fortune-teller machines at the airport," said Fisher.

Tyler frowned.

"Ah, let 'im come, Captain," said the sergeant.

"Isn't up to me," said Tyler.

"That's true," said Fisher. "I can just assign myself."

"Bullshit you can."

"Or I can work through channels, have my general call your general."

"This is Colonel Gorman's operation," said Tyler.

"You really going to let a blue suit tell you what to do?" asked Fisher.

Tyler made a face.

"Tell you what," said Fisher. "I'll play darts for it. I win; you take me."

"I can't do that," said the captain.

"You can't beat me or you can't take me with you?"

"I can beat you."

"Bring the dartboard outside and let's see," said Fisher.

"Outside?"

"Yeah. I don't want to hurt nobody."

The others laughed. Tyler agreed, and the entire barroom soon assembled outside. At Fisher's suggestion the dartboard was mounted on a post overlooking an empty bog.

"You go first," said Tyler.

"Nah, you go," said Fisher. "Throw all your darts."

Shaking his head, Tyler went ahead. He got one bull's-eye and put the others inside the next ring.

"My turn," said Fisher. "Stand back."

"You don't have the darts," said Tyler.

"Don't need 'em," said Fisher, drawing his revolver. His first bullet obliterated the dart as well as the red dot at the center of the board, and the others followed through cleanly. "See you in the a.m. I'll bring the joe."

CHAPTER
4

Megan hesitated a moment, her hand resting on the throttle. They'd built roughly thirty minutes of leeway into her schedule, but only thirty minutes, and once they were airborne her options became extremely limited. She'd have no update on the position of most of the American aircraft involved in the operation.

The plan itself was solid. Even if the monitoring aircraft did something unusual or unanticipated, she'd be able to recover.

In, out. Once back, she and the crew would board the cigarette boat and be gone. A long vacation awaited.

General Bonham's death had shaken her, even though the Web sites were reporting it as an accident. Segrest had sent a BS E-mail to her in response: "Stay with the general's game plan" was the gist of it. She'd thoght of contacting her cousin to get the real story but decided it was safer not to: There was no way to contact him directly using their encrypted system, which deposited J-PEG files on a server in Austria, and any clear text message would inevitably be read by several people before it got to him. Better at the moment to follow through with the plan, such as it was. Once she arrived in Argentina she could begin untangling what was going on.

Megan held the plane against its brakes one last time as she revved the engines, giving the plane its final check. The chief of the three-man crew that had served as the bare-bones ground team gave a quick salute and began running from the edge of the runway, crossing down the dusty access ramp. The crew's boat was waiting in the cove less than a mile away; whatever happened from this moment on, she and her weapons officer were on their own.

"All right," she said over the plane's internal radio system. "You're ready?" she asked the weapons officer.

"Very ready."

"Rogers?"

"Anytime, beautiful."

The Amos/X, an enhanced version of the standard long-range Russian air-to-air missile, added over one thousand pounds to her heavily altered Blackjack's weight. Given the aircraft's size and design, the additional weight might have seemed relatively insignificant, but the short, rough runway complicated the takeoff. Even without the missile, the plane typically dipped off the edge of the island and came perilously close to the waves in a light headwind; Megan guessed there was perhaps a 30-percent chance now that she would crash into the water.

But then it would be over, wouldn't it?

She could accept that. She'd have done her duty.

She nodded to herself, then slapped the throttle bar, revving the engines for takeoff. The time for contemplation was long past: Action was what was needed now.

CHAPTER

5

Though the sea was nearly flat, there was no way for the speedboats to keep up with the two Mi-28 attack helicopters, and every 30 often the man at the helm cursed and gave his throttle a little jab, as if the combination might give him a few more knots of speed. Luksha found the man's curses somewhat amusing but said nothing. The driver was a paratrooper, not a seaman, and seemed unduly anxious about his job; Luksha feared any distraction might be catastrophic.

The island was now ten miles away; he could see the outline of the abandoned oil derrick with his night glasses.

Four other men were crammed into the small boat; a total of twenty-three had been chosen personally by Luksha to accompany him. He had reviewed the records of the crews in the Mi-28s; both pilots had served in Chechnya, and their reputations were impeccable.

If things went well, a Navy patrol vessel with another two dozen men would join them on the island an hour after they landed. A transport helicopter, as well as two large cargo airplanes, could land there within two hours of receiving his command.

The general leaned forward on the seat, his hand braced against the aluminum strut at the side of the boat. It had been years since he had been personally involved in an action like this—so long that it had a surreal quality, as if it were a pleasure outing.

And yet, the stakes were extremely high. Within an hour he should know if the American superweapon was located here.

He might also have it, or at least parts of it, in his possession. But that was being wildly optimistic.

His analysts had mapped out possible mines near the main landing area and gun emplacements on the north and south portions of the island. They also thought it possible that there were antiship missiles as well. Only by landing would they discover if these were all realities or fantasies of overparanoid minds.

In their favor, the analysts had concluded that there were no more than two dozen people there. His force was big enough to overcome them, assuming that the layout of the facility had not been altered. Luksha and his men would feed disabling gas into the bunker ventilation system and then cut the power, entering through two narrow emergency exitways that could not be sufficiently protected. There had not been time to rehearse the operation, but the men with him had a great deal of experience in such matters, and he had no doubt they would succeed.

In the hours since returning from Moscow, Luksha had come to believe the theory that the CIA was hiding the weapon here for future use. Its precision would allow it to be used for many things—including, Luksha thought, targeting the North Korean army. Why they would do that from here rather than a normal base, he could not say.

"Five minutes," said the man at the wheel.

As Luksha fine-tuned his focus on the island, a small pinpoint of light flared on the right. It burst brighter and larger, streaking from right to left, then climbing.

"Hold!" he said. "Hold all the boats!"

Luksha nearly lost his balance as the helmsman threw down the power. In the distance, the aircraft that was taking off continued to climb, its exhaust circles shaping into long ovals.

It was turning.

Luksha put his glasses down and waited. They could all hear the aircraft now.

The men knew of the weapon's capabilities and knew that its heat could burn a hole in the boat, even though it was on the surface of the ocean.

Or it could explode the gas tank or melt the metal rivets. Death had many possibilities.

They waited, listening to the roar of the jet as it overwhelmed the sound of the water knocking against the gunwales of the slightly overloaded vessels.

"Low-power surface radar," said one of his men, monitoring the warning receiver. "Northeast side of the island, probably mounted on or near the derrick."

Luksha nodded. The aircraft was still nearby, though the sound of its engines was receding. They weren't to be targeted after all.

The most critical part of his mission had just been accomplished; he was sure now that their guesses were correct.

He would go ahead, take care of the small contingent on the island, wait for the plane to return. It would be easier once it landed; it would be out of fuel, vulnerable. He could hide his forces on the island, have the helicopters rush in.

Luksha would take the weapon. He would be honored beyond his imagination.

Unless it was now headed on a mission over Russia. In that case, he would be considered a bungler who arrived ten minutes too late.

"Signal that we are going ahead," Luksha told his communications man. "Tell the helicopters to remain as reserves. We may not need them until the plane returns. The less attention we draw now, the better chance we will have for surprise afterwards."

He pointed his finger toward the island for the helmsman and leaned toward the spray as they picked up speed.

CHAPTER

6

Howe and Timmy launched at precisely 0400 local time, the two F/22Es rocketing into the blue twilight with the studied precision of a pair of synchronized swimmers. They climbed out to twenty thousand feet as they arced westward, drawing a sweeping semicircle over the Bering Sea. The Aleutian islands spread out to their left as they flew; the Fox Islands, a small group about midway in the chain, marked the launch point for the test.

The test area was already being patrolled. Howe exchanged pleasantries with a pair of Navy jocks as they pushed south, riding a wide curve that had them roughly parallel to the northern Kuril Islands, a thousand miles off their right wings. The Velociraptors hit the southernmost point of their patrol area, then swept back toward the rendezvous with a tanker. They'd just topped off when the RC-135 with the monitoring gear came on station. There were still two hours left before the first test launch; Jolice's turn was scheduled for two hours after that.

Howe believed there were two possibilities for detecting a plane. The most likely was with the RC-135 equipment, which presumably would catch the laser shot during the test. But he also thought they might find the aircraft prior to the test as it moved into position. Since they knew Cyclops's range and capabilities, they also knew where the plane would have to position itself to fire. The "box"— more like a long rhomboid with rounded edges—ranged nearly a thousand miles, depending on the altitude the laser plane flew and the altitude it engaged its target at. But they thought the position of the Navy ships cordoning off the test area probably narrowed it a great deal—they couldn't be sure, since they didn't know the details of the radar profile—and so the long box was only a hundred miles wide.

Still a lot of area to cover, but not an impossible haystack.

The Navy had two Hawker E-2C radar aircraft covering the southwestern portion of the test zone; an Aegis-equipped cruiser with its powerful SPY-1B phased-array radar and associated systems complemented the airborne radar planes and their carrier group, tracking through an arc of roughly 250 miles. An array of smaller ships, aircraft, and drones formed a thick picket around the area.

Howe answered a query from one of the Hawkeye controllers. Timmy exchanged a few good-natured insults with the Navy jocks. Otherwise their flight south and then back north was almost eerily quiet.

Driving the entire circuit in supercruise took just over an hour, the finely tuned P&Ws humming. A Russian monitoring ship had taken up station at the southwest corner of the test area under the shadow of an American destroyer. Two monitoring aircraft, also Russian, were flying out from Siberia. These were tentatively ID'd by the AWACS as Myasishchev M-55 Geofizia twin-boom spy planes. Known as Mystic Bs in the West, the planes were advertised as high-altitude "environmental research" aircraft and could fly somewhere over 65,000 feet for four or five hours. Odd-looking creatures with swept-back wings and tails vaguely reminiscent of North American Broncos, their capabilities were somewhat comparable to early-model U-2s.

Two F-15s were tasked to shadow the Mystics—*shadow* being the operative word, since the Russian aircraft, though slow and not particularly maneuverable, could operate comfortably several thousand feet higher than the Eagles. Howe didn't envy the F-15 pilots—or the F/A-18 pilot tasked with checking out a small boat spotted at the southern end of the test range by one of the drones a few minutes later.

"Just about an hour to go," said Timmy as they spun back to the south.

"How's the hangover?"

"How do you know I have a hangover?"

"Maybe the fact that you've said three words the whole flight."

Fisher unfolded the large chart on his lap, studying the red *X*'s that were supposed to designate the approximate locations of the surface ships around the test range. He had another small map of the test area that showed the approximate positions for the intercepts, as well as a folder of satellite photos.

None of it was worth very much, though it seemed to impress the Air Force people flying the C-17. Fisher had been granted a seat on the flight deck, which, he gathered, was considered an honor. It was not only padded but swiveled, and if you didn't get too anal about restraints and watched what you were doing, you could stretch your feet against the back of the copilot's seat and a panel on the far right, making for a position nearly as comfortable as the back of a Honda Civic flattened in a rear-end collision.

His headset was not only plugged into the plane's intercom, or "interphone," system but had what looked like an old-fashioned transistor radio wired in that could select any of the myriad frequencies, though it wasn't clear to Fisher what combination of buttons he had to push to actually communicate with anyone.

Fisher looked at his watch. There was now just over a half hour before the test.

He didn't know what was going to happen, but whatever it was, he figured it should have happened by now.

So he was wrong again. Bitch of a losing streak.

Howe listened as a controller in one of the Hawkeyes exchanged a few choice words with a crewman aboard the cruiser about a contact flying out of the south toward the aircraft carrier and test area. The airplane—it appeared to be a civilian airliner, but its Ident gear wasn't working properly—didn't answer hails but finally took a sharp turn southward away from the test area. Howe broke in to request the Hawkeye to detail an aircraft to visually inspect the airliner: It was, after all, at least theoretically large enough to house the Cyclops weapon. The Navy controller replied somewhat sharply that he already had a plane en route.

The seaman at the display of the Aegis air defense system aboard the cruiser started throwing a series of numbers and acronyms out over the air. It sounded almost as if he were speaking in tongues.

"Five minutes to test," said the mission controller, who was aboard a Navy ship just off the Aleutians. Though presented as a simple statement, the words were actually a command: *Shut up and let's get to work.*

Howe felt himself starting to relax. Maybe Fisher was wrong about everything—maybe the wreckage had contained the laser after all.

"*Religion?*" Megan laughed at him.

"*Yeah. Are you religious?*"

"*Are you?*"

"*You sound religious.*"

"*I believe in things.*"

"*I don't see how you can be a pacifist and be involved in a military program.*"

"*How am I a pacifist?*"

"*You want to end war, right?*"

"*Absolutely.*"

"*That's not pacifism?*"

"*See, the word is all fucked up.*"

Howe laughed.

"*It is.*"

"*That word seems strange coming out of your mouth.*"

"*Kiss me, then, and make the strangeness go away.*"

"*I love you.*"

Had he said that?

He couldn't remember now. He must have said it; he must have told her. But he couldn't remember.

She was starting to fade away.

"Asset Mike-Charlie is off the air."

The words seemed to break through a fog, rays of sun separating the clouds.

"Repeat, Asset Mike-Charlie is off the air."

Howe fought against the adrenaline that jerked through his veins. "Monitor, do we have a fire?" he asked the RC-135, which was looking for the laser burst.

"Negative, Bird One. No shot, Colonel."

Voices filled every circuit. Mike-Charlie was a UAV patrolling the southeast quadrant of the test area. Two Navy fighters selected afterburners, hustling in that direction; two others swept around to back them up. The Hawkeye closest to the area reported no contacts. One of the surface ships had a possible visual sighting but then lost it.

The mission boss stopped the ABM launch at T-minus 2:31 as the patrol vessels and aircraft scoured the area where the UAV had been. After a few minutes with no fresh contacts and the covering aircraft now mustered around the area, he let it proceed.

"Still clean," Monitor told Howe as the countdown returned.

"Bird One," acknowledged Howe, starting a bank as he reached the southernmost point of his patrol area.

CHAPTER

7

Megan was now much too far away from the drone to know if the Amos/X missile she'd launched scored a hit or not. She could tell from her passive radar receiver that at least one of the aircraft over the test area was reacting; she took that as a hopeful sign.

She was already too committed to turn back. Following the precisely computed flight plan, she selected afterburner and began to rise from her track fifty feet over the waves. The weapons officer meanwhile acknowledged that the weapon was operational and prepared to fire.

"We have a launch," said the weapons officer. "Their target is airborne."

"Radar's clean," said Rogers.

Megan didn't reply, concentrating on flying her aircraft. The more they climbed on this course, the closer they got to the AWACS radar. She suspected that they would be detected before the ABM missile was fired; she just hoped it was close enough so the launch couldn't be aborted.

Her hand steadied against the stick. Megan thought of her uncle and his last mission over Tokyo. The way he described it, he'd been an automaton, more mechanical than a flight computer.

She was that way now.

"ABM launch," said the weapons officer. "I need ten miles."

He gave her more directions, asking her to take a hard turn to the east and continue climbing. There was no doubt now they would be detected. Megan pushed the stick, making the correction. The maneuver bled speed off the wings, but the plane moved precisely as she wanted, still rising in the air.

"Preparing to fire. I'm locked," said the weapons officer.

Megan reached forward, her thumb edging toward the button that turned control of the plane over to the automatic pilot circuit, allowing the weapon to fly the aircraft on a very straight and predictable path as it fired. She hesitated—it felt almost like a surrender—but there was no way for the laser to fire without pushing that button.

Go, she told her thumb.

A thick bar flashed at the top of her HUD and an icon appeared in the lower part of the screen. Megan leaned back, a passenger in her own jet.

"Firing!" reported the weapons officer. His excitement seemed to shake the aircraft, though it was actually the discharge of the weapon, ramping through the system and unleashing through the clear glass at the tail end.

To fly through that smoke over Tokyo, to kill all those people—you could justify their deaths in the end, add them up in the awful calculus of human survival. But if you didn't resolve to get beyond those grim equations—if you didn't work to end all war—weren't you as guilty as the butchers who had started it all?

That had been her uncle's and her father's arguments. It was her birthright, her debt.

Paid now.

"The missile hit," said the weapons officer.

He said something else but the words garbled in her ears, too far from her thoughts to penetrate. Megan took back control of the aircraft from the computer, rolling her wings and tucking back to the west in a twisting dive that put nearly 9 g's of stress across the frame, overloading even the overengineered Russian design. The Blackjack groaned but held, possibly unaware of the fate that awaited her a little over an hour and a half from now—assuming, of course, they made it back to the base.

Megan pushed the engines into afterburner. Fuel gushed into the engines, taking the semistealthy Blackjack from just under three hundred knots to over nine hundred. Megan had to assume she'd been spotted, and so she needed every second's worth of acceleration to get away. But she could sustain her burst for merely a minute; otherwise she'd consume too much fuel and risk ditching. Megan punched her watch's preset; her arms moved like levers as the time drained to zero.

"Looking good," she told Rogers as she backed off power. "We're on the home stretch."

8

"Bird One, Bird One! We have a positive fire! Positive fire!"

Howe's heartbeat jumped, chasing away the fatigue that just a few moments ago had been pushing him low in the seat.

"Location?" he said, consciously trying to slow his tongue down.

"Working on that."

Howe hailed the AWACS controller, who was reporting a contact to the northwest, maybe 350 miles from the track the ABM target had taken. Meanwhile the mission boss reported the ABM missile had struck home.

"Monitor, you have that vector?" Howe asked the RC-135.

"Definitely north of you," said the crewman. "He should have been out of range, though."

"I'm going north."

"Screw that," said someone over the circuit. "Head toward the Kurils. Got to be."

Howe clicked his mike to ask who had said that, then realized it was Fisher.

"The UAV was a deke, a fakeout," said Fisher. "Don't worry about where they were: Worry about where they're going."

"How do you know where they're going?"

"I don't. We just take our best guess and see what happens."

"Fisher—"

"Don't give up on me now, Colonel."

Howe hesitated for a second, then banked into a turn that would take him in the islands' general direction off the coast of Russia.

* * *

Fisher gripped the map and folder in his hand as he worked his way down the ladder to Tyler.

"Has to be one of these three places," he told the Special Forces captain, pointing at the map. He had the satellite pictures at the top of the folder and took them out. Only two of the islands looked as though they had landing strips, but the photo interpreter had assured Fisher that the third had a long, flat surface as well. In fact, he seemed to feel that what looked like a rock line and hills at the northeast were in fact painted shadows. Like the other two sites, the reconnaissance satellites did not cover the island 24/7, and their schedule could be pinpointed by someone in the know.

"My guess is it's this one with the phony oil rig and the Escher painting in the middle that looks like hills," Fisher told Tyler, pointing at the third and explaining the camouflage. "But they're all long enough. We can land anywhere they can."

"How long will it take?"

"Pilot says a little over an hour," said Fisher.

"I have to talk to Colonel Gorman," said Tyler.

"Tell her I said hello. Hey, are there smoke detectors down here?"

The Velociraptors' long-range scan remained clean. Howe was now roughly three hundred miles from the nearest of the small islands Fisher had claimed the laser plane would be heading toward; he should have it in sight in less than twenty minutes.

Had the laser plane escaped? Or had Fisher simply been wrong?

He checked his course. The Kurils stretched in a semicircle toward the Russian coast, a scythe pointing toward the northernmost island of Japan. Many of the islands were uninhabitable atolls, but a few were large enough for small fishing villages and settlements. Perhaps a dozen or more were somewhere in between and at various times had been used for military installations. Fisher had ID'd three as possible targets, including two that had been used by the Soviet Union during the Cold War.

Howe would sweep over the northernmost target and arc south with Timmy on his tail. He had a search pattern laid out, and they'd already worked out a rendezvous with one of the tankers, which would take up a station to the west.

A flight of F-15s were heading north from Japan to join in the search. They hadn't contacted Howe yet; at last report they would be near the target area about fifteen minutes after he got there, and would probably be too low on fuel to hang around for very long.

The radar kicked up a contact at extreme range, flying at roughly thirty thousand feet; after a few seconds the contact disappeared, their courses taking them in diverging directions.

"Think that was our boy?" asked Timmy.

It was possible, but if so, the plane was heading over Russia. Howe told him to ignore it, and a few minutes later they fell onto the course he'd plotted to overfly the first island. The AWACS plane accompanying the task force was a good distance behind them, and even the nearest Navy aircraft was well outside radar range. They would have little warning if the Russians managed to spot them and decided to jump them.

CHAPTER
9

It took Blitz a few seconds to understand exactly what was going on as the transmissions from the augmented-ABM test barraged into the small secure videoconferencing booth. He turned to McIntyre, who seemed to be in a daze.

"Mac, Fisher was right."

"Yes," said the NSC aide, his voice still far away— probably on the ground in Kashmir, where it had been since his return. Blitz was going to insist on a long rest— and possibly psychological counseling for post-traumatic stress disorder—as soon as this was over.

"Get on the line to the FBI director and tell him to proceed with the shutdown of NADT. We want everything," he added, though the command was superfluous.

"Fisher was right," said McIntyre.

"As incredible as it seems," said Blitz, turning back to the communications board and punching up Colonel Gorman's circuit. "You have full authority to proceed," he told her. "You're answering to the President on this."

CHAPTER
10

Just as the island started to grow in her windscreen, Megan's radar warning receiver flashed to life, picking up transmissions from two planes approaching at high speed. The direction surprised her: They were coming out of Russia.

Her weapons officer ID'd them as Su-35s, afterburners blazing. But at just under a hundred nautical miles away, they weren't going to catch her, not today.

"Prepare for landing," she told Rogers. As she cut her speed and settled into the landing pattern, the wings of the big jet swung outward. The extension increased the radar profile exponentially, but it was immaterial now: They had the lead needed. In less than fifteen minutes the plane and the weapon would be smoldering, and she and the others would be in the water.

"I have something else." The radar operator's voice was practically a yelp.

Megan, lined up and descending toward the runway, glanced at her own radar display and saw the helicopters that were just coming over the edge of the island from the water. But it was too late: She was nearly out of fuel and committed to landing.

"Shit," she said. "Rogers, what is this?"

"Damned if I know," said the copilot. "Russians?"

"Just hang tight," Megan told him, pushing the wheels onto the hardened-lava runway.

CHAPTER

11

Howe finally got a plane on the radar, landing at the third site, sixty-three miles south of him. The AI circuits in the tactical radar targeting system focused their beams and scratched their silicone heads, tentatively IDing the contact as a Blackjack bomber.

"I have it," said Howe.

"I copy," said Timmy. "More contacts: Su-35s."

The planes appeared on his tactical screen, their approximate speed and altitude computed for him. The Russian planes had not yet found the American jets, but if they stayed on their present course, they would beat them to the island.

A combat escort? Or something else?

Another pair of contacts rose near the atoll: helicopters.

Howe tried but couldn't reach Gorman's command plane, or any of the other aircraft in her task force. He gave it another try; when he came up blank he told Timmy they'd shoot over the atoll where the Blackjack had landed and have a look.

"What do you want to do about the Russians?" asked his wingman.

"Tell them to stand off, that we're conducting a test mission."

"Yeah, and when they laugh at us, then what?"

"Splash them if they get in our way."

"What I'm talking about."

CHAPTER
12

Megan trundled through the dust at the far end of the camouflaged strip, heading back over the area she'd just landed on. The explosives were rigged in a grid at the edge of the narrow ramp that led to the hangar elevator; they could not be detonated unless the plane was sitting on one of the large metal plates at the mouth of the elevator. As she approached, a whirlwind kicked across her path. Rocks flew into her nose and smacked hard against the thick glass of her windscreen.

Not rocks: bullets.

The whirlwind turned back. It was a helicopter gunship, a cannon at its chin. The dark green and brown fuselage of an Mi-28 Havoc materialized out of the maelstrom, continuing to fire at her as she rolled. Megan ducked involuntarily as bullets crashed into the right side of the fuselage and wing. She had trouble finding the turnoff but stayed on the hardened ground, pushing the nose around at the last minute but still managing to get in the middle of the plate.

"Out!" she shouted. "Out! Out!"

She fumbled with the lock on her restraints, finally snapping it off as the topside hatchway hissed open. Megan curled over the side, throwing her legs over and then down, releasing herself to the ground. She rolled as she landed, getting up to her feet as one of the helicopters streaked overhead.

CHAPTER

13

Howe saw the helicopters fluttering over the plane as it stopped. They were Russian choppers, Mi-28s or something similar, gunships that might support assault troops. He was moving too fast to target anybody; he began a turn south, hoping to use the time to sort out what was going on down there.

"Bird One, this is Cyclops Control," said Gorman. "Be advised: Several Russian interceptors are approaching you."

No shit, he thought.

"The laser plane is down," Howe told her. Words rattled from his mouth like bullets from the Gatling in the F/A-22V's starboard wing root as he gave her the GPS coordinates, ID'd the plane as a Blackjack with a V-shaped tail and other mods, and then told her about the helos.

"Assault team has an ETA of minus thirty minutes," she said. "We'd like to recover the aircraft if possible. If not, destroy it."

Before Howe could acknowledge, Timmy shouted a warning.

"Missiles in the air! Missiles in the air! Those crazy Russian fucks are gunning for us."

"Can you assess the situation on the ground?" Gorman asked, unable to monitor the communications between the two Velociraptors.

"We're under fire," said Howe, dishing chaff and taking evasive action.

"From the Russians?"

Howe was too busy jinking to make any of the dozen or so retorts that occurred to him.

CHAPTER

14

The dust felt like heavy sackcloth, covering her face. Megan choked as she tried to get up, rubbing her eyes to clear enough grit away so she could get her bearings. She saw her three crewmen collapse behind her, falling as the helicopter made another pass.

Definitely a Russian. The bastards had figured it out somehow—as she had predicted.

"Rogers, blow up the plane," she yelled to her copilot, who was lying next to her. When he didn't move, she pulled at the pocket of his pant leg where the radio detonator was. "Do it! Do it!"

"I can't," he said. "Segrest told me not to blow the plane."

"What?" She didn't believe him, taking the radio device out anyway and pressing it. Nothing happened.

"He wants the laser," said Rogers. "The detonator's not rigged."

"You bastard, these are Russian helicopters. This is Segrest?"

"No," said Rogers. "I don't think so."

"Fuck, come on."

"Where?"

"We can't let them get the plane. We have to blow it up."

"The detonator's not set."

"So help me set it."

As she started to run, something popped in the air a few feet away. There was a roar and a rush of air. Megan felt herself pushed to the ground. One of the helicopters passed somewhere behind her, the ground shaking. Megan scratched forward a few feet, then got up and started to run again. She could hear the crackle of small-arms fire, felt her body becoming wet. She pressed the button on the detonator again and again as Rogers fell on top of her and rolled off, howling in pain, then awfully silent.

Luksha steadied his AK-74 automatic rifle at the fallen figure as he ran. It was the pilot. He had something in his hand, a radio no doubt. The pilot fumbled with it, trying to turn it in his hand.

Luksha kicked it under the jet, then pulled the man away, back to the side of the runway.

Not a man: a woman. The pilot was a woman.

Just like the Americans.

Luksha's men swarmed over the aircraft. There was more gunfire, some shouts; for a moment he feared that more troops had been hiding on the island and they were about to be overwhelmed. The drumming of the helicopters rose and the wind swirled around him.

Then the chaos began to recede. There were no other troops, and there had been only four crewmen, three of whom were now dead. Only the woman remained alive.

Success. All of his planning, the decision to wait until the aircraft took off and returned from another flight—it had all paid off. They were his, considerably more easily than he had hoped.

"Call in the transports and technical crew," Luksha told his communications specialist. He turned to his sergeant, who'd just run up next to him and was hunched over, collecting his breath. "Secure this woman. She is our prisoner, and a very valuable one."

CHAPTER
15

Howe had little trouble ducking the Russian's Alamo missile, a semiactive radar home that had been launched from outside its optimum range. But his defensive maneuvering took up time and forced him to turn to the east; before he could recover and sort out the situation, four more Russian fighters, all MiG-29s, had appeared over the horizon. They had their pedals to the metal as they came to help out the two Super-Flankers that had launched the attack.

Howe's computer buzzed as Timmy fired an AMRAAM at one of the nearby Russians, the missile track dotted in the HUD hologram.

"I have the bandit at the south," Howe told his wingman, starting a turn to cut toward its tail. "Watch out for the four Johnny-come-latelies."

"Oh yeah, copy that. Bring those suckers on," said the wingman. "Got your back."

Howe and the Sukhoi were separated by about five miles, just outside of a good Sidewinder shot. Howe went for more power, needing to accelerate but wary, anticipating that the enemy fighter would try to pull him into a quick turn. He blew a wad of air into his mask. His hand curled tightly on the stick, waiting for the sensor in the missile head to growl at him, indicating that it was ready. Howe told himself to ease off, to relax, to just follow. The missile got a good strong scent of the enemy plane and began screaming at him, telling him to fire. Howe waited a few more seconds, confident now he had him, confident he was gaining sufficiently on the enemy jet.

"Fire," he told the computer.

The missile ripped out from the side bay of the Velociraptor, plunging downward momentarily and then pushing its nose too far to the left as the Sukhoi pilot came hard right. But the circuitry in the all-aspect Sidewinder, refined after generations of dogfights, quickly corrected, driving the missile back toward the big Russian jet and its hot tailpipe. The Sukhoi started to jink east just as the warhead exploded; shrapnel ripped through the left engine and severed the controls to the tailfin, leaving the pilot no option but to bail.

By that time Howe was already turning northward to meet the newcomers.

Timmy swept into the battle eagerly, his hand gripping the stick with the sort of gentle firmness he'd use to guide a date to bed. The encounter shaped up as an almost textbook four-on-two dustup, with the Russian MiG-29s blustering forward, seemingly oblivious to the approaching F/A-22Vs. The two Velociraptors were at fifteen thousand feet, a good five thousand below the MiGs, but that was their only disadvantage; they had an intercept from the east, and even thirty miles away the Russians seemed not to know where they were.

"I'm going to save one of my AMRAAMs in case the laser plane gets off," Howe told him. "I have that lead one on the left."

"Yeah, roger that. I have number two."

Timmy's HUD hologram had the target plane boxed and tied with a bow. He fired about a half-second after Howe, sliding around to get into position for a tailpipe shot on the last two MiGs in the formation. Belatedly, the MiGs began throwing chaff and hitting ECMs.

"Yours on the right," said Howe as the bandits divided.

Timmy started to follow but quickly lost his Russian, who'd taken out a hammer and nailed his throttle on the last stop, burning through his relatively limited store of fuel in his bid to get back home in one piece. Timmy pulled off, circling to the south and looking for Howe.

The Velociraptor's radar system was light-years beyond the primitive scopes that fighter pilots of old had to decipher as they rode their steeds into battle; the unit could select its own modes, interpret its contacts, fight off electronic countermeasures, and paint a three-dimensional picture of the battlefield, all with minimal input from the pilot. But no gee-whiz technology could eliminate the effects of high-g turns, mission fatigue, and what planners referred to as the fog of war. The pilot's instincts and his ability to think clearly under stress were far more important than the convenient cues projected in glorious 3-D on his HUD, or the melodious warning tones of his RWR. Timmy pushed left; then, for some reason he couldn't have explained, he jerked his stick and threw the Velociraptor the other way. The maneuver put him four miles behind one of the MiGs.

"I'm on him," he told Howe.

He had a good closure rate on the enemy, who was just starting to accelerate after a series of maneuvers. The Sidewinder's sensor began to growl; Timmy waited a second or two more, then fired, alerting Howe and once again breaking away, knowing he was northeast of the target island but not sure exactly where.

"Good shot, Two," said Howe as the second Sidewinder tallied. "I want you to come south now. How's your fuel?"

Low, thought Timmy, without even looking. He found Howe three miles southeast of him. The island was roughly ten miles away.

He'd splashed three planes in the space of what, five minutes? Four?

Shit.

Super shit.

Between India and this, he'd lived the life of twenty fighter pilots inside a week. His heart raced in his chest, and his head wasn't more than a half-stride behind.

Shit.

Super shit.

Like winning the Super Bowl, this. People'd be parading him all around, buying drinks. Women—God he was the man, *the* man.

Not that he hadn't been before.

Shit.

Super shit.

"Fuel, Timmy," prompted Howe.

He took a breath and got back to dealing with reality.

"Bird One, what's your situation?" asked Jemma Gorman.

Howe laid it out for her, emphasizing their rapidly diminishing fuel states. The tanker was a little closer than he thought—five hundred miles—but even so, they had at best five minutes before having to head back. A pair of F-15s from the task group had tanked and were coming west, but they were still roughly a half hour away. The Eagles scrambling northward from Kadena were a little closer but still wouldn't be in sight for about twenty minutes, maybe a little less.

Which, in his mind—and in any reasonable mind—meant the assault team should hold off.

"We need to be on that island now," said Gorman. "I need the assault team down there. Take out the helicopters so they can land. Your tanker is en route."

"It's too far," he told her. "Even if we left now, we'd be on a bingo profile. We're way low on fuel."

"Bail out or land on the damn island if you have to," she told him. "Just take out the helicopters and cover the assault team."

"You're out of your fucking mind."

"We need the laser," said Gorman. "We've already tried contacting the Russian forces by radio and they've refused to acknowledge. They're hostile."

"Yeah, no shit they're hostile," said Howe. "I'll take out the plane. I have two small-diameter bombs."

"Take out the helicopters. My orders are to recover the laser intact if we can, and we can. My people want a look at that plane and what mods they've made."

Howe squeezed the side stick, as if that might force the anger from his body. He needed to get rid of the emotion so he could think logically, figure this out.

It was damn easy for Gorman to tell him not to worry about refueling.

"Colonel, please acknowledge," said Gorman.

Howe's fingers were now so tight that his pinkie felt numb, and he'd started to grind his teeth. His head, though, remained clear: He had one of the helicopters hovering off the tip of the island, five miles away. He could go guns, sweep in, and nail it.

"Two, I want you to hang back and try and conserve fuel," he told Timmy. "I'm going to take that chopper there on my left and then see if I can gun out the other bastard quick. Get a fresh ETA from the C-17 with the assault team, see what they're up to."

"Two," acknowledged Timmy without comment.

Howe clicked his arms selector over to Gun and slid into the attack, still too far to fire.

Hitting a helicopter with the cannon could actually be quite difficult, depending on the circumstances; the F/A-22V's speed advantage turned into a liability as it closed for the attack. As Howe pushed into a shallow dive, the chopper spit right. He began to fire, though he was still a little far off; the bullets trailed downward and well behind the helicopter. He let off of the trigger and came around wide, in effect backing off for a better pass. The helicopter, meanwhile, threw out flares and jinked toward the sea, obviously expecting a missile attack. Howe's turn put him in the direction of the helo's course; he got off a shot but was by too fast and at too hard an angle to score a hit. By the time he recovered, the helicopter was headed back toward the island. That was a mistake: Howe, whose speed had slid down through two hundred knots, lined up easily on the helo's tail and began pumping it full of lead. The chopper tipped to the left but Howe had it mastered; he put a burst through the engines and then pulled up to avoid the fireball.

"Missile in the air!" warned Timmy.

Howe shot flares and jinked right. The shoulder-launched SS-16 was a potent little missile, at least arguably the equal of an American Stinger. It caught a whiff of one of the flares as well as the Velociraptor's tailpipes; confused, it decided to explode. Shrapnel from the small warhead flew in an elongated mushroom through the air; two small red-hot pieces struck the back end of Howe's aircraft, though they did little except dent the metal.

The pilot felt nothing, not even aware that the missile had exploded until Timmy told him. He continued to climb, checking his tactical display and then working quickly through his indicators, making sure he remained intact.

"That second helicopter is lifting off," said Timmy.

Howe looked up. The helicopter rose in the right quadrant of his windscreen.

"I have it," Howe said. He switched back to the missiles, deciding at this point there was no reason to save the last Sidewinder: The Backfire was making no sign of getting ready to take off, and he still had the AMRAAM.

The helicopter fired at him as he came in from the west, loosing not only an air-to-air missile but its cannon. Howe had already started a turn, swinging first to the south but then quickly northward, guessing that the helicopter might try to turn inside and take another missile shot; his maneuver would keep the heat-seeker well off his tail. But instead the helicopter ducked back east. It took Howe a few seconds to pick it out, but when he finally did he was almost in perfect position for the Sidewinder shot. He started to close, launched, then pulled back around amid a cascade of flares, anticipating that the bastards on the ground would be taking another shot at him.

"C-17 is less than two minutes off," said Timmy. "I have a boat on the surface, high-speed. Don't think it's ours."

"Take it," said Howe.

"What I'm talking about."

Timmy put the Velociraptor into a shallow dive, letting the patrol boat grow in his sight. Four fat ship-to-ship missile launchers dominated the rear half of the ship, massive gray suitcases jammed into the hull. Timmy lit his cannon, lacing the water as he worked to get the spray into the front quarter of the ship. His bullets found the bow as the twin 30mm AA gun began sparkling; he rode the stream into the gun housing, then the superstructure, tearing across the bridge and off the boat's starboard side.

He dished flares and chaff, starting to recover. The Velociraptor's tail wagged behind him, responding sluggishly to the control inputs. As Timmy got his nose up, warning lights started to pop; he'd taken some hits along the rear fuselage and tailplane. Before he could sort it out, something red flashed in front over him: an SA-N-12 from the patrol boat. Timmy started to turn away, only to be bracketed by two explosions from barrage-launched SA-N-5s, low-altitude heatseekers. The pilot struggled to hold his aircraft.

"Got a problem," he told Howe.

"Come east, Timmy," Howe told him. "Break ninety: Turn, damn it! You're running back into his gunfire."

Timmy couldn't get the plane to turn fast enough to avoid the bubbling black mass as it rose in the sky. Wings peppered by flak, he fought desperately just to stay level. It didn't matter how hard he pushed against the stick or throttle—the controls were electric, not hydraulic—but he muscled them anyway, as if his strength might somehow flow out to the control surfaces and buoy the plane.

From super shit to stuck in shit, all in less than sixty seconds. The cockpit looked like a Christmas display, warning lights flashing. Timmy heard something howling in his ears.

"Out," Howe was saying. "Out!"

"Yeah, baby," said the pilot.

He put his hand down to grab the yellow and black ejection handle. As he gripped it the last SA-N-5 from the patrol boat exploded just under the back end of the plane. Timmy pulled the handles. but it was already too late: He felt a sudden surge of heat behind him; then the world turned black and incredibly, instantly cold.

Howe saw his wingmate's plane explode and felt his hand once more tighten involuntarily around the stick. He stared at the hurtling ball of metal, plastic, and fire, waiting, hoping, expecting the canopy to shoot off and the seat to appear, Timmy hurtling away with his good-ol'-boy chuckle. Howe got ready to note the location, follow the chute down, vector the SAR assets in.

Slowly he realized that wasn't going to happen. The stricken Velociraptor disintegrated before his eyes, imploding from its many wounds. Howe flew on, finally forcing his eyes down to the tactical screen, pushing his head back into the game where it had to be.

The Russian ship was dead in the water, two miles from the island. Black smoke unfurled from the middle of the vessel. He pushed down, looked at the cue in the holographic HUD, the computer automatically drawing the dotted line for him.

"Fire," he said, pressing the trigger as well.

One of his first bullets hit the Styx launcher on the port side; by the time he let off the trigger and began to climb, the rear half of the boat had vaporized.

"The helicopters and patrol boat are down," he said over the shared frequency for the C-17. "If you're coming, now's the time to do it. I'll rake the field."

CHAPTER

16

Fisher leaned over the seat on the flight deck, trying to hear what Tyler and the pilots were saying.

"Once around to see what the layout is," suggested the Special Forces captain.

"That just gives anyone on the ground a shot at us," said the pilot. "Best bet is either parachute in or land right away. One or the other. They fired at least one missile at the Velociraptors. We're a much easier target."

"We'll land, then," said Tyler. The captain turned to Fisher. "We're going to land."

"You think that's a good idea?"

Tyler looked at him as if he hadn't understood, then pushed past to go down to his men. Fisher took his place.

"Hey! Don't touch anything there!" said the copilot, proprietary all of a sudden.

"Stay away from the plane," Fisher told the pilot. "They probably have it rigged for explosives."

"Okay," said the pilot. "But there's not too much to work with. Strip's narrow and short."

"Sounds like a personal problem to me," said Fisher.

CHAPTER

17

Luksha cursed as the transmission from the patrol ship ended in a hiss. The American jets had obviously found the boat; the helicopters had not been able to lead them away.

He suspected that his reinforcements were under fire as well. He'd heard nothing from the transport or its escorts; he had to assume it had turned back.

He still had the four small speedboats they'd used to get to the island, as well as the helicopters waiting on the island thirty miles away, but none of them were big enough to carry off the weapon.

"The pilot," he told his sergeant. "Get her and bring her here."

As the sergeant ran off toward the boat landing, two of the men who were working on dismantling the laser emerged from the plane, carrying a large gray box housing computer gear. Luksha ran to them; one of the men, an engineering specialist, began to explain the significance of the box but Luksha cut him off.

"Put it back in the plane. We're going to fly out of here."

"General—"

"Throw it back in the plane," demanded Luksha. "Then get down to the boats."

* * *

One of the Russians jerked Megan to her feet. For a second she thought he was going to push her over the side of the rocks to the water ten feet below; instead he tugged her up the trail back toward the landing strip.

The plane sat exactly where she had parked it over the charges. If she had a few minutes, she might be able to figure out how to set them by hand, or find a backup device.

She could just as easily grow wings and fly away. Two Russian paratroopers met her guards, forming a cocoon around her as she walked. Rather than going to the bunker as she expected, they took her toward the aircraft.

There were planes overhead: Velociraptors, she thought.

Howe?

God, what if it was him?

The two men in front of her stopped abruptly, standing aside as a Russian officer approached. It was the same one who had informed her earlier she was a prisoner.

"This is Russian land. You are a trespasser," he told her. His accent was thick and it took her a second to cut through it. "You are subject to serious penalties, including death."

Megan guessed what was coming and said nothing.

"Fly us out of here and you are free. You have ten seconds to decide," said the Russian. He reached to his belt and unholstered his pistol.

It was a gift, really: She could take off and crash the plane.

"We need fuel," she told him. "There is an underground pumping system. It's automated, though. We can do it easily. All right?"

His answer was drowned out by the roar of an aircraft approaching the runway.

18

If they were going to have any chance of getting the weapon and plane intact, Howe had to be careful about where he used the bombs. He didn't have much of a target anyway: As he came across the island, he saw perhaps a dozen soldiers scurrying toward the parked Russian jet. There were boats on the other side of the island, but he decided to leave them alone; no sense cutting off their escape if what he really wanted was for them to leave.

Howe gave a few winks from his gun and shot off flares, hoping to suck off any shoulder-launched SAMs they might have left on the ground. He cruised over the strip at roughly seventy-five feet.

"Dozen or so ground people, maybe more," he told the C-17 and Gorman. "They didn't fire any SAMs at me, but that's no guarantee."

"We can get down on the ground and hold them there," said Tyler, the assault team leader. "I can't guarantee that they won't blow up the plane, but the C-17 will block the runway and they won't get off."

"Good. We have reinforcements right behind you," said Gorman. "No more than an hour away."

"Tell them to move faster," said Tyler.

"I'm going to go down again, then lead you in," said Howe. He could see the big transport as it headed in from the northeast. "Once you're down, you're on your own."

In Fisher's experience, landings were always the worst part of any flight. The movie was over, drinks were cut off, and the anticipation of that next cigarette built like the swelling music in a 1930's melodrama, without a violin section. He steadied himself at the side of the plane behind the SF team, admiring their weapons and bullet-proof vests. The landing would take them down the runway away from the concentration of Russian troops; according to the satellite photo, they would have some cover at that end of the atoll from a short run of rocks. But to get to that cover, they would have to run roughly thirty yards.

Then again, he'd run farther when ducking the boss back at headquarters. This would be child's play.

The rear deck of the aircraft opened as they began their descent. The rushing air sucked and pushed him; he felt cold and for some reason wet, as if he'd been thrown into the water. Daku and James, standing at the back of the plane, began dumping smoke grenades as the plane's wheels hit the hard-packed dirt. Flares were being launched by the aircraft. Someone had started to shoot. Bullets ripped through the cargo compartment. The smell of burning metal mixed with the grit.

It *was* a thirties movie.

The plane veered hard to the right, then back, then hard right again.

Someone shouted. The plane resounded with the thump of a grenade launcher being fired.

"Go!" yelled Tyler. "Go!"

Fisher waited a second, then followed outside, crouching protectively to make sure his cigarette stayed lit in the wind. Smoke was everywhere, laid down by the commandos to cover their movements. Fisher looked to his left and saw the pilot and copilot crouching beneath the plane, holding M16s. Impressed, Fisher worked his way back around the other side of the plane, trying to figure out what the hell was going on beyond the thick haze of smoke and dust. The commandos had gone forward to the left but seemed to be holding their fire. The plane that held the laser weapon, meanwhile, was back at the far end of the strip, presumably guarded by the Russian assault team that had landed here ahead of them.

These interagency busts could be a real bitch and a half.

Fisher began trotting in the general direction of the SF team, bending his head down as a concession to the situation, though at the moment no one seemed to be firing. He found Daku at the edge of what looked like a haphazardly formed rock wall. The soldier thumbed him up toward the main group, which had taken position in some rocks about fifty or sixty yards ahead.

Fisher began trotting toward it. One of the SF soldiers grabbed him and nearly threw him down. Stumbling, Fisher caught his balance on the side of a crouched commando, who turned out to be Tyler.

"What the hell are you doing, Fisher?" asked the captain.

"I have to make the arrest," he said.

"Those Russians'll perforate you."

"Won't be the first time," said Fisher.

Tyler grabbed hold of his suit jacket. "You're not going anywhere."

"Careful of the material," said Fisher. "Five of Sears' finest squirrels labored to make this suit."

The captain scowled but let him go.

"Give me the bullhorn," said Fisher. "Let me talk to them."

"You can speak Russian?"

"Only the four-letter words."

Before the soldier carrying the bullhorn could come up, one of the Russians announced in fairly decent English that they were on Russian soil and would be treated as hostile aggressors if they didn't take off immediately.

"Actually, this is Japanese territory," Fisher yelled back, still waiting for the bullhorn. "And we're in pursuit of stolen U.S. property. Which we want back. And also, I'm arresting the people who were flying the plane. Hang on a second, I have to read something to you."

"You aren't fucking going to Mirandize them," said Tyler.

"Got to. Or anything they say won't hold up," said Fisher, pulling the small laminated card from his pocket. He took the bullhorn from James, who'd had it in his pack.

"You're out of your fucking mind," said James.

"That and I'm having a nicotine fit," answered the FBI agent, bringing the megaphone to his mouth. "All right. You have the right to remain silent. . . ."

CHAPTER

19

The combat with the helicopters, the tangle with the patrol boat, and the flyovers to clear the field had all taken their toll on Howe's fuel. He was now well into reserves, and there was no way he was going to make the task force tanker. A second tanker from Kadena was likewise a good way off.

He was just about to break out a map to see about diverting down to Honshu or northern Japan, when he realized he had his own personal divert strip sitting below him. The three thousand feet was usable, thanks to the F/A-22V's wing design. With the C-17 off to the side at the far end, Howe figured he'd have no problem stopping before his feet got wet.

Assuming they could secure the field.

The smoke had cleared somewhat; Howe could see a group of men near the Blackjack, and another group about fifty yards from the C-17. A third group was moving down the southern side of the island, possibly seeking to flank the Russians. From what he could see, nobody was firing.

When he failed to reach the SF troops on the frequency they'd been assigned, he went over to the command channel and asked Gorman what was going on.

"They have them pinned down by the aircraft," she said. "At the moment they're still trying to size up the situation. We have reinforcements en route."

"You think I could land there if I had to?"

They discussed the possibilities as he recalculated his fuel. Depending on how he managed it, he had about a half hour in the air.

The two F-15s sent up from Kadena appeared above him. Howe could divert and land—and in fact he absolutely *should* do so.

But somehow it didn't feel right to turn off. As he circled northward he caught sight of some debris in the water. Timmy's plane had gone in somewhere nearby.

"Colonel, I can't tell you what to do with your aircraft," said Gorman.

Howe started to laugh.

"Thanks, I'll remember that," he told her before punching over to the frequency the new arrivals were using so he could brief them.

As the American FBI agent continued to ramble, Luksha signaled to his communications man. The sergeant ran forward with his satellite radio, wheezing from the dust.

"We'll go down to the boats. Call in the helicopters," he told him. "Tell them we'll be pursued."

"Yes, General."

Megan heard the jet pass again and knew it was the F/A-22V.

It was him. He'd come for her.

To kill her?

He'd hate her by now. He'd think she was a traitor.

"This way," said the Russian, grabbing her wrist.

"Wait, I can fly it," she said. "If we put the fuel in, just enough to get away."

"Don't be absurd. They'll gun us down. Come on."

"No." She pushed her shoulders down, as if clamping her arms to the sides of her body would somehow cement her to the spot.

"It is not an option," said the Russian, and she felt a pair of arms grab her from behind.

"You got that out of your system?" asked Tyler as Fisher finished reading the Miranda warning.

"Hey, the lawyers say you gotta do it."

Davis, on point, waved. The other team had taken up their position at the end of the runway across from the jet.

"All right, let's move out," Tyler told his men. "If that's okay with you, Fisher."

"I'm right behind you," said the FBI agent.

Luksha heard the pop of the smoke canisters behind him. He had decided he would not run: This was, after all, Russian land, disputed or not. Nonetheless, he quickened his pace as his last two soldiers trotted behind him. Up ahead, the men had tied a rope around the American pilot and had begun to lower her down the cliff.

He grabbed the rope. An acrid taste rose from his stomach and burned his chest: He'd been defeated by unlucky circumstance, cheated, and now was being forced to run away with nothing to show for his efforts.

The man to his left slipped on the rocks. Luksha grabbed his arm, pulling him to safety. He saw the fear in the man's eyes.

Yes, he thought to himself.

He smiled, helping the paratrooper grab on to the rocks.

"Another day," Luksha said loudly, before starting downward.

Unable to stop herself from swinging because her hands were tied, Megan banged against the rocks so sharply she lost her breath. She wheezed as she reached the sand, collapsing into the shallow water. Someone picked her up and threw her into the boat. Voices screamed above her, people yelling at her.

She thought of the fire and smoke her uncle had flown through. *Never again,* she thought.

And if the Russians had the weapon too? What then?

They didn't, though. They were leaving without it.

The boat rocked. An engine roared, then another. She thought of trying to throw herself out, then felt a sharp pain in the back of her neck as someone stepped on her as he scrambled into the boat.

Luksha did not realize until the boats had started to back away from the island that some of his men had been cut off by the Americans at the end of the runway. But he was committed now; there was no option but to retreat.

He held on to the rail at the side as the small boat began to pick up speed. The woman pilot was crumpled on the floor beside him. Luksha reached over and helped her into the hard-backed seat.

"We have much to discuss," he told her.

Her mouth moved but she said nothing. Belatedly, Luksha realized she was trying to spit at him.

He raised his hand to slap her but started laughing at her instead.

Howe finally found the right frequency for the SF ground team as he swept across the northern side of the atoll, his speed held back so he could get a good view of what was going on. A cloud of smoke and dust separated the main groups of fighters, or at least seemed to; though he was low and slow, it was still difficult to pick out exactly what was going on. There was movement near some rocks at the base of the island; as he moved past he caught sight of a boat.

"I think you have a group escaping in a boat," he told the ground team as he banked around.

If there was an acknowledgment, it got lost in the general scramble of things as Howe positioned for another pass. The overlong mission had heaped fatigue on the pilot's head like steel weights; his eyes burned and even his most mechanical, practiced motion felt awkward.

"Two boats—three. Coming out of the island. There's another there," he told the commandos as he started toward the island.

He had his gun selected, and the cue lined up in the HUD.

"They have one of the people from the plane, a woman," said the SF commander, taking over from the communications man.

A woman?

Megan.

The realization froze him, as if he'd been hit by a taser. His hands moved; he flew the plane past the island and into a bank.

I can kill her.

I will kill her.

Fisher scrambled to the edge of the rocks and grabbed the line. It wasn't that far down but he didn't want to risk jumping into the water, since he couldn't tell how shallow it was.

He also couldn't swim.

"Where the hell are you going?" yelled Tyler, running to catch up.

"They have my suspect," the FBI agent told him. He pulled off his jacket and wrapped the cloth around the line to keep his hands from burning as he went down. "I want her back."

"We'll never catch up."

"We will if we don't overload the boat."

"You're out of your mind."

"I've heard that," said Fisher, stepping off the rocks.

By the time Fisher got the boat started, Tyler and one of the SF men had made it down as well. Three others stood at the top of the rocks.

"This is all we're taking!" yelled Fisher. "Throw down the megaphone."

"What?" shouted one of the men.

"The loudspeaker!"

Fisher grabbed at the megaphone as it flew through the air. He deflected it into the water but managed to grab it before it sank, just as the boat started in pursuit of the Russians. He dumped the water out and tested it. The squawk seemed a little off-key but it was working.

"You really think they're going to stop?" Tyler asked him.

"If we threaten them, they may throw her overboard."

"How are we going to threaten them?"

Fisher thumbed toward the sky.

"We don't have a radio with us to order in a strike," said Tyler.

"You gonna tell them?"

Tyler nodded. "We'll take this as far as we can," he said. "But we're not going to get ourselves killed."

"Sounds like a plan. Want a cigarette?"

"The Russians are not important," Gorman told Howe. "We have the laser. We have Navy assets en route and we're landing a fresh team on the island. You can let them go."

"Tyler and Fisher are in pursuit," Howe told her, relaying the word the SF people had sent. "The Russians have at least one of the aircraft's crew members."

"He's not important," said Gorman. "We're trying to reach Fisher and tell him to turn back. Leave them."

Howe's radar indicated that there was a helicopter approaching from the northwest. The F-15s had also spotted it; they kicked toward it to check it out.

He could shoot up the boats, no problem. At this point no one was going to question what happened. The whole scrum was too confusing, too fluid.

No one would criticize him for killing a traitor. On the contrary, Fisher and the others were trying to stop her. He was completely justified.

The boat sat in the center of the target box, held there by the computer. He could kill the bitch, have revenge or whatever it was—vent his rage.

She had betrayed his country and everything he believed in.

She had betrayed him.

He pushed his side stick, closing in.

He really did love her, in ways he hadn't understood at the time. And now it was gone. It had shot past him, the way a meteor traveled once through the atmosphere and burned up.

His finger rested lightly on the gun trigger. But something held it back.

Love? Duty? Fear?

He couldn't sort it out. He *had* loved her, and then hated her, and now, as his plane rushed toward the earth, he decided—unconsciously, without words, with thoughts that were fragmentary and fleeting—that it was what *he* had thought that mattered, and what *he* did now that was the important thing. Not Megan: She had made her choice; she was gone. Tearing up the boat, killing her—

that wasn't where his duty lie. Revenge, anger—they weren't who he was or who he would be.

Howe banked the plane sharply in front of the escaping Russian boats. He was less than fifty feet from the surface of the water.

"I have a fuel emergency," he told the SF unit on the island. "I need to land."

Megan watched the F/A-22V as it flew across their path, so low it almost touched the waves. It was Howe—it had to be.

The others ducked as the plane flew by. She stood and stared at him, trembling with sadness.

She could easily throw herself out of the boat; they were concerned with their pursuers, busy trying to reach their helicopter, lining up their weapons on their enemies. She could go over the side, escape.

But there was no real escape for her; she'd known that when she'd agreed with Bonham's original plan, as safe as he had made it sound. There were things worth dying for, and she remained convinced she'd chosen correctly.

The question she couldn't answer was whether there were things worth giving up love for. She'd made the decision before she met Tom Howe, when she had the luxury of not facing the question. Her fate was set with her first decision, with the stories her uncle had told; her beginning became her end.

It tugged at her, though. If duty was more important than love, why did every part of her inside feel choked?

Eliot had said something in "East Coker," his meditation on religion, about your beginning being your end, fate set as duty and meditation. It had been his answer for *The Waste Land*.

Not her answer, but a comfort nonetheless.

She remembered reading *The Waste Land* to Tom once, joking with him at first, then growing serious. The end of the poem came to her now as she stared at her destiny. Eliot had ended by repeating the Sanskrit word for peace, as if he'd had a premonition of Julius Robert Oppenheimer standing at the atomic bomb test, invoking the god of destruction in an effort to find peace.

Peace.

It was possible.

Shantih.

Peace peace peace.

One of the Russian paratroopers jostled against her. The man had slid his pistol back into his holster.

The second she saw it, she threw her whole body toward it.

Luksha saw the bodies tumbling together out of the corner of his eye. He spun toward them, not yet comprehending as the boat slapped hard against the waves. Then he realized that the American was grabbing for his sergeant's gun.

He pressed the trigger of his rifle. The first slug hit her in the side and spun her toward him. There was an explosion: She'd taken the gun from the holster. He fired again, finger nailed on the trigger.

Red and black and cold, cold—the smoke over the city as it burned filled her nose with the acrid scent of things dying, objects burning that were never intended to burn: rocks, dirt, human flesh.

It would never happen again. War had been made obsolete.

Megan felt herself falling into the black abyss. At the last second she recognized it as peace, and closed her eyes.

Fisher saw the bodies falling, one into the back of the boat, the other into the water.

"Aw shit," he said out loud. He threw his cigarette into the ocean. "There goes my case."

The others were silent as they slowed and pulled over to the lifeless body. He reached over and pulled her up with one hand, sliding her onto the boat. He knelt down and, for form's sake, checked her pulse to make sure she was dead.

Howe got his plane down with maybe three ounces of fuel left in the tanks. A planeload of Marines landed right behind him; two minutes after they touched down another group of SF soldiers from Gorman's task force came in a Hercules. Though tired as hell, he found himself supervising the operation to secure the Russian aircraft; not only did it seem flyable but the C-17 pilot had checked it out and thought—*knew*—he could get it off the ground and down to Kadena himself. It seemed a better option than waiting for the Russians to send reinforcements over the horizon, especially once the troopers found that there was fuel in the underground tank farm.

There were also charges set to explode. Taking no chances, the demolition experts made everyone move to the far side of the atoll while they neutralized them.

Which meant that Howe had a good view when the boat with Megan landed. Tyler called for a stretcher, and for a second Howe thought she was alive. His heart began to pound; then her arm dropped off the side, and he realized he didn't have to worry about what he would say to her or how he would feel when she walked past.

"Sucks," said Fisher, walking up from the small dock where they'd tied up.

"Yeah," said Howe. "Sucks."

PART SEVEN

Conspiracy Theory

CHAPTER

1

Howe leaned against the wall, so tired he worried that he might actually fall asleep. Then suddenly he remembered where he was—the hallway of the White House—and he snapped back up, ramrod straight, or at least as close to it as he could manage.

McIntyre, standing a few feet away, gave him an odd look. "You all right?"

"Just tired," said Howe.

"Relax. President's a great guy."

Howe glanced over at the Secret Service agent standing at the end of the hallway. Two men Howe didn't know took up a spot behind him in the hall, nodding as if they recognized him. Howe nodded back.

Dr. Blitz had met him a few hours earlier. He had been full of praise for Cyclops, talking about how revolutionary it was, how important it would be. Big things were happening, the national security advisor said; there seemed even to be an opening for peace finally between Israel and the Palestinians.

"Peace in the Middle East—what a concept," said Blitz.

He'd been sincere, but it sounded like something Timmy would say.

Howe had met his wingman's parents yesterday at the memorial service. The mother seemed pretty stoic; it was his father who was nothing but tears, gripping the folded-up flag.

There'd be no memorial service for Megan. Her immediate family were all dead and Howe hadn't heard whether the body had even been claimed.

Maybe he'd do that.

McIntyre turned toward him, motioning with his head. Howe realized the door to the office had opened; he followed inside, where the President met him in front of his desk. Blitz and the chairman of the Joint Chiefs of Staff were standing at the side, beaming.

"Colonel, very good." The President's grip was strong. "Excellent job. Excellent."

"Thank you, sir."

"Mac, are you looking after him?"

"Oh yes, sir."

"I just wanted to congratulate you personally, thank you for a tremendous effort."

"Yes, sir."

"You married, Colonel?"

"No, sir," said Howe. Where once he would have added, "Divorced," in a tone that suggested he'd sworn off women and relationships completely, he surprised himself by shrugging and thinking that he just hadn't found the right woman; someday he might.

Maybe.

As the President started saying something about the last time he'd been out to Montana during his campaign, Howe realized they wouldn't talk about the Cyclops weapon or the ABM test or even General Bonham.

"Sir, excuse me," he said finally. "Cyclops, and the ABM system—are we safer?"

"Safer?" The President had been taken completely by surprise.

"Dr. Blitz said he thought they were going to bring peace."

Everyone looked at Blitz.

"I think Cyclops, and the ABM system, our present system and the augmented ABMs—they're not a way to end war," said the national security advisor. "They're not even a chance to alter the future. But they are a path we can take—one we have to take—to our better natures."

It sounded like a speech. Howe looked back over to the President. D'Amici smiled. His eyes seemed to open a little wider, as if he were reading Howe's face, looking there to see what it was he needed to hear.

"I think we have an opportunity here. And it's due to you and your efforts," said the President. "People will remember your contribution. *I'll* remember it."

Howe nodded, even as one of the President's aides showed him to the door.

McIntyre waited in Blitz's office in the West Wing, around the corner from the President's. He'd seen Howe off, then gone inside and sat close to the door where he couldn't be seen from the hall. He knew it was better to wait here than in his office. He'd made up his mind and wanted no distractions.

Blitz finally appeared around three o'clock.

"Mac," he said, surprised as he walked into the office.

"Professor. Can I talk to you?"

The national security advisor took a look at his secretary, then signaled for McIntyre to follow him inside. He closed the door behind him.

"The investigation's going to move ahead very smoothly," said Blitz as he sat down. "NADT's been shut down. Jack Hunter's got over a hundred men on the case now. You know, there's a possibility even the secretary of state was involved."

McIntyre said nothing, listening as Blitz outlined the administration's plans to reorganize the Defense Department and services, cutting out the independent agencies and companies, returning to a more traditional structure. The speech sounded a little too well rehearsed, including a few talking points that would likely make their way to the Sunday talk shows, but it was irrelevant now. Besides, McIntyre was convinced of his boss's basic integrity and honesty.

Then again, he'd been convinced of his own as well.

"I have a confession," he said when Blitz finally paused.

Blitz's face blanched.

"It has nothing to do with Jolice or any of that," said McIntyre quickly.

Blitz instantly looked relieved. "Yes?"

"I killed somebody when I was on the ground in Kashmir."

"What?"

McIntyre explained as slowly and carefully as he could.

"Well . . . ," said Blitz when he was done.

McIntyre rose. "I'm resigning. It's all right."

"It sounds like it was an accident, under very difficult circumstances," said Blitz.

"Thanks for saying that, Professor. Thanks." He reached into his pocket and took out the envelope with his formal resignation, sliding it quietly on the desk before he left.

2

Megan York's death did not help the investigation, but it didn't blow it, either. Knowing about the island base not only gave the investigators a shot at tracking through the tangle of dummy and legitimate corporations that had been employed by the core conspirators, it also gave them real charges to use for leverage in the investigation—charges that could be cited in subpoenas and court orders. Bonham's murder was another promising avenue, assuming the trail team on Borg didn't lose the hit man as he hunted for his impersonator.

There were, however, indications that the conspirators were several steps ahead. Despite the flood of agents Hunter had sent to swarm over Jolice and its associated companies, several of its key officers could not be located. Only one board member so far had been interviewed: an eighty-eight-year-old resident of a nursing home in upper Michigan. Megan York's cousin, Congressman Taft, would clearly be hung out to dry, but he was already represented by the best criminal defense lawyers in D.C. Most unpromising of all, Fisher's boss had personally taken over the FBI side of the investigation.

Luckily for Fisher, he was not among the "hundreds and hundreds of agents working the case." Hunter's math had to be divided by three, at least. The boss had notified him that he was needed on more important investigations, which undoubtedly would turn out to be as far away from this one as possible.

Not that he was going to complain. The interesting stuff was all done; from here on out it was just shoe polish and brown-nosing.

Fisher leaned back in his seat, listening as Jemma Gorman finished filling in the rest of the team at the secret base in Montana on what was going on. In the world according to Jemma, the entire universe had been saved by one female colonel who refused to give up.

As Jemma yammered on, Fisher thought about Megan York. He had decided, mostly based on what Howe had told him, that she had been sincere about wanting the weapons developed because they might end war. That wasn't true of the others—greed and power pretty much ruled the day, as always—but it was an interesting exception, the sort of thing that made the rule. Fisher hadn't run up against altruism as a motive for treason before; it would make for the kind of story that could get you a few drinks at the old agents' home when the Social Security money ran out.

"And I think it would be appropriate, now that we're wrapping up, to give credit where credit is due," said Gorman. "Andrew—Mr. Fisher—if you can take your face out of that coffee mug, we'd like to give you a hand. Your work consistently led the way."

Fisher looked at her. She actually seemed sincere.

"I think I'll wait for the medal," said Fisher.

Gorman shook her head. The rest of the room laughed.

"Beer's on," said somebody, and they began filing out to find the mess, where there was indeed free beer.

"I meant it," said Gorman, coming over.

Fisher stood slowly. "Yeah, well, I got most of it wrong all along," he said.

"It's the end that counts."

"Uh-huh. You were almost right about the Russians."

"So you're saying I'm not a nincompoop, huh?" Gorman folded her arms.

"Seventy percent of intelligence is genetic," said Fisher.

"What's your excuse, then?"

"Touché." He reached into his pocket and pounded on the new pack of smokes.

"No comeback? No repartee? What happened? Somebody put decaf in your coffee?" asked Gorman.

Fisher opened the pack and pulled out a cigarette. A whiff of butane, a hint of smoke, a hit of nicotine—his fatigue vanished.

"So, you going to Mom's for Thanksgiving?" asked Gorman.

"Yeah, I guess," Fisher said. "You?"

"Uh-huh. I'm coming in the Sunday before."

"My flight's Saturday. I'll pick you up."

"Thanks." Gorman smiled at him, then took a step to leave. "See you there."

"Not if I see you first."

"Very funny, little brother. You ought to be a comedian."

"You do it so well I'd never want to compete," said Fisher, blowing a perfect ring of smoke into the air.

Visit
❖ Pocket Books ❖
online at

....

www.SimonSays.com

....

Keep up on the latest new
releases from your favorite
authors, as well as author
appearances, news, chats,
special offers and more.

SIMON & SCHUSTER
A VIACOM COMPANY
www.SimonSays.com

Pocket
Books